BUT YOU LIKE REALLY DATED?!

itbooks

AN IMPRINT OF HARPERCOLLINS PUBLISHERS

BUT YOU LIKE REALLY DATED?!

The Celebropedia of Hollywood Hookups

Written and illustrated by Ryan Casey

HarperCollins books may be purchased for educational, business, or sales promotional use. For information please e-mail the Special Markets Department at SPsales@harpercollins.com.

FIRST IT BOOKS EDITION

Designed by Ryan Casey

Library of Congress Cataloging-in-Publication Data is available upon request.

ISBN 978-0-06-226677-4

13   14   15   16   17   QGT   10   9   8   7   6   5   4   3   2

Shout-out to all my ladies and gays.
I dedicate this book to my sisters in the game.

Disclaimer
Legalese to CMA (COVER MY ASS!)

Everyone calm the EFF down! This celebropedia is a work of C.O.M.E.D.Y. Hookup, in this book, is a broad term: it can mean kiss, cuddle, dry hump, bone, or even hold hands. I mean let's face it, no celebrity is going to confirm to ME who they have shared sexy times with. I get my information where everyone else does: television, books, magazines, and blogs. And I believe all of it to be true (everything here comes from more than one source). So don't shoot the messenger. Think of me as a medium, and celebrity news as the higher power.

And if you want more info on any of the topics brought up in the book, do yourself a favor: whip out your smart phone and GOOGLE IT, and you'll see. OH, and tweet me @GoRyanGo with any fun goss' you discover. :)

TTYL, LYLAS

Contents

Sup, Bitches?

(An Introduction, of Sorts)

I'm obsessed with celebrities. I know the names of Reese's kids, and all the dudes she shaved her legs for. Hey, these are my interests, and yes, I'm part of the "problem." Don't judge me. I drool over gossip magazines and refresh celebrity websites faster than Lindsay can light her next Marlboro. Then I go home, turn on *E! News*, read Kim Kardashian's tweets, and scroll through Rihanna's Instagram. I know. It's bad. I also know that you do the same thing! You picked up this book, didn't you?

I have obviously gathered and retained A LOT of useless celebrity information over the years, and frankly, it has become an important aspect of how I live. I'll say the information is "useless" because I should probably learn how to lead a better life through history, meditation, or higher education. Instead, I look to the stars as my guide. I think about how Sandra Bullock lives her life and try to use her infinite wisdom when making my own personal decisions. I believe Sandy's way is the right way—I mean, the woman was cheated on by an undercover freakshow husband who was boning a woman with a forehead tattoo. Sandy fuckin' dealt with that shit like a ninja: she got a new life and a brown baby and barely shed a tear. This wasn't a movie, it was her REAL LIFE, people, and Sandy came out of that shitstorm smelling like the beautiful rose that she is. See—studying the lives of celebrities is not so useless, is it? We should all be looking to Sandy when the chips are down.

Now, let's get back to this little volume you hold in your hands. While Sandy does make an appearance, these pages contain the dirty business of many a dot on the Hollyweird map. Famous people love other famous people. They taste each other's juices, get all love drunk, and think it's forever. Well, it's not. Here's what really happens: they go on a few dates, one of them does an interview, and acts all coy about their new "budding" relashe'. We REGs (regular people) get all obsessed. A few weeks later, someone snaps a photo of the couple together. BOOM! Photographic evidence! It's REAL! But as the Native Americans believe, a photo can suck the soul out of the relationship. Oh, who cares, we're still fascinated.

The truth is, the reason why these famous relationships don't work is EGO. When you put two ego monsters together, that shit gets cray and they BREAK UP, which is why a lot of these celebs have been around the block. The only way to get over a former lover is to get under a new one, and Hollywood stars are doing plenty of that! So much, that I was able to write and illustrate an entire book!

I've documented all the famous dating and the dumping for you! So without further ado, I give you *But You Like Really Dated?! The Celebropedia of Hollywood Hookups*.

Enjoy. You know you will.

xo,

The
DIRTY
Dozen

The following twelve celebs have been spotted around "town" (I mean Hollywood, not your shit-hole town xo) with a, shall we say, vast array of girlfriends, boyfriends, hookups, you name it. They've probably been around more blocks than documented in these pages, but who cares about those losers (because they're not famous). We only care about celebs hooking up with other celebs or super-rich wannabes, right?! So pour some sweet tea, it's time to talk about Hollyweird's sexual superheroes!

1. Paris Hilton

Remember when Paris Hilton was really famous? In 2004, she was included in Barbara Walters's list of Most Fascinating People! What was going on there? Well, those days are done, thank goodness. But Paris is still (in)famous for her taste in men. Take a look.

BRODY JENNER
If you're blonde and on a reality show, Brody may be calling you tonight.

MARK SALLING
Paris was allegedly his welcome gift when he arrived in Hollywood.

COLIN FARRELL
The famous Irish man made a lot of drunken mistakes in his heyday, but, uh, don't we all? Colin's turned his life around and is now sober. Good for him and us...

JARED LETO
This so-called rocker and actor has very questionable taste in hairstyles, eyeliner, and women.

More names in Paris's little black book:

JAMIE KENNEDY
He's supposed to be funny?

JASON SHAW
A male model Paris has dated, twice.

ANDY RODDICK
Andy, you're better than this.

AFROJACK
Some lame DJ.

JAMES BLUNT
Maybe he thought she was beautiful?

BRANDON DAVIS
You don't know who he is? Me neither.

RIVER VIIPERI
A hot-ass male model.

LINDSAY LOHAN
I'm pretty sure these two only hooked up to impress some dudes.

CY WAITS
Nightclub mogul who was busted in Vegas, with Paris, for a DUI.

CRISS ANGEL
Too bad he didn't make Paris disappear.

TODD PHILLIPS
The hilarious and talented director of *The Hangover*. Super weird, right?

VIN DIESEL
Allegedly she made out with him in a dark club.

STAVROS NIARCHOS
Ms. Hilton loved his Greek yogurt. It was money flavored, duh!

OSCAR DE LA HOYA
This famous boxer might have been suffering from a head injury when he went out with Ms. Hilton.

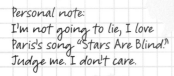

Personal note:
I'm not going to lie, I love Paris's song "Stars Are Blind." Judge me. I don't care.

NICK CARTER
They were kind of perfect together, right?

TOM SIZEMORE
Tom says he hooked up with Paris after a house party. I need to read his memoir!

50 CENT
There are some very curious photos online of Paris and 50 partying together.

FRED DURST
Fred did it for the nookie. What's your excuse, Paris?

KEVIN FEDERLINE
Paris has no shame. Don't you ever forget it.

KID ROCK
He denies it. But Bob Ritchie (his real name) calls himself Kid Rock. He's not the most credible witness, you know?

TRAVIS BARKER
It's very punk rock to hook up with Paris Hilton, ya know?

LEONARDO DiCAPRIO
Ladies, take note: If you're blonde, skinny, and tall, you have a shot with Leonardo!

RICK SALOMON
Hollywood playboy who dated Shannen Doherty (Brenda!) for awhile.

PARIS LATSIS
Oh, the Parises! He's a Greek shipping heir, and Ms. Hilton loves foreign money! These two were meant for each other.

CRISTIANO RONALDO
A sexy metrosexual footballer for Real Madrid. Paris is very international, y'all!

MARK McGRATH
Picturing these two together is what nightmares are made of.

BENJI MADDEN
Her ex BFF, Nicole Richie, is married to his bro Joel. Paris tried to score Benji to rekindle her friendship with Nicole, I bet.

TYLER ATKINS
A hot dude from *The Amazing Race: Australia*.

EDWARD FURLONG
Dated Paris for a year before Edward terminated her, and his career.

ADRIAN GRENIER
He really let her hang with his entourage?

DOUG REINHARDT
A baseballer, reality TV personality, and grade-A tool.

DERYCK WHIBLEY
He dated Paris, then married Avril Lavigne. What's wrong with this dude?

JOSH HENDERSON
Actor from *Desperate Housewives* and the new version of *Dallas*. I expected better from him.

CHAD MICHAEL MURRAY
He costarred with Paris in *House of Wax*. She got stabbed through the head with a spike or something. It was an awesome movie.

SIMON REX
This dude is friends with Charlie Sheen. He clearly doesn't make the best decisions.

VINCENT GALLO
Vincent is not too hipster for her. This probs happened when Paris was new to the scene.

JOE FRANCIS
Paris probably did it with the *Girls Gone Wild* guy, right? 'Cause I mean like why wouldn't she?

HARRY MORTON
Restaurateur, socialite, and connoisseur of lady parts.

HOOK UP **DATED** *WTF*

2. Warren Beatty

Dick Tracy has made it with a lot of Hollywood beauties. Rumor on the street is the number is close to 12,775 women. Dick Crazy, may be more like it.

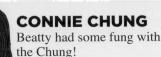

CONNIE CHUNG
Beatty had some fung with the Chung!

MADONNA
Just watch *Truth or Dare*.

RAQUEL WELCH
Did Warren flip her wig?

JANICE DICKINSON
WILD WOMAN.

MARY TYLER MOORE
She was young once, too.

DIANE KEATON
She is a queen. Get it, girl!

More ladies Warren Beatty'd:

DIANE VON FURSTENBERG
Warren Beauty was a freak panty dropper. Don't blame Diane!

DIANE SAWYER
"Show me the receipts, Diane!" Sorry, I had to quote Whitney Houston.

DARYL HANNAH
Part Mermaid, part kooky tree hugger. Go figure.

JULIE CHRISTIE
She's motherfuckin' classy. I hope Warren showed some respect!

BARBARA HERSHEY
Remember her? She's the cancer chick from *Beaches*, and *Black Swan*'s crazy-ass mom!

CARLY SIMON
"You're So Vain" has to be about Warren Beatty, right?!

BRIGITTE BARDOT
French and sexy.

VANESSA REDGRAVE
Stage legend.

DIANE LADD
Laura Dern's mom. I love Laura, so Diane's gotta be cool.

JONI MITCHELL
Did Warren pretend Joni was a river and skate far, far away? Harsh, dude!

JANE FONDA
Rumored communist and exercise queen. JK. Love you, Jane!

PRINCESS MARGARET
Keepin' it classy!

STEPHANIE SEYMOUR
Some model.

MELANIE GRIFFITH
Quirky, kooky, fabulous!

DIANA ROSS
Her afro is filled with secrets!

CANDICE BERGEN
Gettin' down with Murphy Brown!

CHER
Reason #10,104 why Cher rules at life.

BARBRA STREISAND
Oh, the memories! Babs knows how to score a dude.

MORGAN FAIRCHILD
The one who isn't Farrah Fawcett.

GOLDIE HAWN
God bless Goldie, Even if she looks like Bret Michaels now!

NATALIE WOOD
She died on a boat. :(

VIVIEN LEIGH
Won an Oscar for *A Streetcar Named Desire.*

ELLE MACPHERSON
She sucks, literally.

IMAN
This famous model probably shoots lasers out of her vagina. She's fierce!

BIANCA JAGGER
She was married to Mick for six years in the 70s. Warren got his satisfaction!

JOAN COLLINS
The original Lisa Vanderpump.

MAYA PLISETSKAYA
One of the greatest ballerinas of the 20th century.

CHRISTINA ONASSIS
Jackie O's stepdaughter.

BERNADETTE PETERS
Warren got with her after seeing her perform on stage for the first time, so the legend goes.

BARBARA HARRIS
Broadway star turned movie star. Look her up, bitches!

MAMIE VAN DOREN
Supposedly, she was the poor man's Marilyn Monroe.

PRINCESS ELIZABETH OF YUGOSLAVIA
This brings Warren's princess count to two.

LINDA McCARTNEY
After dating Warren, she met the love of her life, Paul.

MARGAUX HEMINGWAY
Model, actress, and Ernest's granddaughter.

CAROL ALT
Some model who eats raw food.

ANNETTE BENING
Annette killed the fun. Warren put a ring on it.

HOOK UP **DATED** **WTF**

7

3. Lindsay Lohan

Oh Lilo, you had so much promise. We are still rooting for you, girlfriend, but seriously, let's make some better life choices!

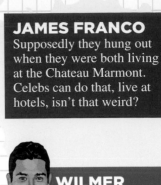

NICK JONAS
The hottest Jonas hands down.

JAMES FRANCO
Supposedly they hung out when they were both living at the Chateau Marmont. Celebs can do that, live at hotels, isn't that weird?

HEATH LEDGER
Hope you are sleeping well, sweet prince.

WILMER VALDERRAMA
He claims "they" are real.

BRUCE WILLIS
Linds, clearly, has daddy issues, and Bruce seems like a really level-headed guy.

More victims Lindsay has claimed:

CRISS ANGEL
Ladies, you really find him attractive?

BRODY JENNER
The fame fucker strikes again!

SEAN LENNON
John Lennon's strange son.

COLIN FARRELL
Paris, Lindsay, Britney. Come on, Colin!

JAMES BLUNT
Please go back to England.

PARIS HILTON
SO MUCH TO SAY, but I don't need to.

LEONARDO DiCAPRIO
You're better than this, Leo!

HARRY MORTON
He owns a restaurant called Pink Taco. Yeah, so there's that.

JARED LETO
Calm down, Jordan Catalano!

EVAN ROSS
Diana Ross's son! Diva, Jr.

VANESSA MINNILLO
Former MTV VJ. Now Mrs. 98°. Do yourself a favor and Googadis (Google this): Lindsay Lohan and knife.

JUDE LAW
Hey Jude, make it better, ok?

ROBBIE WILLIAMS
Wait, he's not gay?

JASON SEGEL
Jason probably thought, "Take a chance, hook up with the messed-up girl."

GERARD BUTLER
Gerry's a wild man. I can understand Lilo's attraction here.

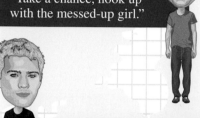

TERRY RICHARDSON
Lilo was the muse of the the super-famous photog at one point. Terry loves freckled boobs!

RYAN PHILLIPPE
When Reese cut him loose, he went ape shit with the ladies.

SAMANTHA RONSON
They were the best together!

BRANDON DAVIS
Remember when he drunkenly slurred about Lilo's fire crotch on that paparazzi video with Paris Hilton? You know you watched it. Stop lying.

RYAN ADAMS
Nashville hipster with an appetite for teen queens. He ended up marrying Mandy Moore.

JAMIE BURKE
He later dated Kelly Osbourne. Movin' up in the world!

DAMIEN FAHEY
MTV VJ from the *TRL* days.

TALAN TORRIERO
Some idiot from *Laguna Beach*.

BRETT RATNER
He claims to be very talented at oral sex and has made girls cry from pleasure. Thanks for sharing, B-Rat.

LANDON BROWN
Gettin' down with Bobby Brown's son!

BENICIO DEL TORO
This dude had a baby with Kim Stewart (Rod Stewart's daughter).

AARON CARTER
Aw, they dated before they both went off the rails.

50 CENT
I bet they watched *Mean Girls* afterwards.

SHAUN WHITE
Can you imagine if Lilo and the Flying Tomato had kids?

 HOOK UP   **DATED**   **WTF**

4. Leonardo DiCaprio

Leo is a talented actor. But his true passion is the ladies.
The Great Gatsby star has pretty much boned every nameless blonde model in the free world, but who cares; he's still a hottie with swag.

JESSICA SIMPSON
Leo was perhaps not in the best place when he hooked up with America's favorite mom jeans model.

I'M THE KING OF THE MODELS!

GISELE BÜNDCHEN
Jizzelle! That's all...

MARIAH CAREY
This must have happened back in the day. Now Mariah is married to Nick Cannon and mom to dem babies!

NOTHING TASTES AS GOOD AS SKINNY FEELS.

KATE MOSS
CoKate! This hookup is probably a blur for both parties.

NAOMI CAMPBELL
Super-famous model and well-known Rageaholic.

More la-la-ladies Leo has known:

LAUREN HOLLY
Some rando ginger chick from *Dumb and Dumber*.

BAR REFAELI
Bar and Leo tried to make it work a couple of times. But Jack Dawson knows there are other models in the sea.

AMBER VALLETTA
No, she's not a pornstar! She's a model turned actress.

HEATHER GRAHAM
A fine actress, of course.

RACHEL HUNTER
Rod Stewart's ex-wife.

EMMA BUNTON
Motherfuckin' Baby Spice, bitches!

ALICIA SILVERSTONE
These days Cher Horowitz is a stone-cold weirdo. She chews food and barfs it into her kid's mouth. Momma bird style. Not kidding.

BRITTANY DANIEL
This actress was on the TV show *Sweet Valley High*. Yeah, so there's that.

DEMI MOORE
Supposedly these two tried to date, twice!

CLAIRE DANES
Romeo and Juliet! They tried in real life but with no success. Hey, at least no one died.

BLAKE LIVELY
These two shared romantic getaways and more. Blake thought it was love. Leo took her to Disneyland for christsakes!

KATE WINSLET
Kate, the constantly nude super talent, tried to take their love from the sea to the streets but failed. But Kate and Leo remain good friends to this day.

LINDSAY LOHAN
Leo, you know this was really wrong, right?!

PARIS HILTON
Leo, please tell us this is not true!

BIJOU PHILLIPS
Kooky Scientologist actress. Hold on for one more day; her sister is in Wilson Phillips!

JULIETTE LEWIS
Mallory Knox! Oh yeah, she was nominated for an Oscar for *Cape Fear* and wore corn rows to the ceremony. FYI.

LIV TYLER
Liv seems pretty normal considering....

SIENNA MILLER
Another British notch to Leo's belt.

HELENA CHRISTENSEN
Supermodel legend. I'll give Leo this one.

TRISHELLE CANNATELLA
Train-wreck Trishelle from the *Real World: Las Vegas!* It had to be noted.

ERIN HEATHERTON
Just another Victoria's Secret Angel who gave Leo her soul.

HOOK UP **DATED** WTF 11

5. Drew Barrymore

Who doesn't love Drew? The girl partied hard at the *E.T.* premiere and she was, what, seven? Josie Grossie is a reformed party girl and 2x rehabber. She is a hippie at heart who has dated her fair share of weirdos. But Drew has transformed from a total disaster with parent issues to a savvy film director, actress, wife, and mom. Take a note, Lindsay Lohan.

JUSTIN LONG
The Mac dude! Maybe Drew was more of a PC?

CHRISTIAN BALE
Oh gooooood for youuuu, Drew! Remember how H.O.T. he was in *American Psycho*?! I hope Drew got with him during THAT.

ANDY DICK
There was no way Drew let this happen. I hope.

COREY FELDMAN
These two were pretty much parentless in Hollywood, so they naturally gravitated toward one another.

More dudes Drew got weird with:

ED WESTWICK
Chuck from *Gossip Girl*. Drew loves a hipster Brit.

FABRIZIO MORETTI
Drummer from The Strokes. Went on to date her friend Kristen Wiig.

ZACH BRAFF
Scrubs actor and all-around nice guy. I liked them together.

ERIC ERLANDSON
Weren't Drew and Courtney Love best friends for a hot second? Well, Ms. Barrymore dated the only dude in Hole.

RICK SALOMON
He got nasty with Paris Hilton and decided to release the infamous sex tape. He's not worthy of Drew, but rumor has it....

EDWARD NORTON
Edward was into damaged girls. It didn't last, 'cause Drew got her shit together.

BILLY IDOL
There are rumors on the interwebz the two hooked up in 1994. They were in *The Wedding Singer* together. You be the judge.

DAVID ARQUETTE
Never Been Kissed is the best movie ever. Just sayin'.

TOM GREEN
The twosome were invited to get married on *Saturday Night Live* in 2000. But they decided to have a private ceremony instead. None of this matters, though, because their love match lasted 163 days.

JASON SEGEL
Hot chicks love this guy; maybe it's because he seems super normal?

LUKE WILSON
He seems like a pretty sweet, slightly boring guy.

SPIKE JONZE
Amazing director. Weird little genius.

JAMIE WALTERS
Actor from *Beverly Hills 90210* and *The Heights*. He also sang the hit song "How Do You Talk to an Angel." Hey, do you think that tune is about Drew?!

SAM ROCKWELL
Costarred with Drew in *Charlie's Angels*. C'mon.

HENRY THOMAS
Um, her brother from *E.T.*?! Say it ain't true, Drew!

BALTHAZAR GETTY
Really, your name is Balthazar? What a mouthful to scream in bed.

WILL KOPELMAN
Winner! Will married Drew in 2012. They now have a daughter, Olive, together. How cute!

 HOOK UP   *DATED*   *WTF*

6. Janice Dickinson

The wacky former *America's Next Top Model* judge is pretty much a maniac. She is also a badass and doesn't take SHIT from any model, let alone any man.

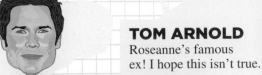

ROB LOWE
He was nuts back in the day. It's possible.

TOM ARNOLD
Roseanne's famous ex! I hope this isn't true.

JACK NICHOLSON
Janice flew over the cuckoo's nest with old Jackie boy.

MICK JAGGER
A jumpin' Janice flash is a gas, gas, gas.

Janice also got down with these peeps:

WARREN BEATTY
I wonder what number Janice was?

KELLY LeBROCK
Lestastic! Janice and Kelly allegedly did some *Weird Science* together!

PRINCE ALBERT OF MONACO
Janice's attempt to become a royal.

RON WOOD
Just one of the MANY rockstars (and not the only Rolling Stone) Janice shared an intimate moment with.

BRUCE WILLIS
Live free, fuck hard.

JOHN CUSACK
He's an undercover playboy who has quite the rap sheet.

GRACE JONES
Lestastic take 2! Janice supposedly got freaky with the original Lady Gaga at Studio 54.

LIAM NEESON
This Irish man was taken by the sultry supermodel.

ROMAN POLANSKI
Janice was of age, at least.

JON LOVITZ
Is Janice a chubby chaser? LOL!

SYLVESTER STALLONE
These two were perfect together! It's a goddamn shame it didn't last.

TOM MORELLO
The guitarist from Rage Against the Machine? Say it ain't so, Tom.

DOLPH LUNDGREN
He's pretty much the Swedish Sylvester Stallone, right?!

JFK JR.
Legend, in every sense.

FRANK ZAPPA
Maybe Janice liked his weird music, IDK?!

HOOK UP   **DATED**   *WTF*   15

7. Cameron Diaz

Does Cammy D really use jizz for hair gel? Well, it has to be famous sperm 'cause girl don't mess around with no middle-class fools. Cameron has expensive taste, y'all!

ALEX RODRIGUEZ
These two made great workout buddies.

VINCE VAUGHN
Let's be real. It's pretty shocking they couldn't make this work. They seem perfect for each other!

JUSTIN TIMBERLAKE
Timberpuss is a full-on momma's boy. It's rumored his mom hated Cameron. You know how that goes.

KEANU REEVES
Cameron broke his heart. Sad Keanu.

ADAM LEVINE
Cam liked his tight-ass yoga body. But Adam knows Victoria's Secret, and it does not involve Ms. Diaz.

More guys spotted with glam Cam:

CRISS ANGEL
His penis has to be magic, right?! Otherwise why is he so busy?

JARED LETO
Cammy tried to tie Jared down. No dice, lady.

TYRESE GIBSON
Get it, girl!

JUDE LAW
Players unite! Remember that piece of shit movie they made together, *The Holiday*? Man, that sucked!

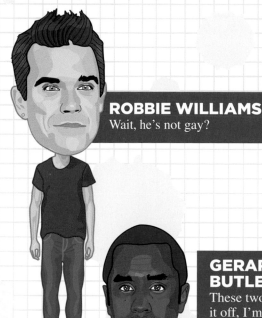

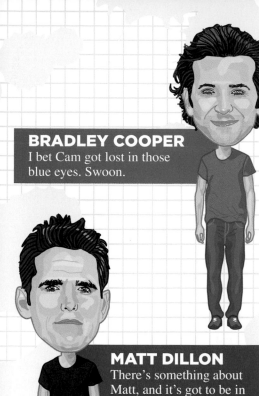

BRADLEY COOPER
I bet Cam got lost in those blue eyes. Swoon.

ROBBIE WILLIAMS
Wait, he's not gay?

MATT DILLON
There's something about Matt, and it's got to be in his pants.

GERARD BUTLER
These two playas hit it off, I'm sure.

P DIDDY
Cameron probably rocked her tightest daisy dukes to score this mogul!

PAUL SCULFOR
A British male supermodel who often fucks famous women.

VINCE NEIL
He's hooked up with a lot of celebs? Who knew?!

DJIMON HOUNSOU
He's dark and sexy. Enough said.

EDWARD NORTON
Cameron is a turbo and Ed is more slo-mo. Therefore, Edward hit it and quit it.

KELLY SLATER
A pro surfer who Cameron "bartered" with for surfing lessons.

 HOOK UP　 *DATED*　*WTF*　17

8. George Clooney

Clooney knows how to score the plooney and by plooney I mean well, you know. From now on, any woman who hooks up with George is called a "Plooney." It started here, folks. Tell your frenemies. Anyway, George is a stand-up guy, and he gives every woman he breaks up with a very expensive parting gift.

KELLY PRESTON

It didn't work out because she is attracted to really manly men who fly planes. And like massages.

KAREN DUFFY

DUFF! One of the best MTV VJs ever. You go, Duff!

RENÉE ZELLWEGER

Long live the Zells, wanton sex goddess.

JULIA ROBERTS

Don't lie!

More ladies who have fallen prey to the Clooney charm:

ELIZABETH DAILY
Some actress.

CAROLE RADZIWILL
Real-life princess and *Real Housewife of NYC*. She said George is a great kisser. We *totally* believe her.

KIMBERLY RUSSELL
She was on *Head of the Class* in the 80s, what a fine bit of television that was.

SARAH LARSON
A random chick.

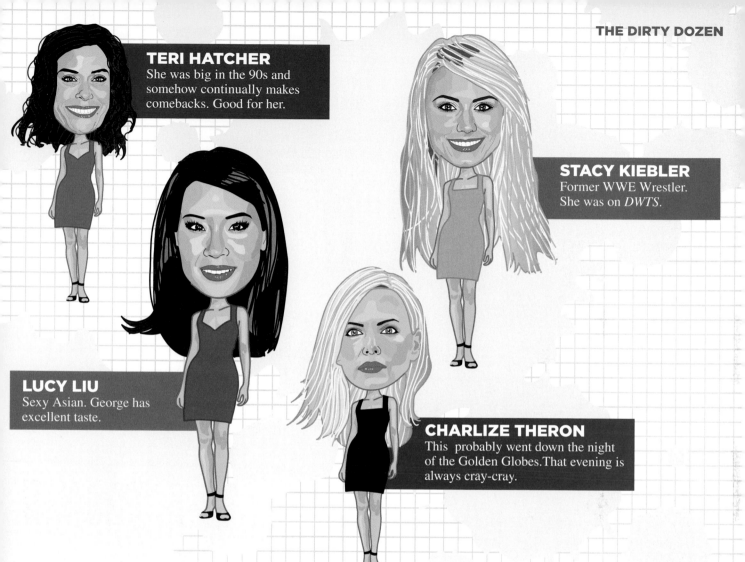

TERI HATCHER
She was big in the 90s and somehow continually makes comebacks. Good for her.

STACY KIEBLER
Former WWE Wrestler. She was on *DWTS*.

LUCY LIU
Sexy Asian. George has excellent taste.

CHARLIZE THERON
This probably went down the night of the Golden Globes. That evening is always cray-cray.

KRISTA ALLEN
A nobody actress.

TRAYLOR HOWARD
She was on that stupid show *Two Guys, a Girl and a Pizza Place* with Ryan Reynolds. Also her name is *Trailer*.

ELISABETTA CANALIS
Um, she dated *Jackass* star STEVE-O after GEORGE CLOONEY? WTF?

HOOK UP　　*DATED*　　WTF

9. Madonna

"I always thought of losing my virginity as a career move." Well said, Madge. Your career boning famous dudes has placed you on The Dirty Dozen. As far as the men Madge has made it with, we can make the assumption she is attracted to men with anger issues, weirdos, and young studs with brown skin.

SEAN PENN
Madge loves a bad boy, and Sean Penn was all that and more in the 80s. Their breakup was anything but amicable. So in 2012, when Sean was seen at Madonna's concert, there were rumors swirling about the two rekindling their romance. Hey, we can only hope.

WARREN BEATTY
Breathless Malone got down with Dick Tracy. VOGUE!

> I STRETCH, I KICK, AND I'M 50! EAT IT!

CARLOS LEON
Madonna and Carlos made a beautiful daughter.

GUY RITCHIE
It's shocking he put up with her as long as he did.

Personal note: In 2008, I saw Madonna in concert from the front row. She pretty much looked like a zombie Dakota Fanning. I couldn't bring myself to look her in the eyes. Bitch is intense.

More of Madge's victims:

BASQUIAT
Genius artist from the 80s. He gives the Material Girl some street cred.

JOSE CANSECO
Steroid enthusiast.

JESUS LUZ
In 2009, Madonna went crazy for this Latin lover.

SANDRA BERNHARD
Sandra could suck the pink out of a salmon. I love her. Too bad they couldn't make it last.

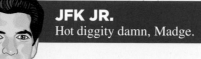

JFK JR.
Hot diggity damn, Madge.

LENNY KRAVITZ
They could have made a cute couple.

VANILLA ICE
Nothing gets better than this hot mess. Holla!

WILLEM DAFOE
Remember *Body of Evidence*, when they poured wax on each other's junk? That was weird, right?

ANTONIO BANDERAS
Madonna's famous crush from *Truth or Dare*, and they later made *Evita*! together

BRITNEY SPEARS
Um, they tongued each other on MTV in front of Brit's ex-boyfriend! You know you remember!

CHRISTINA AGUILERA
Madge gave Xtina the tongue that night, too. Thanks, MTV, for giving us that visual memory.

BRAHIM ZAIBAT
Madge's second boy toy boy joy. He was 24. She was 53.

■ *HOOK UP*　■ *DATED*　WTF

10. Taylor Swift

A round of applause for America's favorite sexually active band geek! Taylor is the youngest member of the Dirty Dozen, and you gotta give the girl some credit. Sure, she's a love junkie, but if you mess around with Taylor and leave her, you're SCREWED 'cause she'll sing about it until your ears bleed, and her bank account has a few more zeros!

TAYLOR LAUTNER
THE TAYLORS. Lautner whipped out his werewolf micro peen and dry humped Swifty's leg.

CORY MONTEITH
RIP! Walmart employee turned Gleetard. These two went on a bowling date together.

JOE JONAS
Joe dumped her ass through a text message. Jerk face.

HARRY STYLES
Hooked up with Tay, then jetted off to Australia to smush with another chick. They rekindled their romance at the end of 2012 but quickly broke it off for good. Look out, Harry, this next song's for you!

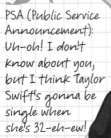

PSA (Public Service Announcement): Uh-oh! I don't know about you, but I think Taylor Swift's gonna be single when she's 32-eh-ew!

Taylor has also been linked to:

GARRET HEDLUND
The *Tron* actor dumped the pop star for a more sullen blonde: Kirsten Dunst.

JUSTIN GASTON
Justin was in Taylor's music video "Love Story."

TOBY HEMINGWAY
Sucked face with TayTay in her music video "Mine." Maybe in real life, too?

LUCAS TILL
Some actor from *Hannah Montana*.

TIM TEBOW
These two may have dated for a hot second. We pray that Taylor had the good sense to say no.

JOHN MAYER
John hit it and quit it. Another name on John's impressive lady list.

EDDIE REDMAYNE
Taylor tried her hardest to land a part in the film version of *Les Misérables*. She didn't get the part, but Eddie helped her through the misery.

ZAC EFRON
God bless Swift for allegedly landing the greatest piece of ass ever.

JAKE GYLLENHAAL
Gwyneth Paltrow set these two up. Jake played head games, dickmatized her, introduced her to his family, then dumped her like a bad habit. And Jakey Poo, just so you don't forget, you are never ever getting back together — LIKE EVER.

CHORD OVERSTREET
The blond, hot one from *Glee*.

PATRICK SCHWARZENEGGER
Arnold's HOT son…not the secret one he had with his Mexican maid.

CONOR KENNEDY
Taylor started dating him before his senior year of high school. They would have had so much fun at the prom.

ED SHEERAN
Odd-looking ginger singer/songwriter who may have been born in Middle Earth. It's hard to imagine, but nonetheless, there's chatter.

HOOK UP　　**DATED**　　*WTF*

11. Demi Moore

Pour the Red Bull! Demi's crazy, crazy fun! The 50-year-old seems like she knows how to party and doesn't give a FUCK about anything. Well, she does give a FUCK about looking young.

Question: Have you ever seen Demi dance? Do yourself a favor and GOOGADIS. It's so embarrassing!

ALEX RODRIGUEZ

Do you think A-Rod played strip poker with Demi?

OWEN WILSON

Gotta love the male version of Ellen DeGeneres.

ASHTON KUTCHER

These two really thought they had it all. RIP @mrskutcher.

ANTHONY KIEDIS

Red hot Demi!

Demi has also canoodled with:

HARRY MORTON

Steakhouse boy strikes again!

EMILIO ESTEVEZ

Mighty Ducks forevah! Forevah, evah!

NIKKI SIXX

The bassist from Mötley Crüe. Really, Demi?

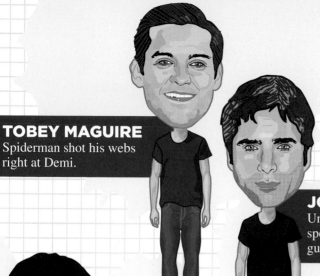

TOBEY MAGUIRE
Spiderman shot his webs right at Demi.

JOHN STAMOS
Uncle Jesse, yogurt spokesperson, hot Greek guy. You go, Demi!

BRAD PITT
Supposedly this happened in 1998, long before he fell into Angie's clutches.

BRUCE WILLIS
The *Die Hard* actor made his exit after having three daughters with Demi.

JOE MANGANIELLO
Touch my mangina-ello!

THOMAS JANE
Have you ever seen how this actor dresses in real life? Something is wrong.

LEONARDO DiCAPRIO
Leo strayed from his normal blonde flavor to give Demi a try, twice.

VITO SCHNABEL
Young art dealer who Demi hung out with after Ashton. Vito is the son of famous artist Julian Schnabel and society page mainstay.

GUY OSEARY
Madonna's manager.

 HOOK UP   *DATED* *WTF* 25

12. Britney Spears

Brit Brit. God bless her with her fourth-grade education. She earned all my respect when she shaved her head. That was some next-level shit. So, let's salute her wild ways!

IT'S BRITNEY, BITCH!

WADE ROBSON
This was the guy Britney allegedly cheated on JT with. CRY ME A FUCKING RIVER! Wade Robson, you ruined everything, get the hell outta here.

TOM BRADY
Britney. Brazilian supermodel. Same diff.

EMINEM
Anger sex, anyone?

JASON ALEXANDER
LOL. JK. Not this Jason Alexander, some nobody who was briefly famous for becoming Mr. Britney Spears for one night.

Oops, Brit Brit, you did it again, and again, and again:

COLIN FARRELL
Brit Brit showed up with him at a red carpet event. The rest is up to our imagination.

ADNAN GHALIB
Some gross paparazzo who was the staple of the pink wig era.

JARED LETO
If Jordan Catalano (*My So-Called Life*, duh) wants it, he gets it.

KEVIN FEDERLINE
Once upon a time, KFed was skinny and kind of cute, but then he started drinking 20 sodas a day.

FRED DURST
He touched the Holy Spearit.

JUSTIN TIMBERLAKE
Never forget that matching denim look on the red carpet. NEVER FORGET.

BEN AFFLECK
Go, Britney! Ben did get engaged to JLo, so he does have a wild side, which makes this a wee bit more believeable.

JASON TRAWICK
Jason was Brit Brit's manager. They got together. He hit the gym. They got engaged. She wanted more kids. Jason had other ideas. Tootles!

DAVID LUCADO
David, a lawyer, got the OK to start dating Ms. Spears after his background check cleared and he signed a confidentiality agreement. Romance!

 **HOOK UP**    **DATED**   *WTF*

*13. Winona Ryder

Gwyneth Paltrow's most famous frenemy! Winona ran into some trouble back in the day with the whole shoplifting thing, but everyone's favorite 90s star is slowly making her way back on the scene! An Oscar is in your future, girl!

ROBERT DOWNEY JR.
Iron man got weird and might have touched Ms. Ryder's Hollywood strip.

KEANU REEVES
These two spent some time in the Matrix together.

MATT DAMON
Remember their famous double dates with Gwyneth and Ben Affleck?!

ADAM DURITZ
Counting Crows? More like Countin' Hoes.

CHARLIE SHEEN
I mean, I guess Charlie was kinda hot back in the day.

More dudes Wino had her way with:

GARY OLDMAN
Did they get close on the set of *Bram Stoker's Dracula*?

CHRIS ISAAK
Winona may have done a bad bad thing with the 90s crooner.

EVAN DANDO
He's from that band the Lemonheads, I believe.

PETE YORN
Winona loves a musician.

DAVE PIRNER
OMG! The lead singer from Soul Asylum?! "Runaway Train" is the jam.

DANIEL DAY-LEWIS
I'm OK with this.

EDWARD BURNS
Oh, he is so cute! And that voice is adorbs.

DAVE GROHL
Hell yeah! Grohl is the coolest.

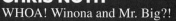

CHRIS NOTH
WHOA! Winona and Mr. Big?!

DAVID DUCHOVNY
I would be very interested in learning
more about their XXX-file, just sayin'.

JOHNNY DEPP
GET BACK TOGETHER. GET BACK
TOGETHER. GET BACK TOGETHER.
GET BACK TOGETHER. GET BACK
TOGETHER. Maybe, if we *Beetlejuice*
this shit it will come true?

TOM GREEN
He's weird. She's weird.
Fun was had by all.

CHRISTIAN BALE
Winona probably hit it when
Mr. Bale was in his prime!

BECK
These two were both raised by hippies,
right? Shocking it did not work out.

JAKOB DYLAN
Anyone could get lost in those blue eyes.

JIMMY FALLON
How can you not fall in love with Jimmy?

JAY KAY
Jamiroquai! "Virtual Insanity" took us and
Winona to another level.

CONOR OBERST
Good ole' Bright Eyes. Winona is so emo.

TRÉ COOL
Some dude from Green Day?!

RYAN ADAMS
These two seem like they would be the
perfect couple, right?

HOOK UP   **DATED**   *WTF*

The History of the SUPER COUPLE

"Oh, look at us, we're sooo famous, we're sooo pretty, we're sooo in love!" *Shut up!* No one cares. Well, maybe we care a little bit. A super couple (real or fictional) is a special phenomenon. To create a power couple, each person needs to be famous or infamous. The chemistry between the two needs to make the public either smile or barf.

THE HISTORY OF THE SUPER COUPLE

BEGINNING OF TIME
ADAM *and* EVE
Eve screwed everything up when she fooled around with a huge snake.

41 BC
CLEOPATRA *and* MARK ANTONY
Mark dropped his third wife and three kids to run off with Ms. Cleo.

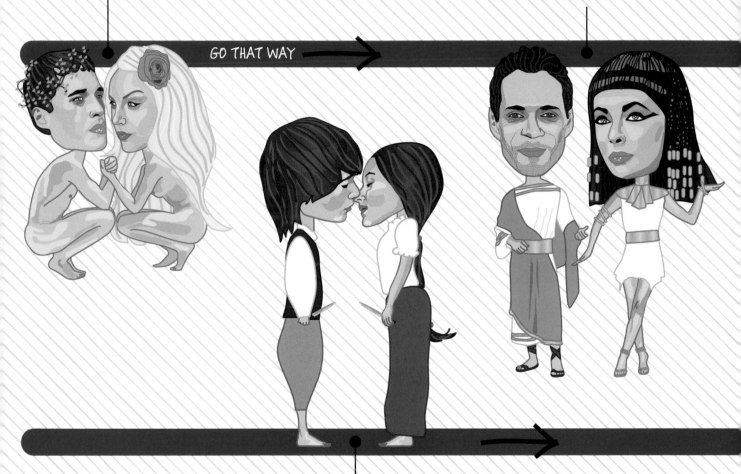

GO THAT WAY →

1597
ROMEO *and* JULIET
Hot young sex on a platter, with a side of suicide!

5 BC
MARY and JOSEPH
Joseph's #1 stunner had an affair with a ghost, and he still stayed with her.

DOWN AND TO THE LEFT, SEXY

FAST FUCKING FORWARD

1607
JOHN SMITH and POCAHONTAS
White boy helping himself to some natives. You bad boy, John.

1938
CLARK KENT and LOIS LANE
The royal couple to comic book nerds makes their debut.

1939
SCARLETT O'HARA and RHETT BUTLER

Gone with the Wind fabulous!

1942
SPENCER TRACY and KATHARINE HEPBURN

Spence was unimpressed when he first met Katharine.
He wasn't into her because of her dirty fingernails.

1951
FRANK SINATRA and AVA GARDNER

Frank had a total of four wives in his life. Ladies loved his blue eyes and uh, microphone.
Ava was his second lady love, and their chemistry capitivated the world.

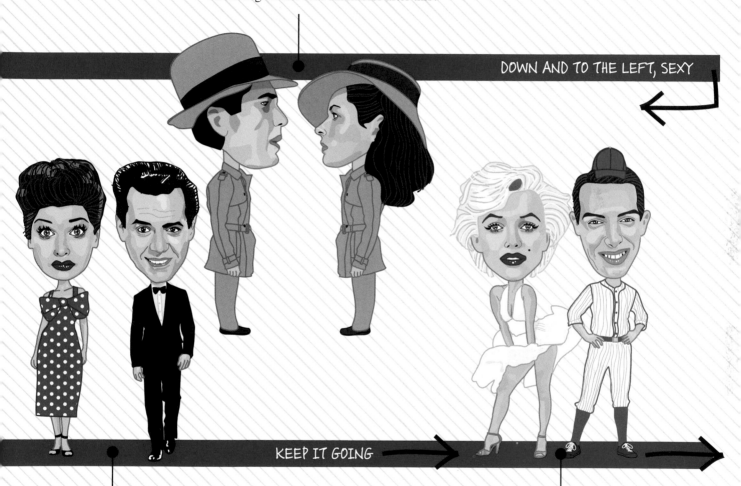

1943
HUMPHREY BOGART
and INGRID BERGMAN

Casablanca is released. Did couples start wearing matching trench coat ensembles after this?

DOWN AND TO THE LEFT, SEXY

KEEP IT GOING

1951
LUCILLE BALL
and DESI ARNAZ

I Love Lucy debuts on October 15. A white girl gettin' down with her Papi. America loved it!

1954
MARILYN MONROE
and JOE DiMAGGIO

Married for 274 days. Still beats 72 days. Suck it, Kim Kardashian!

1958
PAUL NEWMAN *and* JOANNE WOODWARD

Married for 50 years until his death in 2008. There's an amazing quote from Paul about Joanne: "Why fool around with hamburger when you have steak at home?"

1960
JFK *and* JACKIE O

We all know JFK was a skirt chaser. Nonetheless, it did seem like he geniunely loved Ms. Jackie.

THIS IS FUN, RIGHT?

1964
ELIZABETH TAYLOR *and* RICHARD BURTON

These maniacs married and divorced TWICE. That's gotta be true love, I tell you!

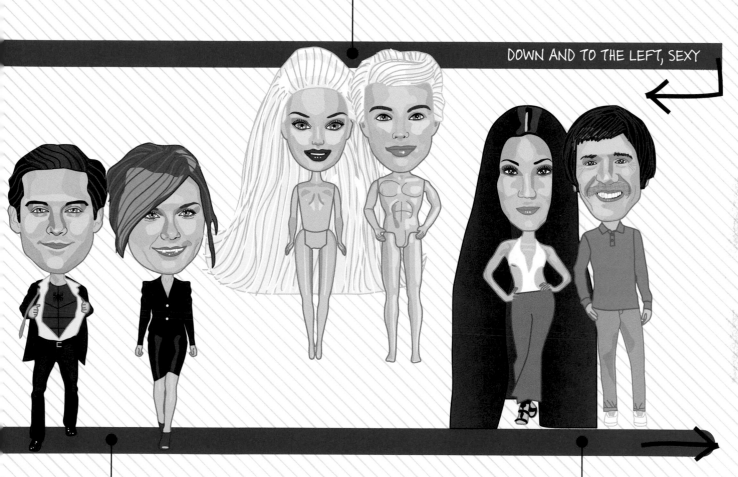

1961
KEN *and* BARBIE

Met on the set of a TV commercial. Soon after, they began rubbing their smooth flat private areas together.

DOWN AND TO THE LEFT, SEXY

1965
PETER PARKER *and* MARY JANE WATSON

The first *Spider-Man* comic is released. Nerds everywhere drop loads.

1965
SONNY *and* CHER

"I Got You Babe" hits #1. In 1974, the famous couple said "See ya, babe!"

THE HISTORY OF THE SUPER COUPLE

1965
TINA and IKE TURNER
Paved the way for Rihanna and Chris Brown.
Love had nothing to do with it!

1967
BONNIE and CLYDE
The movie starring Warren Beatty and Faye
Dunaway is released. The real Bonnie and Clyde
robbed about a dozen banks from 1931 to 1934.

1969
JOHN and YOKO
Lennon marries the woman who will
break up the Beatles.

1976
ROCKY and ADRIAN
Wouldn't *Rocky* have been so much better if
Sylvester Stallone died in the end?

1968
JOHNNY CASH and JUNE CARTER

Johnny marries June. Remember when Reese Witherspoon won an Oscar playing her? That was weird. "Baby, baby, baby!"

1969
MIKE and CAROL BRADY

The Brady Bunch debuts. Their kids Marcia and Greg were pretty squeaky-clean on screen, but off, it sounds like they were having a little too much fun, if ya know what I'm sayin'.

KEEP IT MOVING, PEOPLE

THAT IS A FABULOUS TOP, CAROL!

OH, MIKE.

COME ON, WE'RE NOT DONE

1981
RONALD and NANCY REAGAN

Some people believe politicians are the greatest actors in the game. Well, give Ronnie an honorary Oscar 'cause this guy slayed!

1981
PRINCESS DI *and* PRINCE CHARLES
Attractiveness is finally added to the Royal gene pool!

1981
LUKE *and* LAURA
Luke drunkenly raped Laura, but later she fell in love with him. The two married on *General Hospital* while 30 million viewers watched. The 80s were so weird.

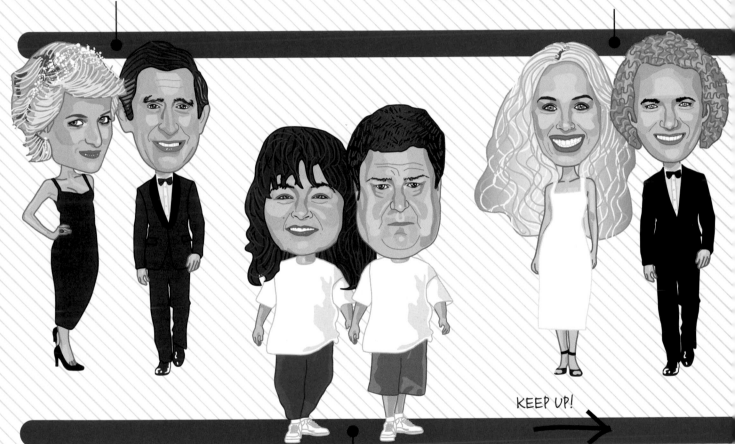

KEEP UP!

1988
ROSEANNE *and* DAN CONNER
Roseanne premieres on October 18. Fat, poor people are the funniest!

1984
CLIFF and CLAIRE HUXTABLE

The Cosby Show debuts. Goofy dancing and ugly sweaters warm the hearts of millions.

1985
BILLY JOEL and CHRISTIE BRINKLEY

Billy proved that homely rich dudes can score supermodels.

BIPPITY BOP BOP MY PUDDING POP!

TURN THE PAGE!

1990
MEG RYAN and TOM HANKS

The first time we see these two onscreen is in *Joe vs. the Volcano*. That one flamed out, but *Sleepless in Seattle* was a modern classic.

THE HISTORY OF THE SUPER COUPLE

1990
SEIGFRIED and ROY

The glittery gay super couple's lion son took a bite right out of Roy's money maker. Sorry, but that's what happens when you have jungle cats as pets.

1990
HOOKER and RICH DUDE

This one time on set Julia got Richard a pet gerbil. JUST KIDDING! Best urban legend EVER, though.

DON'T CALL ME CRAZY!

1994
ROSS and RACHEL

Friends premieres on September 22. Mom jeans and super-layered haircuts become a "look."

1997
ELLEN and ANNE

Anne broke Ellen's heart. Years later Anne lost control of her mind and body somewhere near Fresno, CA.

1991
OPRAH *and* GAYLE

The Oprah Winfrey show debuts in 1986. Gayle King should be given some sort of award, 'cause girl played her cards RICH, uh wait, RIGHT! BESTIES FOREVER!

1993
BILL *and* HILLARY CLINTON

Billy Boy takes office! Let the jokes begin.

1997
JACK *and* ROSE

Titanic is released. Never let go!

1997
WILL SMITH *and* JADA PINKETT SMITH

These two started getting jiggy with each other in 1997.

1997
WILL *and* GRACE

This sitcom premieres September 21. Giving fag hags a voice, finally.

WOO HOO!

1998
BRAD *and* JEN

These two lied to us! We're still mad about it.

1998
CARRIE and MR. BIG

Sex and the City premieres on June 6. Fashion
sluts and actual sluts infiltrate the boob tube.

1998
POSH and BECKS

Victoria turned David into the world's first metrosexual.

WE ARE SO NOT DONE YET

2002
BENNIFER

Ben was clearly brainwashed by the booty! This union
gave birth to the phenomenon of celeb couple monikers.
Thank God Ben wised up.

2002
SHARON *and* OZZY

The Osbournes premieres March 5. Ozzie and Harriet for the new millennium!

2003
NICK *and* JESSICA

Newlyweds premieres in August. America watches and our collective IQ drops 30 points.

2005
TOMKAT

On May 23, Katie was snatched up! Tom scored a twenty-something and decided to celebrate by jumping on Oprah's couch.

2004
J LO and MARC ANTHONY

Skeletor tried to control Jennifer, but that shit did not fly. J Lo dumped his ass and went for a young hot dancer.

2004
ASHTON and DEMI

The cougar and her cub make their debut.

2005
JACK TWIST and ENNIS DEL MAR

Brokeback Mountain premieres on December 9. Jack takes it like a champ and almost wins an Oscar.

2005
BRANGELINA

After meeting on the set of *Mr. and Mrs. Smith*, Brad ditched Jen and started building his child army with Angie Jo.

2005
BOBBY B *and* WHITNEY

The greatest reality show ever, *Being Bobby Brown* premieres.

AIN'T IT SHOCKING WHAT DRUGS CAN DO!

NEXT!

2008
BARACK *and* MICHELLE

Their secret service code names are Renegade and Renaissance. Superstars!

2008
JAY-Z *and* BEYONCÉ

Jay finally put their love on top and married the legend that is Beyoncé, thus creating hip-hop royalty.

READY B?!

DOWN AND TO THE LEFT, HOTTIE

HE UP ON ME, I'M UP ON HIM!

2008
ELLEN *and* PORTIA

Hollywood's sweetest lesbian couple make it official.

2008
GISELE *and* TOM

Gisele claims she can eat whatever she wants, and Tom is raking in the dough playing ball. Try to be happy for them.

2010
NEIL PATRICK HARRIS
and DAVID BURTKA

These two give gays a good name. In 2010, they cemented their love with the arrival of their adorable twin gaybies.

2011
WILLIAM *and* KATE

The two sweethearts tied the knot in April. Diana would be proud. Seriously.

2011
KIM KARDASHIAN
and KRIS HUMPHRIES
The reality couple made $11 million off broadcasting their wedding and divorced after 72 days. GFY (Go Fuck Yourself).

2012
KIMYE
In 2012, they announced they were together, and by 2013 the Kimye spawn landed on earth!

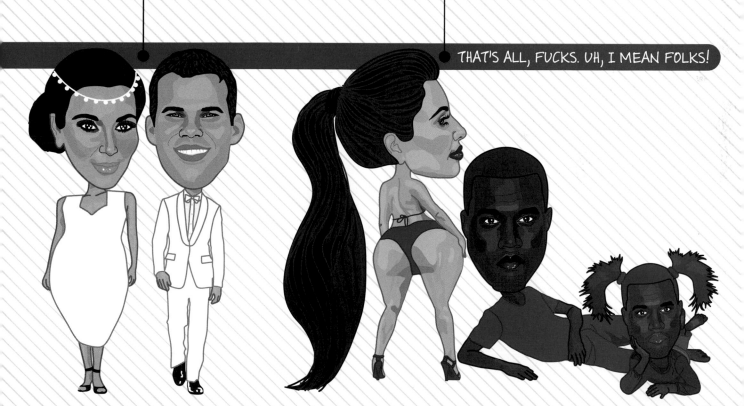

THAT'S ALL, FUCKS. UH, I MEAN FOLKS!

WTF COUPLES

WTF COUPLES

Bust out the defibrillators! You are gonna need those suckers after you get through this chapter. It might feel like you are tripping your balls off on some "Steve Jobs Grade-A" LSD while reading the next few pages, but you aren't; this is real life. Did Shaggy really bone Jennifer Love Hewitt?! Deep breath! Stay with us! BREATHE! OK, want some more? Let's go!

WTF COUPLES

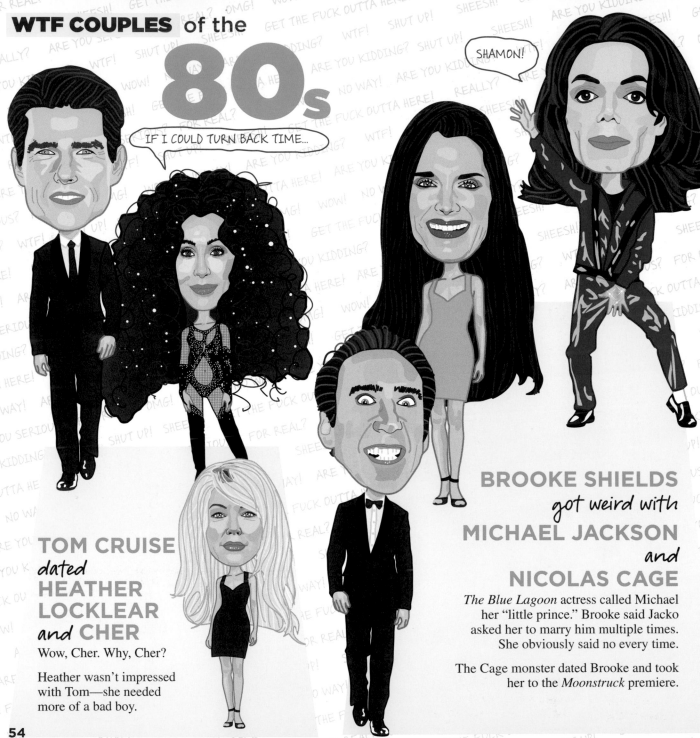

WTF COUPLES of the 80s

IF I COULD TURN BACK TIME...

SHAMON!

TOM CRUISE
dated
HEATHER LOCKLEAR
and **CHER**

Wow, Cher. Why, Cher?

Heather wasn't impressed with Tom—she needed more of a bad boy.

BROOKE SHIELDS
got weird with
MICHAEL JACKSON
and
NICOLAS CAGE

The Blue Lagoon actress called Michael her "little prince." Brooke said Jacko asked her to marry him multiple times. She obviously said no every time.

The Cage monster dated Brooke and took her to the *Moonstruck* premiere.

BRAD PITT

hung with

CHRISTINA APPLEGATE
& ROBIN GIVENS

I'M RIGHT ON TOP OF THAT, ROSE!

Christina would go on to become one of the queens of the 90s. Who needs you, Brad?

Brad got down with Mike Tyson's ex?!

ROGERT EBERT
and
OPRAH

This is when they were both large and in charge. The two probs just shared a romantic meal at Roy Rogers and talked movies. RIP, Mr. Ebert. Oprah and all of us miss your wit and charm!

DREW BARRYMORE
dated
COREY FELDMAN

Hey, it was the crazy 80s!

WTF COUPLES of the 80s

KELLY PRESTON
got down with
CHARLIE SHEEN

Kelly's type is more of a song and dance kind of man, so she moved on from Mr. Sheen.

ROB LOWE
dated
JANET JACKSON

Rob is one of those dudes who hasn't aged since the 80s. Bitch STILL looks good. Janet is due for a major comeback soon, right?

PRINCE
tried to seduce
KIM BASINGER

Back in '89, Prince became obsessed with Kim. They met on the set of Tim Burton's *Batman*. Prince wrote a whole album based on his feelings for Kim. WEIRD, yes, but not for Prince!

56

ROBERT DOWNEY JR.
dated
SARAH JESSICA PARKER

I really hope these two are still friends and schedule playdates with their adorable children.

LARRY KING
wanted
KATIE COURIC

Katie shot down Don Juan King's advances by telling him she wanted to find someone closer to her age. Her loss!

HALLE BERRY
and
DANNY WOOD

Halle knows how to hang tough!

57

WTF COUPLES of the 90s

WHOOPI GOLDBERG
and
TED DANSON

Wait, Whoopi is NOT gay?! While these two were dating, Ted sported black face to roast her at the Friars Club in 1993. Awkward!

ANNA NICOLE SMITH
dated
DONALD TRUMP

There are rumors these two shared a few intimate nights.

> I WON'T BE IGNORED, WOODY!

WOODY HARRELSON
and
GLENN CLOSE

Woody, the weed vaporizing connoisseur, got it on with Glenn in the 90s. Freaky attraction!

MADONNA
vogued for
DENNIS RODMAN
and
VANILLA ICE

Madonna kept it motherfuckin' weird in the 90s with her taste in men.

LISA KUDROW
and
CONAN O'BRIEN

Two comedic geniuses together?! It's a shame it didn't work.

HUH! HUH!

PEE-WEE HERMAN
and
DEBI MAZAR

This is so 90s!

WTF COUPLES of the 90s

SEAN PENN and JEWEL

Who knew Mr. Penn was into yodeling?

ADAM DURITZ spent quality time with COURTENEY COX and JENNIFER ANISTON

Just imagine the three of them smoking weed on the *Friends* set and having a 90s threesome.

COREY HAIM and VICTORIA BECKHAM

Remember the other Corey from the 80s? He was in *Lost Boys* and BFFs with Corey Feldman. The former child actor sadly died at 38. But in 1995, he scored Posh Spice! Granted, this was way before Victoria became a rail-thin fashion powerhouse.

ASHLEY JUDD
and
MICHAEL BOLTON

When a woman loves a man with lady hair, the world wonders why.

EDWARD NORTON
dated
COURTNEY LOVE

This is so odd. I have no words.

JULIA ROBERTS
was once with
MATTHEW PERRY
and
LYLE LOVETT

Let's get real. Julia does not discriminate when it comes to men. She has no problem dating the weirdo or the ugly dude.

61

WTF COUPLES of the 90s

PAULY SHORE and TIFFANI AMBER THIESSEN

The *Son-In-Law* star touched Kelly Kapowski's boobs?

YOU OUGHTA KNOW, UNCLE JOEY!

CENSORED

CENSORED

DAVE COULIER and ALANIS MORISSETTE

Dude, Alanis and Uncle Joey. In a movie theater! He dumped her ass and she wrote a song about it, and became super famous.

CHRISTINE TAYLOR and NEIL PATRICK HARRIS

Ben Stiller's wife got down with Doogie before he went strictly dickly?

DAVID BLAINE
got weird with
FIONA APPLE

Remember when Michael Jackson randomly thanked David Blaine at the VMAs? "David Blaine, I believe in you and your magic is real." This confirms for us regs that David is a weirdo. But so is Fiona. So I can see it.

SHERYL CROW
and
OWEN WILSON

Owen just might be Sheryl's favorite mistake.

MARIAH CAREY *and* LEONARDO DiCAPRIO

I wonder if Mariah thought Leo would always be her baby?

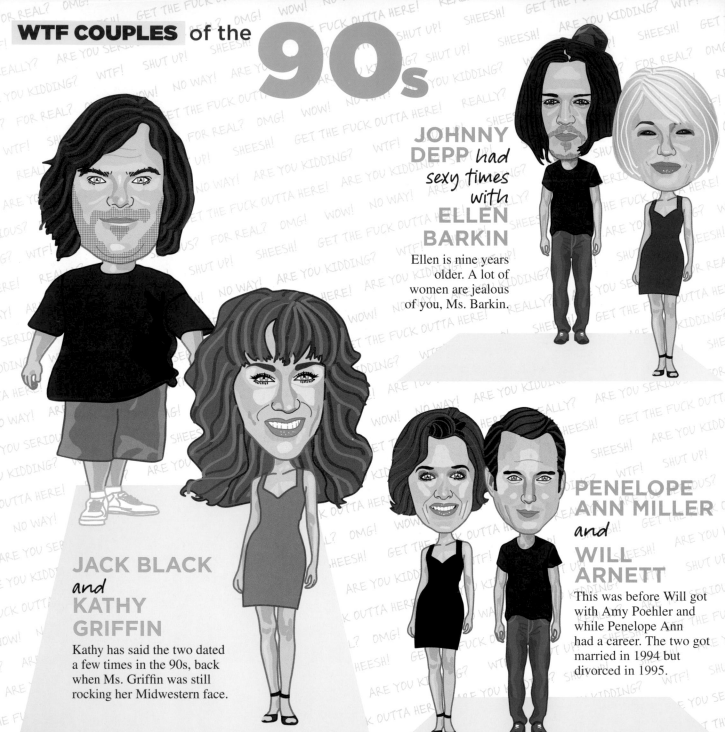

WTF COUPLES of the 90s

JOHNNY DEPP *had sexy times with* ELLEN BARKIN

Ellen is nine years older. A lot of women are jealous of you, Ms. Barkin.

JACK BLACK *and* KATHY GRIFFIN

Kathy has said the two dated a few times in the 90s, back when Ms. Griffin was still rocking her Midwestern face.

PENELOPE ANN MILLER *and* WILL ARNETT

This was before Will got with Amy Poehler and while Penelope Ann had a career. The two got married in 1994 but divorced in 1995.

ROBERT DE NIRO
was seen chatting up
UMA THURMAN, NAOMI WATTS,
even
WHITNEY HOUSTON

Weird, right? Bobby is scary talented but seems so boring IRL (in real life). Ladies really dig him?

KISS MY ASS!

BARBRA STREISAND
and
ANDRE AGASSI

Babs thought Andre's wig was like buttah!

LARA FLYNN BOYLE
dated **JACK NICHOLSON** *and* **ERIC DANE**

This chick rocked a tutu to the Golden Globes. Enough said.

WTF COUPLES of the 90s

MICHAEL JACKSON
and
LISA MARIE PRESLEY

The biggest WTF couple of the 90s, right? Remember when these two kissed at the beginning of the 1994 VMAs? Collective gag, I mean gasp.

JENNIFER LOPEZ
and
WESLEY SNIPES

Wesley was so hot in the 90s. Then he wasn't. Bye bye, J Lo!

SMIZE!

TYRA BANKS
and SEAL

Rumor has it Seal dumped Tyra for Heidi Klum.

MICHELLE WILLIAMS
and
JEREMY JACKSON

PLEASE say you watched *Baywatch*?! Well, apparently Michelle was a guest star back in the day, and she got friendly with Hobie Buchannon!

JUSTIN TIMBERLAKE
and FERGIE

Dude, JT and Fergalicious! Also, never forget Fergie pissed herself on stage while performing with the Black Eyed Pees (uh, Peas).

WTF COUPLES of the 00s

Personal note: If you haven't watched Alanis's naked music video for the song "Thank You," you should, uh, check it out. It's interesting

PARIS HILTON and EDWARD FURLONG

These two hit the club scene hard!

THAT'S HUUUUGE.

RYAN REYNOLDS dated KRISTEN JOHNSON and ALANIS MORISSETTE

Ryan hooked up with the chick from *3rd Rock from the Sun*?!

More importantly, he was ENGAGED to Alanis Morissette for AWHILE. Ryan has strange taste in women. But remember, he is Canadian.

CARSON DALY and TARA REID

Remember this?! I'm still upset that Tara's reality show *Taradise* was cancelled.

JOHN MAYER
serenaded
JESSICA SIMPSON
and
JENNIFER LOVE HEWITT

According to John, Jessica is sexual napalm, and J. Love's body is a wonderland.

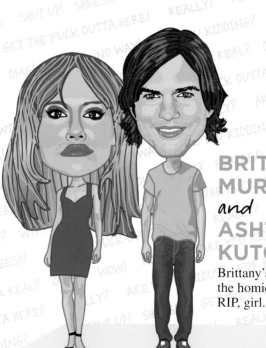

BRITTANY MURPHY
and
ASHTON KUTCHER

Brittany's rollin' with the homies in heaven. RIP, girl.

CHRIS KLEIN
dated
KATIE HOLMES

Katie dated "average Joe" Chris before she slid into the clutches of megastar Cruise.

WTF COUPLES of the OOs

JOSH GROBAN
dated
JANUARY JONES

Word on the street is Josh has a giant set of hairy balls, which would make sense with his deep-ass voice and all.

OH, LANCE! I'M HAVING A BALL!

LANCE ARMSTRONG
and
ASHLEY OLSEN

The professional doper dated one of the fashion trolls!

HEATH LEDGER *dated* HEATHER GRAHAM *and* MARY-KATE OLSEN

Heather got her claws in Heath when he first moved to Hollywood. He wised up pretty quick.

Heath spent his last day on Earth in Mary-Kate's apartment in NYC. I'm still sad about that.

Motherfuckin'!
MOBY
hooked up with
NATALIE PORTMAN

That's right, *Star Wars* nerds.

MACAULAY CULKIN

was with
MILA KUNIS

for a lot longer than Mila would like to remember.

JANET JACKSON
and
MATTHEW McCONAUGHEY

Who knew Ms. Jackson (if you're nasty) was into hot Southern boys?

WTF COUPLES of the OOs

HALLE BERRY
and
FRED DURST

The Oscar winner was in a movie with Mr. Limp Bizkit, and people say they really hit it off.

TIGER WOODS
and
LeANN RIMES

These two CHEATERS went on a few dates in 2002.

JENNIFER LOVE HEWITT
spent some time with
SHAGGY
and
JOHN CUSACK

J. Love has quite *The Client List* of men who have whispered into her ear.

JEFF GOLDBLUM and NICOLE RICHIE

Nicole said she had a childhood crush on Jeff. So he took her on a few dates. How nice!

KEANU REEVES and DIANE KEATON

The two starred in the modern masterpiece *Something's Gotta Give* and tried their story line out in real life.

SOFIA VERGARA dated TOM CRUISE and DONAL LOGUE

Sofia was allegedly vetted by the Church of Scientology to potentially service Cruise's intergalatic penis.

Donal is a pretty famous character actor. It's kind of sweet to think Sofia would give ugly dudes a chance!

WTF COUPLES of the 00s

RIHANNA dated JOSH HARTNETT and SHIA LaBEOUF

Shia and Josh like to party, so sparks flew with the Queen of Barbados.

HILARY DUFF also went on a date with SHIA LaBEOUF

The two have said it was the worst date they have ever been on.

BILLY CORGAN got it on with TILA TEQUILA and JESSICA SIMPSON

Doesn't get any weirder than this, people!

RENÉE ZELLWEGER
sucked face with
KENNY CHESNEY
and
JACK WHITE

Renée Zellweger randomly married Chesney. We still don't know why.

She was also engaged to Jack White, the pale corpse from the White Stripes.

SIENNA MILLER
and
P DIDDY

Diddy gets down with white chicks, so goes the word on the street.

GEOFFREY AREND
and
CHRISTINA HENDRICKS

Yay! Another regular dude scores a hot chick!

WTF COUPLES of the 10s

KIERAN CULKIN
dated
EMMA STONE

Kieran was a revelation in *Home Alone*. "Fuller, GO EASY ON THE PEPSI!" Emma went on to score the fine-ass Andrew Garfield.

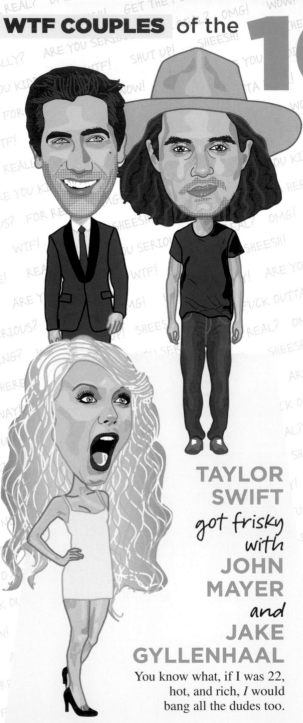

TAYLOR SWIFT
got frisky with
JOHN MAYER
and
JAKE GYLLENHAAL

You know what, if I was 22, hot, and rich, *I* would bang all the dudes too.

SEAN PENN
and
SCARLETT JOHANSSON

A 24-year age difference, people! ScarJo wanted this to stick so bad!

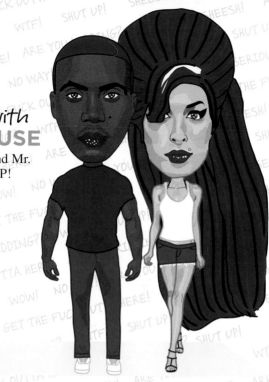

NAS *hooked up with* AMY WINEHOUSE

People think her song "Me and Mr. Jones" is about the rapper. RIP!

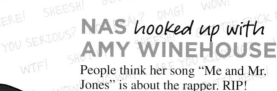

EVAN RACHEL WOOD
gothed out with
MARILYN MANSON

This seriously boggles the mind.

JUSTIN TIMBERLAKE *and* ASHLEY OLSEN

These two were spotted at a few parties together.

WTF COUPLES of the 10s

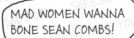

MAD WOMEN WANNA BONE SEAN COMBS!

AMBER TAMBLYN and DAVID CROSS

The Sisterhood of the Traveling Pants actress married the weirdo from *Arrested Development* in the fall of 2012 while guests like Blake Lively and Ryan Reynolds watched in awe.

CAMERON DIAZ spent some QT with P DIDDY

I bet Diddy knows how to wine, dine, and 69 a broad.

ELLEN PAGE had sexy times with ALEXANDER SKARSGÅRD

So it turns out *Juno* is not a hardcore lesbo! Well, you go Junebug, 'cause Mr. Skarsgård is top of the line!

MATTHEW PERRY
and
LIZZY CAPLAN

Chandler Bing is doing it with Janice Ian (DYKE!) from *Mean Girls* in real life, people! This was shocking to me, OK?!

AVRIL LAVIGNE
dumped
BRODY JENNER
for
CHAD KROEGER

Yep, the dude from Nickelback. If these two make music together, we are SCREWED.

CHELSEA HANDLER
dated
50 CENT

The comedienne tried dating 50, but they couldn't find much to talk about.

TALK OF THE TOWN

This chapter is dedicated to all the rumored celeb cheaters, womanizers, pervs, porn-star enthusiasts, hooker lovers, nude pic aficionados, and sex tape superstars. Here's a tip: if you're famous, don't do any of this stuff, because we will find out.

TALK OF THE TOWN

DIAMONDS!

HAPPY BIRTHDAY, MR. PRESIDENT.

JFK

John F. Kennedy was the original Playa President.
He snuck chicks into the Oval Office on the regular.
His most famous conquest was Marilyn Monroe.

ELIZABETH TAYLOR

Shout-out to Dame Elizabeth Rosemond
Taylor Hilton Wilding Todd Fisher Burton
Burton Warner Fortensky. If there is one
thing Liz did not give, it was a FUCK. As
a teenager she tried to seduce a 36-year-old
Ronald Reagan. Dame Liz stole her best
friend Debbie Reynolds's husband.
Elizabeth even tried to trap Frank Sinatra
into marrying her by faking a pregnancy.
Evil genius, or just plain genius?

KRIS KARDASHIAN JENNER

Kris revealed in her memoir
(or as she says, memwaaaaah)
that she cheated on her husband
Robert Kardashian with a much
younger tennis instructor.

YOU'RE A BIT OF A FREAK, CHARLES.

PRINCE CHARLES

Chuck cheated on Diana starting in the late 80s with Camilla Parker Bowles. Charles was so obsessed with Camilla he wanted to be her tampon. Sexy, right, ladies?

BILL CLINTON

"I did not have sexual relations with that woman." LOL, Bill, LOL. President Clinton is a freak.

BILLY BOB THORNTON

Billy Bob left Laura Dern for Angelina Jolie. Those two freakshows got married a year later. Oh, and they wore each other's blood in a vial around their necks… so there's that.

TALK OF THE TOWN

HEY, Y'ALL!

PUT DOWN THE VACUUM.

SI SEÑOR!

ARNOLD SCHWARZENEGGER

Maria Shriver probably married one of the biggest scumbags of our time. Arnold is a cheater. Not only did he cheat with Brigitte Nielsen who is basically Dolf Lundgren in female form, BUT he fucked the maid on the DL for twelve, TWELVE years! AND they had a KIDDDDD!

BRITNEY SPEARS

Brit Brit allegedly cheated on Justin Timberlake with Australian choreographer Wade Robson. Justin then dumped her ass and went on to make the amazing song and video "Cry Me a River." Bad move, Brit Brit.

MEG RYAN

Ms. Ryan was married to ultra hottie Dennis Quaid; then, she filmed some movie with Russell Crowe and suddenly leaves Dennis! WTF? Well, apparently she moved on from both dudes 'cause she is now with John Cougar Mellancamp.

ETHAN HAWKE

Uma is better off. Ethan turned out to be a really creepy-looking dude.

KOBE BRYANT

Supposedly Kobe shared some shady moments with a 19-year-old hotel employee. Wife Vanessa stayed with Kobe and WORKED that shit to her advantage. He showered her with "I'm sorry" jewels.

> YOU WANNA GET INTO THESE MOM JEANS, HUH?!

JUDE LAW

Aww, Jude and Sienna Miller were so cute together and tried to make it work TWICE, but in the end it wasn't meant to be.

JESSICA SIMPSON

Why did Nick and Jessica break up? Does anyone know? In 2006, Jessica was seen wearing Adam's T-shirt on her walk of shame after a night of partying with Mr. Maroon 5.

TOM BRADY

Tom seemed to be really into Bridget Moynahan—oh wait, then he met Gisele. It was game over for Bridge, who was pregnant with his kid.

MARIO LOPEZ

Remember when A.C. Slater was engaged to the Doritos girl? It turns out he wasn't the best fiancé. Ali Landry discovered his wild ways during his bachelor weekend and called off their wedding.

JOHN EDWARDS

Johnny Boy cheated on his wife WHO HAD CANCER with campaign worker Rielle Hunter.

RITA ORA

The poor man's Rihanna supposedly cheated on Rob Kardashian with over 20 dudes. The reality star then blasted the pop star on Twitter. Reports later came up that one of the dudes Rita got freaky with was Jonah Hill!

PETER COOK

Peter fucked his 18-year-old intern, so Christie Brinkley LEFT his ass.

DAVID LETTERMAN

Dave cheated on his wife with REGS who were his staff members. So lame!

> I CALL LEANN "ANGEL FISH" BECAUSE SHE SINGS LIKE AN ANGEL AND DRINKS LIKE A FISH.

EDDIE CIBRIAN *and* LeANN RIMES

Eddie met Leann on the set of some god-awful Lifetime movie. Leann was married to a dancer with a serious case of gay face. Eddie was married to the goddess Brandi Glanville. Eddie and Leann were caught on camera making out at a restaurant. Shit broke loose. Brandi slashed Eddie's tires, got vaginal rejuvenation surgery with his credit card, then left him. Leann stopped eating and dropped her dancer husband like a hot potato. Leann and Eddie tied the knot and lived happily ever after… JK LOL.

DAVID DUCHOVNY

Turns out David plays a sex addict in real life as well as on TV. He and his wife tried to work it out, but eventually Téa cut the strings on that shit.

87

TALK OF THE TOWN

TONY PARKER

Tony was texting with his teammate's wife behind Eva Longoria's back. Allegedly they had an affair soon after. Longwhoria found said sext messages and left his ass.

CLAIRE DANES

Hollywood's ugliest crier weaves a tangled web! Claire started her reign of terror when she cheated on her Aussie boy Ben Lee with dirt dog Billy Crudup — whose wife, Mary Louise Parker, was preggo with their child! Classy! Billy got his a few months later when Claire cheated on him with Hugh Dancy.

LARRY KING

Larry's seventh wife, Shawn, filed for divorce when she thought Larry had tapped the ass of her hotter sister. Larry, YOU OLD DOG! They eventually made up. The jury's still out on whether the sister-fucking is true.

KELSEY GRAMMER

The *Frasier* star has said he gave his wife the privilege of appearing on *The Real Housewives of Beverly Hills* as a parting gift before ending their marriage. He then cheated on her with a fucking flight attendant.

GAVIN ROSSDALE

Courtney Love told Howard Stern in 2010 that Gavin cheated on Gwen Stefani with her. I think Ms. Love was just trying to cause troubs'.

TIGER WOODS

Oh man, this is a crazy-ass scandal. Tiger was on the DL for YEARS. He got with strippers, pornstars, prostitutes, pretty much any-thing that had a vagina. When Elin found out right before Thanksgiving, she took a golf club to his car. She is an American Legend.

MORE ABOUT TIGER AND HIS FILTHY WAYS!

THE MANY HOLES OF TIGER WOODS

Elin Nordegren
Divorced the shit out
of Tiger Woods after
finding out he was
a man whore. She
got a $100,000,000
settlement and started
dating a billionaire!

Lindsey Vonn
The Olympic
medal-winning skier
has obviously fallen
down on the slopes
and hit her head a few
too many times, be-
cause in March 2013
Tiger and Lindsey
announced they were
dating. On Facebook!

90

No one will ever forget this shit show! Tiger Woods was at the top of his game in 2009. The most successful golfer ever, crazy endorsement deals, beautiful wife, kids, the whole nine. Well, when it broke later that year that Tiger Woods was a downlow dirtbag, the world, along with his Swedish model wife Elin Nordegren, lost their damn minds. The press started leaking reports of Tiger's wild ways. He had a group of famous friends who introduced him to the wild Vegas hooker lifestyle. Woods's pussy posse supposedly included Michael Jordan, Derek Jeter, David Boreanaz, and Charles Barkley. Needless to say, Tiger got caught red-handed by the press, and the mistresses of Tiger Woods started stepping forward....

1. Rachel Uchitel The main girl. On November 25, 2009, the *National Enquirer* claimed Tiger was having an affair with Rachel, a nightclub "hostess" (that means hooker, right?). This opened the floodgates for more women to come foward.

2. Devon James Porn Queen.

3. Emma Rotherham Tiger liked her to dress up like a naughty secretary, and he would give it to her on his office desk.

4. Julie Postle Some Florida trash.

5. Jamie Grubbs From the reality show *Tool Academy*. Grubb released a voice mail to *Us Weekly* from Tiger saying his wife knew about all his shady lady business.

6. Susie Ogren A computer technician. A hot nerd, maybe?

7. Mindy Lawton A Perkins waitress. Perkins is a family restaurant, but Tiger saw it as a place to "make" a family.

8. Jamie Jungers With a name like that, she has to have big boobs.

9. Michelle Braun Supposedly ran an escort service.

10. Loredana Jolie Playmate.

11. Theresa Rogers An older lady who says *she* taught Tiger about lady parts.

12. Holly Sampson Another pornstar. How predictable.

TALK OF THE TOWN

BEN MAISANI

New York City was a-chatter when word hit the street that Anderson Cooper and his successful bar owner boyfriend were on the rocks. Ever since the drama, the couple has kept a low profile. Those sneaky gays. We wish them the best!

KRISTEN STEWART
and
RUPERT SANDERS

Twi hard to fuckin' calm down! Fans of the *Twilight* saga lost their shit when *Us Weekly* released amazing photos of Kristen making out in public with her *Snow White and the Huntsman* director Rupert Sanders. She's an idiot. But Robert Pattinson took her back, so he's an idiot. But finally in 2013, Rob came to his senses and dumped Kristen and her perma-sourpuss face.

HEIDI KLUM

Remember how these two used to shove their love down our throats with their Halloween parties, yearly vow renewals, and that steamy music video? Well, they divorced and Heidi was supposedly getting down with her bodyguard. She will NOT always love you Seal…sorry.

JOHNNY DEPP *and* AMBER HEARD

While filming *The Rum Diaries*, these two got CLOSE. At the time, Amber was dating a chick and Johnny was in a 14-year relationship with the corpse model Vanessa Paradis. The word around Hollyweird is that Vanessa was spouting off venomous words about Ms. Amber and her slutty ways. Who knows? Johnny is now single and exercising his boner at a frequent rate.

TIKI BARBER

Ex-football player Tiki Barber began working at NBC as a correspondent and quickly started hanging out with a hot blonde intern. Oh, and Tiki's wife was eight months pregnant. Nice!

INTERN

ASHTON KUTCHER

Ashton Coochie! Rumor has it Demi likes to skinny dip in a certain kind of pond with her boy-toy husbo. Ashton eventually deleted his cougar wife from the equation.

DANNY DeVITO

Don't let the midget love die! Danny was accused of cheating on his wife of 30 years Rhea Perlman with a film extra. But Rhea eventually gave Danny another chance.

TALK OF THE TOWN

MICHAEL JACKSON

The King of Pop was accused multiple times of touching kids' no-no holes but avoided jail time. At the end of his last trial, there was a woman outside the courtroom who released a dove for every "not guilty" that was read. Soon Jacko went to sleep permanently.

ROMAN POLANSKI

The Oscar-winning director's idea of the perfect date is some champagne and a quaalude or two and a good bufu!

JERRY LEE LEWIS

The "Great Balls of Fire" singer married his 13-year-old cousin. This is all sorts of wrong.

Note:
Wow, I just realized my drawing of Jerry Lee Lewis looks like Puck from the Real World: San Francisco. Whatever, I'm into it.

ELVIS PRESLEY

Elvis got weird with Priscilla when he met her in 1959. He was 24 and she was 14.

WOODY ALLEN

Woody and Mia began dating in 1980. Mia entered the marriage with children from a previous marriage including her 10-year-old adopted daughter Soon-Yi. Well, when Soon-Yi was a teenager, she became Woody's new favorite. Well, Mia flipped her shit. The two parted ways, and Woody went on to marry Soon-Yi in 1997.

DOUG HUTCHINSON

The 51-year-old washed-up actor married 16-year-old Courtney Stodden with her parents' permission, of course (?), and set the world on fire.

TALK OF THE TOWN

PAMELA ANDERSON *and* TOMMY LEE

This shit started the celebrity sex tape craze. It also proved that Tommy Lee was QUITE the man.

ROB LOWE

A ménage à trois sex tape was leaked of Robbie boy having sex with two young women (one underage).

TOM SIZEMORE

Heidi Fleiss's favorite client might have an eight-hour sex tape.

PARIS HILTON

While being filmed with a night vision camera, Paris Hilton resembled a raccoon feasting on fresh garbage.

DUSTIN DIAMOND

Yeah, so Screech made a sex tape called *Saved By the Smell*. In the end, he gives his lady friend a dirty sanchez, kid you not!

COLIN FARRELL

Colin makes Irish men proud in his video escapade with a black Playmate.

WITH LEGS WIDE OPEN!

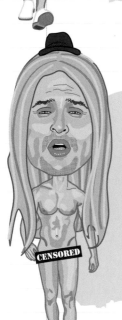

KID ROCK *and* SCOTT STAPP *got it on with* A BUNCH OF GROUPIES

Everyone's favorite Republican rockers have a sex tape! No, they aren't brokebacking it. Rather, they are simultaneously getting blow j's from several groupies.

KIM KARDASHIAN

This is the tape that made Kim a *SUPERSTAR*! With the help of her Momager, Kris Jenner, she was able to earn a profit from the "leaked" sex tape. Once Ryan Seacrest saw Kim's skills, he decided to give Kim and her family a reality show. Now the Kardashian clan rakes in about $60 million a year!

TALK OF THE TOWN

FRED DURST
Watching Fred do it for the nookie will cause your eyeballs to bleed.

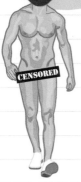

GENE SIMMONS
The KISS bassist shows the world how he tortures his victims.

VERNE TROYER
Someone fucked Mini-Me and for some reason wanted a video to remember it by.

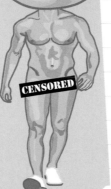

– – – – – – – –
– – – – – – – –

There is gossip that this actress uses her feet in a very curious way. Fun Fact: her mom gave birth to her while in jail.

GUESS WHO?!

DANIELLE STAUB

The Real Housewives of New Jersey star who looks like Jafar from *Aladdin* has a sex tape, and it is pretty much like *The Ring*. If you watch it, you will die in seven days. Do NOT look directly at her giant CLIT ring. It is the size of a doorknocker.

GUESS WHO?!

In 2011, this triple threat's first husband started shopping around an old sex tape of her. It's 20 minutes long and she supposedly flashes her beave at the camera.

TONYA HARDING

Nancy Kerrigan's mortal enemy drunkenly fucks her loser husband on film. What would you rather do: Get shot in the face or watch the ex-figure skater's sex tape *Tonya Harding's Wedding Night*?

REBECCA GAYHEART *and* ERIC DANE

McSteamy and his wife might have a 12-minute sex tape with special guest star. No joke, Mcthreesome.

99

TALK OF THE TOWN

– – – – –

– – – – – – – – –

This male model-turned-actor jerked it online in a chat room with a female model. While he was stroking his weentron he started listing off all the movies he was in.

HULK HOGAN

If you haven't seen the clip of Hulk getting a beej and boning his BEST FRIEND'S wife, please google this. GOOGADIS! It's insane. At one point, Hulk says, "Fuck, I just ate, too. I feel like a pig."

I'M GONNA WRESTLE WITH YO WIFE, BROTHER!

CENSORED

YOU KNOW WHAT YOU DID!

LAUREN CONRAD

While on *The Hills*, Heidi and Spencer started a rumor that there was an LC sex tape. The couple said Lauren's lady bits were anything but bitty, so they dubbed her "Beef Curtains." Ouch.

CENSORED

CENSORED

GUESS WHO?!

– – – – –

– – – – –

Word on the street is that there is a tape of this actress doing the nasty with an ex-boyfriend. It's allegedly 30 minutes long, shot in New Mexico, and the couple is boning to a Brandy album. Random!

OCTOMOM

God save our eyes and her litter kids. Octomom claims to be very sexually inexperienced despite having 14 fuck trophies. The sex tape features Octo diddling her skittle and vibing to electro peen.

CENSORED

CENSORED

KANYE WEST

There is supposedly a sex tape of 'Ye doing the nast with a woman who looks like Kim Kardashian. OH, and this dude also showed his dick off on the web.

CENSORED

GUESS WHO?!

GUESS WHO?!

The gossip rags claim there is a saucy video of this Oscar winner from her "bad girl" days. Her current husband is NOT happy about this.

A dirtbag ex-boyfriend says he has a sex tape featuring this very talented up-and-coming actress.

TALK OF THE TOWN

CHRISTINA HENDRICKS

Nude photos of the *Mad Men* star's tits leaked online and surprisingly it did not break the interwebz.

BLAKE LIVELY

Nude pics of the *Gossip Girl* star leaked in 2011.

GUESS WHO?!

_ _ _ _ _ _ _ _ _ _ _ _

Get naked, maybe?

PRINCE HARRY

The British Ginger God was photographed partying nude in Sin City!

OLIVIA MUNN

What's weird about Olivia's nude pics are that she pretty much made a PowerPoint presentation. She added arrows and messages that were pretty shocking. Girl, cut to the point.

CHRIS BROWN
You can see photos of Chris's long skinny shlong online.

RIHANNA
Nude pics leaked of the star, and a lot of sources believe Chris Brown might have released them in an act of revenge.

VANESSA HUDGENS
Nude photos of the Disney star leaked twice! And she has a giant BLACK BUSH!

KATE MIDDLETON
Some creepy photog snapped topless pics of the Duchess while she was on vacation. She is smoking in some shots, too. Scandalous!

SCARLETT JOHANSSON
Her phone was hacked and naked cell phone pics were exposed! She brought the celebrity hackers to court and won.

TALK OF THE TOWN

HEIDI FLEISS

Bitch is cray. She loves birds and has over a dozen as pets. When Madam Fleiss was 25 she started a Hollywood prostitution ring. She's never revealed the names of her famous clients. Stay classy, Madam!

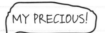

MY PRECIOUS!

HUGH GRANT

Hugh cheated on Elizabeth Hurley with a straight up prostitute. Big ups to Ms. Divine Brown!

ELIOT SPITZER

It's not shocking that Mr. Spitzer paid for 'stutes like Ashley Dupré. He looks like Gollum.

$

JERRY SPRINGER

Police found his name on a check at a "massage parlor."

WINNER WINNER SHEEN DINNER!

CHARLIE SHEEN

How awesome was this maniac's meltdown? Charlie Sheen is from another planet, a martian filled with pure Adonis DNA and tiger blood. The Sheenster welcomes each "goddess" pornstar, like Bree Olson, into his home and even has them babysit his kids. WINNING!

TIGER BLOOD

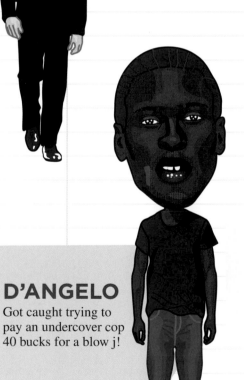

WANNA GET TEABAGGED, EDDIE?

EDDIE MURPHY

Hahahaha! In 1997, Eddie got caught with a tranny hooker.

D'ANGELO

Got caught trying to pay an undercover cop 40 bucks for a blow j!

$

TALK OF THE TOWN

QUENTIN TARANTINO

The talented director is said to have a curious fascination with feet. Hey! Everyone's got their "thing."

MARCIA *and* GREG BRADY

Here's a story: according to Maureen McCormick's memoir, Barry Williams was fucking his on-screen stepsister Marcia, who was a huge cokehead to boot!

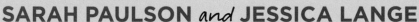

SARAH PAULSON *and* JESSICA LANGE

These two ladies are everything. The *National Enquirer* claimed that Sarah and Jessica were getting frisky while filming *American Horror Story* but Jessica denied it, so my dreams are dead for a super cougar lesbian love affair. :(

RIHANNA *and* CHRIS BROWN

Chris Brown is THE WORST. He beat the shit out of Rihanna. In 2012 the couple rekindled their bad romance.

GERARD BUTLER *and* BRANDI GLANVILLE

When do A-List (OK maybe B-List) actors hook up with reality stars?! The fun part is Gerry had no idea who Brandi was. He was shocked to learn later she was a boozy, "F" bomb-dropping Real Housewife!

TAYLOR SWIFT *and* THE CURIOUS CASE OF THE KENNEDY COUSINS

Reports started surfacing that Tay Tay was doing the dirtay with Arnold Schwarzenegger's son Patrick but then moved on to his cousin Conor Kennedy. Taylor went on to buy a house next to Conor's family's house in Hyannisport. Coincidence? You be the judge.

PEE-WEE HERMAN, FRED WILLARD, and GEORGE MICHAEL

These dudes like to get their freak on in public spots. Pee-Wee likes to jerk it in theaters and so does Fred Willard. George has an affinity for sex in public bathrooms.

JAMES McGREEVEY

"I am a gay American" the NJ governor announced while his WIFE stood next to him. Yep, McGreevey cheated on his wife with a dude. They soon divorced and McGreevey became a full-fledged homo. Welcome to the party, Jimmy!

GAVIN ROSSDALE

When Gavin was 17, he hooked up with a dude. He told *Details* magazine about his experimental phase: "Yeah. That was it. You have to know what you like, and I know what I like."

MEL GIBSON

"You're a dishonest CUNT! You should just SMILE and BLOW ME!" Remember when Radar Online would release a new Mel Gibson voice mail every day that one summer? It was Christmas in July!

LIFE HAS KILLED THE DREAM I DREAMED!

ANNE HATHAWAY *and* RAFFAELLO FOLLIERI

One of Anne's first boyfriends turned out to be a con man! He convinced people he worked for the Vatican and scammed them out of millions. He served time in jail and then was immediately deported back to Italy. Ciao!

MASSEUR #3

MASSEUR #2

MASSEUR #1

MASSEUR #4

MASSEUR #5

JOHN TRAVOLTA

He is a "massage" enthusiast and one of Hollyweird's biggest mysteries!

THE OSCAR **LOVE CURSE**

Win gold, lose love! Reaching the highest professional achievement in Hollywood usually means your love life will soon be in the shitter. Check out who has been affected by the famous curse.

JESSICA LANGE

Jessica won the Best Actress Oscar in 1995 for *Blue Sky*. Soon after, she broke things off with her longtime partner, Sam Shepard.

HELEN HUNT

The TV star turned movie star won Best Actress in 1998 for *As Good As It Gets* and then dumped Hank Azaria for something better.

CHARLIZE THERON

Charlize and Stuart Townsend promised they wouldn't get married until all the gays could legally marry in the USA. Oh, that's sweet. Then Theron won the Oscar for her epic portrayal of Aileen Wournos in *Monster*, and she let Stuart loose.

SUSAN SARANDON

Ms. Sarandon won an Oscar for *Dead Man Walking* in 1996 and made her longtime partner Tim Robbins take a walk.

HILARY SWANK

Well, when Hil won her first Oscar for *Boys Don't Cry,* she forgot to mention her husband Chad Lowe. That is where the problem started. Swank won again in 2005. She thanked Chad, but then soon showed him the door.

HALLE BERRY

After Halle won for playing a topless depressed woman, it was revealed she was leaving her husband Eric Benét. He was a SEX ADDICT!

SANDRA BULLOCK

Why Sandra Bullock married Jesse James is a modern-day enigma. During her Oscar acceptance speech, she cried thanking Jesse. A few weeks later, shit hit the fan...BIG TIME.

DO YOU KNOW WHO I AM?!

REESE WITHERSPOON

After seven years of marriage and Reese's Oscar win, Ryan and Reese announced they were getting divorced because he was supposedly getting side pussy from costar Abbie Cornish.

KATE WINSLET

Kate won for *The Reader* and then kicked her husband Sam Mendes to the curb. Kate went on to marry Richard Branson's nephew Ned, who changed his last name to RocknRoll. Kate RocknRoll?

OTHERS AFFECTED BY THE OSCAR LOVE CURSE

Bette Davis, Ginger Rogers, Joan Crawford, Elizabeth Taylor, Julie Andrews, Barbara Streisand, Maggie Smith, Jane Fonda, Liza Minnelli, Faye Dunaway, Cher, Kathy Bates, Emma Thompson, Goldie Hawn, Mary Steenburgen, Anjelica Huston, Geena Davis, Kim Basinger, Renée Zellweger.

TINY BITS OF
WISDOOM
FOR CELEBRITIES

Celebretards, are you listening? Do you know what's harder than finding fame? Finding love when you're famous. And good luck trying to stay together! We've learned a lot from the dating scandals of Hollywood. Maya Angelou once told Oprah: "When you know better, you do better." So let's do better! Turn down your Beats By Dre headphones and pay attention to a few simple rules.

Don't send naked pics of yourself or for god's sake make a sex tape.

Someone will find that shit and release it. Odds are whomever you are with at the moment of the leak will leave you. And for MOST people, who do not have a crazy momager like Kris Jenner, it will not make you a superstar or land your family a reality show.

Don't win an Oscar if you are in love.

It will FUCK YO SHIT UP. Just stick with those stupid Katherine Heigl RomComs and action flops, um, flicks. Just make money; you don't need industry respect. Is your Oscar going to keep you warm at night when you are 75?

Don't date a whack job.

"When people show you who they really are, BELIEVE THEM." Another life lesson from Oprah's Sister Teacher/Nubian Queen Maya Angelou. Rihanna, honey, are you writing this down?

Don't marry a sex addict.

If you get a weird vibe from your dude or dudet—listen to your heart and dump them immediately.

Don't let your man go to the Victoria's Secret Fashion Show.

It's bad fucking news. You know why? Because those models are hungry and horny. Horngry. They will eat your man's brain and soon you will be dancing like a loser to "Single Ladies" with your forever-alone aunt at your younger cousin's wedding.

Please don't date your costar.

Look at those lovely kids Zac and Vanessa. They tried to bring their *High School Musical* love to the school of life and that shit FAILED. There is on-screen chemistry and off-screen chemistry. You can't have both. CHOOSE.

Never date a comedian (unless they are heavily medicated).

Jim broke Jenny's AND her autistic son's heart. Humor comes from anger, people.

Don't marry a male dancer, ladies.

Britney, LeAnn, and J Lo will tell you. Those dudes are either into other "dancers," undercover lardasses, or bums.

Don't star in a reality show together.

RIP, Jessica and Nick. I'm STILL not over their breakup. AND how many divorces have the *Real Housewives* had now? Oh, 15 divorces in seven seasons, not to mention a murder and a suicide? Stay away.

Lesbians! Don't date bisexual women.

Ellen and Samantha Ronson got sucked into the lies of Heche and Lohan. Don't let this happen to you. These chicks aren't "bisexual," they are "trysexual"—try anything to get more FAMOUS.

Don't have a big expensive extravagant wedding.

That shit is the nail in your marriage coffin. You're just showing off. It's not love, and we all know it.

Never have a threesome. Like never.

Don't have a ménage à trois with your husband. Dudes can't handle it. Soon he will turn those threesomes into twosomes and YOU will be sitting at home, alone.

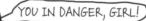

GUESS WHO?!

OUR BODIES ARE FILLED WITH DEAD ALIEN SOULS

Don't marry a religious freak.

Unless, of course, YOU are a religious freak, too; then have at 'em.

Don't match. EVER.

Don't dress alike. Don't get matching highlights. It's practically twincest! You look like assholes, and everyone needs to be their own person. This goes for errbody, gay and straight.

NIC CAGE

married a sushi waitress.

USHER

married a stylist.

ROBERT DE NIRO

married a flight attendant.

TOBEY MAGUIRE

married a jewelry designer.

B-B-BONUS BITCHES!

HERE ARE SOME CELEBS WHO KEPT IT REAL, AND MARRIED REGS!

JULIA ROBERTS

married a camera man.

DAVID SCHWIMMER

married a photographer.

KELSEY GRAMMER

married a flight attendant.

MATT DAMON

married a bartender.

PATRICK DEMPSEY

married a hairdresser.

MARCIA CROSS

married a stockbroker.

JON BON JOVI

married a karate instructor.

VINCE VAUGHN

married a real estate agent.

BUT YOU SHOULD LIKE REALLY DATE!

PERFECT MATCHES

Alright, sluts, let's get our Patti Stanger on. You know the Bravo matchmaker? Whatever, just go with it. Anyway, here's who would be perfect for each other in Hollywood. If these celebs joined forces and private parts, they would reach maximus happiness and become super couples! Trust!

JENNIFER LAWRENCE
&
RYAN GOSLING

Both are SUPER talented. They have great personalities and do not take themselves too seriously.

The internet would most likely break if these two hooked up. Plus, their kids would so hot.

ROBERT PATTINSON
&
SIENNA MILLER

These two both seem like they have a bad attitude. They were both cheated on and have good teeth, despite being British.

JESSE JAMES
&
KRISTEN STEWART

Have you ever seen KStew's parents? They look like they are from that show *Sons of Anarchy*.

CAMERON DIAZ
&
LEONARDO DiCAPRIO

They've both kissed a lot of frogs, so they should just give it up and get together. Can you imagine the yacht they could build together? Mula, baby$!

P DIDDY
&
JENNIFER
LOPEZ

These two were the best together. From the insane Grammy dress to the gun in the nightclub, pure love! They should reunite....

LINDSAY
LOHAN
&
COREY
FELDMAN

This pairing would be magical if they both continue living and were "sober." It would need to be a reality show. The series would be a ratings juggernaut.

MILEY CYRUS
&
JUSTIN BIEBER

These two soul sisters even look alike.
Come on, ladies, make beautiful
music together!

ANDY COHEN
&
ANDERSON COOPER

OH, ANDY! OH, ANDY! This shit would
be so cute! It would excite straight women
across the nation!

TIGER WOODS & RIHANNA

Let's get down to business, Tiger. You like a bad girl, so stop it and get with Rihanna. You KNOW she is down for WHATEVER.

DEMI MOORE & MACAULAY CULKIN

You know it BURNS Demi that Ashton got with Mila Kunis. So D should get with Mila's ex Macaulay. DUH! They could sit around and trash their exes!

CENSORED

TAYLOR SWIFT
&
ADAM LEVINE

If you can't be with Jake, ya gotta
get with his friends.

PIPPA MIDDLETON
&
PRINCE HARRY

You know these two were MEANT for
each other. They are both the badasses in
the family and flirt HARD. Supposedly
Harry calls Pippa COMMANDO. Hot!

DENNIS RODMAN
&
NICKI MINAJ

Isn't it fucking obvious? They could dye each other's hair, wear matching dresses, and just be assholes together!

ALEXANDER SKARSGÅRD
&
CHARLIZE THERON

These two could make beautiful, tall, Swedish, African, blond, model babies!

JON HAMM
&
KRISTEN WIIG

Jon and Kristen need to get it together
and get together! They're hilarious and
would be a super comedy couple, fo' sho.

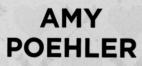

AMY
POEHLER
&
TINA FEY

Ladies, ditch the dudes. It would be
like the modern-day *Brady Bunch* with
laughs and a shit ton of money. You
could snuggle and watch *Homeland*
together. You'll love it! We'll love it!
Pretty please!

JOE SIMPSON & KEN PAVES

Jessica Simpson's dad and her ex-main gay should totally get together.

CHAZ BONO & LANA DEL REY

Alright this is a little out there, but stay with me, Chaz is Cher's transsexual son and Lana is very alternative. They are both sober. Chaz loves video games and Lana sings about them. Can you see it now?

LADY GAGA & MARILYN MANSON

It's gonna be hard for Gaga to find a man to put up with her. She's a freak. A good kinda freak, but she needs another weirdo to make it last.

KATIE HOLMES & BRADLEY COOPER

Katie needs low-key after Tom Cruise. Brad seems very chill, with his head on straight. They could split their time between Ohio and Pennsylvania, and avoid Hollyweird.

BUT I'M LIKE REALLY LOOKING FOR A DATE
an online dating community

Send Amanda a message…

Amanda Bynes

Um, no • Empire State of Mind
Looking for dudes

Long hair, don't care.

Education NICKELODEON

Height ?, I WEIGH 100lbs

Body Type STRIPPER

Diet GUMMY BEARS AND DIET COKE

Drinks YES

Drugs I PLEAD THE 5th, hehe

Profession RETIRED ACTRESS

Hometown NICKELODEON

My self-summary
RAWR! I love makeup. If you say I'm going off the rails, I WILL SUE YOU.

The first thing people usually notice about me
How skinny I am.

Fun fact about me
I survived Hurricane Sandy.

Q & A

What is your spirit animal?
A leopard, because they are sexy and skinny. I like their spots!

The most private thing I'm willing to admit
I wear a DD bra.

I'm really good at
Posing for selfies and working out at the gym.

I spend a lot of time thinking about
Drake. MURDER MY VAGINA!

What I'm doing with my life
Living the dream in NYC. Starting a fashion line.

BUT I'M LIKE REALLY LOOKING FOR A DATE

an online dating community

Send Justin a message...

Justin Bieber

19 • All around the world...
Looking for Mrs. Bieber

Never say never.

Education Self taught

Height I'm still growing

Body Type Rock hard

Diet POUTINE

Drinks NO

Drugs NO WAY ;)

Profession TRIPLE THREAT

Hometown CanaDUH!

My self-summary
GOOGLE ME.

The first thing people usually notice about me
My hair and my SWAG.

Fun fact about me
I have a really long tongue!

Q & A

What is your spirit animal?
A beaver.

The most private thing I'm willing to admit
Sometimes I get really lonely in this world. But then I log onto Twitter and I'm like "Whoa, I have 38 million fans."

I'm really good at
Pleasing a woman.

I spend a lot of time thinking about
Dropping a #2. You can't do that on the tour bus!

What I'm doing with my life
Conquering the world. Michael Jackson's spirit lives on in me.

BUT I'M LIKE REALLY LOOKING FOR A DATE

Send MaStew a message…

Martha Stewart

71, bitch • Business in the city, party in the country
Looking for men

The bigger the peony, the better.

Education Schoolin' Life

Height Tall Enough

Body Type Toned

Diet Gourmet 24/7

Drinks STRAIGHT UP

Drugs I've baked brownies with Snoop Lion.

Profession HBIC (Head Bitch In Charge)

Hometown Jersey Strong

My self-summary
I've done a lot in my life. I've built an empire for christsakes. I'm an avid animal lover and my dogs are champions. Yes, I've spent some time in the clink, but it's only made me stronger. "What doesn't kill you…" right, Kelly Clarkson? I love her! In prison, I was not anyone's bitch. The ladies were quite lovely and they loved calling me MaStew. Please do not message me if you are UNEMPLOYED. *I can't get with that.*

Q & A

What is your spirit animal?
Bald eagle. I fly above the drama. I enjoy a great aerial view so I know when to swoop in and put people in their place.

The most private thing I'm willing to admit
I like to drink pickle juice!

I'm really good at
Poaching eggs, gardening, teaching inmates to knit.

I spend a lot of time thinking about
BRUNCH.

What I'm doing with my life
Um, what I am I NOT doing with my life. My company is Martha Stewart Living OMNIMEDIA.

Fun fact about me
I dated Hannibal Lecter!

BUT I'M LIKE REALLY LOOKING FOR A DATE

an online dating community

Send Bethenny a message...

Bethenny Frankel

40ish • Nueva York
Looking for men

Keep it skinny!

Education National Gourmet Institute

Height I think I've shrunk from all the stress

Body Type Skinnygirl

Diet Nibbler

Drinks Booze = cash

Drugs What? No.

Profession MOGUL

Hometown Ugh, Florida

Q & A

What is your spirit animal?
A chihuahua. I might be small but I've got a bark on me and I'll gnaw your balls off.

The most private thing I'm willing to admit
I literally have sex dreams about red velvet cake.

I'm really good at
Shutting. It. Down.

I spend a lot of time thinking about
The last time I got laid. It's been awhile and I'm afraid if I don't use it, I'll lose it.

What I'm doing with my life
Getting over a divorce.

My self-summary
Believe me, I can swim in the shark tank. Did you see me on *Real Housewives*? Sheesh.

The first thing people usually notice about me
How naturally thin I am.

Fun fact about me
I pissed in a trash can in my wedding dress while I was pregnant!

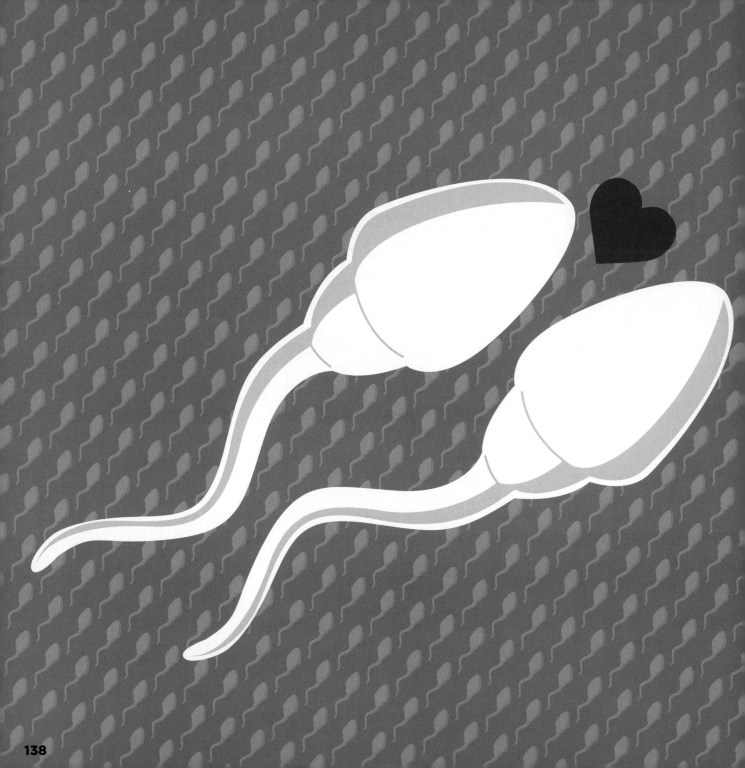

The Children Are Our Future

Teach them well *and* let them lead the way. Pour one out for our fallen homie, Whitney Houston!

These kids need help and they, like their parents, will most likely only date other famous spawn. So, Maddox Jolie-Pitt, if you are reading this, TRUST this book and date Sasha Obama.

Mom
Mama June aka Coupon Queen
Dad
Sugar Bear

Mom
Angelina Jolie
Dad
Brad Pitt

Mom
Teresa Giudice
Dad
Juicy Joe Giudice

Mom
Kourtney Kardashian
Dad
Scott Disick

HONEY BOO BOO
should date
SHILOH JOLIE-PITT

Brad and Angie's gorgeous daughter will want to escape the ego monsters of Hollyweird when she gets older. Honey Boo will be waiting for Shiloh with her go-go juice. A dollar makes her hollah, y'all!

MILANIA GIUDICE
should date
MASON DISICK

All hail Milania. She is the breakout star of *The Real Housewives of New Jersey*. Guidos and guidettes all want the best for Milania. She deserves a man who can spoil her rotten. Mason Disick will be able to bankroll her shopping habit.

Mom
Katie Holmes
Dad
Tom Cruise

Mom
Rachel Zoe
Dad
Rodger Berman

SURI CRUISE
should date
SKYLER BERMAN

Suri is a she-demon. Ms. Cruise needs a man she can boss around. He must be into fashion. So if Rachel Zoe's greatest wish of having a gay son does not come true, he should go for Suri!

Mom
Angelina Jolie
Dad
Brad Pitt

Mom
Michelle Obama
Dad
Barack Obama

MADDOX JOLIE-PITT
should date
SASHA OBAMA

Maddox has traveled around the world. Even before Angie got with Brad, he hung tough with his mom. Mads will know how to treat a woman. He will be smart, political, and passionate. Maddox deserves Sasha Obama.

Mom
Bridget
Moynahan
Dad
Tom Brady

Mom
Jessica
Simpson
Dad
Eric
Johnson

JACK BRADY
should date
MAXWELL JOHNSON

Well, both their dads are footballers! Jack is going to be a lady killer and li'l Maxi will be a Hollywood socialite, fo' sho.

Mom
Beyoncé
Dad
Jay-Z

Mom
Adele
Dad
Who
cares

BLUE IVY
should date
ADELE'S SON

The British powerhouse's full name is Adele Laurie Blue Adkins. So it is written in the stars that Adele's son (who she quietly named Angelo) is going to date hip-hop royalty, Ms. Blue Ivy Carter.

Mom
Michelle
Williams
Dad
Heath
Ledger

Mom
Angelina
Jolie
Dad
Brad
Pitt

MATILDA LEDGER
should date
PAX JOLIE-PITT

Matilda is in our hearts. We want the best for our quirky li'l princess. But she may have a thing for bad boys. Pax Jolie will give her that rush.

Mom
Giuliana
Rancic
Dad
Bill
Rancic

Mom
Tori
Spelling
Dad
Dean
McDermott

EDWARD DUKE RANCIC
should date
HATTIE McDERMOTT

These two could date, get engaged, get married, have a baby, all on reality TV.

Mom
Reese
Witherspoon
Dad
Ryan
Phillippe

Mom
Victoria
Beckham
Dad
David
Beckham

AVA PHILLIPPE
should date
BROOKLYN
BECKHAM

Ava is a little hipster who is going to want an international heartthrob to give her a certain edge. Brooklyn's got it.

Mom
Nicole Richie
Dad
Joel Madden

Mom
Victoria
Beckham
Dad
David
Beckham

HARLOW
MADDEN
should date
ROMEO
BECKHAM

Harlow is going to be a fashion maven with a flair for mischievous boys like her dad. Romeo will break her heart, but in the end will be her soulmate.

Mom
Courteney
Cox
Dad
David
Arquette

Mom
Britney Spears
Dad
Kevin Federline

IT'S SEAN PRESTON, BITCH!

COCO ARQUETTE
should date
SEAN PRESTON FEDERLINE

The Federline boys are tons of fun. Coco loves that. Her dad is David Arquette, after all. These two will hit it off like crazy.

Mom
Jada
Pinkett Smith
Dad
Will Smith

Mom
Lady Gaga
Dad
TBD

WILLOW SMITH
should date
LADY GAGA'S SON

Even if Gaga has a daughter, they could still be besties.

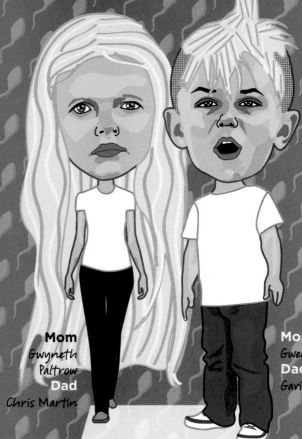

Mom
Gwyneth
Paltrow
Dad
Chris Martin

Mom
Gwen Stefani
Dad
Gavin Rossdale

APPLE MARTIN
should date
KINGSTON ROSSDALE

Two little rockstars! Apple and Kingston can dip dye each other's hair, smoke cigs, and write music together.

Mom
Gwyneth
Paltrow
Dad
Chris Martin

Mom
Nicole
Kidman
Dad
Keith
Urban

MOSES MARTIN
should date
SUNDAY ROSE URBAN

Moses and Sunday are both quiet and shy. They will be romantic and sensitive and rich!

Mom
Madonna
Dad
Carlos Leon

Mom
Sandra Bullock
Dad
???

Mom
Reese
Witherspoon
Dad
Ryan Phillippe

Mom
Jennifer
Garner
Dad
Ben Affleck

LOURDES LEON
should date
LOUIS BULLOCK

You KNOW Lourdes is going to follow in her mom's footsteps and date younger men. Lola will be 15 years Louis's senior. He will be hot, hip, and YOUNG.

DEACON PHILLIPPE
should date
VIOLET AFFLECK

Deacon and Violet will be so cute together! He will be all sporty and she will be all brainy. It will be young love at its best!

CELEBRITY
Rap Sheets

That's right. Takin' names and makin' notes. Don't think you can just hook up with Fred Durst and think everyone will forget about it. WE KNOW. We might not talk about it on a regular basis, but we will never forget, and we're judging you. Get excited! The next few pages list who's hooked up with who in Hollyweird.

50 CENT

Joy Bryant
Kelly Rowland
Kim Kardashian
Naomi Campbell
Eva Longoria
Lindsay Lohan
Nicole Scherzinger
Vanessa Marcil
Ciara
Paris Hilton
Chelsea Handler

ADAM DURITZ

Christina Applegate
Lara Flynn Boyle
Monica Potter
Gwen Stefani
Winona Ryder
Jennifer Aniston
Courteney Cox
Mary-Louise Parker
Samantha Mathis
Trishelle Cannatella
Emmy Rossum

ADAM LEVINE

Jessica Simpson
Maria Sharapova
Cameron Diaz
A shit ton of models

ALEC BALDWIN

Ally Sheedy
Julia Roberts
Cheri Oteri
Janine Turner
Kim Basinger
Kristen Davis
Tatum O'Neal
Lori Singer
Hilaria Thomas

ALEX RODRIGUEZ

Madonna
Kate Hudson
Cameron Diaz
Demi Moore

ALEXANDER SKARSGÅRD

Amanda Seyfried
Evan Rachel Wood
Kate Bosworth

Skarsgård (cont'd)
Elizabeth Olsen
Charlize Theron
Ellen Page

AMANDA BYNES

Drake Bell
Taran Killam
Frankie Muniz
Nick Zano
Channing Tatum
David Cross
Seth MacFarlane
Liam Hemsworth
Kid Cudi

AMANDA SEYFRIED

Emile Hirsch
Alexander Skarsgård
Dominic Cooper
Ryan Phillippe
Josh Hartnett
James Franco
Ben Barnes

ALYSSA MILANO

Corey Feldman
Jonathan Silverman
Kirk Cameron FAIL
Corey Haim

Milano (cont'd)
David Arquette
Eric Nies
Scott Wolf
Justin Timberlake
Fred Durst
Eric Dane

ANGELINA JOLIE

Oliver Stone
Jenny Shimizu
Jonny Lee Miller
Mick Jagger WTF
Timothy Hutton
Billy Bob Thornton
HER BROTHER
Nicolas Cage
Val Kilmer
Brad Pitt

ANNA PAQUIN

Joaquin Phoenix
Logan Marshall-Green
Kieran Culkin
Stephen Moyer

ANNE HATHAWAY

Topher Grace
Scott Sartiano
A Criminal
Adam Shulman

ASHLEE SIMPSON

Josh Henderson
Carson Daly
Ryan Cabrera
Wilmer Valderrama
Pete Wentz
Vincent Piazza

ASHLEY GREENE

Jackson Rathbone
Gerard Butler
Ryan Phillippe
Robert Pattinson
Nick Jonas
Chace Crawford
Seth MacFarlane
Ian Somerhalder
Adrian Grenier
Kellan Lutz
Jared Followill
Brock Kelly
Joe Jonas
Reeve Carney

ASHLEY OLSEN

Jared Leto
Lance Armstrong
Justin Bartha
Johnny Depp

ASHTON KUTCHER

Nelly Furtado
January Jones
Ashley Scott
Brittany Murphy
Monet Mazur
Demi Moore
Mila Kunis

AUDRINA PATRIDGE

Justin Bobby
Chris Pine
Mark Salling
Ryan Cabrera

AVRIL LAVIGNE

Deryck Whibley
Doug Robb HOOBASTANK
Brandon Davis
Wilmer Valderrama
Brody Jenner
Chad Kroeger

I'M COMPLICATED.

B

BEN AFFLECK

Britney Spears REALLY?
Jaime King
Lauren Holly
Salma Hayek
Shoshanna Lonstein
Gwyneth Paltrow
Famke Janssen
Jennifer Lopez UGH
Krista Allen
Jennifer Garner

BEYONCÉ KNOWLES

Mekhi Phifer
Shemar Moore GET IT, GIRL
Mos Def
Eminem
Jay-Z

BLAKE LIVELY

Penn Badgley
Ryan Gosling
Leonardo DiCaprio
Ryan Reynolds

BRAD PITT

Juliette Lewis
Gwyneth Paltrow
Jennifer Aniston
Robin Givens
Christina Applegate
Elizabeth Daily
Thandie Newton
Claire Forlani
Demi Moore
Angelina Jolie

BRADLEY COOPER

Denise Richards WTF
Isabella Brewster
Jennifer Esposito
Cameron Diaz
Renée Zellweger
Olivia Wilde
Jennifer Lopez
Zoe Saldana
Jennifer Aniston
Mélanie Laurent
Sandra Bullock
Lake Bell
Jaime King
Jessica Biel
Scarlett Johansson

BRITNEY SPEARS

Please see pp 26–27 of
THE DIRTY DOZEN

151

BRODY JENNER

Kristin Cavallari
Lindsay Lohan
Nicole Richie
Lauren Conrad
Haylie Duff
Paris Hilton
Jayde Nicole
Avril Lavigne

BROOKE SHIELDS

Woody Harrelson
Scott Baio
Matt Dillon
John Travolta
Michael Jackson
Ted McGinley
John Kennedy Jr.
Dean Cain
George Michael
David Lee Roth
Nicolas Cage
Liam Neeson
Julian Lennon
Michael Bolton
Andre Agassi

BRUCE WILLIS

Janice Dickinson
Estella Warren
Demi Moore
Rachel Hunter
Kim Cattrall
Brooke Burns
Lindsay Lohan

C

CAMERON DIAZ

Please see pp 16–17 of
THE DIRTY DOZEN

CARMEN ELECTRA

Colin Farrell
Mark McGrath
Vin Diesel
Victoria Silvstedt
David Spade
Prince
Dennis Rodman
Fred Durst
Tommy Lee
Leonardo DiCaprio

Electra (cont'd)
Dave Navarro
Joan Jett
Simon Cowell

CHACE CRAWFORD

Shauna Sands REALLY?
Carrie Underwear (UH, UNDERWOOD)
Ashley Greene
Taylor Momsen
Bar Refaeli
Lauren Conrad
Erin Andrews

CHARLIE SHEEN

MAD Pornstars
Robin Wright Penn
Winona Ryder
Heidi Fleiss
Kelly Preston
Stephanie Seymour
Denise Richards
Ashley Dupré
Brooke Mueller

CHARLIZE THERON

David Arquette
Stephan Jenkins
THIRD EYE BLIND
George Clooney

Theron (cont'd)
Stuart Townsend
Keanu Reeves
Jeremy Renner
Ryan Reynolds
Alexander Skarsgård

CHER

Elvis THEY HOOKED UP
IN THE 70s!?
Tom Cruise
Richie Sambora
Warren Beatty
Sonny Bono
David Geffen
Gregg Allman
Gene Simmons
Les Dudek
Val Kilmer
Michael Bolton
Tommy Lee

CHRIS BROWN

Kelly Rowland
Lil Mama
Rihanna MAKE IT STOP!
Karrueche Tran
Nicole Scherzinger

CHRISTIAN BALE

Drew Barrymore
Winona Ryder
Samantha Mathis
Anna Friel

CHRISTINA AGUILERA

Fred Durst
Enrique Iglesias
Jordan Bratman
Pharrell Williams

CHRISTINA APPLEGATE

Steven Adler
Adam Duritz
Richard Grieco
Sebastian Bach
Brad Pitt
Christian Slater
Johnathon Schaech

CLAIRE DANES

Leonardo DiCaprio
Andrew Dorff
Ben Lee
Matt Damon
Billy Crudup
Hugh Dancy

COLIN FARRELL

Britney Spears
Lindsay Lohan
Rosario Dawson
Angelina Jolie
Carmen Electra
Paris Hilton
Michelle Rodriguez
Demi Moore

CORY MONTEITH

Taylor Swift
Lea Michele

COURTENEY COX

Josh Hopkins
Michael Keaton
Kevin Costner
Liev Schreiber
Adam Duritz
David Arquette

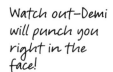

Watch out—Demi will punch you right in the face!

D

DANIEL CRAIG

Kate Moss
Sienna Miller
Rachel Weisz

DAVID SPADE

Carmen Electra
Kristy Swanson
OG BUFFY: VAMPIRE SLAYER!
Julie Bown
Lara Flynn Boyle
Krista Allen
Julie Bowen
Jillian Barberie
Heather Locklear
Pamela Anderson
Nicollette Sheridan
MAD Pornstars

DEMI LOVATO

Joe Jonas
Wilmer Valderrama
Niall Horan

DEMI MOORE

Please see pp 24–25 of THE DIRTY DOZEN

DENISE RICHARDS

John Stamos
Scott Baio
Bradley Cooper
Paul Walker
Patrick Muldoon
Charlie Sheen
Richie Sambora
Nikki Sixx

P DIDDY

Kim Porter
Jennifer Lopez
Naomi Campbell
Sienna Miller
Aubrey O'Day
Cassie Ventura
Cameron Diaz

DREW BARRYMORE

Please see pp 12–13 of THE DIRTY DOZEN

E

ED WESTWICK

Leighton Meester
Drew Barrymore
Jessica Szohr

ELLEN DeGENERES

Anne Heche
Portia de Rossi

EMILY BLUNT

Michael Bublé
John Krasinski

EVA LONGORIA

50 Cent
J.C. Chasez
Tony Parker
Hayden Christensen
Eduardo Cruz
PENELOPE'S BRO

EVA MENDES

Jason Sudeikis
Ryan Gosling
EVA, FALL BACK, BITCH!

EVAN RACHEL WOOD

Edward Norton
Marilyn Manson
Joseph Gordon-Levitt
Shane West
Alexander Skarsgård
Jamie Bell

F

FERGIE

Mario Lopez
Justin Timberlake
Josh Duhamel

FRED DURST

Lauren Holly
Rachel Hunter
Bijou Phillips
Christina Aguilera
Courtney Love

Durst (cont'd)
Tara Reid
Thora Birch
Britney Spears
Alyssa Milano
Halle Berry
Geri Halliwell
Brittany Murphy
Pamela Anderson
Paris Hilton
Jessica Simpson

G

GEORGE CLOONEY

Please see pp 18–19 of
THE DIRTY DOZEN

GERARD BUTLER

Jennifer Aniston
Lindsay Lohan
Jessica Biel
Ashley Greene
Rosario Dawson
Naomi Campbell
Cameron Diaz
Shanna Moakler
Brandi Glanville

GISELE BÜNDCHEN

Rodrigo Santoro
Leonardo DiCaprio
Kelly Slater
Chris Evans
Tom Brady

GWEN STEFANI

Adam Duritz
Tony Kanal
Gavin Rossdale

GWYNETH PALTROW

Scott Speedman
Chris Heinz
Robert Sean Leonard
Brad Pitt
Viggo Mortensen
Ben Affleck
James Purefoy
Bryan Adams
Felipe de Borbón
Aaron Eckhart
Luke Wilson
Chris Martin

Gwynnie goops
diamonds, y'all!

H

HALLE BERRY

Kevin Costner
Danny Wood
Wesley Snipes
David Justice
Shemar Moore
Eric Benet
Fred Durst
Michael Early
Gabriel Aubry
Olivier Martinez

HAYDEN PANETTIERE

SHE'S A LITTLE TROLL!
Stephen Colletti
Milo Ventimiglia
Jess McCartney
Steve Jones
Harry Morton
Kevin Connolly

HEATH LEDGER

Julia Stiles
Heather Graham
Shannyn Sossamon
Naomi Watts
Michelle Williams

Ledger (cont'd)
Helena Christensen
Kate Hudson
Gemma Ward
Mary-Kate Olsen
Lindsay Lohan

HEATHER LOCKLEAR

Scott Baio
Tom Cruise
Mark Harmon
Tommy Lee
Richie Sambora
David Spade
Jack Wagner

HEIDI KLUM

Anthony Kiedis
Jay Kay aka Jamiroquai
Seal
Martin Kirsten
HER BODYGUARD, RIP WHITNEY

HILARY DUFF

Aaron Carter
Shia LaBeouf
Frankie Muniz
Joel Madden
Mike Comrie

J

JACK NICHOLSON

Joni Mitchell
Kelly LeBrock
Marg Helgenberger
Julie Delpy
Heidi Fleiss
Candice Bergen
Angelica Huston
Janice Dickinson
Christina Onassis
Angie Everhart
Lara Flynn Boyle
Kate Moss REALLY?
Jessica Simpson HE ASKED HER OUT ON A DINNER DATE; SHE SAID NO!

JAKE GYLLENHAAL

Camilla Belle
Olivia Wilde
Isabel Lucas
Jenny Lewis
Kirsten Dunst
Natalie Portman
Reese Witherspoon
Rachel Bilson
Taylor Swift
Anna Kendrick
Minka Kelly

JAMES FRANCO

Sienna Miller
Lindsay Lohan
Marla Sokoloff FULL HOUSE, BITCHES!
Roger Garth A DUDE?
Amanda Seyfried

JANET JACKSON

Rob Lowe
Q-Tip
Jermaine Dupri
Matthew McConaughey
Wanya Morris FROM BOYZ II MEN

JANUARY JONES

Ashton Kutcher
Jim Carrey
Brandon Davis
Seann William Scott
Josh Groban
Tommy Alastra
Jeremy Piven
Adrian Brody
Bobby Flay
Jason Sudeikis

JARED LETO

Soleil Moon Frye
PUNKY BREWSTER
Cameron Diaz
Britney Spears
Scarlett Johansson
Tila Tequila EWW
Ashley Olsen
Lindsay Lohan
Sharon Stone REALLY?
Paris Hilton
Lydia Hearst
MAD Models

JENNIFER ANISTON

Tate Donovan
Adam Duritz
Jon Stewart
Brad Pitt
Vince Vaughn
Paul Sculfor
John Mayer
Bradley Cooper
Gerard Butler
Justin Theroux

JENNIFER GARNER

Scott Foley
Michael Vartan
Ben Affleck

JENNIFER LOPEZ

Wesley Snipes
Ojani Nowa
P Diddy
Cris Judd
Ben Affleck
Marc Anthony
Bradley Cooper
Casper Smart

JENNIFER LOVE HEWITT

Joey Lawrence
Will Friedle
Andrew Keegan
Carson Daly
Rich Cronin
Wilmer Valderrama
Patrick Wilson
Enrique Iglesias
Shaggy
John Mayer
Stephen Dorff
John Cusack
Kip Pardue

Love Hewitt (cont'd)
Antonio Sabato Jr.
Jamie Kennedy
John Mallory Asher

JENNY McCARTHY

Chris Hardwick
SINGLED OUT!
Ivan Sergei
John Mallory Asher
WEIRD SCIENCE!
Jenna Jameson REALLY?
Jim Carrey

JESSICA ALBA

Michael Weatherly
Mark Wahlberg
Derek Jeter
Cash Warren

JESSICA BIEL

Chris Evans
Edward Norton
Derek Jeter
Justin
Timberlake
Gerard Butler

JESSICA SIMPSON

Leonardo DiCaprio
Jensen Ackles
Nick Lachey
Adam Levine
Fred Durst
Bam Margera
Dane Cook
John Mayer
Jeremy Renner
Marcus Schenkenberg
Tony Romo
Billy Corgan
Eric Johnson

JESSICA SZOHR

Jason Lewis
Ed Westwick

JOE JONAS

Sky Ferreira
JoJo
Taylor Swift
Camilla Belle
Brenda Song
Demi Lovato
Ashley Greene

JOEL MADDEN

Hilary Duff
Nicole Richie

JOHN CUSACK

Jamie Gertz
Huma Abedin
WEINER'S WIFE?!
Claire Forlani
Janice Dickinson
Lili Taylor
Ione Skye
Gina Gershon
Minnie Driver
Alison Eastwood
Neve Campbell
Shoshanna Lonstein
Jodi Lyn O'Keefe
Jennifer Love Hewitt
Rebecca Romijn
Alexandra Kerry
Brooke Burns

JEFF GOLDBLUM

Geena Davis
Laura Dern
Kristin Davis
Nicole Richie
Tania Raymonde
Lydia Hearst

JOEY LAWRENCE

Keri Russell
FELICITY 4 LIFE!
Katherine Heigl
Jennifer Love Hewitt

JOHN KRASINSKI

Rashida Jones
Renée Zellweger
Emily Blunt

JOHN MAYER

Miley Cyrus
Ke$ha
Vanessa Carlton
Jennifer Love Hewitt
Rhona Mitra
Jessica Simpson
Minka Kelly
Jennifer Aniston
Taylor Swift

Mayer (cont'd)
Giada De Laurentiis
Katy Perry

JOHNNY DEPP

Sherilyn Fenn
Jennifer Grey
Winona Ryder
Traci Lords
Juliette Lewis
Holly Robinson Peete
Juliette Lewis
Ellen Barkin
Kate Moss
Salma Hayek
Naomi Campbell
Vanessa Paradis
Christina Ricci
Eva Green
Ashley Olsen
Amber Heard

JOHN STAMOS

Demi Moore
Natasha Henstridge
Denise Richards
Ingrid Sthare
MAD Models
Chelsea Noble
GROWING PAINS
Lori Loughlin
Marlee Matlin
Paula FUCKING Abdul

Stamos (cont'd)
Julie Anderson
Rebecca Romijn

JOSH DUHAMEL

Kristy Pierce
Nikki Cox
Fergie
Some Stripper

JOSH HARTNETT

Julia Stiles
Natalie Imbruglia
TORN?!
Kirsten Dunst
Scarlett Johansson
Gemma Ward
Sienna Miller
Penelope Cruz
Rihanna
Mischa Barton
Amanda Seyfried

JOSH HUTCHERSON

AnnaSophia Robb
Victoria Justice
Vanessa Hudgens

JUDE LAW

Sophie Monk
Sadie Frost
Scarlett Johansson
Nicole Kidman
Sienna Miller
Cameron Diaz
Natalie Portman
Lindsay Lohan
Kimberly Stewart
Lily Cole

JULIA ROBERTS

Christopher Meloni
Alec Baldwin
Billy Idol
Dylan McDermott
Liam Neeson
Richard Gere
Kiefer Sutherland
Jason Patric
Lyle Lovett
Daniel Day-Lewis
Ethan Hawke
Matthew Perry
Benjamin Bratt
George Clooney
Danny Moder

KATE HUDSON

Matt LeBlanc
Chris Robinson
Owen Wilson
Dax Shepard
Heath Ledger
Lance Armstrong
Alex Rodriguez
Matthew Bellamy

JULIANNE HOUGH

Apolo Ohno
Kevin Connolly
Jared Followill
Dane Cook
Ryan Seacrest

JUSTIN TIMBERLAKE

Elisha Cuthbert
Fergie
Britney Spears
Jenna Dewan-Tatum
Alyssa Milano
Cameron Diaz
Scarlett Johansson
Jessica Biel
Olivia Munn
Olivia Wilde

K

KANYE WEST

Selita Ebanks
Kate Upton
Amber Rose
Kim Kardashian

KATE BOSWORTH

Chris Evans
Ian Somerhalder
Orlando Bloom
Alexander Skarsgård
Michael Polish

KATE MOSS

John Kennedy Jr.
Evan Dando
Jack Osbourne
Leonardo DiCaprio
Johnny Depp
Daniel Craig
Jack Nicholson
Pete Doherty
Jamie Burke
Russell Brand
Rhys Ifans
Jamie Hince

KATE WINSLET

Leonardo DiCaprio
Sam Mendes
Louis Dowler AFTER HER DIVORCE SHE GOT BACK IN THE GAME WITH THIS HOT-ASS MODEL.
Ned Rocknroll

KATHERINE HEIGL

Joey Lawrence
Jason Behr
Josh Kelley

KATIE HOLMES

Joshua Jackson
Chris Klein
Tom Cruise

KATY PERRY

Travie McCoy
Russell Brand
John Mayer

KEANU REEVES

Travie McCoy
Russell Brand
John Mayer

KEIRA KNIGHTLEY

Johnny Depp
Rupert Friend
James Righton

KEITH URBAN

Niki Taylor
Nicole Kidman

KERI RUSSELL

Joey Lawrence
Scott Speedman
Shane Deary

KEVIN CONNOLLY

Nikki Cox
Kelly Carrington
Topaz Page-Green
Nicky Hilton
Haylie Duff
Julianne Hough
Hayden Panettiere
Stacy Keibler
Arielle Kebbel

KEVIN FEDERLINE

Shar Jackson
Britney Spears
Paris Hilton
Kacey Jordan

KHLOE KARDASHIAN

Rashad McCants
Derrick Ward
Lamar Odom

KIM KARDASHIAN

Bret Lockett
50 Cent
TJ Jackson
Damon Thomas
Nick Lachey
Nick Cannon
Ray J
Marques Houston
Evan Ross
Reggie Bush
Cristiano Ronaldo
Shengo Deane
Miles Austin
Gabriel Aubry
Kris Humphries GOD
BLESS KRIS HUMPHRIES.
HE FARTED IN KIM'S
FACE ON NATIONAL TV.
Kanye West

KIRSTEN DUNST

Ben Foster
Tobey Maguire
Jake Gyllenhaal
Josh Hartnett
Orlando Bloom

Dunst (cont'd)
Andy Samberg
Adam Brody
Fabrizio Moretti
Justin Long
Garrett Hedlund

KIRSTIE ALLEY

William Shatner
Parker Stevenson
John Travolta
James Wilder
Jamie Foxx

KOURTNEY KARDASHIAN

Taj Jackson
Joe Francis
Scott Disick

KRISTEN BELL

Drake Bell
Matthew Morrison
Dax Shepard

KRISTEN STEWART

Michael Angarano
Robert Pattinson
Rupert Sanders

KRISTIN CAVALLARI

Stephen Colletti
Talan Torriero
Brody Jenner
Matt Leinart
Nick Zano
Chris Evans
Justin Bobby
Jay Cutler

LADY GAGA

Luc Carl
Taylor Kinney

LAUREN CONRAD

Stephen Colletti
Jason Wahler
Brody Jenner
Chris Richardson
Shawn Pyfrom
Lee Norris
Doug Reinhardt
Kyle Howard
Derek Hough
Chace Crawford

LEA MICHELE

Theo Stockman
Cory Monteith

LeANN RIMES

Jensen Ackles
Andrew Keegan
Tiger Woods
Dean Sheremet
Eddie Cibrian

LEIGHTON MEESTER

Ed Westwick
Sebastian Stan
Justin Long
Garrett Hedlund

LEONARDO DiCAPRIO

Please see pp 10–11 of
THE DIRTY DOZEN

LIAM HEMSWORTH

Amanda Bynes
Miley Cyrus

LINDSAY LOHAN

Please see pp 8–9 of
THE DIRTY DOZEN

LIV TYLER

Joaquin Phoenix
Royston Langdon
Steve Bing
Charlie Hunnam

LUKE WILSON

Drew Barrymore
Gwyneth Paltrow
Joy Bryant

MADONNA

Please see pp 20–21
THE DIRTY DOZEN

MANDY MOORE

Wilmer Valderrama
Brian McFayden
Shane West
Andy Roddick
Zach Braff

MARIAH CAREY

Eddie Griffin
Derek Jeter
Marcus Schenkenberg
Leonardo DiCaprio
Eminem
Trey Songz
Nick Cannon

MARILYN MANSON

Peaches Geldof
Jenna Jameson
Rose McGowan
Dita Von Teese
Evan Rachel Wood
Lana Del Rey
CariDee English

MARIO LOPEZ

Fergie
Tiffani Amber Thiessen
Jaime Pressly
Ali Landry
Karina Smirnoff

MARK WAHLBERG

Nicole Eggert
Trina
Traci Bingham
Shannen Doherty
Reese Witherspoon
China Chow
Rachel Hunter
Jordana Brewster
Jessica Alba

MARY-KATE OLSEN

David Katzenberg
Stavros Niarchos
Max Snow
Heath Ledger
Olivier Sarkozy

MATT DAMON

Minnie Driver
Claire Danes
Winona Ryder
Penelope Cruz

MATTHEW McCONAUGHEY

Ashley Judd
Sandra Bullock
Janet Jackson
Penelope Cruz
Camila Alves

MEGAN FOX

David Gallagher
Brian Austin Green
Shia LeBeouf

MICHELLE WILLIAMS

Jeremy Jackson
Conor Oberst
Bobby Cannavale
Heath Ledger
Spike Jonze
Jason Segel

MILA KUNIS

Macaulay Culkin
Ashton Kutcher

MILEY CYRUS

Jared Followill
Justin Bieber
Nick Jonas
John Mayer
Justin Gaston
Liam Hemsworth

MILO VENTIMIGLIA

Alexis Bledel
Emmy Rossum
Hayden Panettiere
Isabella Brewster

MISCHA BARTON

Brandon Davis
Cisco Adler THE BALLS
Josh Hartnett

N

NAOMI CAMPBELL

50 Cent
Lars Ulrich
Quincy Jones
Lenny Kravitz
Mike Tyson
John Kennedy Jr.
Robert De Niro
Eric Clapton
Sylvester Stallone
Johnny Depp
Damon Dash
P Diddy
Tommy Lee
Usher

Campbell (cont'd)
Terrence Howard
Gerard Butler
André Balazs

NAOMI WATTS

Heath Ledger
Robert De Niro
Liev Schreiber

NATALIE PORTMAN

Natalie Portman
Andy Sandberg
Lukas Haas
Hayden Christensen
Moby
Gael García Bernal
Jake Gyllenhaal
Jude Law
Devendra Banhart
Rodrigo Santoro
Benjamin Millepied

NEIL PATRICK HARRIS

Robyn Lively TEEN WITCH/ BLAKE LIVELY'S SISTER
Christine Taylor
David Burtka

CELEBRITY RAP SHEETS

NICK LACHEY

Jessica Simpson
Kim Kardashian
Cheryl Burke
Vanessa Minnillo

NICOLE KIDMAN

Tom Cruise
Russell Crowe
Jude Law
Q-Tip
Lenny Kravitz
Robbie Williams
Keith Urban

NICOLE RICHIE

Jason Mewes
Adam Goldstein DJ AM
Steve-O
Jeff Goldblum
Brody Jenner
Joel Madden

OLIVIA MUNN

Bryan Greenberg
HOT PIECE FROM THE MOVIE PRIME
Jamie Foxx
Chris Pine
Justin Timberlake
Brett Ratner
Matthew Morrison
Brad Richards
Joel Kinnaman

OLIVIA WILDE

Jonathan Tucker
Jake Gyllenhaal
Bradley Cooper
Ryan Gosling
Justin Timberlake
Jason Sudeikis

OPRAH WINFREY

John Tesh
Steadman Graham
Roger Ebert
Don Johnson

ORLANDO BLOOM

Sienna Miller
Kate Bosworth
Helena Christensen
Kirsten Dunst
Vanessa Minnillo
Penelope Cruz
Miranda Kerr

OWEN WILSON

Sheryl Crow
Gina Gershon
Demi Moore
Kate Hudson

P

PAMELA ANDERSON

Slash
Mario Van Peebles
Scott Baio
Eric Nies
David Charvet
Vince Neil
Antonio Sabato Jr.
Bret Michaels
Arsenio Hall
Tommy Lee

Anderson (cont'd)
Kelly Slater
Marcus Schenkenberg
Kid Rock
Fred Durst
Stephen Dorff
Mark McGrath
Ray J
Usher
David Spade
Rick Salomon
Criss Angel

PARIS HILTON

Please see pp 4–5 of *THE DIRTY DOZEN*

PAULA ABDUL

Jackie Jackson
Arsenio Hall
John Stamos
Emilio Estevez
Corey Clark
AMERICAN IDOL CONTESTANT! HE WROTE AN AMAZING SONG ABOUT THEIR RELATIONSHIP CALLED "PAULATICS"

PENELOPE CRUZ

Nicolas Cage
Matt Damon
Tom Cruise
Matthew McConaughey
Orlando Bloom
Josh Hartnett
Javier Bardem

PENN BADGLEY

Blake Lively
Zoe Kravitz

PETE WENTZ

Michelle Trachtenberg
Ashlee Simpson

P!NK

Carey Hart
Tommy Lee

R

RACHEL BILSON

Adam Brody
Hayden Christensen
Jake Gyllenhaal

RACHEL McADAMS

Ryan Gosling
Josh Lucas
Michael Sheen

BUT YOU'RE LIKE REALLY PRETTY.

REBECCA ROMIJN

John Stamos
John Cusack
Jerry O'Connell

REESE WITHERSPOON

Jeremy Sisto
Chris O'Donnell
Stephen Dorff
Mark Walhberg
Ryan Phillippe
Jake Gyllenhaal
Jim Toth

RENÉE ZELLWEGER

Jim Carrey
George Clooney
Jack White
Kenny Chesney
Luke Perry
John Krasinski
Paul McCartney
André Balazs
Dan Abrams
Bradley Cooper
John Stamos

RICHARD GERE

Diana Ross
Barbra Streisand
Priscilla Presley
Kim Basinger
Julia Roberts
Cindy Crawford
Uma Thurman
Carey Lowell

RIHANNA

Ashton Kutcher
Josh Henderson
Shia LaBeouf
Omarion Grandberry
Josh Harnett
Chris Brown
Drake
Ryan Phillippe
Rob Kardashian
Travis Barker
Dudley O'Shaughnessy
Dane Cook

ROBERT DOWNEY JR.

Farrah Fawcett
Jennifer Jason Leigh
Sarah Jessica Parker
Winona Ryder
Marissa Tomei
Calista Flockhart
Susan Downey

ROBERT PATTINSON

Ashley Greene
Camilla Belle
Nikki Reed
Kristen Stewart

ROSARIO DAWSON

Jay-Z
Joshua Jackson
Colin Farrell
Jason Lewis
Quentin Tarantino
Eli Roth
Gerard Butler
Danny Boyle
Michael Fassbender

RUMER WILLIS

Chord Overstreet
Zac Efron

RYAN GOSLING

Sandra Bullock
Famke Janssen
Rachel McAdams
Kat Dennings
Blake Lively
Olivia Wilde
Eva Mendes

RYAN PHILLIPPE

Ashley Greene
Reese Witherspoon
Nikki Reed
Abbie Cornish
Lindsay Lohan
Jessica White
Alexis Knapp
Amanda Seyfried
Rihanna
Demi Lovato

RYAN REYNOLDS

Traylor Howard
Kristen Johnston
Rachael Leigh Cook
Alanis Morissette
Scarlett Johansson
Sandra Bullock
Charlize Theron
Blake Lively

RYAN SEACREST

Sheryl Crowe
Teri Hatcher
Sophie Monk
Julianne Hough

S

SANDRA BULLOCK

Tate Donovan
Keanu Reeves
Troy Aikman
Matthew McConaughey
Ryan Gosling
Jesse James
Ryan Reynolds

SALMA HAYEK

Ben Affleck
Antonio Banderas
Johnny Depp
Edward Norton
Josh Lucas
François Pinault

SARAH JESSICA PARKER

Michael J. Fox
Robert Downey Jr.
JFK Jr.
Nicolas Cage
Matthew Broderick

SARAH MICHELLE GELLAR

David Boreanaz
Jerry O'Connell
Freddie Prinze Jr.

SCARLETT JOHANSSON

Jack Antonoff *LATER DATED LENA DUNHAM FROM GIRLS.*
Jude Law
Benicio Del Toro
Patrick Wilson
Jared Leto
Josh Hartnett
Justin Timberlake
Ryan Reynolds
Sean Penn

SELENA GOMEZ

Mark Salling
Logan Lerman
Nick Jonas
Taylor Lautner
Justin Bieber

I LOVE YOU LIKE A LOVE SONG.

SHERYL CROW

Eric Clapton
Owen Wilson
Kid Rock
Josh Charles
Lance Armstrong
Ryan Seacrest *REALLY?*
Hank Azaria

DIDN'T SHERYL SAY SHE WIPED HER ASS WITH ONLY ONE PIECE OF TOILET PAPER?

SHIA LaBEOUF

Hilary Duff
Rihanna
Megan Fox
Carey Mulligan

SIENNA MILLER

Leonardo DiCaprio
Orlando Bloom
Jude Law
Daniel Craig
James Franco
Hayden Christensen
Josh Hartnett
P Diddy
Jamie Burke
Matthew Rhys
Rhys Ifans
Balthazar Getty
Tom Sturridge

SOFIA VERGARA

Tom Cruise
Tyrese Gibson
Donal Logue

STEPHEN DORFF

Milla Jovovich
Reese Witherspoon
Alicia Silverstone
Bridget Hall
Jennifer Love Hewitt
Pamela Anderson
Sarah Harding

T

TAYLOR LAUTNER

Emma Roberts
Selena Gomez
Victoria Justice
Taylor Swift
Lily Collins
Ashley Benson

TAYLOR MOMSEN

Jack Osbourne
Chace Crawford

TAYLOR SWIFT

Please see pp 22–23 of
THE DIRTY DOZEN

TERI HATCHER

Richard Dean Anderson
MOTHERFUCKIN'
MACGYVER!
Michael Bolton
Dean Cain
Jon Tenney

Hatcher (cont'd)
John Salley
George Clooney
Ryan Seacrest
Jason Lewis

TIGER WOODS

Please see pp 90–91
THE MANY HOLES OF
TIGER WOODS

TOM BRADY

Mariah Carey
Britney Spears
Tara Reid
Bridget Moynahan
Gisele Bündchen

TOM CRUISE

Melissa Gilbert
Heather Locklear
Rebecca De Mornay
Cher
Mimi Rogers
Nicole Kidman
Penelope Cruz
Nazanin Boniadi
Sofia Vergara
Katie Holmes

TOMMY LEE

MAD PORNSTARS
Tawny Kitaen
Heather Locklear
Cher
Pamela Anderson
Jenna Jameson
Carmen Electra
Blu Cantrell
P!nk
Naomi Campbell
Tara Reid
Kimberly Stewart
Shauna Sand

TORI SPELLING

Jean-Claude Van
Damme REALLY?
Brian Austin Green
Vince Neil
Julian Lennon
Patrick Muldoon
Vincent Young
Charlie Shahnaian
Dean McDermott

TYRA BANKS

Will Smith
Hype Williams
Tyler Perry
Rick Fox
John Singleton
Seal
Chris Webber
John Utendahl

V

VANESSA HUDGENS

Zac Efron
Josh Hutcherson
Austin Butler

VANESSA MINNILLO

Derek Jeter
Orlando Bloom
Lindsay Lohan
Topher Grace
Nick Lachey

U

USHER

Monica
Brandy, WAS
"THE BOY IS MINE"
ABOUT USHER?
Chilli from TLC
Naomi Campbell
Joy Bryant

VANESSA WILLIAMS

Michael Jordan
Rick Fox

VINCE VAUGHN

Joey Lauren Adams
Cameron Diaz
Jennifer Aniston

W

WILL SMITH

Tyra Banks
Garcelle Beauvais
Nia Long
Jada Pinkett Smith

WINONA RYDER

Please see pp 28–29 of
THE DIRTY DOZEN

WILMER VALDERRAMA

Christina Milian
Ariana Richards
FROM *JURASSIC PARK*
Jennifer Love Hewitt
Mila Kunis
Mandy Moore
Lindsay Lohan
Ashlee Simpson
Avril Lavigne
Demi Lovato
Minka Kelly

Z

ZACH BRAFF

Drew Barrymore
Sarah Chalke
Bonnie Somerville
Mandy Moore
Shiri Appleby

ZAC EFRON

Vanessa Hudgens
Taylor Swift
Emma Roberts
Rumer Willis
Lily Collins

ZOOEY DESCHANEL

Martin Freeman
Ben Foster
Chris Kattan REALLY?
Jason Schwartzman
Ben Gibbard
Jamie Linden

COMMERCIAL BREAK!
Brought to you by
Zac Efron's hot body.

Alright, you good?
Turn the page.

GAMES, TRIVIA & MORE

DATE, DUMP, *Marry*

1. **KIM KARDASHIAN**
   KHLOE KARDASHIAN
   KOURTNEY KARDASHIAN

2. **BEYONCÉ**
   RIHANNA
   BRITNEY SPEARS

3. **OPRAH**
   ELLEN DeGENERES
   ROSIE O'DONNELL

4. **RYAN GOSLING**
   JAKE GYLLENHAAL
   RYAN REYNOLDS

5. **MEGAN FOX**
   SCARLETT JOHANSSON
   JESSICA BIEL

6. **OJ SIMPSON**
   CHRIS BROWN
   IKE TURNER

7. **TAYLOR SWIFT**
   KATY PERRY
   MILEY CYRUS

8. **KEVIN FEDERLINE**
   VANILLA ICE
   EMINEM

9. **MARIAH CAREY**
   CHRISTINA AGUILERA
   NICKI MINAJ

10. **KANYE WEST**
    JAMIE FOXX
    JAY-Z

11. **KRIS JENNER**
    DINA LOHAN
    TISH CYRUS

12. **KRISTEN WIIG**
    AMY POEHLER
    TINA FEY

13. **MARY-KATE OLSEN**
    ASHLEY OLSEN
    ELIZABETH OLSEN

14. **CAMILLE GRAMMER**
    LISA VANDERPUMP
    BRANDI GLANVILLE

15. **JENNIFER ANISTON**
    REESE WITHERSPOON
    SANDRA BULLOCK

16. **TERESA GIUDICE**
    DANIELLE STAUB
    CAROLINE MANZO

17. **DONALD TRUMP**
    NICOLAS CAGE
    CHRIS CHRISTIE

18. **SARAH PALIN**
    HILLARY CLINTON
    MARTHA STEWART

19. **JUSTIN BIEBER**
    HARRY STYLES
    ASHTON KUTCHER

20. **GEORGE CLOONEY**
    LEONARDO DiCAPRIO
    BRADLEY COOPER

21. **ANDY COHEN**
    ANDERSON COOPER
    NEIL PATRICK HARRIS

Name That Celeb!

1. Who is Taylor Swift's song "We Are Never Getting Back Together" supposedly about?

2. What was the name of the dude that Britney Spears allegedly cheated on Justin Timberlake with?

3. Name the celeb who really really enjoys a nice massage.

4. What celeb went on a date with Tiger Woods before he married Elin?

5. Name three celebs who married regular people.

6. Which famous director has a curious fascination with feet?

7. This reality TV star hooked up with hunky actor Gerard Butler.

8. Johnny Depp got her name tattooed on his body, then later had it altered.

9. Lindsay Lohan and Hilary Duff both dated and fought over him.

10. Name the director Kristen Stewart cheated on Robert Pattinson with.

11. Which actor is rumored to have slept with over 12,000 women?

12. Who almost tied the knot on *Saturday Night Live*?

13. What rap star did Amy Winehouse allegedly hook up with?

14. Who is the most famous pornstar in the world? Think about it for a second...

ANSWERS: 1. Jake Gyllenhaal **2.** Wade Robson **3.** John Travolta **4.** LeAnn Rimes **5.** See page 121 **6.** Quentin Tarantino **7.** Brandi Glanville **8.** Winona Ryder **9.** Aaron Carter **10.** Rupert Sanders **11.** Warren Beatty **12.** Drew Barrymore and Tom Green **13.** Nas **14.** Kim Kardashian, duh.

171

50 Shades

JOHNNY WEIR
Queerest of the queer. Literally floats on air.

GAYEST!

CHRISTIAN SIRIANO
Trickity Tranny from Transylvania.

RICHARD SIMMONS
Everyone's favorite exercise/workout queen!

CARSON KRESSLEY
Sashay'd the gay into the hearts of women everywhere!

ROSS MATHEWS
TV personality and red carpet host. His voice may be higher that a fifth-grade girl's.

GEORGE MICHAEL
Huge fan of public sex.

BOY GEORGE
Was never afraid to let his freak flag fly. Lady boy was a pioneer!

CHRIS COLFER
Sings like a nightingale on *Glee*.

NATHAN LANE
He was hilarious in *The Birdcage*, right?

DAVID BOWIE
Did he put the moves on Jagger?

MATT BONER, ah sorry, BOMER
GDILF.

NEIL PATRICK HARRIS
Doogie likes dudes!

LANCE BASS
Out of Sync is the title of his memoir. Totally nailed it!

BRUNO TONIOLI
The *DWTS* judge purrs and coos like a jungle cat in heat!

GAAAY!

ANDERSON COOPER
Have you heard Coop giggle like a school girl?

RYAN MURPHY
Hollywood power gay!

SARAH GILBERT
We were all right, Darlene is a lesbo.

JESSE TYLER FERGUSON
Ginger gay!

JANE LYNCH
She knows how to deliver a one-liner and find a lady's g-spot.

TIM GUNN
May lose gay card if he doesn't end his 29-year sexual dry spell.

JIM PARSONS
Geeky gay from *The Big Bang Theory*!

DAVID HYDE PIERCE
Frasier sucks, it's for old people, and he was so irritating on it.

KELLY McGILLIS
She was in *Top Gun*! And, it turns out, women take her breath away.

MEREDITH BAXTER
Yep, the mom from *Family Ties* is a carpet muncher IRL.

IAN McKELLEN
Gandalf likes dick. Deal with it.

# of Gay

The gay scale of Hollyweird!

FREDDIE MERCURY
Legend.

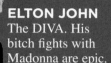

ELTON JOHN
The DIVA. His bitch fights with Madonna are epic.

RICKY MARTIN
Father to twin gaybies. Those hips don't lie!

PEREZ HILTON
Draws jizz on celebs.

SEAN HAYES
OMG, Ms. Hayes on *Will & Grace* is everything.

ANDY COHEN
A fag hag's dream date.

GAYER!

ADAM LAMBERT
Screamer.

CLAY AIKEN
Dorkiest gay in the game.

RUFUS WAINWRIGHT
Very gay and very into opera.

RACHEL MADDOW
There is an amazing rumor that she wears mesh shorts (under the desk) while she does her news show.

ALAN CUMMING
Won at life when he released his fragrance *Cumming*.

MARC JACOBS
Wears a skirt A LOT.

ROSIE O'DONNELL
Remember when Boy George dared her to get that crazy dykey haircut?!

RUPERT EVERETT
Every girl in the 90s hoped for a gay bestie like Rupe.

ZACHARY QUINTO
Leading the next generation of gays.

CYNTHIA NIXON
Miranda is a big ol' dyke, y'all!

NATE BERKUS
Interior designer who survived a tsunami. He's now with hottie Jeremiah Brent.

JONATHAN KNIGHT
I always knew there was a gay one in New Kids on the Block!

GEORGE TAKEI
Oh, myyyyyy. George is always the best on *The Howard Stern Show*.

MELISSA ETHERIDGE
Bitch knows how to shred guitars and panties.

SUZE ORMAN
Smart investments and hot chicks give Suze a ladyboner.

TOM FORD
Eats a Snickers every day and prefers to take baths rather than showers.

VICTOR GARBER
Jennifer Garner's main gay. He was in *Titanic* and *Alias*, remember?

SAMANTHA RONSON
Dittles girls' skittles and spins records.

CHAZ BONO
Tougher than all these homos.

GAY!

THE APPENDICKS

Face it, you've always wanted to know who has a big shlong in Hollyweird!

LIAM NEESON
Janice Dickinson said it is the size of an Evian bottle.

DAVID BOWIE
Iman would not mess around with a teenie weenie.

VINCENT GALLO
Weird guys like Vincent are always packing a creeper shlong.

JAY-Z
Beyoncé's song "Ego" talks about J's beer can sized dong not fitting.

TOMMY LEE
We've all seen it, right?

MILTON BERLE
People would not shut up about Milton's monster cock.

FRANK SINATRA
Ol' Blue Eyes was equipped with a very large trouser snake.

MATT DILLON
There's something about Matty D.

JON HAMM
Was asked to please wear underwear on the set of *Mad Men*, 'cause his *HUGE* vagina ripper was distracting the crew.

BILLY BOB THORNTON
Scored AngieJo and his face is nothin' to look at.

MICHAEL FASSBENDER
Rent the movie *Shame*.

PETER ANDRE
Married Katie Price aka Jordan, who said it is the size of a television remote control.

COLIN FARREL
In his sex tape, the beautiful black Playmate is very impressed.

JAMES WOODS
Creeper with a 12"cock. He dates 20-year-olds.

TED DANSON
Whoopi almost married this fool, and Whoopi can only get off with 10+ inches.

BENEDICT CUMBERBATCH
His eyes are so far apart he MUST be rocking an extra large turtleneck.

BRANDON ROUTH
His dick was supposedly so big in the Superman suit the director had to digitally alter Routh's monster.

ANTHONY KIEDES
Has a big chili pepper.

TONY DANZA
Do you know who's the boss? Tony's long penis.

DAN RATHER
Legendary newsman is HUGE. Look at his ears.

SIMON REX
Filmed a solo vid where he showed off his manhood.

TOBEY MAGUIRE
Easy, *Seabiscuit*! Tobey's a dork packin' some serious heat.

JARED LETO
Young starlets say he's "Hollywood's Biggest."

MARC ANTHONY
Could J Lo not handle his wrist-thick cock anymore?

THE APPENDICKS

ANDERSON COOPER

A long one. Go, Coop! Bloop! Bloop!

TIM ROBBINS

You can catch glimpses of his penis outline in *Shawshank* and shit is REAL.

LYLE LOVETT
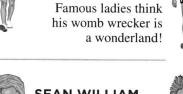
Julia Roberts don't like no short dick man.

JOHN MAYER
Famous ladies think his womb wrecker is a wonderland!

SEAN WILLIAM SCOTT

Stifler has a large stifler!

MATT LeBLANC
How YOU doin, Joey?

ERIC BANA

HUGE. Again, ladies and gays, check the ears.

DON JOHNSON

Hung like a porn king.

DAVID BOREANAZ

You can't handle his boner! I mean *Bones*!

TAYE DIGGS
He can get any woman's groove back.

ORLANDO BLOOM

Legolas means "third leg" in elvish.

DAVID BECKHAM

Posh's favorite and sometimes only meal of the day!!

EWAN McGREGOR

Packin a large piece of haggis under his kilt.

MICK JAGGER

Forget about the moves, most dudes want a dick like Jagger!

WILLEM DAFOE
He's got a flesh goblin in his pants!

OWEN WILSON

Was photographed in wet boxers and was packin' serious HEAT.

DANIEL CRAIG

Judi Dench said, "It's an absolute monster, watch out!"

ROBERT DE NIRO
Black chicks are into him, and they do not mess around.

ALEXIS ARQUETTE

Born with an extra large skin flute but may have cut it off.

MILO VENTIMIGLIA
A little guy with a HUGE surprise.

VANILLA ICE
10". Pulled it out to prove it. Madonna approved.

SCOTT DISICK
A Kardashian had two babies with him.

LAMAR ODOM

A Kardashian married him.

KANYE WEST
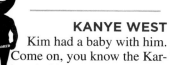
Kim had a baby with him. Come on, you know the Kardashians are size queens!

176

SEE YOU LATER,

MASTURBATOR!

Thanks, Bitches!

Thank you to my parents, Mollie and John, for empowering me to achieve my dreams. Shout-out to my sisters, Colleen and Anna, who showed me love with a healthy splash of cruelty. Don, you are my constant support, my everything, my forever. Thank you to my friends for sharpening my wit and for the constant laughs. I love you all!

Carrie Thornton, Kevin Callahan, and everyone at HarperCollins/It Books, I can never thank you enough for this opportunity, but more importantly for believing in me and letting me be myself! Big ups to the weirdos on the internet, Howard Stern, reality television, Kim Kardashian, and the people of the world who don't take themselves too seriously.

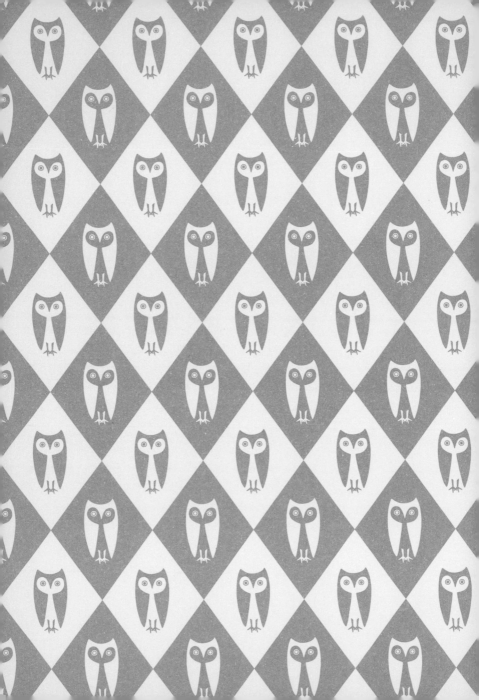

Image Credits
Cover illustrations: *Owl* CSA-Archive/Getty Images; *Bookshelves* Shanina/Getty Images
Illustrations on page viii: *Monkey* goodzone/Shutterstock; *Cities* Courtesy David Taylor;
Hand Pretty Vectors/Shutterstock; *Deer* Panda Vector/Shutterstock; *Giraffe* WladD/
Shutterstock; *Buffalo* Sloth Astronaut/Shutterstock
All other illustrations: The Noun Project

ISBN 978-1-62145-560-8 (paperback)
ISBN 978-1-62145-561-5 (e-pub)

We are committed to both the quality of our products and the service we provide to our
customers. We value your comments, so please feel free to contact us.

Reader's Digest Adult Trade Publishing
44 South Broadway
White Plains, NY 10601

For more Reader's Digest products and information, visit our website:
www.rd.com

Printed in China
10 9 8 7 6 5 4 3 2 1

is
BRAIN POWER

*More Than
100 Quick Quizzes
& Fun Facts*

Reader's
Digest

New York / Montreal

CONTENTS

INTRODUCTION

You might say it got off to a *spurious* start. "Spurious" was the very first stumper in the inaugural Word Power quiz, published in the January 1945 issue of *Reader's Digest*. (Correct definition: "false.") The column was the brainchild of author, publisher, and lifelong word nerd Wilfred J. Funk—whose father was the "Funk" of Funk & Wagnalls encyclopedias.

Wilfred conjured nearly 5,000 words in 20 years of writing "It Pays to Increase Your Word Power." Then he passed the dictionary to his son Peter Funk, who later upgraded the title to "It Pays to Enrich Your Word Power." ("Enrich"—that's such a Word Power word.)

As Peter Funk wrote in his introduction to the *Word Power Quiz Book* (a collection of Word Power challenges published in 2007):

> *My many years as a lexical semanticist (a scholar who studies the meaning of words) have led me to adapt Wittgenstein's observation to my own experience: The limits of the size and quality of our vocabulary form the limits of our minds.*

And I especially stress quality over sheer size.

For example, concept words are quality words having to do with ideas. They stimulate us to think in new ways.

Whenever we learn a new word, it is not just dumped into our "mental dictionary." Our brain creates neuron connections between the new word and others relevant to our interest. It develops new perceptions and concepts.

More recent research indicates that a large vocabulary may lead to a more resilient mind by fueling what scientists call cognitive reserve. One way to think about this reserve is as your brain's ability to adapt to damage. Just as your blood cells will clot to cover a cut on your knee, cognitive reserve helps your brain cells find new mental pathways around areas damaged by stroke, dementia, and other forms of decay.

This could explain why, after death, many seemingly healthy elders turn out to harbor advanced signs of Alzheimer's disease in their brains despite showing few signs in life. It's their cognitive reserve, researchers suspect, that may allow some seniors to seamlessly compensate for hidden brain damage.

How does one build up cognitive reserve? That's more good news

"Today, more than 50 years later, I always check out 'It Pays to Enrich Your Word Power' first when *The Digest* comes each month. I have learned that a word can work a small miracle—if it's the right word, in the right place, at the right time."

—Lee Iacocca (1924-2019), former chairman of Chrysler, who remembered vocabulary tests based on Word Power in ninth grade

"BUFFALO BUFFALO BUFFALO BUFFALO BUFFALO BUFFALO BUFFALO BUFFALO" IS A REAL SENTENCE. HOW?

Let's break it down, starting with a simple phrase:

Monkeys from Pisa bully deer from London.
OK, admittedly it's an implausible scenario, but it's a grammatically fine sentence. In English we can use place names as adjectives, so let's shorten the sentence a little.

Pisa monkeys bully London deer.
Now we'll throw in some giraffes from Paris to even the score with those mean monkeys.

Pisa monkeys, whom Paris giraffes intimidate, bully London deer.
English is peculiar in that you can omit relative pronouns, e.g., "the person whom I love" can be expressed as "the person I love." Let's do that to this sentence.

Pisa monkeys Paris giraffes intimidate bully London deer.
This kind of pronoun removal can be a little more difficult to grasp when written than when spoken. Saying the above sentence with pauses after monkeys and intimidate can help. Now we need to replace both of the verbs, intimidate and bully, with their (admittedly uncommon) synonym, buffalo:

Pisa monkeys Paris giraffes buffalo buffalo London deer.
Again, pauses help keep the meaning in mind: Put a pause after monkeys and the first buffalo. Now we'll replace all the worldwide place names with the second-largest city in New York State: Buffalo. (That's Buffalo's tallest building, One Seneca Tower, below.)

Buffalo monkeys Buffalo giraffes buffalo buffalo Buffalo deer.
You can probably guess what the next step is. But before we replace all the animals with the common name for the American bison, note how the capital letters in the above sentence help you keep the place names separate from the other usages of the word. OK, here goes:

Buffalo buffalo Buffalo buffalo buffalo buffalo Buffalo buffalo.
One last thing: This exceptional sentence is possible because the plural of the animal buffalo is buffalo, not buffaloes, otherwise all the words wouldn't be identical. English is strange and wonderful! prooffreader.com

for word lovers. Vocabulary is notoriously resistant to aging, and having a rich one, according to researchers from Spain's University of Santiago de Compostela, can significantly delay the manifestation of mental decline. When the team analyzed vocabulary test scores of more than 300 volunteers ages 50 and older, they found that participants with the lowest scores were between three and four times more at risk of cognitive decay than participants with the highest scores.

And the more you love learning about words, the more it will help. "You have to increase levels of the feel-good brain chemical dopamine in order to generate brain-cell growth," explains neuroscientist William Shankle, MD, medical director of the Pickup Family Neurosciences Institute of the Hoag Hospital Network in Newport Beach, California. "Don't do things you don't like because they're supposed to boost brainpower. Pick something you love. Keep learning about it and doing it. It takes passion to get benefits."

Luckily, you won't find a funner way of improving your vocabulary than this all-new collection of Word Power quizzes—and yes, "funner" is really a word! There's a reason the column remains one of the most popular in the magazine, after all. Along the way, you'll also learn some enlightening tidbits about English grammar, such as the fact that one single word (at left), repeated eight times, can make a complete sentence. Whether you want to sound smarter in business meetings, ace that standardized test, or finally beat your brainy uncle in Scrabble, this book will help you increase your word power and your brain power—for life. ●

HOW TO MAKE THE MOST OF THIS BOOK

**THROUGH THE QUIZZES AND
ARTICLES IN THIS BOOK, YOU WILL:**

- learn myriad new words
- refresh your memory of those words that you know but haven't used for a while
- discover how certain words relate to the lives and thoughts of famous personalities
- read about the fascinating etymologies that add so much to word lore
- find a host of words that are relative newcomers to the English language

**HERE ARE A FEW HELPFUL TIPS TO
RETAIN YOUR NEW KNOWLEDGE:**

MAKE FLASH CARDS on which to write new words, with illustrations or examples of their usage. Include origins, for they can be an aid to remembering a word. The English language has never been on a leash. It has roamed freely, returning home with "friends" from all over the world as well as from science, technology, the arts, and many other professions and pastimes.

ADD ONE OR TWO SYNONYMS to gain a sense of the word's range. English, more than any other language, has vast numbers of synonyms. A synonym gives a slightly different slant to the meaning of a word, adding precision to thinking and communicating. A synonym is to a writer or speaker what a shade of color is to a painter. **USE THESE WORDS** as often as possible, for the first week or so, in your speaking and writing.

TAKE OUR WORD POWER CHALLENGE:

At the end of each Word Power quiz, you'll find a place to record your score. Once you've completed all the quizzes in the book, add up your scores to see how much of a brainiac you are. Are you a word learner or a word grandmaster? Use the score sheet on page 201 to find out!

GO ONLINE FOR MORE:

If you're hungry for more Word Power, visit our website for interactive quizzes that you can share with friends! Scan the QR code at right to find them.

ALL IN THE MIND

Don your thinking cap before you take this quiz
on words about all matters cerebral. Are you
feeling the brain strain? Turn the page
for answers that will expand your mind.

1. ken

(ken) *n.*

A hunch.

B attention span.

C range of knowledge.

2. abstruse

(ab-'stroos) *adj.*

A scatterbrained.

B hard to comprehend.

C obvious to anyone.

3. cogent

('koh-jent) *adj.*

A from a man's
perspective.

B convincing.

C of two minds.

4. construe

(kon-'strew) *v.*

A interpret.

B baffle.

C refuse to believe.

5. erudition

(er-uh-'di-shun) *n.*

A clear speech.

B extensive learning
through books.

C loss of memory.

6. nescient

('neh-shee- or 'neeh-see-
unt) *adj.*

A showing good
judgment.

B having foresight.

C lacking knowledge.

7. discerning

('di-ser-ning) *adj.*

A beyond belief.

B showing insight.

C mentally stimulating.

8. métier

('me-tyay) *adj.*

A measure of
intelligence.

B doubt.

C area of expertise.

9. recondite

('re-kon- or ri-'kahn-diyt) *adj.*

A triggering a memory.

B skeptical.

C deep or obscure.

10. untenable

(un-'te-ne-bul) *adj.*

A impossible to defend.

B not open to question.

C obtuse.

11. autodidact

(aw-toh-'diy-dakt or -'dakt) *n.*

A demanding teacher.

B complete thought.

C self-taught person.

12. empirical

(im-'peer-ih-kul) *adj.*

A all-knowing.

B widely accepted.

C from experience
rather than theory.

13. polymath

('pah-lee-math) *n.*

A teacher.

B person of great and
varied learning.

C numerical puzzle.

14. cogitate

('kah-je-tayt) *v.*

A think deeply.

B become confused.

C take a guess.

15. pundit

('pun-dit) *n.*

A humorist.

B pupil.

C critic or airer of
opinions.

1

"ALL IN THE MIND" ANSWERS

1. ken
c *range of knowledge.*
Sorry, but the care and feeding of anything with eight legs is a little outside my ken.

2. abstruse
B *hard to comprehend.*
Do you find the rules of British cricket a bit abstruse?

3. cogent
B *convincing.*
Alice did not consider the Mad Hatter's reasoning to be all that cogent.

4. construe
A *interpret.*
It's hard to construe a politician's real meaning through all the bluster.

5. erudition
B *extensive learning through books.*
Despite her erudition, Jen was prone to commonsense blunders in her love life.

6. nescient
c *lacking knowledge.*
"How can you offer the contract to that nescient neophyte?" Dan whined.

7. discerning
B *showing insight.*
To demonstrate what a discerning reader he was, Joe recited Persian poetry.

8. métier
c *area of expertise.*
Etiquette was Emily's purported métier, but it certainly didn't show at the state dinner last night.

9. recondite
c *deep or obscure.*
Nothing, Jimmy's mom joked, is as recondite as the password for her son's tree house.

10. untenable
A *impossible to defend.*
The row of dug-up flower beds put Andy's new puppy in a most untenable position.

11. autodidact
c *self-taught person.*
In the field of foot-in-mouth, unfortunately, I'm an autodidact.

12. empirical
c *from experience rather than theory.*
Jill has empirical evidence that microwaving a plate full of marshmallows is not a wise idea.

13. polymath
B *person of great and varied learning.*
A true polymath, Randi was acing every question on *Jeopardy!*

14. cogitate
A *think deeply.*
"To solve this case, Watson," said Sherlock Holmes, "one must cogitate over a pipeful of tobacco."

15. pundit
c *critic or airer of opinions.*
I'm getting swamped by all the talking-head pundits on TV.

YOUR SCORE:
___ / 15

IN WORDS WE TRUST

The United States can take credit for many contributions to the world's lexicon: Rock 'n' roll, software, teddy bear, and even A-OK are all-American additions. Here are some lesser-known gems with U.S. roots.

1. borax
('bor-aks, -iks) *n.*
A cheap or shoddy merchandise, usually furniture.
B wooden dam.
C creature in folklore.

2. highbinder
('hiy-biyn-der) *n.*
A type of moonshine.
B 19th-century gun.
C corrupt politician.

3. Holy Joe
('ho-lee jo) *n.*
A meat sandwich.
B clergyman.
C exclamation.

4. ponderosa
(pahn-deh-'roh-suh) *n.*
A a gold mine.
B pine tree.
C mountain range.

5. alewife
('ayl-wiyf) *n.*
A rudimentary log cabin.
B kinship.
C herring common to the Atlantic Coast.

6. blackstrap
('blak-strap) *n.*
A type of molasses.
B early horse saddle.
C gambling house.

7. slimsy
('slim-zee, -see) *adj.*
A questionable.
B frail.
C slippery.

8. blatherskite
('bla-thr-skiyt) *n.*
A double-edged knife.
B one who speaks nonsense.
C red rock indigenous to North America.

9. sockdolager
(sahk-'dah-li-jer) *n.*
A decisive blow or answer.
B counselor.
C nickname for a banker.

10. jag
(jag) *n.*
A stone step.
B unrestrained activity.
C insult.

11. piker
('pi-ker) *n.*
A one who gambles with a small amount of money or does something cheaply.
B one who likes to walk.
C nickname for a logger.

12. simon-pure
(si-men-'pyur) *adj.*
A fresh.
B immoral.
C of untainted integrity.

13. callithump
('ka-le-thump) *n.*
A noisy band or parade.
B carnival game.
C type of rabbit.

14. deadhead
('ded-hed) *n.*
A traveler who has not paid for a ticket.
B slang for male witch.
C a weed.

15. copacetic
(koh-puh-'seh-tik) *adj.*
A very satisfactory.
B satirical.
C pepped up.

"IN WORDS WE TRUST" ANSWERS

1. borax
A *cheap or shoddy merchandise, usually furniture*
"What a borax of a table!" cried Alison as its legs collapsed.

2. highbinder
C *corrupt politician*
While seemingly not an evil man, the mayor was at the very least a highbinder.

3. Holy Joe
B *clergyman*
The anxious privates all went to visit the Holy Joe before shipping out.

4. ponderosa
B *pine tree*
The name of this North American tree has roots (pun intended) in the word "ponderous."

5. alewife
C *herring common to the Atlantic Coast*
Art prefers alewife to typical sea herring.

6. blackstrap
A *type of molasses*
Fran's must-have ingredient for his beans? Blackstrap molasses.

7. slimsy
B *frail*
"I can't knit with that," Emilie said. "The cotton is so slimsy!"

8. blatherskite
B *one who speaks nonsense*
"Can't anyone silence that blatherskite?!" exclaimed Michael.

9. sockdolager
A *decisive blow or answer*
His editor was looking for a sockdolager of a story but Matt just couldn't think of anything powerful enough.

10. jag
B *unrestrained activity*
Joy went on a whining jag after losing her phone.

11. piker
A *one who gambles with a small amount of money or does something cheaply.*
Always the family's piker, Aunt Ruthie played only three dollars at the craps table.

12. simon-pure
C *of untainted integrity*
Alessia's reputation as a writer? She's simon-pure.

13. callithump
A *noisy band or parade*
At the much-anticipated callithump, the Colts celebrated their gridiron win.

14. deadhead
A *traveler who has not paid for a ticket*
"Does that deadhead really work for the airline?" asked the disgruntled passenger after he was moved from first class to coach.

15. copacetic
A *very satisfactory*
Mama's smile told him that everything was copacetic.

YOUR SCORE:
___ / 15

THE I'S HAVE IT

What do whiz kids, fish sticks, miniskirts, and film critics have in common? Their only vowel is the letter i. So grab your skim milk, put on your string bikini, and hit this list.

1. grissini
(grih-'see-nee) *n.*
A Italian breadsticks.
B carved inscriptions.
C figure skating jump.

2. dirndl
('dern-duhl) *n.*
A needle for darning.
B full skirt.
C spinning top.

3. limpid
('lihm-pihd) *adj.*
A hobbling.
B perfectly clear.
C like a mollusk.

4. schism
('skih-zuhm) *n.*
A separation.
B pithy quotation.
C deep hole.

5. kimchi
('kihm-chee) *n.*
A logic puzzle.
B throw rug.
C pickled dish.

6. skinflint
('skihn-flihnt) *n.*
A scam artist.
B penny-pincher.
C fire starter.

7. insipid
(ihn-'sih-pihd) *adj.*
A bland.
B just getting started.
C undrinkable.

8. fizgig
('fihz-gihg) *n.*
A plan that fails.
B large swarm of bees.
C hissing firework.

9. jib
(jihb) *n.*
A sharpened pencil point.
B bird's beak.
C triangular sail.

10. philippic
(fih-'lih-pihk) *n.*
A international treaty.
B charitable gift.
C tirade.

11. viscid
('vih-sid) *adj.*
A sticky.
B transparent.
C wickedly cruel.

12. krill
(kril) *n.*
A tiny crustaceans.
B peacock tail feathers.
C knitting pattern.

13. pippin
('pih-pihn) *n.*
A apple.
B migrating songbird.
C thumbtack.

14. pidgin
('pih-juhn) *n.*
A trapshooter's target.
B toe turned inward.
C simplified language.

15. niblick
('nih-blihk) *n.*
A comic routine.
B iron golf club.
C pocket flask.

"THE I'S HAVE IT" ANSWERS

1. grissini
A *Italian breadsticks.*
Daryl wished the child at the next table would stop playing drums with the grissini.

---

2. dirndl
B *full skirt.*
For her role in the musical, Christina is donning a dirndl and learning to yodel.

---

3. limpid
B *perfectly clear.*
The water in the bay was warm and limpid—ideal for an afternoon of snorkeling.

WHY WIKI?
Ever wonder how the reference site Wikipedia got its name? In 1995, programmer Ward Cunningham called a user-editable website he'd created WikiWikiWeb, after the Wiki-Wiki shuttle buses he'd seen at the Honolulu airport. (*Wikiwiki* means "quickly" in Hawaiian.) That was the very first wiki—a site that allows contributions or corrections by its users.

4. schism
A *separation.*
There is quite a schism between your idea of good coffee and mine.

---

5. kimchi
C *pickled dish.*
Annie used to hate Korean food, but now she loves kimchi.

---

6. skinflint
B *penny-pincher.*
Our skinflint of an uncle never tips a dime.

---

7. insipid
A *bland.*
No insipid love ballads for this band; we're here to rock!

---

8. fizgig
C *hissing firework.*
The wedding reception ended with a celebratory fizgig display.

---

9. jib
C *triangular sail.*
Harry is an amateur when it comes to sailing—he doesn't know the jib from the mainsail.

---

10. philippic
C *tirade.*
We accidentally goaded Joaquin into one of his wild philippics about his ex-wife.

---

11. viscid
A *sticky.*
The massive spider in my greenhouse has caught many a hapless fly in its viscid snare.

---

12. krill
A *tiny crustaceans.*
One blue whale can consume up to four tons of krill each day.

---

13. pippin
A *apple.*
"Ten bucks says I can knock that pippin right off your head," said William Tell.

---

14. pidgin
C *simplified language.*
Sean relies on pidgin to communicate when he travels abroad.

---

15. niblick
B *iron golf club.*
Emma cursed her niblick as her ball splashed in the pond.

YOUR SCORE:
 ___ / 15

WEATHER FACTS

You can't change the weather, but you can at
least talk about it sensibly and intelligently.
Here's a flurry of useful terms you can try sprinkling
into your everyday chitchat.

1. inclement
(in-'kle-ment) *adj.*
A comfortably warm.
B severe.
C ever-changing.

2. temperate
('tem-pret) *adj.*
A marked by
moderation.
B steamy.
C frigid.

3. aridity
(ah-'ri-de-tee) *n.*
A harshness.
B blazing sunshine.
C drought.

4. nimbus
('nim-bus) *n.*
A frostbite.
B rain cloud.
C weather vane.

5. doldrums
('dohl-drumz) *n.*
A sounds of booming
thunder.
B stagnation or
listlessness.
C weather map lines.

6. inundate
('ih-nen-dayt) *v.*
A overheat or melt.
B form icicles.
C flood.

7. abate
(uh-'bayt) *v.*
A decrease in force, as
rain.
B increase, as wind.
C pile up, as snow.

8. convection
(kun-'vek-shen) *n.*
A cyclonic movement.
B hot air rising.
C meeting of
weatherpersons.

9. striated
('striy-ay-ted) *adj.*
A jagged, as hail.
B banded, as clouds.
C patchy, as fog.

10. hoary
('hor-ee) *adj.*
A hazy.
B white with frost or
age.
C lightly sprinkling.

11. leeward
('lee-werd) *adj.*
A by the shore.
B out of balance.
C not facing the wind.

12. graupel
('grauw-pel) *n.*
A snow pellets.
B mudslide.
C warm-water current.

13. insolation
(in-soh-'lay-shen) *n.*
A sunstroke.
B shade.
C winter clothing.

14. permafrost
('per-muh-frost) *n.*
A dusting of powdery
snow.
B stalled front.
C frozen subsoil.

15. prognosticate
(prahg-'nahs-ti-kayt) *v.*
A forecast.
B chill.
C take shelter.

"WEATHER FACTS" ANSWERS

1. inclement
B *severe.*
Today's kite festival has been canceled due to inclement weather.

2. temperate
A *marked by moderation.*
After that cold snap, we could really use some temperate conditions.

3. aridity
C *drought.*
If this aridity continues, I swear I'll do my rain dance.

4. nimbus
B *rain cloud.*
We took one glance at the looming nimbus and headed straight for shelter.

5. doldrums
B *stagnation or listlessness.*
FYI, the everyday use of doldrums refers to the area around the equator where prevailing winds are calm.

6. inundate
C *flood.*
After the storm, our tiny shop was inundated with water and debris.

7. abate
A *decrease in force, as rain.*
"I do believe," said Noah, "that the downpour is about to abate."

8. convection
B *hot air rising.*
Sea breezes are a common weather effect of convection.

9. striated
B *banded, as clouds.*
You could almost climb the ladder suggested by those striated cirrus clouds.

10. hoary
B *white with frost or age.*
Professor Parker's beard was almost as hoary as the windshield he was scraping.

11. leeward
C *not facing the wind.*
We huddled on the leeward side of the island, well out of the stiff breeze.

12. graupel
A *snow pellets.*
As I heaved my shovel in the winter nor'easter, graupel stung my cheeks like BBs.

13. insolation
A *sunstroke.*
Insolation is a serious threat during summer football practices.

14. permafrost
C *frozen subsoil.*
Excavating the permafrost in Alaska often requires a jackhammer.

15. prognosticate
A *forecast.*
We might not always appreciate his opinion, but nobody can prognosticate like Punxsutawney Phil.

YOUR SCORE:
___ / 15

THE QUEEN'S ENGLISH

Americans and Brits speak the same language—
or do they? Test your knowledge of the Queen's English with
this quiz, which features a bevy of British words. No need to
hop across the pond for the answers; just turn the page.

1. fiddly
('fih-duh-lee) *adj.*
A set to lively music.
B needing close
   attention.
C insignificant.

2. knackered
('na-kerd) *adj.*
A clever.
B exhausted.
C cluttered.

3. brolly
('brah-lee) *n.*
A umbrella.
B young man.
C streetcar.

4. pitch
(pich) *n.*
A grassy plain.
B playing field.
C stiff collar.

5. ta
(tah) *interj.*
A oh dear.
B to your health.
C thanks.

6. posh
(pahsh) *adj.*
A squishy.
B fancy.
C disdainful.

7. cack-handed
('kak-han-ded) *adj.*
A guilty.
B clumsy.
C made-to-order.

8. aubergine
('oh-ber-zheen) *n.*
A plum.
B zucchini.
C eggplant.

9. argy-bargy
(ar-jee-'bar-jee) *n.*
A pint of beer.
B argument.
C royal carriage.

10. chuffed
(chuft) *adj.*
A polished.
B discarded.
C delighted.

11. dog's breakfast
(dawgz 'brek-fuhst) *n.*
A confusing mess.
B savory pie.
C morning walk.

12. clanger
('klang-er) *n.*
A church bell.
B copycat.
C blunder.

13. nick
(nik) *v.*
A shove.
B rush.
C steal.

14. chin-wag
('chin-wag) *n.*
A close shave.
B friendly chat.
C goatee.

15. poppet
('pah-pet) *n.*
A little one.
B bauble.
C tea biscuit.

"THE QUEEN'S ENGLISH" ANSWERS

1. fiddly
B *needing close attention.*
I hate sewing on buttons; it's such fiddly work.

2. knackered
B *exhausted.*
Knackered after a long week, Giles ordered pizza instead of going to the gym.

3. brolly
A *umbrella.*
Bring your brolly and wear your boots—it's going to pour today!

4. pitch
B *playing field.*
The Reds dominated the game from the moment they stepped onto the pitch.

5. ta
C *thanks.*
"Ta, Dad!" Imogen yelled as she grabbed her lunch and ran out the door.

6. posh
B *fancy.*
My wife wants to go camping for our anniversary, but I'd prefer a weekend in a posh hotel.

LET'S CONSULT SPELL-CHEQUE

Why do Brits and Yanks write some words differently? For his American dictionary, 19th-century lexicographer Noah Webster tweaked some terms to match our pronunciation: colour lost its "u," centre became center, and defence switched to defense. Not all of his proposed alterations made their way into our books: He wanted to change tongue to tung.

7. cack-handed
B *clumsy.*
"Why am I always so cack-handed?" Susan grumbled, picking up shards of glass.

8. aubergine
C *eggplant.*
The chef chopped squash, aubergine and garlic for the stir-fry.

9. argy-bargy
B *argument.*
I don't agree with you, but let's not get into an argy-bargy about it.

10. chuffed
C *delighted.*
Arthur was chuffed when his painting won first place.

11. dog's breakfast
A *confusing mess.*
Dr. Cornwell's filing system is a complete dog's breakfast; I don't

know how she finds anything.

12. clanger
C *blunder.*
After a series of on-air clangers, the newscaster was fired.

13. nick
C *steal.*
I can't believe someone would nick my laptop!

14. chin-wag
B *friendly chat.*
George and Nigel meet at the pub for a chin-wag every Wednesday.

15. poppet
A *little one.*
"Give your granny a kiss, poppet."

YOUR SCORE:
___ / 15

BEAUTY OF WORDS

What makes a word beautiful? Is it a melodious sound?
An exotic meaning? For whatever reason, the words below
appeal to our sense of beauty—though their meanings
may not all be pellucid (a pretty word for "clear").

1. lavaliere

(lah-vuh-'leyr) *n.*

A magma outflow.
B pendant on a chain.
C rider with a lance.

2. flan

(flan) *n.*

A pizzazz.
B custard dessert.
C mirror reflection.

3. panoply

('pa-nuh-plee) *n.*

A impressive array.
B bouquet.
C folded paper art.

4. gambol

('gam-buhl) *v.*

A stake money on a horse.
B frolic about.
C sing in rounds.

5. chalice

('cha-luhs) *n.*

A goblet.
B ankle bracelet.
C glass lamp.

6. languorous

('lan-guh-ruhs) *adj.*

A of the tongue.
B in the tropics.
C lackadaisical or listless.

7. pastiche

(pas-'teesh) *n.*

A thumbnail sketch.
B fabric softener.
C artistic imitation.

8. opulent

('ahp-u-lent) *adj.*

A right on time.
B pertaining to vision.
C luxurious.

9. penumbra

(peh-'nuhm-bruh) *n.*

A something that covers or shrouds.
B drowsiness.
C goose-feather quill.

10. tendril

('ten-druhl) *n.*

A wooden flute.
B spiraling plant sprout.
C clay oven.

11. imbroglio

(im-'brohl-yoh) *n.*

A complicated mix-up.
B Asian palace.
C oil-painting style.

12. dalliance

('dal-lee-ents) *n.*

A frivolous or amorous play.
B flourish on a trumpet.
C blinding light.

13. mellifluous

(meh-'lih-fluh-wuhs) *adj.*

A having broad stripes.
B milky white.
C sweet sounding.

14. diaphanous

(diy-'a-fuh-nuhs) *adj.*

A marked by a fine texture.
B having two wings.
C romantic.

15. recherché

(ruh-sher-'shay) *adj.*

A elegant or rare.
B well-practiced.
C silent.

"BEAUTY OF WORDS" ANSWERS

1. lavaliere
B *pendant on a chain.*
The lavaliere around the princess's neck caught the eye of her suitor.

2. flan
B *custard dessert.*
We went to a dozen restaurants in search of the perfect flan.

3. panoply
A *impressive array.*
Eli was mesmerized by the panoply of dinosaur fossils at the museum.

4. gambol
B *frolic about.*
Our dogs love to gambol in the snow.

CELLAR DOOR

The fantasy writer J. R. R. Tolkien maintained that the loveliest combination of sounds—with the r's and l's that people find lyrical—is the phrase cellar door. Try repeating it aloud. It ends with an open o sound, which Edgar Allan Poe called the "most sonorous" of the vowels (sonorous meaning "full sounding").

5. chalice
A *goblet.*
One chalice contains deadly poison; the other, an all-healing elixir—now choose!

6. languorous
C *lackadaisical or listless.*
The winter chill made Sara long for the languorous hours of summer.

7. pastiche
C *artistic imitation.*
You call his work a pastiche; I call it a knockoff.

8. opulent
C *luxurious.*
Sally was awed by the store's opulent entrance.

9. penumbra
A *something that covers or shrouds.*
As he entered the cave, the explorer fell under a penumbra of fear.

10. tendril
B *spiraling plant sprout.*
The alien pod wrapped its tendrils around the captain's ankle.

11. imbroglio
A *complicated mix-up.*
Too many films are based around a much-expected imbroglio.

12. dalliance
A *frivolous or amorous play.*
The couple's early dalliance was marked by subtle flirting and letter writing.

13. mellifluous
C *sweet sounding.*
Nothing is so mellifluous as the jingle of a bell on our Christmas tree.

14. diaphanous
A *marked by a fine texture.*
My wife wore a diaphanous veil on our wedding day.

15. recherché
A *elegant or rare.*
Alison wondered if her grandmother's bejeweled shoes were too recherché for the office party.

YOUR SCORE:
___ / 15

SHORT ON TIME

There's never enough time, or words to describe it.
Get out your stopwatch to see how long it takes
you to do our quiz. If you just can't wait to
find out the answers, turn the page.

1. anachronism
(uh-'nak-ruh-niz-um) *n.*
A brief interval.
B grandfather clock.
c thing misplaced in time.

2. concurrent
(cun-'cur-unt) *adj.*
A occasional.
B simultaneous.
c in the nick of time.

3. temporize
('tem-puh-rise) *v.*
A evade in order to delay.
B get up-to-date.
c put on a schedule.

4. ephemeral
(ih-'fem-uh-rul) *adj.*
A short-lived.
B antique.
c improving with age.

5. dormancy
('door-mun-see) *n.*
A incubation period.
B curfew.
c state of inactivity.

6. incipient
(in-'sip-ee-unt) *adj.*
A cyclical.
B just beginning.
c out of sync.

7. equinox
('ee-kwuh-nocks) *n.*
A when day is longest.
B when day is shortest.
c when day and night are the same length.

8. pro tempore
(pro-'tem-puh-ree) *adv.*
A in good time.
B ahead of time.
c for the time being.

9. juncture
('junk-chur) *n.*
A midyear.
B point in time.
c gap in the geologic record.

10. erstwhile
('urst-wile) *adj.*
A past.
B present.
c future.

11. dilatory
('dill-uh-tor-ee) *adj.*
A early.
B tardy.
c occurring at ever-widening intervals.

12. moratorium
(more-uh-'tore-ee-um) *n.*
A half a century.
B suspension of activity.
c clock tower.

13. perpetuate
(pur-'peh-chuh-wate) *v.*
A happen again.
B speed up.
c make everlasting.

14. horologe
('hore-uh-loje) *n.*
A astronomical calendar.
B timepiece.
c dusk.

15. Olympiad
(uh-'lim-pee-ad) *n.*
A four-year interval.
B international date line.
c Greek sundial.

"SHORT ON TIME" ANSWERS

1. anachronism
c *thing misplaced in time.*
I'm pretty sure that the wireless earbuds Mona Lisa is wearing are an anachronism.

2. concurrent
B *simultaneous.*
The soundings of the dinner bell and the fire alarm were concurrent in the house where we grew up.

3. temporize
A *evade in order to delay.*
Asked what had happened to the plate of sugar cookies that had been on the counter, Jeremy temporized by telling his mother she looked beautiful.

4. ephemeral
A *short-lived.*
The New England spring is as ephemeral as a mayfly.

5. dormancy
c *state of inactivity.*
In the middle of the big sales meeting, Stanley emerged from dormancy with a loud snort.

6. incipient
B *just beginning.*
Clem slathered on the herbal concoction and then examined his pate for any incipient hairs.

7. equinox
c *when day and night are the same length.*
Arlene has the brownest of thumbs, but every spring equinox, she pores over all the nursery catalogs she can find.

8. pro tempore
c *for the time being.*
They told me I could have the job pro tempore, until they find someone qualified.

9. juncture
B *point in time.*
James realized he had come to an important juncture in his life when he lost his job and won the lottery on the same day.

10. erstwhile
A *past.*
Our city's erstwhile mayor now makes his residence in the upstate penitentiary.

11. dilatory
B *tardy.*
Stacy apologized for being dilatory in sending thank-you notes.

12. moratorium
B *suspension of activity.*
My brother-in-law and I are observing a moratorium on political discussions.

13. perpetuate
c *make everlasting.*
His self-flattery perpetuates the myth that he's actually competent.

14. horologe
B *timepiece.*
Obsessed with horologes, my aunt stuffs her house with sundials, hourglasses, and cuckoo clocks.

15. Olympiad
A *four-year interval.*
They're a very frugal couple; they eat out once an Olympiad.

YOUR SCORE:
___ / 15

MIXING AND MINGLING

The rules of social engagement are always changing. But whether you interact mouse-to-mouse or face-to-face (now, there's a novel idea), it helps to speak the language of social harmony. Here's a primer on words concerned with schmoozing, mixing, and mingling.

1. diffident
('di-fuh-dent) *adj.*
A argumentative.
B unmatched.
C shy.

2. comity
('kah-me-tee, ko-) *n.*
A hilarious misunderstanding.
B social harmony.
C lack of respect.

3. interlocutor
(in-ter-'la-kyu-ter) *n.*
A formal escort.
B meddler.
C person in a conversation.

4. gregarious
(gri-'gar-ee-us) *adj.*
A a little tipsy.
B fond of company.
C markedly rude.

5. accost
(a-'kost) *v.*
A aggressively approach.
B offer to pay.
C decline to join.

6. propriety
(pra-'pri-a-tee) *n.*
A home of a host.
B good social form.
C tendency to gossip.

7. fulsome
('ful-sem) *adj.*
A broad-minded.
B physically attractive.
C excessively flattering.

8. confabulate
(kon-'fa-byu-layt) *v.*
A chat.
B get things backward.
C greet with a hug.

9. brusque
(brusk) *adj.*
A clownish.
B discourteously blunt.
C full of questions.

10. decorum
(di-'kor-um) *n.*
A high praise.
B dignified behavior or speech.
C showy jewelry or makeup.

11. unctuous
('ung(k)-che-wus, -chus, -shwus) *adj.*
A avoiding eye contact.
B on pins and needles.
C smug.

12. urbane
(er-'bayn) *adj.*
A suave and polished.
B known by everyone.
C pertinent to the subject.

13. malapert
(ma-la-'pert) *adj.*
A socially awkward.
B bold and saucy.
C disappointed.

14. audacity
(aw-'da-sa-tee) *n.*
A long-windedness.
B good listening skills.
C gall.

15. genteel
(jen-'teel) *adj.*
A polite.
B macho.
C timid.

"MIXING AND MINGLING" ANSWERS

1. diffident
c *shy.*
I would hardly call Veronica diffident—she's the center of attention at every party she attends.

2. comity
b *social harmony.*
Ducking for cover as the food fight intensified, Millie realized all comity at her table was lost.

3. interlocutor
c *person in a conversation.*
Ever the gentleman, Professor Windham was sure to give other interlocutors time to speak.

4. gregarious
b *fond of company.*
Dad is so gregarious, it's all we can do to keep him from hugging total strangers.

5. accost
A *aggressively approach.*
Ariana can't even walk across the room without someone accosting her for an autograph.

6. propriety
b *good social form.*
"Someone should tell your daughter that propriety dictates that she eat her spaghetti with a fork," the hostess said, groaning.

7. fulsome
c *excessively flattering.*
When meeting Bev's mom, Eddie praised her with such fulsome remarks that she rolled her eyes.

8. confabulate
A *chat.*
Luca wants to confabulate a bit about the new office's blueprints.

9. brusque
b *discourteously blunt.*
Alice did her best to hold her tongue after listening to the coach's brusque advice.

10. decorum
b *dignified behavior or speech.*
In a surprising show of decorum, the tipsy best man gave an endearing toast.

11. unctuous
c *smug.*
Ramona, don't believe a thing that unctuous, money-grubbing sneak tells you.

12. urbane
A *suave and polished.*
Cary's urbane persona was obvious as soon as he stepped into the room.

13. malapert
b *bold and saucy.*
After the audition, Jenny gave the director a wink in a most malapert manner.

14. audacity
c *gall.*
Did you hear the gossip that Eli had the audacity to repeat?

15. genteel
A *polite.*
Clare had to remind the twins to be genteel around their grandparents.

YOUR SCORE:
___ / 15

GOING IN CIRCLES

We're throwing you a curve ball with a vocabulary roundup of a circular nature. Can you roll with the roundhouses, or are you out of the loop? Give this quiz a whirl, and then take a spin to the next page for answers.

1. rouleau
(roo-'lo) *n.*
A roll of coins.
B mushroom cap.
C crystal ball.
_____

2. ellipse
(ih-'lips) *n.*
A crater.
B oval.
C revolution.
_____

3. gyre
('jy-er) *n.*
A spiral motion.
B ring of fire.
C pirouette.
_____

4. rotund
(roh-'tund) *adj.*
A curled.
B plump.
C rotating.
_____

5. circuitous
(ser-'kew-uh-tuss) *adj.*
A winding.
B surrounded.
C eclipsed.

6. bobbin
('bah-bin) *n.*
A life preserver.
B spare tire.
C spindle for thread.
_____

7. aureole
('or-ee-ohl) *n.*
A pearl.
B seed.
C halo.
_____

8. cupola
('kyew-puh-luh) *n.*
A bald spot.
B espresso mug.
C roof dome.
_____

9. roundelay
('rown-duh-lay) *n.*
A traffic circle.
B song with a refrain.
C barber pole.
_____

10. chapati
(chuh-'pah-tee) *n.*
A flatbread.
B eye patch.
C tasseled belt.

11. hora
('hor-uh) *n.*
A clockface.
B circular folk dance.
C burial mound.
_____

12. maelstrom
('mayl-strum) *n.*
A eye of a hurricane.
B water cycle.
C whirlpool.
_____

13. aperture
('ap-er-chur) *n.*
A orbit.
B hole.
C wine cork.
_____

14. ovate
('oh-vayt) *adj.*
A coiled.
B wearing a crown.
C egg-shaped.
_____

15. oculus
('ah-kyuh-luss) *n.*
A gun barrel.
B spinal disk.
C round window.

"GOING IN CIRCLES" ANSWERS

1. rouleau
A *roll of coins.*
Anand organizes his spare change into rouleaus, but he always forgets to take them to the bank.

---

2. ellipse
B *oval.*
I'm drawing your face as a greenish ellipse—no offense.

---

3. gyre
A *spiral motion.*
In a widening gyre, the drone rose over the field.

A VERY ROUND NUMBER

As a symbol, it can be a circle or an oval, but the word zero comes from the Latin *zephirum* and the Arabic *sifr* (empty). For a term that means, well, nothing, it has a lot of synonyms: cipher (also from *sifr*), zilch, naught, and nil, to name a few. Some sports have their own terms: 1860s baseball gave us the goose egg, and in tennis it's love, probably from the idea of playing for nothing but "the love of the game."

4. rotund
B *plump.*
"Rover is getting a bit rotund; how many treats do you feed him?" the veterinarian asked.

---

5. circuitous
A *winding.*
The hikers followed the circuitous trail through the forest.

---

6. bobbin
C *spindle for thread.*
My great-grandmother's vintage sewing machine is missing the bobbin.

---

7. aureole
C *halo.*
The sun shone behind Diana, making her blond hair a glowing aureole.

---

8. cupola
C *roof dome.*
A white marble cupola tops the mosque's towering minaret.

---

9. roundelay
B *song with a refrain.*
The singer-songwriter's new album is full of soothing roundelays.

---

10. chapati
A *flatbread.*
Dad whipped up vegetable curry and fresh-baked chapati for dinner.

---

11. hora
B *circular folk dance.*
If you're attending a wedding in Israel, be ready to do the hora!

---

12. maelstrom
C *whirlpool.*
The small fishing boat was nearly pulled into the powerful maelstrom.

---

13. aperture
B *hole.*
The wily fox slipped into the henhouse through an aperture in the wall.

---

14. ovate
C *egg-shaped.*
Before his fall, Humpty Dumpty had maintained an ovate physique.

---

15. oculus
C *round window.*
The stained glass in the chapel's oculus dates to the 1920s.

YOUR SCORE:
___ / 15

Q & A

Warning: This quiz—a question-and-answer session featuring the letters q and a—may leave you in a quagmire. So if you're stumped by our q's, just turn the page for the a's.

1. qua
(kwah) *prep.*
A from top to bottom.
B beforehand.
C as, in the capacity of.

2. quay
(key) *n.*
A wharf.
B game played with mallets.
C fox hunted by hounds.

3. quaff
(kwahf) *v.*
A swing and miss.
B drink deeply.
C sing Christmas carols.

4. quasi
('kway- or 'kwah-zi) *adj.*
A from a foreign country.
B having some resemblance.
C feeling seasick.

5. quahog
('co- or 'kwah-hog) *n.*
A edible clam.
B half penny.
C motorcycle sidecar.

6. quantum
('kwahn-tum) *n.*
A type of comet.
B specified amount.
C Australian marsupial.

7. quaver
('kway-ver) *v.*
A change your vote.
B sink down low.
C sound tremulous.

8. quinoa
('keen-wah or 'kee-no-eh) *n.*
A grain from the Andes.
B beehive shape.
C chewable resin gum.

9. quondam
('kwahn-dem) *adj.*
A enormous.
B former.
C backward or upside down.

10. quetzal
(ket-'sall) *n.*
A bow-shaped pasta.
B tropical bird.
C mica used in mirrors.

11. quatrain
('kwah-train) *n.*
A end-of-semester test.
B underground railroad.
C four-line verse.

12. quiniela
('kwin-ye-la) *n.*
A type of bet.
B porcupine's bristle.
C cheesy Mexican dish.

13. quotidian
(kwoh-'ti-dee-en) *adj.*
A janitorial.
B occurring every day.
C showing off one's knowledge.

14. quacksalver
('kwak-sal-ver) *n.*
A ointment.
B glue.
C phony doctor.

15. quinquennial
(kwin-'kwen-nee-el) *adj.*
A of thigh muscles.
B flowing freely.
C occurring every five years.

"Q & A" ANSWERS

1. qua
c *as, in the capacity of.*
"Try to judge the short stories qua short stories, not as landmarks of literature," the student pleaded.

2. quay
A *wharf.*
The passengers moaned as the new captain tried to meet the quay in the storm.

3. quaff
B *drink deeply.*
Make three wishes and then quaff this mysterious elixir.

4. quasi
B *having some resemblance.*
The credit offer is from a quasi company: There's an employee but no address.

5. quahog
A *edible clam.*
As the crew team's lead vanished, the coach just sat there like a placid quahog.

6. quantum
B *specified amount.*
Showing off after physics class, Carly said, "That's an extreme quantum of homework, don't you think?"

7. quaver
c *sound tremulous.*
Every time you try to tell a lie, your voice quavers.

8. quinoa
A *grain from the Andes.*
When the waiter said it was tilapia and arugula on a bed of quinoa, Lauren asked for an English translation.

9. quondam
B *former.*
As soon as Harry's quondam girlfriend spotted him, she burst into a quasi fit of joy.

10. quetzal
B *tropical bird.*
Thinking the affair was a costume party, Andy showed up with an eye patch, a peg leg and a quetzal on his shoulder.

11. quatrain
c *four-line verse.*
As a hardworking poet, Jill needs to rest and raid the refrigerator after every quatrain.

12. quiniela
A *type of bet.*
To win a quiniela, you need to pick the first- and second-place horses, but you don't need to specify the order of the finish.

13. quotidian
B *occurring every day.*
Set in her quotidian routine, the puppy begged for an extra treat after breakfast and dinner.

14. quacksalver
c *phony doctor.*
That quacksalver I go to prescribes calamine lotion for every complaint.

15. quinquennial
c *occurring every five years.*
Um, darling, I think it's time for your quinquennial bourbon and ginger.

YOUR SCORE:
___ / 15

SUMMER FAMILY FUN

Before you splash in a pool, bask on a beach, or putter in
your garden, master this list of summertime words.
You won't find a lemonade stand on the next page,
but you will find the answers.

1. torrid

('tohr-ihd) *adj.*

A blooming.

B scorching.

C perspiring.

2. deluge

('dehl-yooj) *n.*

A heavy downpour.

B squirt gun.

C greenhouse.

3. verdant

('vurh-dint) *adj.*

A sandy.

B green.

C buggy.

4. tack

(tak) *v.*

A hook a fish.

B upend a raft.

C change direction
   when sailing.

5. pyrotechnics

(py-ruh-'tek-niks) *n.*

A sunspots.

B fireworks.

C heat waves.

6. chigger

('chih-ger) *n.*

A fastball.

B biting mite.

C beer garden.

7. estivate

('eh-stuh-vayt) *v.*

A lounge outdoors.

B nurture until grown.

C spend the summer.

8. pattypan

('pa-tee-pan) *n.*

A playground.

B heat rash.

C summer squash.

9. alfresco

(al-'freh-skoh) *adv.*

A with cheese sauce.

B outdoors.

C in a fresh state.

10. hibachi

(hih-'bah-chee) *n.*

A raincoat.

B charcoal griller.

C Asian eggplant.

11. pergola

('per-guh-luh) *n.*

A umbrella.

B trellis.

C paid vacation.

12. glamping

('glam-ping) *n.*

A cave exploring.

B glamorous camping.

C sunbathing.

13. plage

(plahzh) *n.*

A lawn tennis.

B lightning strike.

C beach at a resort.

14. espadrilles

('eh-spuh-drillz) *n.*

A rope-soled shoes.

B hedge pruners.

C pair of matching
   beach chairs.

15. horticulture

('hohr-tih-kul-cher) *n.*

A seaside community.

B pond wildlife.

C science of growing
   plants.

"SUMMER FAMILY FUN" ANSWERS

1. torrid
B *scorching.*
This has been the most torrid August I can remember!

2. deluge
A *heavy downpour.*
Tatiana threw on her black slicker and headed out into the deluge.

3. verdant
B *green.*
Vermont is famous for its verdant mountain ranges.

4. tack
C *change direction when sailing.*
The catamaran had to tack quickly to avoid the floating debris.

5. pyrotechnics
B *fireworks.*
Every Fourth of July, my neighbors set off pyrotechnics in their yard until three a.m.

6. chigger
B *biting mite.*
Miranda doused herself in bug spray before her hike to ward off chiggers.

THE IDIOMS OF SUMMER

When it comes to coining notable phrases, baseball is in a league of its own. If you think that claim is off base, we'll list the evidence right off the bat. Consider pinch-hit, in the ballpark, throw a curve ball, and rain check. Still think we haven't covered our bases? Then step up to the plate and name another sport that has hit more syntactical home runs.

7. estivate
C *spend the summer.*
The Myers family estivates by the ocean.

8. pattypan
C *summer squash.*
Has that pesky rabbit been nibbling my pattypan again?

9. alfresco
B *outdoors.*
"Whose idea was it to dine alfresco?" Ira grumbled, flicking an ant off his sandwich.

10. hibachi
B *charcoal griller.*
Come on over; I'm going to throw some burgers on the hibachi tonight.

11. pergola
B *trellis.*
Legend has it that couples who kiss under this pergola will live happily ever after.

12. glamping
B *glamorous camping.*
Hayden goes glamping with every amenity.

13. plage
C *beach at a resort.*
I never hit the plage until I'm completely slathered in sunscreen.

14. espadrilles
A *rope-soled shoes.*
Melissa used to live in flip-flops every summer, but now she prefers espadrilles.

15. horticulture
C *science of growing plants.*
The coveted Horticulture Award is a statuette of a green thumb.

YOUR SCORE:
___ / 15

FEELING IT

Love is in the air every February 14, but why limit yourself to just one emotion? You'll experience a wide range of feelings in this vocabulary quiz. If you're in the mood, check the next page for answers.

1. ebullient
(ih-'bull-yent) *adj.*
A tranquil.
B haughty.
C enthusiastic.

2. pique
(peek) *n.*
A resentment.
B self-importance.
C whimsy.

3. bonhomie
(bah-nuh-'mee) *n.*
A nostalgia.
B friendliness.
C peace of mind.

4. dour
('dow-er) *adj.*
A guilty.
B generous.
C gloomy.

5. amatory
('am-uh-tohr-ee) *adj.*
A irritable.
B romantic.
C easygoing.

6. timorous
('tih-muh-rus) *adj.*
A affectionate.
B fiery.
C fearful.

7. wistfully
('wist-fuh-lee) *adv.*
A with sad longing.
B dreamily.
C in defiance.

8. belligerent
(buh-'lij-uh-rent) *adj.*
A hostile.
B regretful.
C sympathetic.

9. fervor
('fer-ver) *n.*
A aggravation.
B strong preference.
C passion.

10. compunction.
(kum-'punk-shun) *n.*
A remorse.
B exasperation.
C doubt.

11. umbrage
('uhm-brij) *n.*
A indignant displeasure.
B destructive rage.
C meditative state.

12. schadenfreude
('shah-den-froy-duh) *n.*
A tearfulness.
B timidity.
C joy at another's pain.

13. querulous.
('kwair-yuh-lus) *adj.*
A hyperactive.
B fretful.
C fickle.

14. blithesome
('blyth-sum) *adj.*
A unconcerned.
B guarded.
C merry.

15. lugubrious
(luh-'goo-bree-us) *adj.*
A chatty.
B mournful.
C disgusted.

"FEELING IT" ANSWERS

1. ebullient
C *enthusiastic.*
Nina has such an ebullient personality, I can't believe she was ever shy!

2. pique
A *resentment.*
After being passed over for a promotion, Manuel left the office in a fit of pique.

3. bonhomie
B *friendliness.*
There's an absence of bonhomie between the rival basketball teams.

4. dour
C *gloomy.*
How can you be so dour on this sunny morning?

COME ON, FORGET YOUR TROUBLES

Our vote for the best emotion of them all: happy. You might be as happy as a clam or as happy as Larry. An easygoing person is happy-go-lucky, while a reckless one is trigger-happy. And if you're still not feeling the joy, well, you can just head to happy hour or some other happy place.

5. amatory
B *romantic.*
Some people claim that chocolate can put you in an amatory mood.

6. timorous
C *fearful.*
Bernard is usually timorous around large dogs, but he loves our three golden retrievers.

7. wistfully
A *with sad longing.*
"I miss when my friends would call me on my birthday; now they just text," Monica said wistfully.

8. belligerent
A *hostile.*
The sightseers were chased from the pond by a belligerent swan.

9. fervor
C *passion.*
Nicole's fervor for local honey led her to open a beekeeping business.

10. compunction
A *remorse.*
The con man showed no compunction about fleecing unsuspecting investors.

11. umbrage
A *indignant displeasure.*
Elvira took umbrage at being called a wicked witch.

12. schadenfreude
C *joy at another's pain.*
We all felt some schadenfreude when our boorish manager was finally fired.

13. querulous
B *fretful.*
I don't recommend traveling overseas with Lisa; she gets querulous on long flights.

14. blithesome
C *merry.*
There is nothing so blithesome as a summer day at the beach with the children.

15. lugubrious
B *mournful.*
This lugubrious violin solo isn't doing much to raise my spirits.

YOUR SCORE:
___ / 15

ANIMAL INSTINCTS

Do you know your budgies from your whippets?
Your alpacas from your yaks? Test your knowledge of all
creatures great and small.

1. ailurophile

(i-'lur-i-fiyl) *n.*

A lover of cats.

B one who fears is afraid of animals.

C collector of snakes.

---

2. leporine

('lep-o-riyn, -ren) *adj.*

of or relating to...

A a parrot.

B a goat.

C a hare.

---

3. Komodo dragon

(ka-'mo-do 'dra-gen) *n.*

A Chinese dog.

B Indonesian lizard.

C North American toad.

---

4. card (kard) *v.*

A breed for docility.

B brush or disentangle fibers, as of wool.

C demand to know a dog's pedigree.

---

5. cosset

('kah-set) *v.*

A pamper or treat as a pet.

B selectively breed.

C grow more docile.

6. stridulate

('stri-ju-layt) *v.*

A shed a coat.

B mate.

C make a shrill noise by rubbing together body structures, as a cricket does.

---

7. clowder

('klau-der) *n.*

A fish food.

B group of cats.

C wooden dog toy.

---

8. brindled

('brin-duld) *adj.*

A streaky, as a coat.

B vaccinated.

C on end, as neck hairs.

---

9. komondor

('ka-men-dor, 'ko-) *n.*

A Hungarian sheepdog.

B mythical lizard.

C trained falcon.

---

10. caudal

('ka-dul) *adj.*

A having pointed ears.

B born as twins.

C taillike.

11. vibrissa

(viy-'bri-suh) *n.*

A whisker.

B horse's hoof.

C tortoise's lower shell.

---

12. grimalkin

(gri-'mol-ken, -'mal-) *n.*

A frog pond.

B hip injury in dogs.

C old female cat.

---

13. feral ('fe-rul) *adj.*

A rabid or diseased.

B pregnant or in heat.

C not domesticated.

---

14. zoolatry

(zo-'ah-le-tree) *n.*

A animal worship.

B system for grouping animals.

C study of animal communication.

---

15. ethology

(ee-'tha-le-jee) *n.*

A proper treatment of animals.

B science of genetics.

C study of animal behavior.

"ANIMAL INSTINCTS" ANSWERS

1. ailurophile
A *lover of cats.*
Being an ailurophile is one thing, but building an entire wing for your feline friend is another.

2. leporine
C *of or relating to a hare.*
"So much for the judges' leporine bias," boasted the tortoise as he studied the instant replay.

3. Komodo dragon
B *Indonesian lizard.*
The Komodo dragon's name is justified: This carnivore is the heaviest living species of lizard in the world.

4. card
B *brush or disentangle fibers, as of wool.*
At the rate Beth is carding that yarn, she'll have half a sweater by Easter!

5. cosset
A *pamper or treat as a pet.*
Uncle Paul cossets his nieces. They don't have to lift a finger.

6. stridulate
C *make a shrill noise by rubbing together body structures, as a cricket does.*
The insects continued to stridulate, forcing sleep-deprived Fran to don earplugs.

7. clowder
B *group of cats.*
Testing a new catnip recipe, Leslie fled the room pursued by a crazed clowder.

8. brindled
A *streaky, as a coat.*
Camouflaged in her costume, Marti hid among the brindled barnyard cows.

9. komondor
A *Hungarian sheepdog.*
"Maybe I'll have your komondor do double duty as a kitchen mop!" Ms. Gulch growled.

10. caudal
C *taillike.*
Waving her arms in a ludicrously caudal fashion, Ann did her best to illustrate the puppy's excitement.

11. vibrissa
A *whisker.*
Constantly hurrying, the nervous White Rabbit still took time to fuss over each vibrissa.

12. grimalkin
C *old female cat.*
We weren't sure who was creepier: the old lady or the bedraggled grimalkin on her lap.

13. feral
C *not domesticated.*
When Liz said, "Smile for the camera," her son bared his teeth like a feral hound.

14. zoolatry
A *animal worship.*
Do you think naming your cocker spaniel Your Majesty is taking zoolatry too far?

15. ethology
C *study of animal behavior.*
Natalie needs to complete her ethology degree before she can join the monkey expedition.

YOUR SCORE:
___ / 15

PRO AND CON

Pro and con don't just mean "for" and "against." That would be too easy, and English is anything but. Here are some pros and cons that show there's no arguing with the sheer variety of the mother tongue.

1. protract
(pro-'trakt) v.
A draw up a legal document.
B stick out.
C lengthen.

2. contrite
(kun-'trite) adj.
A boring.
B sorry for a wrong.
C twisted into strands.

3. protuberant
(pro-'too-buh-rent) adj.
A pointing upward.
B turned downward.
C bulging outward.

4. consternation
(con-stur-'nay-shun) n.
A inability to process sound.
B paralyzing dismay.
C puff of air.

5. propinquity
(pro-'ping-kwuh-tee) n.
A nearness in place or time.
B knowledge of all things.
C fussiness.

6. consummate
('con-suh-mit) adj.
A skilled.
B engrossing.
C born at the same time.

7. profuse
(pruh-'fyoos) adj.
A about to catch fire.
B easily agreeable.
C abundant.

8. conflagration
(con-fluh-'gray-shun) n.
A ceremonial banner folding.
B enormous fire.
C joining of rivers.

9. prognosis
(prog-'no-sus) n.
A nose job.
B state of half-sleep.
C forecast.

10. convex
(con-'veks) adj.
A curved inward.
B curved outward.
C broken in half.

11. prostrate
('pros-trate) adj.
A lying at anchor.
B lying flat.
C lying through one's teeth.

12. convivial
(kun-'viv-ee-ul) adj.
A tangled.
B transparent.
C merry.

13. probity
('pro-buh-tee) n.
A juvenile court.
B secret investigation.
C moral uprightness.

14. consensus
(kun-'sen-sus) n.
A blend of perfumes.
B group agreement.
C awareness of one's own surroundings.

15. prolix
(pro-'liks) adj.
A westward.
B wealthy.
C wordy.

"PRO AND CON" ANSWERS

1. protract
c *lengthen.*
The meal was protracted by Mary's failure to take into account the cooking time for the turkey.

2. contrite
B *sorry for a wrong.*
She dropped the china bowl, but at least she was contrite about it.

3. protuberant
c *bulging outward.*
Ida's protuberant eyes make her seem perpetually surprised.

4. consternation
B *paralyzing dismay.*
To our mother's consternation, Ida's Pekingese was not housebroken.

5. propinquity
A *nearness in place or time.*
"When deciding the Thanksgiving seating plan," Grandmother had warned me, "be vigilant for any unfortunate propinquities."

6. consummate
A *skilled.*
A consummate parallel parker, Alfred somehow maneuvered the Winnebago into our crowded driveway.

7. profuse
c *abundant.*
Joey dreaded the arrival of the aunts, with their profuse kisses and lipstick.

8. conflagration
B *enormous fire.*
After last year's conflagration, we decided not to let Aunt Norma cook dinner anymore.

9. prognosis
c *forecast.*
Uncle Irv's confident prognosis that he'd be in shape for the 5K Turkey Trot turned out to be premature.

10. convex
B *curved outward.*
His necktie clung to his convex belly like a snake sliding down a beach ball.

11. prostrate
B *lying flat.*
Prostrate on the kitchen floor, Dad cried, "Who spilled the gravy?"

12. convivial
c *merry.*
My sister-in-law has a talent for making even the most convivial gathering seem like a funeral.

13. probity
c *moral uprightness.*
When coffee was served, Grandpa produced a dozen sugar packets he had taken from restaurants—a habit Grandmother said demonstrated a lack of probity.

14. consensus
B *group agreement.*
My nieces' consensus was that pumpkin pie is technically a vegetable dish and that dessert should consist of double-chocolate brownies.

15. prolix
c *wordy.*
Great-Uncle Cliff always puts us to sleep with his prolix tales of his youth in the old neighborhood.

YOUR SCORE:
___ / 15

MYTHS AND MEANING

Like the month of March—which is named for the Roman war god, Mars—the words in this quiz all have their origins in mythology. Muse upon them, then consult the fates for answers. (Or just turn the page.)

1. odyssey
('ah-duh-see) *n.*
A peculiarity.
B long journey.
C sea monster.

2. nemesis
('neh-muh-sis) *n.*
A pen name.
B memory loss.
C archenemy.

3. delphic
('del-fik) *adj.*
A ambiguous.
B underground.
C greedy.

4. vestal
('veh-stuhl) *adj.*
A springlike.
B fierce.
C chaste.

5. narcissistic
(nar-suh-sih-'stik) *adj.*
A forgetful.
B generous.
C self-obsessed.

6. mercurial
(mer-'kyoor-ee-uhl) *adj.*
A changeable.
B famished.
C combative.

7. aurora
(uh-'roh-ruh) *n.*
A dawn.
B hearing.
C lions.

8. cornucopia
(kor-nuh-'koh-pee-uh) *n.*
A abundance.
B madness.
C herd.

9. calliope
(kuh-'ly-uh-pee) *n.*
A echo.
B shooting star.
C steam-whistle organ.

10. ambrosial
(am-'broh-zhuhl) *adj.*
A delicious.
B of the blood.
C golden.

11. paean
('pee-in) *n.*
A beetle.
B song of praise.
C kinship.

12. venerate
('veh-nuh-rayt) *v.*
A shine.
B hunt.
C worship.

13. myrmidon
('mer-muh-don) *n.*
A half dolphin, half man.
B loyal follower.
C huge crowd.

14. lycanthrope
('ly-cuhn-throhp) *n.*
A sailboat.
B werewolf.
C wine bottle.

15. plutocracy
(ploo-'tah-kruh-see) *n.*
A government by the rich.
B remote solar system.
C chemical reaction.

"MYTHS AND MEANING" ANSWERS

1. odyssey
B *long journey.*
My five-minute errand turned into a day-long odyssey.

2. nemesis
C *archenemy.*
"Ah, my old nemesis—we meet again!" the supervillain cackled.

3. delphic
A *ambiguous.*
Dan was not impressed by the fortune-teller's delphic predictions.

4. vestal
C *chaste.*
The ritual required vestal maidens to dance around the fire.

MIXED-UP MONTHS
Though March comes third in our modern calendar, the Roman calendar originally had only ten months, running from March to December. (January and February were added later.) That's why September, October, November, and December are named for the Latin *septem* (seven), *octo* (eight), *novem* (nine), and *decem* (ten).

5. narcissistic
C *self-obsessed.*
Does posting five selfies a day make me narcissistic?

6. mercurial
A *changeable.*
New England weather certainly is mercurial.

7. aurora
A *dawn.*
The hikers paused to admire the beautiful pink aurora before continuing on the trail.

8. cornucopia
A *abundance.*
"What can I get you? We have a cornucopia of craft beers on tap," the bartender said.

9. calliope
C *steam-whistle organ.*
What's a circus without a calliope?

10. ambrosial
A *delicious.*
An espresso milkshake would taste ambrosial about now!

11. paean
B *song of praise.*
Mom composed a paean for us to perform for Dad's birthday.

12. venerate
C *worship.*
Juliana goes to every Green Bay Packers game—she practically venerates the team.

13. myrmidon
B *loyal follower.*
The emperor's myrmidons cater to his every whim, no matter how outlandish.

14. lycanthrope
B *werewolf.*
My boyfriend always disappears when there's a full moon; do you think he's a lycanthrope?

15. plutocracy
A *government by the rich.*
Only the wealthy can afford to run for mayor—this town has become a plutocracy!

 YOUR SCORE:
____ / 15

Hardest Words to Spell in the English Language

SPELLING CAN BE a difficult pursuit at the best of times, and some words don't make it easy. Sometimes "i" doesn't go before "e," vowels are silent, and consonants harmonize to create sounds they shouldn't be capable of making. Here we've gathered together ten tricky words and explained why it's so hard to get them right on the first try.

Nauseous

THERE SURE ARE a lot of vowels in "nauseous," and it can be tricky to remember what order they go in. Even if you have the vowels straight, you may still second-guess yourself about the consonants. The "sh" sound makes it sound as if there should be a "c" in the word somewhere, as in "conscious."

Sherbet

TIME TO SETTLE this sweet dispute once and for all— there is no such word as "sherbert." Many people understandably, but inaccurately, assume that "sherbet" (or "sherbert," as it's often pronounced) is just an Americanization of "sorbet." While the words both come from the Turkish word *erbet*, sherbet and sorbet actually are different desserts. The difference between them is worth an entire article on its own, but the bottom line is that there's only one "r" in "sherbet."

Bologna

THERE'S A REASON many meat packages spell it "baloney." The word "bologna" derives from Bologna, Italy, since a similar (but fancier) type of sausage comes from that city. If you want to mimic this fanciness, that "-gn" at the end should be pronounced with a "nyuh" sound.

Acquiesce

LOOKING QUICKLY AT this word, which means "comply or agree reluctantly but without question or protest," you might not think that the first "c" needs to be there; it isn't in words like "aquatic" or "aquiver." You may also be tempted to throw a double "s" on the end in lieu of the "sc," or just write the "s" with no "c." But you will just have to acquiesce to the illogical spelling of this word.

Minuscule

NOPE, IT'S NOT "mini-scule," no matter how much logic would suggest. It bears no linguistic relation to "mini" or "miniature," but actually comes from the Latin *minus*, meaning "less."

Playwright

HERE'S ANOTHER ONE that's not that hard to spell but is just counterintuitive. You write a play, so why aren't people who write plays called playwrites? (Or playwriters?) It's because when the word was coined, in the late 1600s, people who produced plays were considered workers who wrought plays rather than wrote them. And if you wrought something, you were considered a wright. The fact that "wright" is a homophone for "write" is just a salt-in-the-wound coincidence.

Fuchsia

BOTH THE PAIRS of letters "sc" and "sh" have been known to make the sound that starts the second syllable of "fuchsia." But "fuchsia" uses neither of those pairings. The plant, whose flowers give the name to the color, was named after German botanist Leonhard Fuchs.

Orangutan

THESE POOR BORNEAN primates are the subject of much linguistic confusion. According to Merriam-Webster, their name is the amalgamation of two words in the Malay pidgin language: *orang* for "man" and *hutan* for "forest." But many people prefer pronouncing an anglicized version that adds another "g" to the end. As if that wasn't confusing enough, some variations hyphenate the word and/or add an "o" before the "u," creating "orang-outan."

Gubernatorial

SERIOUSLY...WHAT?! The word "governor" has no "u," "b," or "t" in it. So where did we get this wacky, hard-to-spell word that means "of or relating to a governor"? As it turns out, "gubernatorial" is actually much closer than "governor" to the origin of the word. Both words come from the Latin *gubernātōr*.

Paraphernalia

INSTEAD OF ADDING a letter like in the case of "orangutan," people pronouncing this already-tricky word tend to skip over the second "r" altogether. This mouthful actually comes from a nearly identical Latin word, *paraphernālia*, which referred to the belongings or property of a bride-to-be, similar to a dowry. Needless to say, this word has modernized, as now it can describe everything from ski gear to musical amplifiers to cell phone chargers.

SPORTING

Test your gaming vocabulary with this playful quiz. There's no harm, no foul, and no penaltyfor flipping to the next page for the answers.

1. aficionado
(uh-fish-ee-uh'nah-doh) *n.*
A referee.
B expert.
C buff.

2. wheelhouse
('weel-howse) *n.*
A batter's ideal swinging range.
B overhand pitch.
C cycling stadium.

3. laugher
('laff-er) *n.*
A close game.
B lopsided win.
C joker in a deck.

4. gambit
('gam-bit) *n.*
A opening maneuver.
B single inning.
C intense rival.

5. arbitrate
('ahr-bi-trayt) *v.*
A protest a call.
B serve as umpire.
C settle for a tie.

6. chaff
(chaf) *v.*
A tease.
B discard.
C advance a pawn.

7. thimblerig
('thim-buhl-rig) *n.*
A party platter.
B con game.
C handspring.

8. see
(see) *v.*
A match, as a poker bet.
B leapfrog over.
C strike and open a piñata.

9. ludic
('loo-dik) *adj.*
A following the rules.
B playful.
C easy to learn.

10. baize
(bayz) *n.*
A pool-table fabric.
B long-range pass.
C sculling boat.

11. maffick
('maf-ik) *v.*
A celebrate joyfully.
B enter a raffle.
C play solitaire.

12. cat's game
('kats 'gaym) *n.*
A tie in tic-tac-toe.
B Parcheesi.
C yo-yo trick.

13. token
('toh-kin) *n.*
A loss of a turn.
B signal to a partner.
C game piece.

14. ruff
(ruhf) *v.*
A sail on a new tack.
B play a trump card.
C drive a ball off the fairway.

15. hat trick
(hat trik) *n.*
A fancy outfield catch.
B three hockey goals by one player.
C "grand slam" of tennis.

"SPORTING" ANSWERS

1. aficionado
c *buff.*
A nascent fishing aficionado, Jonathan insists on using spinning lures instead of worms as bait.

2. wheelhouse
A *batter's ideal swinging range.*
To his chagrin, the pitcher threw into the slugger's wheelhouse and cost his team a run.

3. laugher
B *lopsided win.*
Even though the game was a laugher, the victors graciously greeted the losing team.

4. gambit
A *opening maneuver.*
That sneaky gambit might earn you a four-move checkmate, but it will cost you willing opponents.

5. arbitrate
B *serve as umpire.*
When an argument broke out over the team's last cupcake, a coach stepped in to arbitrate.

6. chaff
A *tease.*
Chloe chaffs Alex each time she beats him at badminton.

7. thimblerig
B *con game.*
Tom thought he could outsmart the thimblerig, but he lost his temper and $5.

8. see
A *match, as a poker bet.*
I'll see your pie bet with some ice cream.

9. ludic
B *playful.*
Fans of the Harlem Globetrotters enjoy their ludic antics on the basketball court.

10. baize
A *pool-table fabric.*
Eddie is such a billiards fanatic that his man cave is carpeted in baize.

11. maffick
A *celebrate joyfully.*
The team mafficked its victory by rushing the field.

12. cat's game
A *tie in tic-tac-toe.*
It took a hasty, careless move to break the longstanding series of cat's games.

13. token
c *game piece.*
My family plays Parcheesi with buttons because the official tokens were lost long ago.

14. ruff
B *play a trump card.*
I smiled at her taunts, knowing I would ruff on the next hand.

15. hat trick
B *three hockey goals by one player.*
After Gretzky's hat trick, the ice was littered with fans' caps.

YOUR SCORE:
___ / 15

LAST BUT NOT LEAST

Here are some zippy words starting with the last letter of the alphabet. Proceed with zeal and zest, and when you need to check your answers, zoom over to the next page.

1. zabaglione

(zah-buhl-'yo-nee) *n.*

A canvas sack.

B stage villain.

C whipped dessert served in a glass.

2. zaftig

('zahf-tihg) *adj.*

A charmingly witty.

B pleasingly plump.

C completely famished.

3. zax

(zacks) *n.*

A roofing tool.

B music synthesizer.

C caffeine pill.

4. zephyr

('zeh-fer) *n.*

A ancient lute.

B gentle breeze.

C crown prince.

5. zeta

('zay-tuh) *n.*

A prototype.

B sixth letter of the Greek alphabet.

C great beauty.

6. zetetic

(zuh-'tet-ik) *adj.*

A arid.

B investigative.

C made of hemp.

7. ziggurat

('zih-guh-rat) *n.*

A lightning bolt.

B pyramidal tower.

C flying squirrel.

8. zinfandel

('zin-fuhn-del) *n.*

A narrow valley.

B heretic.

C red wine.

9. zircon

('zer-kahn) *n.*

A gas-powered blimp.

B gemstone.

C traffic cone.

10. zloty

('zlah-tee) *n.*

A airhead.

B Polish currency.

C earphone jack.

11. zoetrope

('zoh-ee-trohp) *n.*

A optical spinning toy.

B sun-loving flower.

C exaggeration.

12. zori

('zohr-ee) *n.*

A antelope.

B flat sandal.

C seaweed wrap.

13. zydeco

('zy-deh-koh) *n.*

A music of southern Louisiana.

B magnifying glass.

C secret password.

14. zygomatic

(zy-guh-'mat-ik) *adj.*

A related to the cheekbone.

B mysterious.

C of pond life.

15. zyzzyva

('ziz-uh-vuh) *n.*

A type of weevil.

B tricky situation.

C fertilized cell.

"LAST BUT NOT LEAST" ANSWERS

1. zabaglione
c *whipped dessert served in a glass.*
I hate to waste a good zabaglione, but I'm on a diet.

2. zaftig
B *pleasingly plump.*
Anne was a bit zaftig, thanks to her chocolate habit.

3. zax
A *roofing tool.*
Kamal built this entire cabin himself, trimming every roof tile with a zax.

4. zephyr
B *gentle breeze.*
On stressful days, I like to fantasize I'm on a tropical beach with a cool zephyr blowing through my hair.

5. zeta
B *sixth letter of the Greek alphabet.*
The up-and-coming tech firm uses a zeta as its logo.

6. zetetic
B *investigative.*
"My zetetic methods," said Sherlock Holmes, "are quite elementary, my dear Watson."

7. ziggurat
B *pyramidal tower.*
The king ordered his subjects to build a great ziggurat in his honor.

8. zinfandel
c *red wine.*
Do you think zinfandel pairs well with nachos?

9. zircon
B *gemstone.*
She thought he gave her a diamond engagement ring, but those gems were just zircons.

10. zloty
B *Polish currency.*
How is the zloty holding up against the euro these days?

11. zoetrope
A *optical spinning toy.*
You can get the illusion of motion from a zoetrope's whirling images.

12. zori
B *flat sandal.*
After the strap on her zori snapped, Joelle had to go barefoot.

13. zydeco
A *music of southern Louisiana.*
Ian became a big fan of zydeco on his last trip to New Orleans.

14. zygomatic
A *related to the cheekbone.*
Many football players use a zygomatic stripe of greasepaint to reduce glare.

15. zyzzyva
A *type of weevil.*
There are zyzzyvas in the quinoa!

WHAT'S FUNNY ABOUT JOHNNY?

In Italian comedies of the 16th to 18th centuries, a clown named Giovanni (the Italian equivalent of John) was a stock figure. Typically a servant who mocked other characters, this clown became known by the nickname Zanni. Eventually Zanni became the adjective "zany," which we use today to mean kooky and madcap.

YOUR SCORE:
___ / 15

TALKING POLITICS

Before you hit the polls, make sure you've mastered the lingo of the campaign trail. Try this quiz to see how politically correct your vocabulary is, then consult the next page for answers.

1. demagogue
('deh-meh-gog) *n.*
A pollster.
B meeting.
c rabble-rouser.

2. plebiscite
('pleh-beh-siyt) *n.*
A statement of loyalty.
B volunteer.
c countrywide vote.

3. chauvinist
('sho-veh-nist) *n.*
A promoter of monarchy.
B political pundit.
c excessive patriot.

4. reactionary
(ree-'ak-shuh-nary) *adj.*
A very liberal.
B very conservative.
c undecided.

5. canvass
('kan-vas) *v.*
A solicit voters.
B stretch a budget.
c attempt a cover-up.

6. hustings
('huhs-tingz) *n.*
A nominee's supporters.
B proceedings or locale of a campaign.
c ballot punch-outs.

7. gravitas
('gra-veh-tahs) *n.*
A perks and freebies.
B local leanings.
c serious bearing.

8. snollygoster
('snah-lee-gah-ster) *n.*
A unprincipled but shrewd person.
B loud argument.
c close vote.

9. incendiary
(in-'sen-dee-er-ee) *adj.*
A illegal.
B tending to excite or agitate.
c rising in power.

10. suffrage
('suh-frij) *n.*
A right to vote.
B media exposure.
c civil disobedience.

11. jobbery
('jah-beh-ree) *n.*
A works program.
B false persona.
c corruption in office.

12. éminence grise
('ay-may-nahns 'greez) *n.*
A confidential agent.
B diplomat.
c elite class.

13. laissez-faire
(le-say-'fair) *adj.*
A proactive.
B opposing government interference.
c suave.

14. abnegate
('ab-ni-gayt) *v.*
A decline to vote.
B speak out of turn.
c relinquish or renounce.

15. junket
('juhn-ket) *n.*
A government-paid trip.
B smear campaign.
c bad loan.

"TALKING POLITICS" ANSWERS

1. demagogue
c *rabble-rouser.*
The senator's campaign turned ugly once the unofficial demagogue became manager.

2. plebiscite
c *countrywide vote.*
We're having a plebiscite on whether countrywide votes are legitimate.

3. chauvinist
c *excessive patriot.*
The governor is a true chauvinist: He wears Stars and Stripes boxers to bed. (The term, from purported 19th-century French nationalist Nicolas Chauvin, didn't take on the extremist "male chauvinist" meaning until the 1970s.)

4. reactionary
B *very conservative.*
Larry is so reactionary, he won't even consider amending the education bill.

5. canvass
A *solicit voters.*
Ever the all-American, Sally canvassed door-to-door toting a flag.

6. hustings
B *proceedings or locale of a campaign.*
He doesn't really care if he wins; he just likes the bus rides to the various hustings.

7. gravitas
c *serious bearing.*
How can you assume political gravitas with a name like Duckwill?

8. snollygoster
A *unprincipled but shrewd person.*
There's something of a snollygoster in Governor Tooney's public persona.

9. incendiary
B *tending to excite or agitate.*
My youngest girl is composing an incendiary speech about unionizing.

10. suffrage
A *right to vote.*
So I told her, no, she doesn't have suffrage on matters of bedtime.

11. jobbery
c *corruption in office.*
It isn't really jobbery

if my friends all just happened to get on the payroll, is it?

12. éminence grise
A *confidential agent.*
It says Joey's Lemonade Stand, but Ella is the éminence grise of the business.

13. laissez-faire
B *opposing government interference.*
Joan seems to have a laissez-faire attitude about controlling her classroom.

14. abnegate
c *relinquish or renounce.*
By passing this law, Congress abnegated its responsibility to uphold the Consistution.

15. junket
A *government-paid trip.*
I hear the boss went on a Busch Gardens junket using our pension fund!

YOUR SCORE:
___ / 15

FIRST HALF

What do an academic, a debacle, and a Miami Beach clambake have in common? They are words spelled with letters from only the first half of the alphabet, a to m—like all those in this quiz.

1. affable
('af-uh-bull) *adj.*
A easygoing.
B humorless.
c qualified.

2. filial
('fih-lee-uhl) *adj.*
A ornamental.
B of sons and daughters.
c on horseback.

3. edifice
('eh-duh-fiss) *n.*
A steep cliff.
B inspiration.
c large building.

4. calcified
('kal-sih-fyd) *adj.*
A hardened.
B wasted away.
c rusted through.

5. malleable
('mal-ee-uh-bull) *adj.*
A cruel.
B sickly.
c pliable.

6. Gallic
('gal-ik) *adj.*
A Scottish.
B French.
c Roman.

7. allege
(uh-'lej) *v.*
A compare and contrast.
B approach cautiously.
c assert without proof.

8. fallible
('fal-uh-bull) *adj.*
A autumnal.
B fertile.
c imperfect.

9. kalimba
(kuh-'lim-buh) *n.*
A tea service.
B thumb piano.
c motor scooter.

10. blackball
('blak-ball) *v.*
A exclude socially.
B demand money.
c cancel without notice.

11. ebb
(eb) *v.*
A rise slowly.
B decrease.
c encourage.

12. jackal
('jak-uhl) *n.*
A wild dog.
B trickster.
c thatched hut.

13. addled
('ad-uhld) *adj.*
A egg-shaped.
B confused.
c extra.

14. imam
(ih-'mom) *n.*
A electronic message.
B atomic particle.
c Muslim prayer leader.

15. fiddlehead
('fih-duhl-hed) *n.*
A edible fern.
B large crab.
c violinist.

"FIRST HALF" ANSWERS

1. affable
A *easygoing.*
Guillermo is always affable, even when facing big deadlines at work.
___

2. filial
B *of sons and daughters.*
"Is some filial respect too much to ask around here?" Mom joked.
___

3. edifice
C *large building.*
The Gothic edifice will be restored by a team of experts.
___

4. calcified
A *hardened.*
Mary's political opinions only calcified as she grew older.
___

5. malleable
C *pliable.*
After her first yoga class, Emily found that her muscles weren't all that malleable.
___

6. Gallic
B *French.*
Crepes are a classic Gallic dish.
___

7. allege
C *assert without proof.*
At the time you allege my dog dug up your azaleas, he actually was at the vet.
___

8. fallible
C *imperfect.*
The captain may think he's always right, but even his judgment is fallible sometimes!
___

9. kalimba
B *thumb piano.*
My niece taught herself to play Mozart sonatas on the kalimba.
___

10. blackball
A *exclude socially.*
E.J. was blackballed from the gardening club after she missed four meetings in a row.
___

11. ebb
B *decrease.*
Tamika's enthusiasm for knitting began to ebb after she made a few misshapen scarves.
___

12. jackal
A *wild dog.*
What is the mayor's office going to do about the pack of jackals on the loose in our town?
___

13. addled
B *confused.*
Uncle Paul can get addled when he doesn't take his medications.
___

14. imam
C *Muslim prayer leader.*
Local imams, rabbis, and priests formed a task force to promote religious tolerance.
___

15. fiddlehead
A *edible fern.*
We're serving salmon on a bed of sautéed fiddleheads for lunch.
___

HALF-TIME NOTES
Three different prefixes can signal a half: There's semi- (as in semicircle), hemi- (hemisphere), and demi- (demigod). As it happens, all three prefixes occur in music—and in one case, in the same word. A hemidemisemiquaver is a 64th note, or a half of a half of a half of an eighth note, which is called a quaver. The shorter the note, the longer the name!

YOUR SCORE:
___ / 15

ELEMENTARY

This quiz is for fans of the BBC series and Netflix favorite *Sherlock*, as well as readers of the original mystery tales by Sir Arthur Conan Doyle. Follow the trail to the next page for answers.

1. connoisseur
(kah-neh-'sir) *n.*
A swindler.
B expert.
C paid informant.

2. faculties
('fa-kuhl-teez) *n.*
A powers.
B intricate details.
C sudden insights.

3. infallible
(in-'fa-leh-buhl) *adj.*
A never wrong.
B remaining questionable or unsolved.
C carefully balanced.

4. minatory
('min-uh-tor-ee) *adj.*
A unethical.
B with a menacing quality.
C subversive.

5. furtive
('fer-tiv) *adj.*
A nervous.
B sneaky.
C tall and thin.

6. untoward
(uhn-'toh-uhrd) *adj.*
A illogical.
B strongly opinionated.
C not favorable.

7. facilitate
(fuh-'sih-luh-tayt) *v.*
A make easier.
B confront.
C unravel.

8. incisive
(in-'siy-siv) *adj.*
A urgent.
B doubtful.
C impressively direct.

9. tenacious
(tuh-'nay-shus) *adj.*
A persistent.
B well concealed.
C supremely rational.

10. desultory
('deh-suhl-tor-ee) *adj.*
A yielding no clues.
B hot and humid.
C having no plan.

11. proficiency
(pruh-'fih-shun-see) *n.*
A right-handedness.
B likelihood.
C great skill.

12. illustrious
(ih-'luhs-tree-uhs) *adj.*
A graphic.
B eminent.
C deceiving.

13. injunction
(in-'junk-shun) *n.*
A order.
B coincidence.
C shot of medicine or drugs.

14. truculent
('truh-kyuh-luhnt) *adj.*
A cruel or harsh.
B puzzled.
C of few words.

15. sardonic
(sahr-'dah-nik) *adj.*
A carelessly dressed.
B threatening.
C mocking.

"ELEMENTARY" ANSWERS

1. connoisseur
B *expert.*
"Can you recommend an art connoisseur?" the detective asked after the robbery at the museum.

2. faculties
A *powers.*
The prosecution set out to test the full faculties of the defense team.

3. infallible
A *never wrong.*
"Our key witness has an infallible memory," the lawyer said.

4. minatory
B *with a menacing quality.*
The thief gave his victim a minatory gaze before leaving her in the alley.

CALLING ALL DETECTIVES

The term "private eye" alludes simply to "private i" (short for investigator). You may also call such a person a tec (short for detective), a gumshoe (from quiet, rubber-soled footwear), or a sleuth (from an Old Norse word for "trail").

5. furtive
B *sneaky.*
I didn't for one second trust the suspect—he has a furtive look.

6. untoward
C *not favorable.*
"Barring untoward circumstances," said the judge, "we'll have a decision by week's end."

7. facilitate
A *make easier.*
The sergeant needed one more lead to facilitate the investigation.

8. incisive
C *impressively direct.*
"Guilty," the juror offered in a most incisive tone.

9. tenacious
A *persistent.*
Officer Bluntley can be as tenacious as a bulldog.

10. desultory
C *having no plan.*
After finding no clues at the crime scene, the police began a desultory search for evidence.

11. proficiency
C *great skill.*
"I claim no proficiency at lab work—but I am a huge *CSI* fan!"

12. illustrious
B *eminent.*
After an illustrious 30-year career, Detective Klein finally retired.

13. injunction
A *order.*
For failing to follow the injunction, Thomas was ordered to serve 90 days of community service.

14. truculent
A *cruel or harsh.*
The witness was unscathed by the prosecutor's truculent remarks.

15. sardonic
C *mocking.*
"Catch me if you can!" cried the felon with a sardonic laugh.

YOUR SCORE:
___ / 15

EAT YOUR WORDS

Gastronomy—the art of eating—is a rich source of vocabulary. See how many culinary words you know, even if you can't boil water.

1. eupeptic
(yoo-'pep-tick) *adj.*
A perfectly ripe.
B having a peppery flavor.
c promoting good digestion.

2. dim sum
(dim sum) *n.*
A dark meat of a duck.
B made with a blended soy sauce.
c small portions of a variety of foods.

3. sommelier
(sum-ull-'yay) *n.*
A wine steward.
B head chef.
c light salad dressing.

4. dredge
(drej) *v.*
A lightly coat, as with flour.
B grind into meal.
c bind the wings and legs of a fowl.

5. sapid
('sap-ud) *adj.*
A flavorful.
B syrupy.
c stale.

6. julienne
(joo-lee-'en or zhoo-) *v.*
A season with herbs.
B steam.
c cut into thin strips.

7. roux (roo) *n.*
A spicy stew containing okra.
B bead-shaped grain.
c thickener for sauces.

8. coddle
('cod-dull) *v.*
A unmold candy.
B beat with a whisk.
c cook gently in hot water.

9. bain-marie
(ban-muh-'ree) *n.*
A cheese slicer.
B double boiler's lower pot.
c small pastry tip.

10. nori
('noh-ree or 'nor-ee) *n.*
A dipping bowls.
B seaweed wrapper for sushi.
c drink made from fermented rice.

11. macerate
('mass-uh-rate) *v.*
A sizzle.
B soften by steeping.
c break into crumbs.

12. tandoori
(tahn-'dure-ee) *adj.*
A flavored with curries.
B sweetened with tamarind.
c roasted in a charcoal oven.

13. trencherman
('tren-chur-mun) *n.*
A hearty eater.
B salad chef.
c waiter's assistant.

14. clabber
('clab-ur) *n.*
A gristle.
B curdled milk.
c corn whiskey.

15. Florentine
('floor-un-teen or -tine) *adj.*
A prepared with a cream sauce.
B prepared with spinach.
c prepared with mozzarella.

"EAT YOUR WORDS" ANSWERS

1. eupeptic
C *promoting good digestion.*
Dad claims that watching the Super Bowl after a big meal is eupeptic.

---

2. dim sum
C *small portions of a variety of foods.*
It's not worth it to take Paige out for dim sum—one dumpling and she's full.

---

3. sommelier
A *wine steward.*
When Harry ordered a wine spritzer, the sommelier turned pale.

---

4. dredge
A *lightly coat, as with flour.*
Rodney dredged everything in the kitchen but the chicken.

---

5. sapid
A *flavorful.*
This soup is about as sapid as dishwater.

---

6. julienne
C *cut into thin strips.*
The puppy methodically julienned every pillow in the house.

7. roux
C *thickener for sauces.*
If the gravy won't pour, you've used too much roux.

---

8. coddle
C *cook gently in hot water.*
His joke's punch line was "Cannibals don't coddle their children."

---

9. bain-marie
B *double boiler's lower pot.*
I won't make any recipe that calls for a bain-marie—my most exotic kitchen utensil is a pizza cutter.

---

10. nori
B *seaweed wrapper for sushi.*
In his full-body wet suit, Uncle Ned emerged from the water looking like a jumbo shrimp wrapped in nori.

---

11. macerate
B *soften by steeping.*
For dessert, our hostess served Anjou pears macerated in 25-year-old Armagnac, but we would have preferred Twinkies.

12. tandoori
C *roasted in a charcoal oven.*
The restaurant's unrestrained menu included both steak fajitas and tandoori chicken.

---

13. trencherman
A *hearty eater.*
Our teenage son, with his trencherman's appetite, will eat us out of house and home.

---

14. clabber
B *curdled milk.*
Searching the fridge shelves for a little milk for my coffee, I found only a carton full of clabber.

---

15. Florentine
B *prepared with spinach.*
We don't use the word "spinach" in front of our five-year-old; instead we call it a Florentine dish.

YOUR SCORE:
___ / 15

SECOND HALF

This quiz features the likes of nuns, protons, sprouts, and soupspoons— words made exclusively from the second half of the alphabet, letters n to z. If they make you feel topsy-turvy, turn the page for answers.

1. stuporous
('stoo-puh-russ) *adj.*
A hunched over.
B leaking.
C impaired.

2. wry
(ry) *adj.*
A ironically humorous.
B disrespectful.
C made with flour.

3. purport
(per-'port) *v.*
A transfer.
B commit a crime.
C claim.

4. tryst
(trist) *n.*
A final audition.
B natural disaster.
C lovers' meeting.

5. wonton
('wahn-tahn) *n.*
A wild abandon.
B Chinese dumpling.
C great quantity.

6. spoor
(spoor) *n.*
A animal tracks.
B rude rejection.
C plant cell.

7. yurt
(yert) *n.*
A custard dish.
B buffoon.
C circular tent.

8. usurp
(yoo-'serp) *v.*
A puree.
B flip over.
C seize.

9. sop
(sahp) *n.*
A thick syrup.
B bribe.
C wetland.

10. tosspot
('toss-paht) *n.*
A tantrum.
B windstorm.
C drunkard.

11. punt
(punt) *n.*
A linebacker.
B flat-bottomed boat.
C smallest of a litter.

12. tortuous
('tor-choo-us) *adj.*
A clumpy.
B winding.
C painful.

13. onyx
('ah-nicks) *n.*
A antelope.
B gemstone.
C primrose.

14. tyro
('ty-roh) *n.*
A rookie.
B felt hat.
C whirlwind.

15. ouzo
('oo-zoh) *n.*
A firearm.
B Greek liqueur.
C slow drip.

"SECOND HALF" ANSWERS

1. stuporous

c *impaired.*
I can't take medicine for my hay fever—just one pill leaves me sleepy and stuporous.

2. wry

A *ironically humorous.*
Mr. Russo's students loved his wry sense of humor and unusual lesson plans.

3. purport

c *claim.*
Jack purports to be a bad singer, but he always brings down the house at karaoke.

W, X, Y, AND Z ... AND &

The letter z wasn't always last. Up into the 1800s, the alphabet ended with the symbol &, called an ampersand. It meant "and" then, too—like "a" and "i," it was both a character and a word. No one knows for sure when & was booted from the alphabet, but it didn't make the cut when the "Now I know my ABCs" ditty was copyrighted in 1835.

4. tryst

c *lovers' meeting.*
Clara and Luis planned a midnight tryst in the garden.

5. wonton

B *Chinese dumpling.*
I see you've left all the broth and eaten just the wontons.

6. spoor

A *animal tracks.*
The park ranger followed the fox's spoor back to the den.

7. yurt

c *circular tent.*
Hannah teaches meditation workshops in her backyard yurt.

8. usurp

c *seize.*
"I left for one minute—and that guy usurped my seat!" exclaimed Alessandro.

9. sop

B *bribe.*
If you give the doorman a few bucks as a sop, he'll let you in.

10. tosspot

c *drunkard.*
I spent much of my 20s in bars, but I wasn't exactly a tosspot.

11. punt

B *flat-bottomed boat.*
The travelers steered their punt down the Thames.

12. tortuous

B *winding.*
The trail is tortuous and steep, but the reward is a spectacular view from the summit.

13. onyx

B *gemstone.*
Harold gave Esme a black onyx ring for her birthday.

14. tyro

A *rookie.*
I'm a tyro when it comes to social media; can you explain again what "tweet" means?

15. ouzo

B *Greek liqueur.*
"I'd like to propose a toast!" said Nick, lifting his glass of ouzo.

YOUR SCORE:
___ / 15

IN SHORT

Here, we celebrate all things diminutive. Zip through this quiz in short order, then baby step to the next page for answers.

1. transient
('tran-shee-nt or -zee-ent) *adj.*
A short-range.
B short-handed.
C short-lived.

2. vignette
(vin-'yet) *n.*
A small glass.
B short literary sketch or scene.
C thin line.

3. bagatelle
(ba-geh-'tel) *n.*
A child's rucksack.
B cell nucleus.
C something of little value.

4. scintilla
(sin-'ti-luh) *n.*
A short vowel.
B minute amount.
C minor crime.

5. myopic
(miy-'oh-pik) *adj.*
A too tiny for the naked eye.
B shortsighted.
C early.

6. irascible
(i-'ra-se-bul) *adj.*
A small-minded.
B narrow-waisted.
C marked by a short temper.

7. expeditiously
(ek-speh-'di-shes-lee) *adv.*
A promptly and efficiently.
B incompletely.
C tersely or rudely.

8. tabard
('ta-bird) *n.*
A short-sleeved coat.
B booklet of verses.
C dwarf evergreen.

9. arietta
(ar-ee-'eh-tuh) *n.*
A tot's playpen.
B miniature figurine.
C short melody.

10. niggling
('nih-gehling) *adj.*
A petty.
B stunted.
C short-winded.

11. aphorism
('a-feh-ri-zuhm) *n.*
A concise saying.
B shorthand writing.
C cut-off sentence.

12. staccato
(ste-'kah-toh) *adj.*
A of cemented fragments.
B formed into droplets.
C disconnected.

13. nib
(nib) *n.*
A crumb on a plate.
B point of a pen.
C matter of seconds.

14. exiguous
(ig-'zi-gye-wes) *adj.*
A inadequate, scanty.
B momentary.
C reduced by one tenth.

15. truncate
('trun-kayt) *v.*
A compress by squeezing.
B speed up.
C shorten by lopping off.

"IN SHORT" ANSWERS

1. transient
c *short-lived.*
The first-quarter lead proved transient, as the Ravens racked up 42 points in the second.

2. vignette
B *short literary sketch or scene.*
Dickens created characters from prose vignettes like little photographs.

3. bagatelle
c *something of little value.*
My stories aren't prized works, just personal bagatelles.

4. scintilla
B *minute amount.*
There's not one scintilla of evidence against my client.

5. myopic
B *shortsighted.*
Kim's myopic view of the project surely led to its collapse.

6. irascible
c *marked by a short temper.*
If Jack were any more irascible, he'd have smoke coming out of his ears.

7. expeditiously
A *promptly and efficiently.*
As a pick-me-up, a triple espresso works expeditiously.

8. tabard
A *short-sleeved coat.*
My entire Hamlet costume consists of a wooden sword and this tabard.

9. arietta
c *short melody.*
The goldfinch trilled an arietta, reminding us that spring would come soon.

10. niggling
A *petty.*
Mom, you're driving me bonkers with your niggling complaints!

11. aphorism
A *concise saying.*
My father has an aphorism for any situation.

12. staccato
c *disconnected.*
Lucy's hilarious laugh comes in sharp, staccato dog barks.

13. nib
B *point of a pen.*
A faulty nib, Beth complained, ruined her first pass at her final drawing project.

14. exiguous
A *inadequate, scanty.*
Ever a big eater, Art found even the jumbo burger a bit exiguous.

15. truncate
c *shorten by lopping off.*
According to mythology, the gruesome Procrustes would truncate his guests if they were too long for the bed.

YOUR SCORE:
___ / 15

LATIN ROOTS

Latin is not the official language of any country today, but far from defunct, it's thriving in hundreds of our common English expressions. Whether it's alias ("somewhere else") or veto ("I forbid"), Caesar's language is entwined with ours.

1. verbatim
(ver-'bay-tuhm) *adv.*
A slowly and carefully.
B without stopping.
C word for word.

2. mea culpa
(may-uh 'kul-puh) *n.*
A congratulations.
B acknowledgment of fault.
C wavering decision.

3. bona fide
('boh-nuh fiyd) *adj.*
A genuine.
B secret.
C at home.

4. non sequitur
(nahn 'seh-kwuh-tuhr) *n.*
A odd man out.
B comment that doesn't follow logically.
C failure to obey.

5. ad infinitum
(ad in-fuh-'niy-tuhm) *adv.*
A imitating.
B without end.
C making a bold display.

6. status quo
(sta-tuhs 'kwoh) *n.*
A good reputation.
B current state of affairs.
C complete sentence.

7. magnum opus
('mag-nuhm 'oh-puhs) *n.*
A masterpiece.
B large debt.
C giant squid.

8. per capita
(per 'ka-puh-tuh) *adv.*
A financially.
B in block letters.
C for each person.

9. ergo
('er-goh) *adv.*
A as soon as.
B therefore.
C otherwise.

10. circa
(suhr-'kuh) *prep.*
A about or around.
B after.
C between.

11. persona non grata
(per-'soh-nuh nahn 'grah-tuh) *adj.*
A fake.
B thankless.
C unwelcome.

12. semper fidelis
(sem-per fuh-'day-luhs) *adj.*
A at attention.
B innocent.
C always loyal.

13. carpe diem
(kar-peh 'dee-uhm) *interj.*
A happy anniversary!
B seize the day!
C listen, please!

14. pro bono (proh 'boh-noh) *adj.*
A in support of artists.
B at no cost.
C part time.

15. quid pro quo
(kwid proh 'kwoh) *n.*
A something given or received for something else.
B vote in favor.
C generous tip.

"LATIN ROOTS" ANSWERS

1. verbatim
C *word for word.*
If you don't repeat the magic spell verbatim, the cave door won't open.

---

2. mea culpa
B *acknowledgment of fault.*
Whenever Art misses a fly ball, he says, "Mea culpa!"

---

3. bona fide
A *genuine.*
I was waiting for a bona fide apology after my argument with customer service.

---

4. non sequitur
B *comment that doesn't follow logically.*
We were discussing the film when Taylor threw in a non sequitur about her new kitchen.

---

5. ad infinitum
B *without end.*
Don't get my sister started on politics, or she'll start hurling her opinions ad infinitum.

---

6. status quo
B *current state of affairs.*
The new CEO's structural moves have changed the status quo for the better.

TRIVIAL PURSUIT

The word "trivia" is from the Latin for "three roads" (*tri* + *via*). In ancient times, at a major crossroads there was typically a kiosk listing regional information. Or local gossipers might be there. Travelers could learn facts at these intersections—but the information might have seemed commonplace.

---

7. magnum opus
A *masterpiece.*
I think of "Good Vibrations" as Brian Wilson's magnum opus.

---

8. per capita
C *for each person.*
Mom said, "Just one lollipop per capita, kids."

---

9. ergo
B *therefore.*
The groom was late; ergo, the bride appeared unsettled.

---

10. circa
A *about or around.*
It was circa 1978 that Juliana first started collecting Peanuts memorabilia.

---

11. persona non grata
C *unwelcome.*
After I didn't call my best friend for years, he declared me persona non grata.

---

12. semper fidelis
C *always loyal.*
Jack typically shortens the U.S. Marines motto (*Semper Fidelis*) to a yell of "Semper fi!"

---

13. carpe diem
B *seize the day!*
Don't sit around procrastinating, you sluggard—carpe diem!

---

14. pro bono
B *at no cost.*
The lawyer enjoys doing pro bono work to help immigrant children.

---

15. quid pro quo
A *something given or received for something else.*
Offer me trading advice, and I'll chip in some tech help; it's a quid pro quo.

YOUR SCORE:
____ / 15

MORNING PAPERS

From the strange to the straightforward, newspaper
names from around the world form this quiz.

1. chronicle
('krah-ni-kul) *n.*
A daily ritual.
B widely held belief.
C account of events.

2. repository
(ri-'pah-zi-tor-ee) *n.*
A paper shredder.
B medication-delivery device.
C container used for storage.

3. clarion
('kler-ee-un, 'kla-ree-) *adj.*
A high-pitched.
B partially obscured.
C loud and clear.

4. epitaph
('e-pi-taf) *n.*
A editorial.
B clever headline.
C tombstone inscription.

5. ledger
('le-jur) *n.*
A accounting book.
B illustration.
C address book.

6. excelsior
(ik-'sel-see-er, -or) *adj.*
A ever faithful.
B ever upward.
C ever changing.

7. flume (floom) *n.*
A seabird with a wingspan four times its body length.
B narrow gorge with a stream.
C warm summer wind.

8. Whig
(hwig, wig) *n.*
A staunch conservative.
B member of historical British political party.
C news editor appointed by the queen.

9. derrick
('der-ik) *n.*
A serif font.
B woody tropical plant.
C framework over an oil well.

10. gleaner ('gleen-er) *n.—*
someone who...
A makes predictions.
B gathers information.
C classifies data.

11. dominion
(di-'mi-nyen) *n.*
A control.
B large group of people.
C wisdom.

12. delta
('del-ta) *n.*
A high-altitude plain.
B triangular object.
C appointed officer.

13. laconic
(la-'kah-nik) *adj.*
A concise.
B weekly.
C circular.

14. hub (hub) *n.*
A last-minute assignment.
B center of activity.
C funny caption.

15. tribune
('tri-byoon, tri-'byoon) *n.*
A payment made by one state or ruler to another.
B an official in ancient Rome.
C river or stream flowing into a larger river or lake.

"MORNING PAPERS" ANSWERS

1. chronicle
c *account of events.*
Tom's election chronicle included a time line.

2. repository
c *container used for storage.*
Donnie kept photos of the house's history in a wooden repository.

3. clarion
c *loud and clear.*
The pollution exposé was a clarion call to recycle.

4. epitaph
c *tombstone inscription.*
Jed's epitaph made the mourners cry.

5. ledger
a *accounting book.*
The auditor recorded the baker's expenses in his ledger.

6. excelsior
b *ever upward.*
Climbing Mount Everest, Debbie exclaimed, "Excelsior!" to urge herself on.

7. flume
b *narrow gorge with a stream.*
Dejected, Doris watched the water rush down the flume and considered tossing in her failed first draft.

8. Whig
b *member of historical British political party.*
His right-wing friends often joked that liberal-leaning John would have made a great Whig.

9. derrick
c *framework over an oil well.*
Sunlight on the derrick cast a fitting shadow over the oil town.

10. gleaner
b *someone who gathers information.*
A natural gleaner of racy details, Jane was the perfect choice for editor of the new gossip blog.

11. dominion
a *control.*
As owner of both the newspaper and the bank, Morgan held the town under his dominion.

12. delta
b *triangular object.*
The group of friends would often gather in secret at the sandy delta where the river splits.

13. laconic
a *concise.*
Laconic yet creative: That was Colin's MO when he sat down to write captions.

14. hub
b *center of activity.*
After sundown, the beach town's lone restaurant became the hub for tourists and locals alike.

15. tribune
b *official in ancient Rome.*
The tribunes of the plebeians served to protect the interests of the people.

YOUR SCORE:
___ / 15

A IS FOR

The letter a is so much more than the alphabet's leader: music note, blood type, Hawthorne favorite, mark of excellence, and stardom vehicle for Mr. T. This quiz is about words whose only vowel is a.

1. banal
(buh-'nal or 'bay-nuhl) *adj.*
A disallowed.
B uptight.
C trite.

2. annals
('a-nulz) *n.*
A catacombs.
B chronicles.
C long johns.

3. arcana
(ar-'kay-nuh) *n.*
A mysterious or specialized knowledge.
B travel journal.
C rainbow.

4. masala
(mah-'sah-la) *n.*
A Chilean wine.
B Indian spice blend.
C Italian antipasto.

5. llama
('lah-muh) *n.*
A beast of burden.
B heroic escape.
C priest or monk.

6. bazaar
(buh-'zar) *n.*
A weird event.
B marketplace.
C wailing siren.

7. paschal
('pas-kel) *adj.*
A of computer languages.
B in a Gothic style.
C relating to Easter.

8. amalgam
(uh-'mal-gum) *n.*
A mixture.
B volcanic rock.
C back of the throat.

9. plantar
('plan-ter) *adj.*
A vegetative.
B paved with asphalt.
C of the sole of the foot.

10. catamaran
(ka-teh-meh-'ran) *n.*
A Bengal tiger.
B black olive.
C boat with two hulls.

11. balaclava
(ba-leh-'klah-vuh) *n.*
A knit cap.
B Greek pastry.
C Russian mandolin.

12. avatar
('a-veh-tar) *n.*
A mythological sibling.
B incarnation of a god.
C computer language.

13. spartan
('spar-tn) *adj.*
A desertlike.
B marked by simplicity and lack of luxury.
C of classical theater.

14. allay
(a-'lay) *v.*
A refuse.
B take sides.
C calm.

15. lambda
('lam-duh) *n.*
A Greek letter.
B Brazilian dance.
C college degree.

"A IS FOR" ANSWERS

1. banal
c *trite.*
Whenever the teacher says something too banal, Dorothy rolls her eyes.

2. annals
B *chronicles.*
In the annals of sports idiocy, that was the biggest bonehead play I've ever seen!

3. arcana
A *mysterious or specialized knowledge.*
I'd rather not know all the deep arcana of your arachnid research.

4. masala
B *Indian spice blend.*
Easy on the masala—Sarah doesn't have the stomach for spicy dishes.

---

5. llama
A *beast of burden.*
The llama has been used as a meat and pack animal by Andean cultures since the pre-Columbian era.

6. bazaar
B *marketplace.*
During her hunt at the bazaar, Sally found a turn-of-the-century compass that had belonged to her great-grandfather.

7. paschal
c *relating to Easter.*
Terri spent hours on her paschal bonnet—it started as a flowerpot!

8. amalgam
A *mixture.*
Our team is a strong amalgam of raw youth and seasoned leadership.

9. plantar
c *of the sole of the foot.*
"What do these plantar prints tell us, Holmes?" asked Watson.

10. catamaran
c *boat with two hulls.*
Jack thinks he's Admiral Nelson now that he has won the marina's annual catamaran race.

11. balaclava
A *knit cap.*
Hang your balaclava in the foyer and grab some stew.

12. avatar
B *incarnation of a god.*
In Hindu mythology, Rama is the seventh avatar of the god Vishnu.

13. spartan
B *marked by simplicity and lack of luxury.*
We didn't expect such spartan conditions in the honeymoon suite.

14. allay
c *calm.*
Yesterday's board meeting did more than just allay our fears—it gave us an uptick of hope!

15. lambda
A *Greek letter.*
Invert a "V," and you've got a Greek lambda—or Bob's mustache.

 YOUR SCORE:
___ / 15

HOLY WORDS

This contemplative quiz is full of words that refer to holy, soulful, or meditative practices. After you've pondered, ascend to the next page for answers.

1. canticle
('kan-tih-kuhl) *n.*
A sacred flame.
B small chapel.
C Biblical song.

2. asana
('ah-suh-nuh) *n.*
A sweat lodge.
B yoga pose.
C spiritual guide.

3. halal
(huh-'lahl) *adj.*
A in a trance.
B on a pilgrimage.
C fit or lawful.

4. mezuzah
(muh-'zoo-zah) *n.*
A scroll hung by a door.
B golden halo.
C organ composition.

5. vespers
('veh-sperz) *n.*
A evening service.
B silent worship.
C winged cherubs.

6. genuflect
('jen-yoo-flekt) *v.*
A donate.
B ponder.
C kneel.

7. ecclesiastic
(ih-klee-zee-'a-stik, eh-) *adj.*
A relating to a prayer.
B humble.
C of or relating to a church.

8. halcyon
('hal-see-on) *adj.*
A awesome.
B peaceful.
C mythical.

9. atone
(uh-'tohn) *v.*
A begin fasting.
B bow down to.
C make up for.

10. ashram
('ah-shrum) *n.*
A burial mound.
B Nativity scene.
C religious retreat.

11. homily
('hah-muh-lee) *n.*
A sermon.
B hymn.
C parish.

12. thaumaturgist
('thaw-muh-ter-jist) *n.*
A miracle worker.
B congregation head.
C nonbeliever.

13. supplicate
('suh-plih-kayt) *v.*
A pray.
B obey.
C consume.

14. kinara
(kih-'nah-ruh) *n.*
A enlightenment.
B set of seven candles.
C scripture.

15. psyche
('sy-kee) *n.*
A soul.
B guide.
C rite.

"HOLY WORDS" ANSWERS

1. canticle
c *Biblical song.*
The choir sang a canticle to begin Sunday's service.

2. asana
B *yoga pose.*
Barbara's favorite asana is downward-facing dog.

3. halal
c *fit or lawful.*
My family is Muslim, so we've always followed a halal diet.

4. mezuzah
A *scroll hung by a door.*
The Rosens bought that pretty mezuzah on a family trip to Israel.

5. vespers
A *evening service.*
If we don't eat dinner soon, we'll be late to Christmas Eve vespers.

6. genuflect
c *kneel.*
After my knee surgery, I couldn't genuflect for a month.

7. ecclesiastic
c *of or relating to a church.*
The council confined

THAT'S THE SPIRIT(S)

Most examples of spirit are ethereal, such as a person's soul or mood, or even a ghost. But what about that most earthly of spirits—aka alcohol? That meaning may have originated as a term for the vapors produced by distillation; *spiritus* is Latin for "breath." Or it could be linked to the final product of distillation: pure alcohol, the "spirit" of the original liquid.

itself to debating only ecclesiastic matters.

8. halcyon
B *peaceful.*
I adore those halcyon moments that happen as the sun comes up.

9. atone
c *make up for.*
Ellen will be atoning for breaking Mom's camera for years.

10. ashram
c *religious retreat.*
Ashrams are usually associated with Hinduism.

11. homily
A *sermon.*
Can I just borrow the car without all the usual homilies?

12. thaumaturgist
A *miracle worker.*
That man who "cures"

blindness with a touch of his hand says he's a thaumaturgist, but he's really just a huckster.

13. supplicate
A *pray.*
Before his big presentations, Boris would supplicate to the gods of public speaking.

14. kinara
B *set of seven candles.*
The first kinara, used to celebrate Kwanzaa, was created 55 years ago.

15. psyche
A *soul.*
Why do so many politicians seem to have the psyche of a potted plant?

YOUR SCORE:
____ / 15

WORD INVENTION

What's in a name? Sometimes a new word. This
quiz features words inspired by real people.

1. salchow

('sow-cow) *n.*

A heavy-coated dog
  breed.

B vegetable stew.

c figure skating jump.

---

2. martinet

(mar-tuh-'net) *n.*

A woodland songbird.

B gossipy neighbor.

c strict disciplinarian.

---

3. mesmerize

('mez-muh-rise) *v.*

A stimulate with a
  shock.

B predict the future.

c spellbind.

---

4. quisling

('kwiz-ling) *n.*

A medicinal tea.

B traitor.

c whim.

---

5. Beaufort scale

('bo-furt) *n.*

A measure of wind
  force.

B measure of
  earthquakes.

c measure of rainfall.

6. theremin

('ther-uh-mun) *n.*

A dome-topped house.

B iron-rich supplement.

c electronic musical
  instrument.

---

7. Queensberry rules

('kweenz-ber-ee) *n.*

A principles of poker.

B boxing regulations.

c bylaws of diplomacy.

---

8. bowdlerize

('bode-luh-rise or bowd-) *v.*

A talk in circles.

B develop land for
  commercial use.

c censor prudishly.

---

9. Snellen chart

('snel-un) *n.*

A calorie-rating
  system.

B measure of bridge
  capacity.

c test for eyesight.

---

10. draconian

(dray-'ko-nee-un) *adj.*

A severe.

B affected by the full
  moon.

c unnecessarily
  complicated.

11. maudlin

('mawd-lun) *adj.*

A sentimental.

B trendy.

c average.

---

12. curie

('kyur-ee) *n.*

A small fruit-filled
  pastry.

B unit of radioactivity.

c object provoking
  wonderment.

---

13. Machiavellian

(mah-kee-uh-'vel-ee-un) *adj.*

A traveling at the speed
  of sound.

B politically dishonest.

c ornate, as of
  architecture.

---

14. Mae West

(may west) *n.*

A inflatable life jacket.

B curves on a woman.

c bawdy woman.

---

15. jeremiad

(jer-a-'miy-ed, -ad) *n.*

A crybaby.

B a pessimist.

c prolonged complaint.

"WORD INVENTION" ANSWERS

1. salchow
c *figure skating jump.*
(Swedish skater Ulrich
Salchow.) Larry never
mastered the salchow.

2. martinet
c *strict disciplinarian.*
(French army officer
Jean Martinet.) My Latin
teacher was such a
martinet.

3. mesmerize
c *spellbind.*
(German physician
Franz Anton Mesmer.)
The new show
mesmerized us.

4. quisling
b *traitor.*
(Vidkun Quisling,
pro-Nazi Norwegian
politician.) When Johnny
Damon left the Sox for
the Yankees, Dad called
him a quisling.

5. Beaufort scale
a *measure of wind force.*
(British admiral Sir
Francis Beaufort.) A 10
on the Beaufort scale is
too high for kite flying.

6. theremin
c *electronic musical
instrument.*
(Russian engineer

Leon Theremin.) The
otherworldly sound in
"Good Vibrations" was
made by a theremin.

7. Queensberry rules
b *boxing regulations.*
(John Sholto Douglas,
9th Marquess of
Queensberry.) Pugsy
wore cleats in the ring,
in clear violation of the
Queensberry rules.

8. bowdlerize
c *censor prudishly.*
(English editor Thomas
Bowdler.) The church's
bowdlerized version
of *A Streetcar Named
Desire* lacked punch.

9. Snellen chart
c *test for eyesight.*
(Dutch ophthalmologist
Herman Snellen.) This
book is so hard to read,
it might as well be a
Snellen chart.

10. draconian
a *severe.*
(Athenian lawmaker
Draco.) The draconian
condo association bans
window boxes.

11. maudlin
a *sentimental.*
(Mary Magdalene.)

Instead of a maudlin
wedding song, the
couple chose Led
Zeppelin.

12. curie
b *unit of radioactivity.*
(French chemists Pierre
and Marie Curie.) How
many curies of radiation
is safe?

13. Machiavellian
b *politically dishonest.*
(Italian political
philosopher Niccolò
Machiavelli.) The garden
club president, in her
Machiavellian rise to
power, gave first place
to a member's violet.

14. Mae West
a *inflatable life jacket.*
(American actress.)
Servicemen in World
War II relied on their
Mae Wests to stay safe.

15. jeremiad
c *prolonged complaint.*
(Prophet Jeremiah.) The
book is nothing more
than a jeremiad against
the ruling class.

YOUR SCORE:
___ / 15

ALL THAT GLITTERS

Break out your bling—Word Power is going glam!
We're shining the spotlight on glittery words related
to jewelry. Will your score be as good as gold?
Turn the page for the answers.

1. bauble
('bah-bull) *n.*
A showy trinket.
B flawed gemstone.
C set of bracelets.

2. gilt
(gilt) *adj.*
A silver-plated.
B finely carved.
C covered in gold.

3. carat
('kehr-uht) *n.*
A unit of weight.
B measure of clarity.
C depth of color.

4. amulet
('am-yoo-let) *n.*
A watchband.
B protective charm.
C adjustable clasp.

5. iridescent
(eer-uh-'dess-ent) *adj.*
A rustproof.
B having rainbow
   colors.
C made of glass.

6. alloy
('al-oy) *n.*
A mixture of metals.
B gray pearl.
C precious mineral.

7. solitaire
('sah-luh-tayr) *n.*
A loop in a chain.
B gem set alone.
C white metal.

8. girandole
('jeer-en-dohl) *n.*
A pendant earring.
B rare moonstone.
C cuff link.

9. citrine.
(sih-'treen) *n.*
A pink sapphire.
B yellow quartz.
C green topaz.

10. adorn
(uh-'dorn) *v.*
A determine value.
B make beautiful.
C bend into shape.

11. baguette
(bag-'et) *n.*
A beaded purse.
B cocktail ring.
C rectangular stone.

12. filigree
('fih-luh-gree) *n.*
A vintage brass.
B impurity.
C delicate metalwork.

13. palladium
(puh-'lay-dee-um) *n.*
A fool's gold.
B pinkie ring.
C silver-white metal.

14. facet
('fass-et) *n.*
A surface on a cut gem.
B nose stud.
C price per ounce.

15. rondelle
(ron-'del) *n.*
A heavy brooch.
B long necklace.
C jeweled ring.

"ALL THAT GLITTERS" ANSWERS

1. bauble
A *showy trinket.*
Most of my accessories are baubles I found at yard sales.

2. gilt
c *covered in gold.*
Lenore slipped a gilt barrette into her long dark hair.

3. carat
A *unit of weight.*
The famous Hope Diamond weighs a whopping 45 carats!

4. amulet
B *protective charm.*
Clutching the amulet around his neck, Rowen faced the evil sorcerer.

5. iridescent
B *having rainbow colors.*
Kelly's iridescent opal bracelet sparkled in the sunshine.

6. alloy
A *mixture of metals.*
Rose gold is actually an alloy of gold, silver, and copper.

7. solitaire
B *gem set alone.*
"Will you marry me?" asked the duke, slipping the diamond solitaire ring onto his beloved's finger.

8. girandole
A *pendant earring.*
In the 19th century, a fashionable lady might wear ornate girandoles to dinner.

9. citrine
B *yellow quartz.*
Citrine's distinctive color comes from traces of iron.

10. adorn
B *make beautiful.*
The fortune-teller's wrists were adorned with countless bangles.

11. baguette
c *rectangular stone.*
"May I suggest a baguette, rather than an oval cut?" the salesperson said.

12. filigree
c *delicate metalwork.*
The queen's tiara features Victorian filigree.

13. palladium
c *silver-white metal.*
Palladium looks similar to platinum, but it's lighter and less expensive.

14. facet
A *surface on a cut gem.*
When a gem is expertly cut, facets create beautiful patterns.

15. rondelle
c *jeweled ring.*
Chaya's most prized possession is a rondelle that belonged to her grandmother.

NAMING CONVENTIONS

The names of gemstones may reflect their appearance. Ruby comes from Latin's *rubeus* (red), diamond is from the Latin *adamantem* ("hardest metal"), and tanzanite was discovered in Tanzania. Meanwhile, amethyst descended from the Greek *amethystos* (not drunk), as drinking from an amethyst goblet was thought to prevent intoxication.

YOUR SCORE:
___ / 15

WITHIN REGION

Here are some of our favorites from the five-volume *Dictionary of American Regional English,* which feature words and phrases that vary from place to place. (We've added the primary regions for each.)

1. pinkletink
('pink-ul-tink) *n.*, Martha's Vineyard
A piano.
B light rain shower.
c spring peeper frog.

---

2. king's ex (kings eks)
exclam., Gulf states, west of Mississippi River
A get lost!
B good luck!
c time out!

---

3. snail
(snayl) *n.*, California
A cinnamon roll.
B boyfriend.
c strange sound.

---

4. noodle
('noo-dul) *v.*, Arkansas, Missouri, Oklahoma
A catch fish bare-handed.
B drink from a flask.
c visit neighbors.

---

5. all-overs
(ahl 'o-vers) *n.*, South
A one-piece suit.
B nervous feelings.
c gossip.

6. on the carpet
(ahn thuh 'kar-pit) *adj.*, South
A under arrest.
B ready to marry.
c exhausted.

---

7. remuda
(ri-'moo-duh, -'myoo-) *n.*, Southwest
A herd of horses.
B dry gulch.
c bunk.

---

8. punee
('poonay-ay) *n.*, Hawaii
A loose dress.
B couch or sofa.
c outflow of lava.

---

9. pungle
('pun-gul) *v.*, West
A bollix.
B pay up.
c make verbal jokes.

---

10. givey
('giv-ē) *adj.*, Mid- and South Atlantic
A humid or moist.
B too talkative.
c up for anything.

11. rumpelkammer
('rum-pel-ka-mer) *n.*, Wisconsin
A thunderstorm.
B storage closet.
c unruly child.

---

12. mug-up
(mug up) *n.*, Alaska
A mascara kit.
B coffee break.
c robbery.

---

13. berm
(berm) *n.*, West Virginia
A shoulder of a road.
B tip jar.
c big poker hand.

---

14. hook Jack
(huk jack) *v.*, New England
A come up empty.
B add cheese to a dish.
c skip school.

---

15. silver thaw
('sil-ver thaw) *n.*, Oregon, Washington
A brook trout.
B freezing rain.
c 50th wedding anniversary.

"WITHIN REGION" ANSWERS

1. pinkletink
C *spring peeper frog.*
By May, the pinkletinks are in their full-throated glory.

2. king's ex
C *time out!*
As soon as the dentist reached for his drill, Bucky yelled, "King's ex!"

3. snail
A *cinnamon roll.*
The edge went off my appetite when I found a hair in my favorite bistro's snail.

4. noodle
A *catch fish bare-handed.*
For a guy who used to noodle, Jeremy sure has clumsy mitts.

5. all-overs
B *nervous feelings.*
I get the all-overs when my brother lets his pet tarantula loose.

6. on the carpet
B *ready to marry.*
Max is on the carpet, but Grace is still on the fence.

7. remuda
A *herd of horses.*
My brother's two kids hit the house during visits like a galloping remuda.

8. punee
B *couch or sofa.*
Lounging supine on her punee, Clare spends the day watching soaps and eating poi chips.

9. pungle
B *pay up.*
If you don't pungle soon, they're going to send Biff to visit you.

10. givey
A *humid or moist.*
The givey August weather left us drawn down and listless come midday.

11. rumpelkammer
B *storage closet.*
When we played hide-and-seek, nobody could find little Waldo in the rumpelkammer.

12. mug-up
B *coffee break.*
Maria gets nothing done because she yaks through a mug-up every ten minutes.

13. berm
A *shoulder of a road.*
Thoroughly exhausted by the drive from Portland, Alice pulled to the berm for a break.

14. hook Jack
C *skip school.*
Whenever there's an algebra test, Moe and I hook Jack and head for the river.

15. silver thaw
B *freezing rain.*
Hoping to lighten the mood, Audrey did her best Gene Kelly, singing and dancing in the silver thaw.

YOUR SCORE:
___ / 15

10

Fancy Words That Make You Sound Smarter

IF YOU'RE LONGING to impress your friends and flex your linguistic muscles in conversation, this list is for you. From "despondent" to "effervescent," we've rounded up ten words that will impress even your most brilliant coworker. And to boost your brain power, we've included definitions and examples, too.

Vitriolic

IF YOU NEED a fancy word for "mean," try "vitriolic." The word "vitriol" originally referred to sulfates. It evolved over time, but kept the corrosive and destructive connotations from its association with sulfuric acid. Now, it's used to describe a nasty, scathing comment or action.

Effervescent

USE THIS WORD for "enthusiastic" when you want to find a fancier way to describe your bubbly, excitable best friend. Effervescence literally means having the property of forming bubbles, so "effervescent" is a terrific adjective choice for that happy-go-lucky person in your life.

Granular

THIS WORD ALLUDES to the minuscule detail of small particles, and it can help describe a meticulous level of detail in your own work, thinking, or planning. If you literally thought of everything, then you got granular with your thinking!

Confluence

USE THIS WORD when discussing a meeting of minds, a group of ideas, or a coming together of diverse people for a gathering. Confluence can describe, for example, an event in which musicians from different genres perform together at an awards show. That said, it also often is used when describing streams or rivers joining together in nature.

Pithy

A PERFECT WORD for when you talk about how your friend replied to her dating app prospect with a brief, clever, and forceful remark. She wasn't short with that bathroom-mirror selfie guy—she was pithy!

Despondent

IF YOU'RE READY for the weekend but it's 10 a.m. on Monday, why not try a fancy word to indicate your hopelessness? Reserve "depressed" for a medical diagnosis and instead use "despondent" to articulate your extreme sadness.

Lucid

PUT A LITERARY SPIN on your clear-mindedness. Because "lucid" derives from the Latin adjective *lucidus,* meaning "shining," it's the perfect word for intelligent thinking that lets light shine through the confusion.

Diatribe

THIS IS DEFINED as a nasty (and usually lengthy) tirade, whether spoken or written. Are you prone to diatribes when you're upset? They are the perfect excuse to use fancy words that the person you're ranting at may not understand.

Resplendent

THE OFFICIAL DEFINITION in Merriam-Webster is "shining brilliantly: characterized by a glowing splendor." This word is sure to make that special someone swoon when she's all dressed up for a night on the town.

Aplomb

THIS WORD MEANS total composure and self-assurance. If aplomb is something you lack, sprinkling more fancy words into your conversations could give you a boost of confidence.

SHAPELY

You already know that staying in shape is a key to good health. But just as important: keeping your vocabulary finely tuned and toned. Try this quiz about shapes of the literal sort.

1. gangling
('gan-gling) *adj.*
A loose and lanky.
B bulging with muscles.
c short in stature.

2. helix
('hee-liks) *n.*
A pointed tip.
B warped outline.
c spiral.

3. deltoid
('del-toyd) *adj.*
A triangular.
B circular.
c squared off.

4. trefoil
('tree-foyl) *adj.*
A pliable.
B having a three-leaf design.
c tapering narrowly.

5. conical
('kah-nih-kul) *adj.*
A like an igloo.
B like a cone.
c like a tunnel.

6. pentacle
('pen-tih-kul) *n.*
A star.
B crescent moon.
c square.

7. elliptical
(ih-'lip-tih-kul) *adj.*
A slanted.
B embossed.
c oval.

8. sigmoid
('sig-moyd) *adj.*
A crossed like an "X."
B curved like a "C" or an "S."
c bent like an "L."

9. whorl
(hworl) *n.*
A well-rounded muscle.
B flat surface.
c circular pattern.

10. serrated
('seh-rayt-ed) *adj.*
A interconnected, as with circles or rings.
B elongated.
c having notched edges.

11. cordate
('kor-dayt) *adj.*
A stringlike.
B heart shaped.
c free-form.

12. svelte (svelt) *adj.*
A undulating.
B lean.
c in a checked or repeating pattern.

13. parabola
(pah-'ra-bo-la) *n.*
A bowl-like shape.
B moldable, like putty.
c seedlike.

14. lozenge
('lah-zunj) *n.*
A 90-degree angle.
B level used in architectural design.
c diamond.

15. ramify
('ra-meh-fiy) *v.*
A become solid, as cement.
B jut out.
c split into branches or parts.

"SHAPELY" ANSWERS

1. gangling
A *loose and lanky.*
The protagonist of *The Legend of Sleepy Hollow* was the gangling pedagogue.

2. helix
C *spiral.*
Judy is a DNA researcher, so she's getting a tattoo of a double helix.

3. deltoid
A *triangular.*
The pyramids' architects obviously knew a thing or two about the stability of deltoid structures.

4. trefoil
B *having a three-leaf design.*
The gardening club uses a trefoil symbol as its logo.

5. conical
B *like a cone.*
My favorite conical item? Why, the ice-cream cone, of course.

6. pentacle
A *star.*
Hey, this tarot deck is missing all the cards with pentacles!

WHAT'S THE ANGLE?

In geometry, you find various shapes called polygons, from the Greek *poly-* for "many" plus *gonia* for "angle." Hence, a pentagon has five angles (and sides), a hexagon has six, a heptagon has seven, an octagon has eight, and so on.

7. elliptical
C *oval.*
Just two times around the elliptical running track, and Rebecca was wiped out.

8. sigmoid
B *curved like a "C" or an "S."*
On Superman's chest sits a single scarlet sigmoid symbol.

9. whorl
C *circular pattern.*
To find the treasure, walk 50 paces east from the tree with the whorl in its trunk.

10. serrated
C *having notched edges.*
I'm not sure that old serrated knife is best for carving the turkey.

11. cordate
B *heart shaped.*
Sarah is baking cordate cookies for her cardiologist boyfriend.

12. svelte
B *lean.*
The holidays pose a serious challenge to my svelte frame!

13. parabola
A *bowl-like shape.*
The ball traveled in a parabola before swooshing into the basket.

14. lozenge
C *diamond.*
The boys dug up the grass to create a makeshift lozenge so they could play ball.

15. ramify
C *split into branches or parts.*
"We need to ramify this department to keep productivity high!" Kerrie announced.

YOUR SCORE:
___ / 15

DOUBLE ENTENDRE

Many common words have secondary meanings that
aren't widely known. Here are 15. Can you identify their
other definitions? For answers, turn the page.

1. pen
(pen) *n.*
A snowcapped
mountain.
B female swan.
C story with a moral.

2. fetch
(fech) *n.*
A bosom buddy.
B ghost.
C swamp.

3. rack
(rak) *v.*
A run at a fast gait, as
a horse.
B print in capital
letters.
C meet at right angles.

4. ounce
(auns) *n.*
A feeling of well-being.
B short argument.
C snow leopard.

5. burden
('ber-den) *n.*
A refrain of a song.
B footnote.
C reflection in a mirror.

6. troll
(trol) *v.*
A walk with a limp.
B travel by canoe.
C sing heartily.

7. poke
(pok) *n.*
A tree stump.
B black top hat.
C sack or bag.

8. painter
('payn-ter) *n.*
A false compliment.
B drinking song.
C line for mooring a
boat.

9. panic
('pa-nik) *n.*
A raccoon-like animal.
B kind of grass.
C symbol for 0.

10. shy
(shiy) *v.*
A con out of money.
B peel the skin of.
C sling or hurl.

11. murder
('mer-der) *n.*
A uphill trail.
B group of crows.
C mindless repetition.

12. patch
(pach) *n.*
A fool or clown.
B doctor or nurse.
C copy or clone.

13. bark
(bark) *v.*
A lift over one's head.
B turn from back to
front.
C bump or scrape.

14. lore
(lor) *n.*
A small tropical fruit.
B space between a
bird's eye and bill.
C uncharted territory.

15. rote
(roht) *n.*
A pang of anxiety.
B sound of the surf.
C thick coat of fur.

"DOUBLE ENTENDRE" ANSWERS

1. pen
B *female swan.*
The artist took out her pen and quickly sketched the pair of swans: a cob and a pen.

2. fetch
B *ghost.*
"Quick! Go fetch an exorcist!" yelled Lenny. "There's a fetch in the attic!"

3. rack
A *run at a fast gait, as a horse.*
The two boys racked toward the candy rack before their mothers could stop them.

4. ounce
C *snow leopard.*
"This spotted Asian ounce weighs 100 pounds," said the zookeeper, "give or take an ounce."

5. burden
A *refrain of a song.*
Janie is burdened by having the burden of "It's a Small World" stuck in her head.

6. troll
C *sing heartily.*
On YouTube, you can hear a recording of J.R.R. Tolkien trolling "Troll Sat Alone on His Seat of Stone."

7. poke
C *sack or bag.*
Poking around in her suitcase-size poke, Edna found everything but her car keys.

8. painter
C *line for mooring a boat.*
Hired to refinish the yacht's deck, the painter failed to tie the painter and slid out to sea with the boat.

9. panic
B *kind of grass.*
"Don't panic!" the landscaper said to his assistant. "That's not poison sumac, it's just woolly panic grass."

10. shy
C *sling or hurl.*
Never one to shy away from a challenge, George Washington shied a silver dollar across the Potomac.

11. murder
B *group of crows.*
Perched in the autumn branches, the murder of crows, not unlike the ones in Hitchcock's *The Birds,* looked entirely capable of murder.

12. patch
A *fool or clown.*
The king's merry patch wore patchwork breeches.

13. bark
C *bump or scrape.*
Dad barked his shin on the coffee table and gave a bark of pain.

14. lore
B *space between a bird's eye and bill.*
In ornithological lore, the great egret's lores turn a brilliant lime green during breeding season.

15. rote
B *sound of the surf.*
Listening to the rote outside her window, Agnes recited the last ten verses of "The Rime of the Ancient Mariner" by rote.

YOUR SCORE:
___ / 15

OOH LA LA

Thousands of English words, from "archery" to "zest," have their origins in French. Think you're a word connoisseur? Take a tour through this petite list of terms, then sashay to the next page for answers.

1. raconteur
(ra-kahn-'ter) *n.*
A skillful storyteller.
B blackmailer.
C court jester.

2. faience
(fay-'ans) *n.*
A false pretenses.
B fidelity.
C glazed pottery.

3. couturier
(koo-'tuhr-ee-er) *n.*
A head chef.
B fashion designer.
C museum guide.

4. avant-garde
(ah-vant-'gard) *adj.*
A festive.
B new or experimental.
C done by women.

5. cabal
(kuh-'bahl) *n.*
A plotting group.
B young horse.
C crystal wineglass.

6. fait accompli
(fayt ah-cahm-'plee) *n.*
A done deal.
B lucky charm.
C partner in crime.

7. au courant
(oh kuh-'rahn) *adj.*
A on the contrary.
B with cherries on top.
C up-to-date.

8. interlard
(ihn-ter-'lahrd) *v.*
A encroach on.
B vary by intermixing.
C fluctuate in weight.

9. soupçon
(soop-'sohn) *n.*
A wooden ladle.
B swindle.
C small amount.

10. milieu
(meel-'yeu) *n.*
A environment.
B thousand.
C armed force.

11. aubade
(oh-'bahd) *n.*
A gold pendant.
B babysitter.
C morning song.

12. pince-nez
(pahns-'nay) *n.*
A clipped-on eyeglasses.
B rude interruption.
C narrow hallway.

13. sangfroid
(sahn-'fwah) *n.*
A intense heat wave.
B composure under strain.
C mind reading.

14. fracas
('fray-kuhs) *n.*
A wool scarf.
B noisy quarrel.
C utter failure.

15. roué
(roo-'ay) *n.*
A thick meat sauce.
B rakish man.
C illegal gambling game.

"OOH LA LA" ANSWERS

1. raconteur
A *skillful storyteller.*
No one would call me
a raconteur. I tend to
ramble and say "um"
a lot.

2. faience
C *glazed pottery.*
Catherine hoped to sell
the rare faience she'd
found at the tag sale for
a huge profit.

3. couturier
B *fashion designer.*
Couturiers such as
Christian Dior and
Jean-Paul Gaultier have
shaped fashion history.

4. avant-garde
B *new or experimental.*
In our family, Mom's the
avant-garde thinker,
while Dad is more
traditional.

5. cabal
A *plotting group.*
There's a cabal among
the dictator's aides, who
are all vying for control
of the country.

6. fait accompli
A *done deal.*
Well, we've painted the
bedroom dark purple.
It's a fait accompli.

WATCH YOUR TONGUE
The Académie Française, which has set France's linguistic
standards for centuries, has a special distaste for English
tech terms. It nixed "email" and "software" in favor of *courriel*
and *logiciel.* And in 2013, francophones were urged to slash
"hashtag." The French version: *mot-dièse* (*mot* for "word,"
"*dièse*" for a musical sharp symbol).

7. au courant
C *up-to-date.*
To stay au courant,
Rafael snaps up all the
newest apps.

8. interlard
B *vary by intermixing.*
Why did the filmmaker
interlard the narrative
with those bizarre
dream sequences?

9. soupçon
C *small amount.*
Dylan detected a
soupçon of sarcasm
in his teenage son's
remark.

10. milieu
A *environment.*
"The briar patch," said
Brer Rabbit, "is my
natural milieu."

11. aubade
C *morning song.*
Ah, the tuneful aubade
of my alarm!

12. pince-nez
A *clipped-on eyeglasses.*
I've never understood
how you keep your
pince-nez on your nose
while you dance.

13. sangfroid
B *composure under
strain.*
We admired Magda's
sangfroid as she stood
up to her boss.

14. fracas
B *noisy quarrel.*
I wouldn't call it a
fracas. It's just a
difference of opinion.

15. roué
B *rakish man.*
Steer clear of that guy;
he's a shameless roué.

YOUR SCORE:
___ / 15

OPPOSITES ATTRACT

This quiz brings you extremes and polar opposites.
So go all out (but don't overexert yourself!).

1. nethermost

('neth-er-mohst) *adj.*

A coldest.

B thinnest.

c lowest.

---

2. extravagant

(ik-'stra-vi-gent) *adj.*

A all gone.

B irate.

c over the top.

---

3. acme

('ak-mee) *n.*

A verge.

B highest point.

c overflow.

---

4. culminate

('kul-mih-nayt) *v.*

A fly into space.

B hit the bottom.

c reach a climax.

---

5. acute

(uh-'kyoot) *adj.*

A intense, urgent.

B tiny, insignificant.

c pretty, appealing.

6. precipice

('preh-sih-pis) *n.*

A very steep side of a cliff.

B earliest moment.

c towering spire.

---

7. superlative

(soo-'per-leh-tiv) *adj.*

A outstanding.

B excessive.

c final.

---

8. antithesis

(an-'ti-theh-sis) *n.*

A exact opposite.

B end of time.

c extremely negative reaction.

---

9. surfeit

('sur-fet) *n.*

A utter wreck.

B more than needed.

c intense heat.

---

10. exorbitant

(ig-'zor-bih-tent) *adj.*

A on a shore's edge.

B at a mountain's summit.

c far exceeding what is fair or reasonable.

11. overweening

(oh-ver-'wee-ning) *adj.*

A arrogant.

B too fond of food.

c severely strict.

---

12. optimal

('ahp-tih-mul) *adj.*

A best.

B surplus.

c out of sight.

---

13. penultimate

(peh-'nul-teh-mit) *adj.*

A next to last.

B most recent.

c cream of the crop.

---

14. maximal

('mak-sih-mul) *adj.*

A greatest possible.

B conflicting.

c most important.

---

15. zealotry

('ze-luh-tree) *n.*

A extreme greed.

B overdone fervor.

c excess of noise.

"OPPOSITES ATTRACT" ANSWERS

1. nethermost
c *lowest.*
No one dares explore the nethermost dungeons of this castle.

2. extravagant
c *over the top.*
How can Monty afford to throw such extravagant parties?

3. acme
B *highest point.*
Going to the top of the Empire State Building was literally the acme of our trip.

4. culminate
c *reach a climax.*
Nearly every scene with the Stooges in a cafeteria culminates in a pie fight.

EARTHLY EXTREMES

At its farthest point from the sun, Earth reaches its apogee; when nearest the sun, Earth is at its perigee. In these examples, *gee* means "Earth." Meanwhile, in Greek, *apo* means "far from," and *peri* means "near to."

5. acute
A *intense, urgent.*
Joey has an acute hankering for chocolate.

6. precipice
A *very steep side of a cliff.*
As Alex peered over the precipice, he developed a sudden case of acrophobia.

7. superlative
A *outstanding.*
Despite Willie's superlative effort to catch the ball, it landed in the bleachers.

8. antithesis
A *exact opposite.*
Slovenly Oscar is the antithesis of a neatnik.

9. surfeit
B *more than needed.*
We have a surfeit of nachos, but absolutely no salsa!

10. exorbitant
c *far exceeding what is fair or reasonable.*
I nearly fainted from sticker shock when I saw the exorbitant price.

11. overweening
A *arrogant.*
I enjoy the art class, but not Professor Prigg's overweening attitude.

12. optimal
A *best.*
Now is not the optimal time to pester the boss about a raise.

13. penultimate
A *next to last.*
My penultimate finish in the marathon was my best showing ever.

14. maximal
A *greatest possible.*
"OK" is maximal praise from that old curmudgeon.

15. zealotry
B *overdone fervor.*
Zealotry gets attention on TV, but it rarely brings compromise.

YOUR SCORE:
___ / 15

SNUGGLE UP

Button up your overcoat and put on your thinking cap. This quiz is meant to keep you out in the cold.

1. arctic
('ark-tik, 'ar-tik) *adj.*
A like the North Pole.
B extremely windy.
C located at the top of an igloo.

2. hibernate
('hi-ber-nayt) *v.*
A to hike in snowshoes.
B lie sleeping through the winter.
C come down as sleet.

3. rime (riym) *n.*
A slush.
B frosty coating.
C thin outer layer of an Eskimo Pie.

4. Iditarod
(iy-'di-te-rahd) *n.*
A annual dogsled race in Alaska.
B inventor of the snowmobile.
C world-famous ice fisherman.

5. frappe
(fra-'pay) *n.*
A hockey slap shot.
B wool topcoat.
C milk shake with ice cream.

6. floe (flo) *n.*
A flat mass of ice at sea.
B row of icicles.
C diner waitress who brings you ice water.

7. glacier
('glay-sher) *n.*
A outdoor thermometer.
B ground that stays frozen all year.
C large body of ice.

8. gelato
(je-'lah-toh) *n.*
A Italian ice cream.
B large hailstone.
C hooded pullover jacket.

9. mogul
('moh-gul) *n.*
A bump on a ski slope.
B figure skating jump.
C sculpture with snowballs.

10. toboggan
(te-'bah-gen) *n.*
A sled without runners.
B mountain cabin in the Alps.
C indoor skating rink.

11. boreal
('bor-ee-ul) *adj.*
A frosted, as cornflakes.
B of the north.
C overcast.

12. sitzmark
('sits-mark, 'zits-) *n.*
A blizzard.
B avalanche.
C indent left in snow by a skier falling backward.

13. tundra
('tun-druh) *n.*
A powdery snow.
B hot Nordic drink.
C cold, treeless plain.

14. crampon
('kram-pahn) *n.*
A waterproof glove.
B ice climber's spiked footwear.
C frostbite.

15. gelid
('je-lid) *adj.*
A squishy, like jelly.
B stoic.
C icy.

"SNUGGLE UP" ANSWERS

1. arctic
A *like the North Pole.*
Grandpa is always talking about how he trekked to school in arctic conditions.

2. hibernate
B *lie sleeping through the winter.*
Many hibernating bears actually take a series of long naps.

3. rime
B *frosty coating.*
After the ice storm, the rime-encrusted tree branches had an eerie look.

4. Iditarod
A *Alaskan dogsled race.*
The winner of the Iditarod usually takes about ten days to finish the course.

5. frappe
C *milk shake with ice cream.*
In Boston you can order a frappe; in other parts of the country, this treat is called a frosted, a velvet, or a cabinet.

6. floe
A *flat mass of ice at sea.*
A floe may taste salty if you lick it because it's made of frozen seawater.

7. glacier
C *large body of ice.*
Scientists worry that global warming is causing glaciers in Alaska to thaw and crumble.

8. gelato
A *Italian ice cream.*
That hip new ice cream shop has all kinds of gelato flavors, including tomato-basil.

9. mogul
A *ski slope bump.*
My brother went right from the bunny slope to the mogul field. Want to sign his cast?

10. toboggan
A *sled without runners.*
The doomed lovers in the novel *Ethan Frome* steer their toboggan into a tree.

11. boreal
B *of or located in the north.*
Billions of birds fly through the U.S. to the boreal forests to breed in the spring.

12. sitzmark
C *indent left in snow by a skier falling backward.*
Uncle Harry said his ample sitzmark was a snow angel.

13. tundra
C *cold, treeless plain.*
The explorer spotted a gray wolf across the tundra.

14. crampon
B *ice climber's spiked footwear.*
The mountaineer dug his crampons into the icy cliff face.

15. gelid
C *icy.*
Passengers on the *Titanic* perished in the gelid waters of the North Atlantic.

YOUR SCORE: ___ / 15

BIBLIOPHILE'S DREAM

If you love reading, test your literacy with these book-related words, then flip to the next page for answers.

1. abridged
(uh-'brijd) *adj.*
A adapted.
B shortened.
c translated.

---

2. riffle
('rih-full) *v.*
A skim.
B brainstorm.
c copy from.

---

3. saga
('sah-guh) *n.*
A beach read.
B memoir.
c heroic tale.

---

4. prosaic
(pro-'zay-ik) *adj.*
A uplifting.
B dull.
c overly wordy.

---

5. omnibus
('ahm-nih-bus) *n.*
A road atlas.
B collection.
c paperback.

6. scrivener
('skrih-vuh-ner) *n.*
A critic.
B writer.
c bookbinder.

---

7. stanza
('stan-zuh) *n.*
A romance.
B library shelf.
c poem part.

---

8. lexicon
('leks-ih-kahn) *n.*
A dictionary.
B villain.
c twisty plot.

---

9. hyperbole
(hi-'per-buh-lee) *n.*
A overstatement.
B understatement.
c nonsense word.

---

10. elegy
('el-uh-jee) *n.*
A scientific paper.
B mournful poem.
c beautiful quotation.

11. tome
(tohm) *n.*
A horror story.
B poetry slam.
c large book.

---

12. folio
('fo-lee-oh) *n.*
A comedic play.
B page number.
c reading glasses.

---

13. analogy
(uh-'nal-uh-jee) *n.*
A travel blog.
B symbolism.
c comparison.

---

14. epigraph
('eh-puh-graf) *n.*
A opening quotation.
B illustrated guide.
c words said for the dead.

---

15. synopsis
(suh-'nop-suss) *n.*
A Greek drama.
B brief summary.
c cast of characters.

"BIBLIOPHILE'S DREAM" ANSWERS

1. abridged
B *shortened.*
Peter read an abridged version of *War and Peace* right before his book club meeting.

2. riffle
A *skim.*
Work has been so busy, I've barely had time to riffle through my in-box.

3. saga
C *heroic tale.*
The latest *Avengers* saga was a box office smash.

4. prosaic
B *dull.*
Mina can make even the most prosaic subjects feel profound.

5. omnibus
B *collection.*
Priya settled into an armchair with an omnibus of medieval poetry.

6. scrivener
B *writer.*
An amateur scrivener since middle school, Tim published his first bestseller in his 50s.

WHEN A BOOK IS A BOUQUET

A collection of poems, essays, or stories is an anthology. From the Greek *anthos* (flower) and *logia* (collection), it perhaps refers to the gathering of flowery verses into one volume.

7. stanza
C *poem part.*
What does the imagery in the second stanza tell us?

8. lexicon
A *dictionary.*
Armed with a bilingual lexicon and a pot of coffee, Ginny spent all night cramming for her French final.

9. hyperbole
A *overstatement.*
Since you're my only sibling, I can say without hyperbole that you're the best brother I've ever had!

10. elegy
B *mournful poem.*
Billy composed an elegy for Lee—his dearly departed goldfish.

11. tome
C *large book.*
I can't believe you're using my Tolkien tome as a doorstop.

12. folio
B *page number.*
In this experimental novel, the publisher deliberately left off the folios.

13. analogy
C *comparison.*
As a longtime football coach, my dad often uses the sport as an analogy for life.

14. epigraph
A *opening quotation.*
The book's epigraph comes from a Stevie Wonder song.

15. synopsis
B *brief summary.*
Here's a synopsis of *Moby Dick*: It's about a whale.

 YOUR SCORE:
___ / 15

TECH TIME

Don't use your cell phone or computer without first testing your knowledge of telecom terms.

1. malware ('mal-wayr) *n.*
A defective computer.
B defective software.
C software designed to interfere with a computer's normal functioning.

2. flame (flaym) *v.*
A make prank calls.
B be abusive in a chat room.
C lose one's connection.

3. bluesnarfing (bloo-'snarf-ing) *n.*
A despairing over a dead cell phone.
B cursing in public.
C using Bluetooth to steal info from a wireless device.

4. top up (tahp up) *v.*
A buy more minutes for a phone.
B end a chat abruptly.
C be the first to post.

5. clamshell ('klam-shel) *n.*
A phone that flips open.
B private space.
C lurker in a chat room.

6. ROFL ('ro-ful) *interj.*
A reply of four letters.
B running out for lunch.
C rolling on floor laughing.

7. faceplate ('fays-playt) *n.*
A large cell phone.
B cell phone cover.
C state of being glued to a computer.

8. phish (fish) *v.*
A use a private line.
B con out of private info.
C send musical message.

9. phreak (freek) *v.*
A lose one's temper.
B tamper with phone systems.
C chat online in a secret language.

10. viral ('vi-rul) *adj.*
A fast-spreading on the web.
B transmitted by phone.
C moving hacker to hacker.

11. chatterbot ('cha-ter-bot) *n.*
A taped conversation.
B simulation of a person talking.
C constant yakker.

12. digerati (di-je-'ra-tee) *n.*
A modem signals.
B letters represented as numbers.
C people versed in computer technology.

13. wonky ('wahng-kee, 'wong-) *adj.*
A not working right.
B highly technical.
C addicted to texting.

14. bandwidth ('band-with) *n.*
A capacity for data transfer.
B space for a band.
C amount of memory a computer has.

15. cache (kash) *n.*
A a large amount.
B computer memory with short access time.
C hiding place.

"TECH TIME" ANSWERS

1. malware
C *software designed to interfere with a computer's normal functioning.*
If your computer is running slowly, it could be the result of malware.

2. flame
B *be abusive in a chat room.*
The online pyromaniacs club hates it when guys from the firefighters group flame them.

3. bluesnarfing
C *using Bluetooth to steal info from a wireless device.*
Joe got my now ex-girlfriend's number by bluesnarfing me.

4. top up
A *buy more minutes for a phone.*
Barb forgot to top up her cell for vacation.

5. clamshell
A *phone that flips open.*
Nick opted for the clamshell because it reminded him of *Star Trek*.

6. ROFL
C *rolling on floor laughing.*
He's a burglar named Joey Lox? ROFL!

7. faceplate
B *cell phone cover.*
Be brutal: Does my new designer faceplate make me look fat?

8. phish
B *con out of private info.*
Mom, don't give your password to that sleaze; he's just phishing.

9. phreak
B *tamper with phone systems.*
Jim got free long distance until he was busted for phreaking.

10. viral
A *fast-spreading on the web.*
The last thing the senator needed was a viral video of the affair.

11. chatterbot
B *simulation of a person talking.*
The forum host I was flirting with turned out to be a chatterbot.

12. digerati
C *people versed in computer technology.*
You call yourself one of the digerati? Ha! You still use a manual typewriter.

13. wonky
A *not working right.*
Ever since I ran over my cell, it's been wonky.

14. bandwidth
A *capacity for data transfer.*
A photo requires more bandwidth to email than plain text does.

15. cache
B *computer memory with short access time.*
If your laptop is running slow, try clearing your cache.

YOUR SCORE:
___ / 15

INDIGENOUS LANGUAGE

Some indigenous words adopted into English are as common as a backyard chipmunk (that's from the Ojibwa tribe), but there are plenty that are as unusual as a manatee in a mackinaw. For answers and etymology, turn to the next page.

1. mackinaw
('ma-kuh-naw) *n.*
A mountain creek.
B makeshift bed.
C wool coat.

2. dory
('dohr-ee) *n.*
A dry gulch.
B flat-bottomed boat.
C small red potato.

3. hogan
('hoh-gahn) *n.*
A town meeting.
B log home.
C ceremonial pipe.

4. punkie
('puhn-kee) *n.*
A wooden sled.
B biting bug.
C runt of a litter.

5. dowitcher
('dow-ih-chur) *n.*
A wading bird.
B widow.
C gifted healer.

6. Podunk
('poh-dunk) *n.*
A small town.
B swimming hole.
C fried cake.

7. manatee
('ma-nuh-tee) *n.*
A carved face.
B sea cow.
C hard-fought contest.

8. pogonip
('pah-guh-nihp) *n.*
A ball game.
B organic snack.
C cold fog.

9. potlatch
('paht-lach) *n.*
A straw hat.
B red pigment.
C celebratory feast.

10. kachina
(kuh-'chee-nuh) *n.*
A rain shower.
B wooden doll.
C drum.

11. savanna
(suh-'va-nuh) *n.*
A voyage on foot.
B expression of adoration.
C grassland.

12. terrapin
('tehr-uh-pin) *n.*
A spring flower.
B swampland.
C turtle.

13. hackmatack
('hak-muh-tak) *n.*
A larch tree.
B machete.
C ambush.

14. sachem
('say-chum) *n.*
A hex or curse.
B puff of smoke.
C leader.

15. chinook (shih-'nook) *n.*
A convicted thief.
B warm wind.
C campfire.

"INDIGENOUS LANGUAGE" ANSWERS

1. mackinaw
c *wool coat.*
Joseph wears his
mackinaw even
on warm days.
(Algonquian)

2. dory
b *flat-bottomed boat.*
Susan loves fishing
from her dory on the
bay. (Miskito)

3. hogan
b *log home.*
The doorway of a
traditional hogan faces
east. (Navajo)

4. punkie
b *biting bug.*
Whether you call them
midges, no-see-ums, or
punkies, they're all out
for blood! (Delaware)

5. dowitcher
a *wading bird.*
That bird is a long-billed
dowitcher. (Iroquois)

6. Podunk
a *small town.*
Who imagined that this
kid from Podunk would
make it big? (Algonquian)

7. manatee
b *sea cow.*
Manatees use their

SAY THAT AGAIN?
We can thank the Nipmuc people of Massachusetts for the
longest place name in America. With 45 letters and 14 syllables,
Lake Chargoggagoggmanchauggagoggchaubunagungamaugg
certainly presents a challenge to sign painters. Fortunately, it's
also known by a shorter name: Webster Lake.

flippers to "walk"
along the seabed.
(Cariban)

8. pogonip
c *cold fog.*
Thanks to this
morning's pogonip, I
have ice crystals in my
eyebrows. (Shoshone)

9. potlatch
c *celebratory feast.*
Geno's mac and cheese
is a favorite at his
family's annual potlatch.
(Nootka)

10. kachina
b *wooden doll.*
The museum has
quite a collection of
hand-carved kachinas.
(Hopi)

11. savanna
c *grassland.*
On his tour of African
savannas, Eli spotted
elephants, zebras, and
rhinos. (Taino)

12. terrapin
c *turtle.*
On summer days,
terrapins sun
themselves on flat
rocks. (Algonquian)

13. hackmatack
a *larch tree.*
Will you have a picnic
under the hackmatack
with me? (Algonquian)

14. sachem
c *leader.*
The CEO may sit in the
corner office, but the
marketing director
is the real sachem.
(Narragansett)

15. chinook
b *warm wind.*
The chinook melted the
last of the winter snow.
(Chehalis)

YOUR SCORE:
___ / 15

SHARP DRESSER

This time, we challenge your fashion sense—
that is, your knowledge of words about clothing and
style. Fit to be tied? Turn the page for answers.

1. décolletage
(day-kah-le-'tazh) *n.*
A low-cut neckline.
B school uniform.
C clothing sale.

2. sartorial
(sar-'tor-ee-ul) *adj.*
A relating to a tailor or
  tailored clothes.
B relating to shoes.
C made out of wool.

3. ruched
(roosht) *adj.*
A tied in a bow.
B pleated or bunched.
C dyed blue.

4. argyle
('ar-gyl) *adj.*
A in pinstripes.
B in diamond patterns.
C polka-dotted.

5. twee
(twee) *adj.*
A spotted with stains.
B having a veil over the
  face.
C excessively dainty or
  cute.

6. salopettes
('sal-eh-pets) *n.*
A wooden shoes.
B skier's overalls.
C cuff links.

7. caparison
(ke-'per-uh-sun) *n.*
A selection of hats.
B ornamental covering
  for a horse.
C jester's costume.

8. bouffant
(boo-'fahnt or 'boo-fahnt) *adj.*
A flowery.
B puffed-out.
C skin-tight.

9. ikat
('ee-kaht) *n.*
A head scarf.
B shoelace tip.
C tie-dyed fabric.

10. bespoke
(bih-'spohk) *adj.*
A custom-made.
B color-coordinated.
C with circular designs.

11. clew
(klew) *n.*
A ball of yarn.
B run in a stocking.
C alligator skin.

12. regalia
(ri-'gayl-yeh) *n.*
A everyday wear.
B magnificent attire.
C lingerie.

13. panache
(puh-'nash or -'nahsh) *n.*
A handkerchief.
B untucked shirttail.
C flamboyance in style.

14. prink
(prink) *v.*
A perforate.
B dress carefully.
C go down one size.

15. sporran
('spor-en) *n.*
A lobster bib.
B pouch worn with
  a kilt.
C ruffed collar or
  sleeve.

"SHARP DRESSER" ANSWERS

1. décolletage
A *low-cut neckline.*
A stray rolling pea disappeared down Lady Buxton's décolletage.

2. sartorial
A *relating to a tailor or tailored clothes.*
If you had any sartorial respect, you wouldn't dunk my Burberry jacket sleeve in gravy.

3. ruched
B *pleated or bunched.*
Taking a trend too far, Lucy had ruched tablecloths, curtains, and slipcovers.

4. argyle
B *in diamond patterns.*
Roy found that his argyle socks worked well as meatball catapults.

5. twee
C *excessively dainty or cute.*
That pink dress might suit you, but isn't it a bit twee for the barbecue?

6. salopettes
B *skier's overalls.*
Carl's salopettes may have stood out on the slope, but they did nothing to enhance his downhill performance.

7. caparison
B *ornamental covering for a horse.*
The "medieval" battle looked authentic to us, right down to the caparisons for the horses.

8. bouffant
B *puffed-out.*
The gown's bouffant skirt was the perfect complement to the bride's hairdo.

9. ikat
C *tie-dyed fabric.*
In head-to-toe ikat, Rufus looked rather psychedelic.

10. bespoke
A *custom-made.*
Lyle enjoyed showing off his bespoke ten-gallon hat at dinner last night.

11. clew
A *ball of yarn.*
Follow this unraveled clew far enough and you'll find Casper, my tabby kitten.

12. regalia
B *magnificent attire.*
Eva's regalia sure made a statement at last night's state dinner.

13. panache
C *flamboyance in style.*
Yes, Charlie leads an exciting, outrageous life, but he doesn't quite have the panache of a Hollywood playboy.

14. prink
B *dress carefully.*
Lauren prinks for hours before each date.

15. sporran
B *pouch worn with a kilt.*
Rushing out the door for the parade, my brother shouted, "Has anyone seen my sporran?"

YOUR SCORE:
___ / 15

SEARCH FOR MEANING

Endings like "-ism" (belief), "-mania" (obsession), and "-phobia" (fear) can tell you a lot about a word's meaning. As you navigate this quiz, pay close attention to the suffix of each term for helpful clues. At your wit's end? Turn the page for answers.

1. cryptology
(krip-'tah-luh-jee) *n.*
A raiding of tombs.
B series of puzzles.
c study of codes.

2. empathetic
(em-puh-'theh-tik) *adj.*
A showing understanding or sensitivity.
B sad.
c numb.

3. ovoid
('oh-voyd) *adj.*
A egg-shaped.
B empty.
c passionate.

4. deify
('dee-uh-fiy) *v.*
A treat as a god.
B bring back to life.
c disregard.

5. perspicacious
(puhr-spuh-'kay-shuhs) *adj.*
A finicky.
B of acute mental vision.
c fortunate or lucky.

6. indigenous
(in-'dih-juh-nuhs) *adj.*
A poor.
B native.
c mixed.

7. herbicide
('er-bih-siyd) *n.*
A greenhouse.
B skin lotion.
c agent used to inhibit or kill plant growth.

8. pachyderm
('pa-kih-duhrm) *n.*
A elephant.
B jellyfish.
c butterfly.

9. Kafkaesque
(kahf-kuh-'esk) *adj.*
A nightmarishly complex.
B gigantic.
c left-wing.

10. atrophy
('a-truh-fee) *v.*
A waste away.
B win a prize.
c speak out against.

11. knavish
('nay-vish) *adj.*
A sticky.
B sharply honed.
c deceitful or dishonest.

12. legalese
(lee-guh-'leez) *n.*
A passage of laws.
B strict rules.
c legal language.

13. patriarch
('pay-tree-ark) *n.*
A Roman vault.
B father figure.
c homeland.

14. obsolescent
(ob-soh-'leh-sent) *adj.*
A teenage.
B quite fat.
c going out of use.

15. solarium
(soh-'lar-ee-uhm) *n.*
A sunroom.
B private nook.
c answer to a problem.

"SEARCH FOR MEANING" ANSWERS

1. cryptology
c *study of codes*
(-ology = "study").
The Enigma code was cracked by aces in cryptology.

2. empathetic
A *showing understanding or sensitivity*
(-pathy = "feeling").
Are women more empathetic than men?

3. ovoid
A *egg-shaped*
(-oid = "resembling").
Jay's ovoid physique made him a shoo-in for the role of Falstaff.

4. deify
A *treat as a god*
(-fy = "make into").
First we deify pop stars, then we tear them down.

5. perspicacious
B *of acute mental vision*
(-acious = "with a quality of").
She's too perspicacious to fall for their hoax.

6. indigenous
B *native*
(-genous = "producing").
Chemical testing will disrupt the island's indigenous species.

7. herbicide
c *agent used to inhibit or kill plant growth*
(-cide = "killing").
Mother Nature is not fond of lawn herbicides.

8. pachyderm
A *elephant*
(-derm = "skin").
Cartoonist Thomas Nast drew the first Republican pachyderm.

9. Kafkaesque
A *nightmarishly complex*
(-esque = "resembling").
Getting my passport back involved a Kafkaesque maze of bureaucracies.

10. atrophy
A *waste away*
(-trophy = "nourishment").
Without rehab, Alison's knee muscles will atrophy.

11. knavish
c *deceitful or dishonest*
(-ish = "like").
Who's the knavish sneak who swiped my drink?

12. legalese
c *legal language*
(-ese = "language style").
Please, cut the legalese and speak plain English.

13. patriarch
B *father figure*
(-arch = "chief").
That loudmouth is the patriarch of all spin doctors.

14. obsolescent
c *going out of use*
(-escent = "becoming").
Our landline is now obsolescent.

15. solarium
A *sunroom*
(-arium = "place").
Let us retire to my solarium for a little more inspiration.

YOUR SCORE:
___ / 15

THE X FILES

With this quiz, we reach into our lexicon for words beginning or ending with the letter x. For answers, turn the page.

1. hallux

('ha-luhks) *n.*

A lance-bearing soldier.

B lake carved by a glacier.

C big toe.

2. Xanadu

('zan-uh-doo) *n.*

A happy, beautiful place.

B evil Greek sorceress.

C treasure sought by Sir Galahad.

3. xeric

('zeer-ik) *adj.*

A dry, like a desert.

B vast, like an ocean.

C green, like a jungle.

4. crux

(kruks) *n.*

A influence.

B main feature, as of an argument.

C type of stone.

5. vertex

('vur-teks) *n.*

A whirling current.

B waistband for a tuxedo.

C highest point.

6. Xanthippe

(zan-'thi-pee) *n.*

A decisive battle.

B giant sea serpent.

C scolding wife.

7. pollex

('pah-leks) *n.*

A male part of a flower.

B star that guides a traveler.

C thumb.

8. xyloid

('zy-loid) *adj.*

A robotic.

B resembling wood.

C having the shape of a pyramid.

9. faux

(foh) *adj.*

A fake or artificial.

B new or original.

C sly or cunning.

10. xanthic

('zan-thik) *adj.*

A yellowish.

B acting like a clown.

C sticky, as an adhesive.

11. coccyx

('kahk-siks) *n.*

A female acrobat.

B hub of a spinning wheel.

C tailbone.

12. xenophobic

(ze-nuh-'foh-bik) *adj.*

A fearing loud noises.

B fearing ants or bees.

C fearing foreigners or strangers.

13. vortex

('vor-teks) *n.*

A whirling current.

B waistband for a tuxedo.

C highest point.

14. cox (kahks) *n.*

A overconfident person.

B rooster.

C person steering a boat.

15. xanthan gum

('zan-then gum) *n.*

A a tree that makes gum.

B a thickening agent used in prepared foods.

C an Australian dessert.

"THE X FILES" ANSWERS

1. hallux
c *big toe.*
Dexter wears sandals because his hallux is too big for Nikes.

2. Xanadu
A *happy, beautiful place.*
Bixby's backyard would be a veritable Xanadu if it weren't for the toxic dump next door.

3. xeric
A *dry, like a desert.*
Those transplanted Ohioans keep trying to grow phlox here in New Mexico's xeric landscape.

4. crux
B *main feature, as of an argument.*
The crux of the issue is that the teachers have not had adequate training.

5. vertex
c *highest point.*
As he slipped off the rocky crag, Felix was heard exulting, "At last, the verteeeex!"

6. Xanthippe
c *scolding wife* (married to Socrates).
Xenophon emulated Socrates, but drew the line at marrying his own Xanthippe.

7. pollex
c *thumb.*
Little Jack Bollix stuck in his pollex and pulled out a purple plum.

8. xyloid
B *resembling wood.*
After Tex failed shop class six years in a row, friends determined that he possessed a xyloid head.

9. faux
A *fake or artificial.*
Maxine sports fake eyelashes, false teeth, and faux pearls.

10. xanthic
A *yellowish.*
If you ask me, Xena's roots are more brunette than xanthic.

11. coccyx
c *tailbone.*
At the rink, Dixie executed a triple axel but landed smack on her coccyx.

12. xenophobic
c *fearing foreigners or strangers.*
Roxanne is so xenophobic, she hid in a closet the entire time she vacationed in France.

13. vortex
A *whirling current.*
One untruth led to another until the politician got caught in a vortex of lies.

14. cox
c *person steering a boat.*
As cox for the crew team, Alex yelled at the rowers to pull hard.

15. xanthan gum
B *a thickening agent used in prepared food.*
Xanthan gum is commonly used in sauces and dressings.

YOUR SCORE:
___ / 15

APRIL FOOLERY

If you love jokes, pranks, and sneaky tricks, get ready for a vocabulary quiz full of words about clowning, foolery, frauds, and cons.

1. quip
(kwip) *n.*
A witty remark.
B magician's box of gear.
C butt of a joke.

2. antic
('an-tik) *adj.*
A like a clown.
B like a thief.
C like a medicine man.

3. wily
('wy-lee) *adj.*
A easy to fool.
B overly cautious.
C cleverly deceptive.

4. jape
(jayp) *n.*
A look of shock and surprise.
B practical joke.
C one dressed in a gorilla suit.

5. deadpan
('ded-pan) *adj.*
A caught red-handed.
B showing no emotion.
C hit in head by a skillet.

6. shtick (shtik) *n.*
A pie fight.
B comedy routine.
C long, thin object used to stir drinks.

7. ribald
('ri-buld) *adj.*
A funny in a coarse way.
B funny in an odd way.
C with a shaved head.

8. flimflam
('flim-flam) *n.*
A audience paid to laugh.
B potion or elixir.
C deception or swindle.

9. lampoon
(lam-'poon) *v.*
A to mock or riddle in a satire.
B catch in an embarrassing situation.
C remove a performer from the stage.

10. jocular
('jah-kyu-ler) *adj.*
A agile and athletic.
B astride a unicycle.
C wisecracking.

11. sleight
(sliyt) *n.*
A insulting jab.
B dexterity.
C trick that backfires comically.

12. motley
('maht-lee) *adj.*
A old stock of jokes.
B good sense of humor.
C many-colored.

13. shill
(shil) *n.*
A high-pitched laugh.
B stage prop.
C con-game decoy.

14. humbug
('hum-bug) *n.*
A lack of any sense of humor.
B tricky impostor.
C nonsense song with a droning chorus.

15. cozen
('kuh-zen) *v.*
A to hoodwink.
B imitate.
C marry into a neighbor family.

"APRIL FOOLERY" ANSWERS

1. quip
A *witty remark.*
Our bowling team captain is always ready with a punchy quip.

2. antic
A *like a clown.*
If you invite Bozo the Clown to your party, you can only hope your guests will enjoy his antic behavior.

3. wily
C *cleverly deceptive.*
You just can't trust that wily old slyboots.

4. jape
B *practical joke.*
An exploding cigar is some people's idea of a funny jape.

5. deadpan
B *showing no emotion.*
It's hard to remain deadpan when chewing a piece of rubber bacon.

6. shtick
B *comedy routine.*
A good comedian has a well-honed shtick.

7. ribald
A *funny in a coarse way.*
The censors weren't too happy about my ribald jokes.

8. flimflam
C *deception or swindle.*
The agent won't fall for his flimflam.

9. lampoon
A *to mock or ridicule in a satire.*
On TV, it's common to see comedians lampoon our political leaders.

10. jocular
C *wisecracking.*
That Transylvanian guy in accounting is so funny, we call him Count Jocular.

11. sleight
B *dexterity.*
A magician will try to fool his audience with sleight of hand.

12. motley
C *many-colored.*
The king's fool cavorted about the place dressed in a motley, patched-together outfit.

13. shill
C *decoy in a con game.*
The swindler's partner was just a shill pretending to be a customer.

14. humbug
B *tricky impostor.*
Better not take investment advice from that broker; he's just a humbug.

15. cozen
A *to hoodwink.*
That's one game designed to cozen you out of your paycheck.

YOUR SCORE:
____ / 15

LOVE DRAMA

Shakespeare's princely Hamlet is the character who mopes about muttering, "Words, words, words." Here, from the venerable play by the Bard, are some words (in their root form) you can actively employ today. If, tragically, you need answers, consult the next page.

1. impetuous
(im-'peh-choo-wes) *adj.*
A full of questions.
B scheming.
C rash.

2. traduce
(truh-'doos) *v.*
A shame using lies.
B parry with a sword.
C exchange for a profit.

3. whet
(wet) *v.*
A sharpen or stimulate.
B moisten.
C hasten.

4. rub
(ruhb) *n.*
A piece of gossip.
B difficulty.
C good-luck charm.

5. germane
(jer-'mayn) *adj.*
A poisonous.
B relevant.
C ghostly.

6. incorporeal
(in-kor-'por-ee-uhl) *adj.*
A using military might.
B having no body.
C full of tiny holes.

7. wax
(waks) *v.*
A grow smaller.
B grow larger.
C grow a mustache.

8. paragon
('par-uh-gahn) *n.*
A mounted soldier.
B five-sided figure.
C example of excellence.

9. calumny
('ka-luhm-nee) *n.*
A row of pillars.
B disaster.
C character attack.

10. beguile
(bih-'giyl) *v.*
A bond or form a union.
B deceive.
C leave stranded.

11. felicity
(fih-'lih-suh-tee) *n.*
A ill fortune.
B faithful devotion.
C happiness.

12. sully
('suh-lee) *v.*
A answer back smartly.
B drizzle.
C defile or tarnish.

13. malefactor
('ma-luh-fak-tuhr) *n.*
A masculine quality.
B one who commits an offense.
C swear word.

14. exhort
(ig-'zort) *v.*
A dig up.
B overthrow or dethrone.
C urge strongly.

15. quintessence
(kwin-'teh-sents) *n.*
A most typical example.
B one-fifth.
C fluidity in language or spoken word.

"LOVE DRAMA" ANSWERS

1. impetuous
C *rash.*
Jenny walks up and impetuously hugs complete strangers.

2. traduce
A *shame using lies.*
Jed loves to watch politicians on TV traducing each other with bogus statistics.

3. whet
A *sharpen or stimulate.*
The aroma of turkey whet my appetite.

4. rub
B *difficulty.*
Playing hooky is easy, but not getting caught—there's the rub.

5. germane
B *relevant.*
"Your Honor, my client's nickname, Light Fingers, is not germane to this case of theft."

6. incorporeal
B *having no body.*
Grandfather believes incorporeal beings haunt his house.

7. wax
B *grow larger.*
Noah's hopes for a

picnic waxed as the rain began to wane.

8. paragon
C *example of excellence.*
The poet's debut collection was a paragon of eloquence.

9. calumny
C *character attack.*
If you can't win a debate with reason, try outright calumny.

10. beguile
B *deceive.*
Don't let the mermaids beguile you with their siren songs.

11. felicity
C *happiness.*
Nothing could diminish the felicity of the family's first holiday together in years.

12. sully
C *defile or tarnish.*
It would take only one

blowhard to sully the mayor's reputation.

13. malefactor
B *one who commits an offense.*
Upon seeing someone pulled over by a traffic cop, my dad used to announce, "There goes another malefactor!"

14. exhort
C *urge strongly.*
The candidate exhorted the crowd to make the right choice come Election Day.

15. quintessence
A *most typical example.*
The human rights speaker was the quintessence of humility.

DARK DOINGS
The moody Hamlet is often called the melancholy Dane. Melancholy means gloomy, but it literally refers to "black bile." You might recognize its root parts in *melan* (a dark pigment) and *chole* (gall or ill temper). In medieval times, bodily "humors" like black bile were thought to influence our moods.

YOUR SCORE:
___ / 15

POWER WORDS

You might say we're using strong language. This vocabulary quiz features words about power—having it, getting it, or lacking it. After flexing your mental muscles, turn to the next page for answers.

1. anneal
(uh-'neel) *v.*
A toughen.
B weaken gradually.
C submit to authority.

2. doughty
('dow-tee) *adj.*
A hesitant.
B willing to yield power.
C stouthearted.

3. enervated
('eh-nur-vay-ted) *adj.*
A lacking vigor.
B strengthened.
C glorified.

4. dint
(dint) *n.*
A heavyweight.
B power.
C electrical unit.

5. proxy
('prahk-see) *n.*
A strong liking.
B authority to act for another.
C king's royal guard.

6. thew
(thoo) *n.*
A muscular strength.
B castle wall.
C term of surrender.

7. buttress
('buh-tress) *v.*
A shore up.
B challenge head-to-head.
C dethrone.

8. preponderate
(pre-'pahn-duh-rayt) *v.*
A seize control.
B influence by insidious means.
C have greater importance.

9. duress
(du-'rehss) *n.*
A queen's sister.
B sovereign rule.
C compulsion by threat.

10. puissant
('pwee-sahnt) *adj.*
A powerful.
B subdued by fear.
C cowardly.

11. arrogate
('ehr-uh-gayt) *v.*
A supply with weapons.
B seize unjustly.
C crown.

12. effete
(eh-'feet) *adj.*
A marked by weakness.
B brawny.
C able to get things done.

13. attenuate
(uh-'ten-yoo-wayt) *v.*
A make firmer.
B make longer.
C make weaker.

14. coup
(coo) *n.*
A strong signal.
B head honcho.
C power grab.

15. ex officio
(eks uh-'fih-shee-oh) *adj.*
A out of power.
B by virtue of position.
C abstaining from a vote.

"POWER WORDS" ANSWERS

1. anneal
A *toughen.*
Fans of the Chicago Cubs were annealed by decades of misery.

---

2. doughty
C *stouthearted.*
Prince Ari grew up to be a doughty warrior.

---

3. enervated
A *lacking vigor.*
My bout with the flu left me enervated for weeks.

---

4. dint
B *power.*
Chloe doesn't have

THE GOLDEN ARCH

Why do we call someone an archbishop, an archduke, or an archenemy? The Greeks gave us *arkhos*, meaning "leader," and we've attached it to things good (archangel) and bad (archfiend). The ending *–archy* (rule) appears in the kingly "monarchy" (*mon-* = one), the fatherly "patriarchy" (*pater-* = father), and the chaotic "anarchy" (*an-* = without).

an ear for languages, but she has become proficient in German by dint of hard work.

---

5. proxy
B *authority to act for another.*
Tweedledum couldn't attend the vote, so he gave Tweedledee his proxy.

---

6. thew
A *muscular strength.*
That guy Biff is all thew and no brains.

---

7. buttress
A *shore up.*
My puny allowance isn't doing much to buttress my savings.

---

8. preponderate
C *have greater importance.*
Online news outlets now preponderate over print newspapers.

---

9. duress
C *compulsion by threat.*
Indira will eat broccoli, but only under duress.

---

10. puissant
A *powerful.*
Octogenarians can still be plenty puissant—

think Warren Buffett or Queen Victoria.

---

11. arrogate
B *seize unjustly.*
When my mother comes to visit, she immediately arrogates my kitchen.

---

12. effete
A *marked by weakness.*
With every failure, Wile E. Coyote's schemes seem more effete.

---

13. attenuate
C *make weaker.*
We wear earplugs to attenuate the upstairs neighbors' midnight stomping.

---

14. coup
C *power grab.*
The empress had the two conspirators arrested after their attempted coup.

---

15. ex officio
B *by virtue of position.*
All department heads are ex officio members of the company softball team.

YOUR SCORE:
___ / 15

BODY LANGUAGE

Do you know your patella from your pate? This quiz tests
your knowledge of words related to the human body.

1. mental
('men-tul) *adj.*
of or relating to...
A the navel.
B the chin.
C the hands or feet.

2. visage
('vi-zij) *n.*
A face.
B lens of the eye.
C type of birthmark.

3. hirsute
('her-soot, 'heer-, her-'soot,
heer-) *adj.*
A bent over with hands
  on knees.
B barrel-chested.
C hairy.

4. pectoral
('pek-ta-rul) *adj.*
A of the side.
B of the back.
C of the chest.

5. corpulent
('kor-pyu-lent) *adj.*
A of or relating to the
  skull.
B bulky or stout.
C frail, as a bone.

6. alopecia
(a-lo-'pee-shee-uh) *n.*
A skin reddening.
B baldness.
C mythological beauty.

7. nuque
(nyuk) *n.*
A back of the neck.
B arch of the foot.
C tip of the tongue.

8. hemic
('hee-mik) *adj.*
A of the liver.
B of the blood.
C of the stomach.

9. sinewy
('sin-yoo-wee, 'si-noo-) *adj.*
A infected.
B bunched, as nerves.
C tough.

10. ossicles
('ah-si-kulz) *n.*
A small bones in
  the ear.
B nerves attached to
  the eye.
C eyelashes.

11. columella
(kal-ya-'me-luh) *n.*
A kneecap.
B thumb.
C bridge between the
  nostrils.

12. ventral
('ven-trul) *adj.*
A around the stomach.
B leaving the body, as
  exhaled air.
C fully developed, as
  a muscle.

13. axilla
(ag-'zi-la, ak-'si-) *n.*
A network of nerves
  along the spine.
B long bone of the leg.
C armpit.

14. cerumen
(se-'roo-men) *n.*
A type of leg brace.
B essential protein.
C earwax.

15. fontanel
(fahn-ta-'nel, 'fahn-ta-nel) *n.*
A bone in the finger.
B lower-back muscle.
C soft spot in a young
  skull.

"BODY LANGUAGE" ANSWERS

1. mental
B *of or relating to the chin.*
The boxing vet gave the cocky kid a little mental reminder halfway through the first round.

2. visage
A *face.*
Harlan stared hard at the visage in the painting, curious about its smile.

3. hirsute
C *hairy.*
"That is a great costume," Alan said. "But you're missing the hirsute hobbit feet."

4. pectoral
C *of the chest.*
The weight lifter flexed his pectoral muscles in a truly Hulkian spectacle.

5. corpulent
B *bulky or stout.*
Tara wouldn't call her brother overweight, just a little corpulent.

6. alopecia
B *baldness.*
Arthur has been shaving his head since he was 21, hoping to hide his worsening alopecia.

7. nuque
A *back of the neck.*
Grazing Mary's nuque, Hugo thought, was a subtle sign of affection. She disagreed.

8. hemic
B *of the blood.*
Would it be fair to say the *Twilight* characters have a slight hemic obsession?

9. sinewy
C *tough.*
The wrestler looked unimposing but his sinewy arms helped him win the match.

10. ossicles
A *small bones in the ear.*
"For extra credit, what are the smallest bones in the human body?" Mr. Griffin asked. "The ossicles!" Tad shouted out.

11. columella
C *bridge between the nostrils.*
If you have a hanging columella, you may want to have surgery to correct it.

12. ventral
A *around the stomach.*
His ventral fat, *The Biggest Loser* contestant hoped, would be the first to go.

13. axilla
C *armpit.*
The second grader's favorite gag involved his cupped hand and his axilla.

14. cerumen
C *earwax.*
"I certainly doubt cerumen is keeping you from hearing me," the instructor barked, glaring at her student's headphones.

15. fontanel
C *soft spot in a young skull.*
"Mind his fontanel," the new mom said, handing her son to his nervous father.

YOUR SCORE:
___ / 15

10

Essential Grammar Facts and Tricks You Need to Know

DO YOU JOLT AWAKE in the middle of the night, petrified you've used the wrong form of "your" in a work e-mail? Does the prospect of placing an apostrophe make you perspire? There's no way to sugarcoat it: Grammar can be complicated. Worry not, though. This list of rules breaks down key grammar tips and misconceptions and offers easy-to-understand explanations and examples.

Know When to Use "Me" or "I"

IF YOU UTTERED "Me and Mike went to the store," someone probably admonished, "Mike and I!" But don't overcorrect. Here's an easy way to know when to use "me" or "I": Take out the other person, and see whether "me" or "I" makes sense. "Me went to the store" is incorrect, but "Mom met me at the store" is perfectly fine.

Start Sentences with "And," "But," or "So"

IF YOU'VE BEEN DOING mental gymnastics to avoid starting a sentence with a conjunction, sweat no longer. According to the grammar experts at the *Chicago Manual of Style*, this is perfectly acceptable. "There is a widespread belief—one with no historical or grammatical foundation—that it is an error to begin a sentence with a conjunction such as *and, but,* or *so,*" they write. "In fact, a substantial percentage (often as many as 10 percent) of the sentences in first-rate writing begin with conjunctions. It has been so for centuries, and even the most conservative grammarians have followed this practice."

Become a Master at "Your" vs. "You're"

WORD AFICIONADOS GET particularly irked with this grammar snafu despite the irony in reading such examples as "Your an idiot!" or "You're jokes are terrible!" Remember that "you're" is a contraction meaning "you are." Got it? Great! You're smart. "Your" is the possessive form of "you," as in "your big brain," "your gorgeous prose," or "your annoying error."

End Sentences with Prepositions

THIS IS ONE RULE that grammar sticklers love to argue about. (See what we did there?) Because the word "preposition" derives from a Latin word meaning "to place before," some insist that prepositions should always go before their prepositional objects. However, while that's true in Latin grammar, dictionary.com claims that "English grammar is different from Latin grammar, and the rule does not fit English." The sentence "This is one rule about which grammar sticklers love to argue" just doesn't flow the way "… love to argue about" does. And yet, the debate rages on.

Place an Apostrophe

WRITERS FREQUENTLY POP apostrophes where they don't belong. Katy Koontz, writer and editor-in-chief of *Unity Magazine*, offers up this example: "The Smith's aren't coming to dinner. The Smiths are, though. An apostrophe shows possession, it doesn't make a word plural. This shows up with decades a lot—the 1960s were tumultuous, not the 1960's."

Use "Everyday" Correctly Every Day

HAVE YOU EVER written "everyday" when what you really mean is "every day?" It's an everyday error that you might notice every day. Do you see the difference? "Everyday," one compound word, is usually used as an adjective that means daily or ordinary. In contrast, the two separate words indicate "each day." Kendra Stanton Lee, an instructor of humanities at Benjamin Franklin Institute of Technology in Boston, tells her students, "the way to remember if it's two words is to test whether the sentence makes sense to say 'every single day.'"

Choose Between "Good" and "Well"

THE BIG QUANDARY here is that "good" primarily is an adjective (though it could be a noun), and "well" is an adverb. When people say, "I'm doing good," they're using "good" as an adverb to modify the verb "doing." Technically, "I'm doing well" is the correct phrase, and "I'm doing good" actually means that you're doing good deeds like a superhero.

Say How Much, Exactly, You Care

"I COULDN'T CARE LESS" means exactly that. You care so little that you could not care any less. Not so confusing! What is confusing about this one is the fact that people seem to think that "could care less" means the same thing, when it's really the exact opposite. Harvard professor Stephen Pinker has suggested that people started saying "I could care less" sarcastically, meaning that they actually couldn't care less, and that this version of the expression—without the intentional sarcasm—stuck.

Know When to Use "An"

IF YOU USE "an" only in connection with words that start with a vowel ("an octopus") and "a" for everything else ("a telephone"), that's only partly correct. You also should use the word "an" before words that start with vowel sounds. For example, "I'm thinking of starting an herb garden" is grammatically sound because the "h" is silent in "herb."

Be a Whiz at "Lay vs. Lie"

WHEN IT COMES TO commonly confused words, there may not be a more understandably mixed-up pair than "lay" and "lie." The words aren't interchangeable, though many people use them that way. "Lay" needs an object, while "lie" doesn't take one. Saying "I need to lay down" is incorrect, because you have to lay something down. "Please lay that expensive book down on the table carefully" is the correct use of "lay." But the real confusion comes from the fact that the past tense of "lie" is … "lay"! "He wasn't feeling well, so he lay down" is correct. The past tense of "lay," meanwhile, is "laid."

STAY ON TRACK

Feeling lost? These vocabulary words are all about giving you directions: up or down, near or far, east or west, on and on. To locate the answers, navigate to the next page.

1. starboard

('star-berd) *n.*

A ship's right side.

B ship's left side.

c ship's front.

2. transpose

(trans-'pohz) *v.*

A cut straight across.

B turn sharply.

c move to another place.

3. terminus

('ter-mi-ness) *n.*

A end point of a route.

B type of train.

c airport.

4. anterior

(an-'teer-ee-er) *adj.*

A at the midpoint.

B behind.

c in the front.

5. circumnavigate

(ser-kum-'na-va-gayt) *v.*

A be indirect.

B go around.

c encircle.

6. sinistral

('sih-nih-struhl) *adj.*

A from the south.

B underground.

c left-handed.

7. periphery

(puh-'rih-fuh-ree) *n.*

A great distance.

B close range.

c outer edges.

8. apex

('ay-peks) *n.*

A clockwise motion.

B uppermost point.

c needle on a compass.

9. aweigh

(uh-'way) *adj.*

A over the side.

B off the bottom.

c trailing behind.

10. egress

('ee-gress) *n.*

A entrance.

B exit.

c shortcut.

11. recede

(rih-'seed) *v.*

A pass underneath.

B lean to the right.

c move back.

12. laterally

('lat-uh-ruh-lee) *adv.*

A sideways.

B backward.

c upward.

13. polestar

('pohl-star)*n.*

A western route.

B North Star.

c southern tip.

14. adjacent

(uh-'jay-sent) *adj.*

A at the fore.

B neighboring.

c pressing down.

15. abaft

(uh-'baft) *prep.*

A to the rear of.

B on the border of.

c downstream from.

"STAY ON TRACK" ANSWERS

1. starboard
A *ship's right side.*
Looking out over the ark's starboard, Noah scanned the horizon.

2. transpose
C *move to another place.*
Kyle's novel is a retelling of Hamlet, transposed to modern-day England.

3. terminus
A *end point of a route.*
Frankfurt is the terminus for the westbound train.

GETTING ORIENTED

The Latin word *orientem*, meaning "the rising sun" or "the east," gave us the historical name for the world's eastern lands: the Orient. The Occident refers to the west, from the Latin *occidentem* (sunset). Things such as winds and auroras are boreal from the north and austral from the south—hence the name of that down-under continent.

4. anterior
C *in the front.*
"I see that you've been flossing your anterior teeth, but you need to pay attention to your molars," said Dr. Kim.

5. circumnavigate
B *go around.*
Google Maps always helps me circumnavigate the congested areas.

6. sinistral
C *left-handed.*
Did you know that the United States has had just eight sinistral presidents?

7. periphery
C *outer edges.*
My puppy is a bit shy—she tends to linger at the periphery of the dog park.

8. apex
B *uppermost point.*
The Hollywood actress had reached the apex of fame by age 18.

9. aweigh
B *off the bottom.*
"Anchors aweigh, boys!" the captain shouted.

10. egress
B *exit.*
Are you sure this hedge maze has an egress?

11. recede
C *move back.*
When the floodwaters recede, the cleanup will begin.

12. laterally
A *sideways.*
Good basketball players must be able to move well laterally as well as down the court.

13. polestar
B *North Star.*
Once I catch sight of the polestar, I can get my bearings again.

14. adjacent
B *neighboring.*
The sisters lived in adjacent houses on Chestnut Drive.

15. abaft
A *to the rear of.*
The private jet has a ritzy master suite abaft the main cabin.

YOUR SCORE:
___ / 15

SPIRITED

After Prohibition went into effect in 1920,
Americans suffered through a long dry spell—
save for the occasional dip into the bathtub gin.
Take your best shot at this spirited vocabulary.

1. speakeasy
('speek-ee-zee) *n.*
A expert bartender.
B chatty drunk.
C illegal bar.

2. swill
(swil) *v.*
A smuggle.
B age in barrels.
C drink freely.

3. aperitif
(uh-pair-uh-'teef) *n.*
A apricot brandy.
B predinner cocktail.
C swizzle stick.

4. blotto
('blah-toh) *adj.*
A with a splash of
   water.
B intoxicated.
C bubbly.

5. distill
(dih-'still) *v.*
A purify a liquid.
B add a mixer.
C flavor with bitters.

6. wassail
('wah-suhl) *n.*
A hot spiced beverage.
B headache cure.
C public house.

7. bootleg
('boot-leg) *adj.*
A made in small
   batches.
B produced unlawfully.
C watered down.

8. katzenjammer
('kat-sun-jam-er) *n.*
A beer garden.
B corkscrew.
C hangover.

9. snifter
('snif-ter) *n.*
A small goblet.
B nightcap.
C hip flask.

10. Nebuchadnezzar
(neh-byuh-kud-'neh-zer) *n.*
A enormous wine
   bottle.
B tequila-based drink.
C Egyptian chalice.

11. aqua vitae
(ak-wuh 'vy-tee) *n.*
A sparkling seltzer.
B medicinal syrup.
C strong liquor.

12. inebriated
('i-nee-bree-ay-ted) *adj.*
A drunk.
B sloppy.
C excited.

13. rathskeller
('rot-skeh-ler) *n.*
A drinking game.
B basement tavern.
C dark ale.

14. repeal
(ree-'peel) *v.*
A put an end to.
B garnish with lemon.
C legalize.

15. dram
(dram) *n.*
A barstool.
B small drink.
C brewery.

"SPIRITED" ANSWERS

1. speakeasy
c *illegal bar.*
Speakeasies popped up in cities across America in the 1920s.

2. swill
c *drink freely.*
Mimi plans to spend her spring break sunbathing on the beach and swilling margaritas.

3. aperitif
B *predinner cocktail.*
After a round of aperitifs, the couple ordered filet mignon and a bottle of cabernet.

4. blotto
B *intoxicated.*
You're going to college to learn, not to get blotto with your friends.

5. distill
A *purify a liquid.*
Most rum is distilled from molasses.

6. wassail
A *hot spiced beverage.*
A wassail is just the thing to warm you up on a chilly evening.

7. bootleg
B *produced unlawfully.*
According to family lore, Grandpa sold bootleg whiskey from the back of his general store.

8. katzenjammer
c *hangover.*
I had a whopping katzenjammer the day after I turned 21!

9. snifter
A *small goblet.*
Hassan collects vintage snifters and highball glasses.

10. Nebuchadnezzar
A *enormous wine bottle.*
Should I bid on that Nebuchadnezzar of champagne at the museum gala?

11. aqua vitae
c *strong liquor.*
Lakshmi has sworn off aqua vitae until she finishes her doctoral thesis.

12. inebriated
A *drunk.*
The inebriated sailors started to sing very loudly.

13. rathskeller
B *basement tavern.*
The inn offers a cozy rathskeller just below the formal dining room.

14. repeal
A *put an end to.*
Congress ratified the 21st Amendment in 1933, which repealed Prohibition.

15. dram
B *small drink.*
For dessert, I'll have the cherry cheesecake and a dram of amaretto, please.

TIPPLING TONIGHT? TEE-TOTALLY NOT

A teetotaler—aka someone who doesn't drink alcohol—is not necessarily a tea drinker, as the name suggests. The word likely came from the phrase "tee-total abstinence," with the first syllable used simply to emphasize the "t" sound, similar to how you might say, "You're in trouble, with a capital T!"

YOUR SCORE:
___ / 15

ABCs

Here, we get down to the ABCs of words—
the letters—with a quiz about their myriad
faces, sounds, and symbols.

1. serif

('ser-ef) *n.*

A X to represent a kiss.

B a short line at the end of any of a letter's strokes.

C double letter.

2. zed

(zed) *n.*

A dot over an "i."

B British "z."

C underlined character.

3. cursive

('ker-siv) *adj.*

A rounded, as B or C.

B in flowing penmanship.

C left-facing.

4. schwa

(shwah) *n.*

A unstressed vowel.

B misspelled word.

C one-letter word.

5. aspirate

('as-peh-rayt) *v.*

A end in -ess.

B start with an "a."

C pronounce with an H sound.

6. majuscule

('ma-jes-kyewl) *n.*

A italic letter.

B boldface letter.

C uppercase letter.

7. assonance

('a-suh-nents) *n.*

A with the same vowel sound.

B using mixed fonts.

C hard to pronounce.

8. tilde

('til-duh) *n.*

A squiggle over an "n."

B two dots over an "o."

C accent mark.

9. alliteration

(ah-li-te-'ray-shun) *n.*

A an autograph.

B the space following a colon.

C the repetition of the same initial consonant sound.

10. decussate

(de-'kuh-sayt) *v.*

A slur.

B mispronounce.

C intersect; form an X.

11. logogram

('law-ge-gram) *n.*

A picture writing.

B symbol standing for a word.

C set of initials.

12. burr

(ber) *n.*

A rolled or trilled R sound.

B printing error.

C repeated vowel.

13. sibilant

('sih-bih-lent) *adj.*

A similar in sound.

B in alphabetical order.

C having an S or hissing sound.

14. guttural

('guh-tuh-rel) *adj.*

A from the throat.

B having a hard G sound.

C emphasized.

15. orthoepy

('or-theh-weh-pee) *n.*

A code.

B proper pronunciation.

C sign language.

"ABCs" ANSWERS

1. serif
B *a short line at the end of any of a letter's strokes.*
There isn't a serif font in this whole book.

2. zed
B *British "z."*
Since returning from London, Zooey has spelled her name out loud to us a dozen times using a zed.

3. cursive
B *in flowing penmanship.*
I had to admire the lovely cursive of Mary's "Dear John" letter.

4. schwa
A *unstressed vowel.*
In case you're wondering, the "e" in vowel is a schwa.

5. aspirate
C *pronounce with an H sound.*
Eliza Doolittle didn't aspirate when she spoke of "'Enry 'Iggins."

6. majuscule
C *uppercase letter.*
Alex thinks he's so great, he signs his name in all majuscules.

7. assonance
A *with the same vowel sound.*
The only thing Bob and Dot have in common is their names' assonance.

8. tilde
A *squiggle over an "n."*
Nuñez barked when the maître d' forgot the tilde in his name.

9. sigmoid
C *shaped like an S.*
I tried to skate a figure 8 but slipped and left a sigmoid trail instead.

10. decussate
C *intersect; form an X.*
The pirate let two strokes decussate on the map to mark his hidden treasure.

11. logogram
B *symbol standing for a word.*
The Artist Formerly Known as Prince used a fancy logogram instead of his actual name.

12. burr
A *rolled or trilled R sound.*
When Scotty says "rump roast," the burrs are like a purring motor.

13. sibilant
C *having an S or hissing sound.*
Certain sibilant sounds struck Sussman as excessively snaky.

14. guttural
A *from the throat.*
To illustrate guttural consonants, Professor Fenn literally growled at his students.

15. orthoepy
B *proper pronunciation.*
Tongue-twisters like "rubber baby buggy bumper" are good exercises in orthoepy.

YOUR SCORE:
___ / 15

ONLY U

Words with no vowels except u form a peculiar group—or, one might say, a rum bunch. Take a run (but not a bum's rush) through this quiz, which features words with the vowel exclusively.

1. fugu
('foo-goo) *n.*
A African dance.
B flintstone.
C poisonous fish.

2. susurrus
(su-'sir-us) *n.*
A whispering sound.
B low layer of clouds.
C magic elixir.

3. tub-thump
('tub-thump) *v.*
A challenge.
B support loudly.
C fail disastrously.

4. plumb
(plum) *adj.*
A purplish-red.
B exactly vertical.
C exhausted.

5. mugwump
('mug-wump) *n.*
A politically independent person.
B sad child.
C punch or fight.

6. kudzu
('kood- or 'kud-zoo) *n.*
A two-masted ship.
B fast-growing vine.
C rabbit-like rodent.

7. luff
(luhf) *v.*
A change your mind.
B deal a poker hand.
C turn a ship to the wind.

8. jumbuck
('juhm-buck) *n.*
A Australian sheep.
B silver dollar.
C tangled mess.

9. succubus
('suc-cu-bus) *n.*
A skin pore.
B double-decker trolley.
C female demon.

10. usufruct
('yoo-zuh- or 'yoo-suh-frukt) *n.*
A stubborn person.
B legal right of use.
C light-bending prism.

11. chum
(chuhm) *n.*
A gritty buildup.
B bait for fish.
C trill of a bird.

12. lutz
(luhtz) *n.*
A ice-skating jump.
B unit of electric power.
C World War II bomber.

13. subfusc
(sub-'fuhsk) *adj.*
A using espionage.
B drab or dusky.
C too wet to ignite.

14. durum
('der-uhm) *n.*
A wild bull.
B pause in poetry reading.
C kind of wheat.

15. pung
(pung) *n.*
A military takeover.
B hole in a barrel.
C box-shaped sleigh.

"ONLY U" ANSWERS

1. fugu
C *poisonous fish.*
Does Dad know he has to cut out the toxic parts of the fugu?

2. susurrus
A *whispering sound.*
The susurrus of night winds lulled the sentry to sleep.

3. tub-thump
B *support loudly.*
Our pushy kids are tub-thumping for a raise in their allowance.

4. plumb
B *exactly vertical.*
Is it just me, or does that old tower in Pisa look not quite plumb?

5. mugwump
A *politically independent person.*

SO UNCLEAR
Forming the negatives of words can be tricky, and often it's best to avoid our star vowel. Consider: inadvisable, infrequent, and atypical. But sometimes the u's have it: uncontrollable and unalterable.

Despite being a mugwump, Gary takes his civic duty seriously come Election Day.

6. kudzu
B *fast-growing vine.*
My roommate's stuff is taking over the dorm quicker than a kudzu in Georgia.

7. luff
C *turn a ship to the wind.*
A yachtsman knows how to luff without knocking all the passengers overboard.

8. jumbuck
A *Australian sheep.*
In the song "Waltzing Matilda," it's a jumbuck that the swagman catches beside the billabong.

9. succubus
C *female demon.*
According to folklore, a succubus often appears in dreams to seduce men.

10. usufruct
B *legal right of use.*
Last night, the lawyer asked his son, "Hey, who gave you the usufruct to play with my phone?"

11. chum
B *bait for fish.*
"Chief, best drop another chum marker," Quint utters as the crew hunts down the famous predator in *Jaws*.

12. lutz
A *ice-skating jump.*
Carol's lutz was less than perfect.

13. subfusc
B *drab or dusky.*
Every year, Clarice waits for a subfusc winter morning to reread *Wuthering Heights*.

14. durum
C *kind of wheat.*
I hate to tell you, but your all-durum diet is not gluten-free.

15. pung
C *box-shaped sleigh.*
"Oh, what fun it is to ride in a ... pung!" just doesn't have the same ring, does it?

YOUR SCORE:
___ / 15

LOVE CONNECTION

This quiz is all about the language of love. We hope you'll feel ardor for these words of the heart.

1. nuptial
('nup-shul, -chul) *adj.*
A forced to elope.
B named after the mother.
c pertaining to a marriage.

---

2. Casanova
(ka-za-'no-va, -sa-) *n.*
A inn where honeymooners stay.
B man with many love affairs.
c nagging spouse.

---

3. rendezvous
('rahn-di-voo, -dah-) *n.*
A meeting, as between lovers.
B formal engagement.
c romantic view.

---

4. ardor
('ar-der) *n.*
A fierce heartbeat.
B heat of passion.
c garden with a love seat.

---

5. spoon (spoon) *v.*
A to fall deeply in love at first sight.
B go Dutch.
c kiss and caress.

6. rapture
('rap-cher) *n.*
A secret love note.
B state of bliss.
c full bridal gown.

---

7. ogle ('oh-gul) *v.*
A to stare at wolfishly.
B howl at the moon.
c rub noses affectionately.

---

8. coquette
(koh-'ket) *n.*
A young lady who flirts.
B heart-shaped pastry.
c lawn game for couples.

---

9. nubile
('noo-bye-el, 'nyoo-, -bul) *adj.*
A hard to catch.
B of marrying age.
c posing while nude.

---

10. miscegenation
(mi-se-ji-'nay-shun, -si-) *n.*
A marriage between cousins.
B marriage between people of different races.
c marriage between people of different ages.

11. banns (banz) *n.*
A music at weddings.
B announcement of marriage.
c divorce proceedings.

---

12. unrequited
(un-ri-'kwiy-ted) *adj.*
A not returned, as affections.
B broken off, as an engagement.
c having no bridesmaids.

---

13. agape (a-'gah-pay) *n.*
A benevolent love.
B endearing poem.
c openmouthed kiss.

---

14. conjugal
('kan-ji-gul) *adj.*
A priestly.
B relating to a husband and wife.
c of a brassiere.

---

15. shivaree
(shi-va-'ree, 'shi-va-ree) *n.*
A courtesy toward women.
B excited feeling.
c loud music played outside a newlywed couple's window.

"LOVE CONNECTION" ANSWERS

1. nuptial
c *pertaining to a marriage.*
Everyone at the church was elated to see Matilda sob happily as she recited her nuptial vows.

2. Casanova
b *man with many love affairs.*
The singer is such a playboy, just like his famous Italian ancestor Giovanni Casanova.

3. rendezvous
a *meeting, as between lovers.*
Without telling their parents, Pierre and Marie arranged an ardent rendezvous.

4. ardor
b *heat of passion.*
If two jurors fell in love, there would be ardor in the court.

5. spoon
c *to kiss and caress.*
Under the moon in June, sweethearts spoon and swoon.

6. rapture
b *state of bliss.*
After his first kiss, Woody walked around in a rapture for days.

7. ogle
a *to stare at wolfishly.*
Dexter, an incorrigible lout, couldn't help but ogle the lady walking by.

8. coquette
a *young lady who flirts.*
A winking coquette might distract even the most earnest croquet player.

9. nubile
b *of marrying age.*
Felicity is not allowed to get engaged until she's nubile.

10. miscegenation
b *marriage between people of different races.*
Laws prohibiting miscegenation were declared unconstitutional in 1967.

11. banns
b *announcement of marriage.*
The couple were going bananas waiting for the priest to read the banns.

12. unrequited
a *not returned, as affections.*
My heart is ignited, but I'm blue because my love is unrequited.

13. agape
a *benevolent love.*
I gape at the selfless purity of agape.

14. conjugal
b *relating to a husband and wife.*
A conjugal deal may be sealed with a kiss.

15. shivaree
c *loud music played as a joke outside a newlywed couple's window.*
It may have been fun for their pals, but the earsplitting shivaree gave Erica and Ethan a honeymoon headache.

YOUR SCORE:
___ / 15

MELTING POT

From "aria" to "zucchini," Italian words add beauty and flavor to everyday English. Celebrate these words with Italian roots, and then take a gondola ride to the next page for answers.

1. fiasco
(fee-'a-skoh) *n.*
A rowdy celebration.
B complete failure.
C big fire.

2. al dente
(all-'den-tay) *adj.*
A seasoned with salt.
B eaten outdoors.
C cooked until firm.

3. incognito
(in-kog-'nee-toh) *adv.*
A well traveled.
B excessively complex.
C with a concealed identity.

4. vendetta
(ven-'deh-tuh) *n.*
A layered cake.
B blood feud.
C sales booth.

5. patina
(puh-'tee-nuh) *n.*
A high priest.
B lawn bowling.
C sheen produced by age.

6. dilettante
('dih-luh-tahnt) *n.*
A coffee cup.
B dabbler.
C secret note.

7. belvedere
('bel-vuh-deer) *n.*
A head butler.
B set of chimes.
C structure with a view.

8. cameo
('ka-mee-oh) *n.*
A small role.
B almond cookie.
C sofa bed.

9. sotto voce
('sah-toh 'voh-chee) *adv.*
A under one's breath.
B drunkenly.
C in the open.

10. bravura
(bruh-'vyur-ah) *n.*
A encore.
B battle cry.
C display of brilliance.

11. amoretto
(a-muh-'reh-toh) *n.*
A hazelnut flavoring.
B cherub.
C waistcoat.

12. forte
('for-tay) *adj.*
A loud.
B masculine.
C built on a hill.

13. bruschetta
(broo-'sheh-tuh) *n.*
A grilled bread appetizer.
B thumbnail sketch.
C short story.

14. campanile
(kam-puh-'nee-lee) *n.*
A bell tower.
B army troop.
C best friend.

15. brio
('bree-oh) *n.*
A cold spell.
B donkey.
C gusto.

"MELTING POT" ANSWERS

1. fiasco
B *complete failure.*
Though its premiere was a fiasco, the Broadway musical became the smash of the season.

2. al dente
C *cooked until firm.*
I like my noodles al dente, but these are practically raw!

3. incognito
C *with a concealed identity.*
The spy traveled incognito, using an assumed name.

4. vendetta
B *blood feud.*
Romeo and Juliet's love affair was doomed by their families' vendetta.

5. patina
C *sheen produced by age.*
You can tell this writing desk is an antique by its beautiful patina.

6. dilettante
B *dabbler.*
The maestro seeks a professional singer, not some weekend dilettante.

NAME THAT NOODLE

A noodle's name often tells you its shape—at least when you go back to its Italian-language roots. Rigatoni, from *riga*, or "line," has grooves; bucatini, from *buca*, or "hole," is hollow. Other varieties include bow-tie-shaped farfalle (*farfalla*, "butterfly"), pointed penne (*penna*, "quill"), spiraled fusilli (*fuso*, "spindle"), and long, thin spaghetti (*spago*, "string").

7. belvedere
C *structure with a view.*
From the domed belvedere, we could watch Mount Etna erupting.

8. cameo
A *small role.*
Francesca blew her audition for the lead, but she has a cameo as a taxi driver.

9. sotto voce
A *under one's breath.*
"I always speak sotto voce," whispered Sophia, "to make sure people are listening."

10. bravura
C *display of brilliance.*
The defense lawyer delivered the closing argument with bravura.

11. amoretto
B *cherub.*
Why don't you paint a little amoretto above the kissing couple?

12. forte
A *loud.*
In my opinion, a trombone serenade is too forte to be romantic.

13. bruschetta
A *grilled bread appetizer.*
The bruschetta has too many carbs for my diet!

14. campanile
A *bell tower.*
The village's campanile has been standing since medieval times.

15. brio
C *gusto.*
After just one sip of Chianti, I feel my brio returning.

YOUR SCORE:
___ / 15

WORDS OF YESTERYEAR

This group probably is well-known to grandparents, if not to today's whippersnappers.

1. cordial
('kor-jel) *n.*
A garden party.
B fruit-flavored liqueur.
C flower for buttonhole.

2. gumption
('gump-shen) *n.*
A foolhardiness.
B resourcefulness.
C stickiness.

3. ragamuffin
('ra-guh-muh-fen) *n.*
A child in dirty clothes.
B pie made with fruit and stale crumbs.
C abandoned house pet.

4. jalopy
(ja-'lah-pee) *n.*
A beat-up car.
B vacant building.
C elderly gentleman.

5. ewer
('yoo-er) *n.*
A wide-mouthed water jug.
B hand-crank pump.
C paddock for sheep.

6. lollygag
('la-lee-gag) *v.*
A play a trick on someone.
B wolf down food.
C dawdle.

7. bustle
('buh-sel) *v.*
A padding at the rear of a woman's skirt.
B undergarment used to constrict the waist.
C strapless bodice.

8. rapscallion
(rap-'skal-yen) *n.*
A bitter vegetable.
B mischievous person.
C musical style.

9. gumshoe
('gum-shoo) *n.*
A detective.
B burglar.
C athlete.

10. gitches
('gich-ez) *n.*
A arguments.
B underwear.
C silly people.

11. apothecary
(uh-'pah-thi-ker-ee, -ke-ree) *n.*
A fortune teller.
B pharmacist.
C evangelical minister.

12. balderdash
('bohl-der-dash) *n.*
A slang.
B exaggeration.
C nonsense.

13. dickey ('di-kee) *n.*
A chest pocket on overalls.
B false shirtfront.
C high-necked cape.

14. pedal pushers
('pe-dul 'pu-sherz) *n.*
A bicycle gears.
B calf-length trousers.
C two-tone shoes.

15. humdinger
('hum-ding-er) *n.*
A laughable.
B modern.
C someone or something extraordinary.

"WORDS OF YESTERYEAR" ANSWERS

1. cordial
B *fruit-flavored liqueur.*
Only favored guests were offered Aunt Millie's homemade raspberry cordial.

---

2. gumption
B *resourcefulness.*
The Wright brothers sure had gumption to make and fly their planes.

---

3. ragamuffin
A *child in dirty clothes.*
After picking up Arnie from the petting zoo, Grandma proclaimed, "He looks like the ragamuffin Oliver Twist!"

---

4. jalopy
A *beat-up car.*
A constant eyesore, our neighbor's jalopy is more than ready for the junkyard.

---

5. ewer
A *widemouthed water jug.*
A basin and ewer predate the modern bathroom sink.

6. lollygag
C *dawdle.*
Don't lollygag on the way to school or you'll be late.

---

7. bustle
A *padding at the rear of a woman's skirt.*
The bustle added some unneeded curves to her profile.

---

8. rapscallion
B *mischievous person.*
That rapscallion tricked everyone into doing all his chores for him.

---

9. gumshoe
A *detective.*
Who is your favorite gumshoe, Philip Marlowe or Sam Spade?

---

10. gitches
B *underwear.*
It was so warm outside that little Sammy stripped down to his gitches.

---

11. apothecary
B *pharmacist.*
Check with the apothecary about side effects before taking that drug.

12. balderdash
C *nonsense.*
In response to vehement claims that the earth is flat, Galileo would always yell, "What balderdash!"

---

13. dickey
B *false shirtfront.*
My great-uncle wore a dickey, saving my great-aunt from heaps of shirt washing.

---

14. pedal pushers
B *calf-length trousers.*
The costume designer had her hands full making pedal pushers for the play's revival.

---

15. humdinger
C *something or someone extraordinary.*
That was a real humdinger of a storm last night.

YOUR SCORE:
___ / 15

EDUCATION COUNTS

Sharpen your pencil and put on your thinking cap—it's time to head back to school. We've selected a roster of words that will challenge learners of all ages. Will you make the grade or draw a blank? Turn the page for answers.

1. parochial
(puh-'roh-kee-uhl) *adj.*
A rigorous.
B elementary.
C run by a church.

2. conscientious
(kon-shee-'en-shuhs) *adj.*
A extremely careful.
B alert.
C well educated.

3. pore
(pohr) *v.*
A quote at length.
B study intently.
C write by hand.

4. carrel
('kehr-uhl) *n.*
A library nook.
B songbook.
C punctuation mark.

5. catechism
('ka-teh-ki-zem) *n.*
A major disaster.
B religious school.
C series of fixed questions and answers used for instruction.

6. pedantic
(pih-'dan-tik) *adj.*
A misbehaving.
B making a show of knowledge.
C highly poetic.

7. curriculum
(kuh-'rih-kyuh-luhm) *n.*
A lecture hall.
B highest grade.
C set of courses.

8. rudiments
('roo-duh-ments) *n.*
A wrong answers.
B small classes.
C beginner's skills.

9. syntax
('sin-tax) *n.*
A dictionary.
B sentence structure.
C math equation.

10. semantic
(sih-'man-tik) *adj.*
A related to meaning in language.
B collegiate.
C in essay form.

11. pedagogy
('peh-duh-goh-jee) *n.*
A art of teaching.
B debate tactic.
C study of children.

12. syllabus
('sih-luh-buhs) *n.*
A word part.
B class outline.
C textbook.

13. woolgathering
('wool-ga-thuh-ring) *n.*
A taking notes.
B memorizing.
C daydreaming.

14. cognizant
('cog-nuh-zent) *adj.*
A engrossed.
B aware.
C automated.

15. empirical
(im-'peer-ih-kul) *adj.*
A theoretical.
B quick to learn.
C based on observation.

"EDUCATION COUNTS" ANSWERS

1. parochial
C *run by a church.*
Wearing parochial school uniforms left me hating plaid.

2. conscientious
A *extremely careful.*
Carly is conscientious—this sloppy report isn't like her.

3. pore
B *study intently.*
Sam pored over his history notes the night before the midterm.

4. carrel
A *library nook.*
In graduate school, I'd practically sleep in a carrel before exams.

NONWORKING CLASS

The word school comes from the Greek *shkole*, meaning "idleness." In ancient Greece, shkole referred to how the well-to-do spent their spare time: in philosophical discussion. Shkole became the Latin *schola* ("meeting place for teachers and students"), which in turn gave us school.

5. catechism
C *series of fixed questions and answers used for instructtion.*
Shauna taught catechism classes at her church for years.

6. pedantic
B *making a show of knowledge.*
I find Mr. Riordan's bookish teaching style a bit pedantic.

7. curriculum
C *set of courses.*
The first class in the cooking curriculum is Soups and Stews.

8. rudiments
C *beginner's skills.*
First-year students at Hogwarts must learn the rudiments of wizardry.

9. syntax
B *sentence structure.*
This sentence a rather tortured syntax has.

10. semantic
A *related to meaning in language.*
"What's the semantic difference between clown and fool?" our English teacher asked.

11. pedagogy
A *art of teaching.*
"There are no lucrative awards for pedagogy," said Mr. Wilcox, "but I find it very rewarding."

12. syllabus
B *class outline.*
This syllabus has no homework assignments listed—woo-hoo!

13. woolgathering
C *daydreaming.*
If you hadn't been woolgathering in class, you wouldn't have flunked.

14. cognizant
B *aware.*
"I'm cognizant of the facts of your case," the vice principal told Mason, "but they don't excuse cheating."

15. empirical
C *based on observation.*
Brody's science project presents empirical evidence that eating chocolate is good for you.

YOUR SCORE:
___ / 15

TWO OF A KIND

Whether you're from Walla Walla, Washington, or Wagga Wagga, Australia, we double-dare you to master this quiz. It's all about words with repeating sets of letters. (Don't go gaga, though.)

1. baba
('bah-bah) *n.*
A rum-soaked cake.
B maternal relative.
C mild bruise or scrape.

2. muumuu
('moo-moo) *n.*
A radical militant.
B lagoon in an atoll.
C long, loose dress.

3. pupu
('poo-poo) *n.*
A tree with yellow fruit.
B sea breeze.
C Asian appetizer.

4. meme
(meem) *n.*
A perfect imitation.
B recycling symbol.
C idea or trait that spreads within a culture.

5. Isis
('eye-sis) *n.*
A fiery river of Hades.
B Egyptian nature goddess.
C rainbow personified.

6. furfur
('fer-fer) *n.*
A about 1.25 miles.
B dandruff.
C bow-shaped pasta.

7. tsetse
('set-see or 'teet-) *n.*
A type of fly.
B Greek hierarchy.
C opposing force of energy or gravity.

8. chop-chop
(chop-'chop) *adv.*
A sarcastically.
B intently.
C promptly.

9. nene
('nay-nay) *n.*
A endangered state bird of Hawaii.
B forbidden behavior.
C cheap trinket.

10. tam-tam
('tam-tam) *n.*
A pouty look.
B gong.
C skiing maneuver.

11. chin-chin
('chin-chin) *n.*
A broom.
B type of dog.
C salutation or toast.

12. juju
('joo-joo) *n.*
A West African music style.
B trophy.
C candy.

13. couscous
('coos-coos) *n.*
A semolina dish.
B Moroccan beach strip.
C Congolese dance.

14. chichi
('shee-shee) *adj.*
A frigid, icy.
B loose, lanky.
C showy, frilly.

15. bulbul
('bull-bull) *n.*
A songbird.
B knobbed head on a cane.
C croak of a male frog.

"TWO OF A KIND" ANSWERS

1. baba
A *rum-soaked cake.*
Nothing completes a holiday feast like Becky's homemade baba.

---

2. muumuu
C *long, loose dress.*
Natalie was jealous of the authentic muumuu her sister brought back from her honeymoon.

---

3. pupu
C *Asian appetizer.*
Art's favorite part of the meal? The pupu platter of fried shrimp and egg rolls.

---

4. meme
C *idea or trait that spreads within a culture.*
The abuse of the word "like" is an unfortunate meme dating back to the '80s.

---

5. Isis
B *Egyptian nature goddess.*
Certainly, Bob Dylan was inspired by the mystical Isis when he penned his famous song.

---

6. furfur
B *dandruff.*
"I have a great remedy for that furfur on your dog's coat," Tiffany offered.

---

7. tsetse
A *type of fly.*
Sleeping sickness, a disease marked by lethargy and confusion, is transmitted by the tsetse fly.

---

8. chop-chop
C *promptly.*
Yes, the soup arrived chop-chop, but I seriously doubt it's homemade.

---

9. nene
A *endangered state bird of Hawaii.*
A bird lover, Marty was delighted to see the nene up close during his trip.

---

10. tam-tam
B *gong.*
Lauren was fascinated by the tam-tam player in the orchestra.

---

11. chin-chin
C *salutation or toast.*
Neville looked forward to saying "chin-chin" to his classmates at the reunion.

---

12. juju
A *West African music style.*
Featuring a breathtaking beat, Alec's juju composition relies on heavy percussion.

---

13. couscous
A *semolina dish.*
Our family's couscous recipe goes back five generations.

---

14. chichi
C *showy, frilly.*
As we'd predicted, Lucy got just what she wanted: an over-the-top, chichi engagement ring.

---

15. bulbul
A *songbird.*
The bulbul makes frequent appearances in Persian poetry, Emily learned during her graduate studies.

YOUR SCORE:
___ / 15

A WONDERFUL WORLD

How well do you know the peaks and valleys of planet Earth?
Can you tell a bluff (that's a cliff) from a gulch (a narrow ravine)?
Circumnavigate your way through this list of words.

1. biosphere
('by-uh-sfeer) *n.*
A gases around Earth.
B parts of Earth that support life.
C planet's outer crust.

2. strata
('stray-tuh) *n.*
A rock layers.
B low clouds.
C seabed.

3. bayou
('by-oo) *n.*
A tropical island.
B deep cavern.
C marshy waterway.

4. arroyo
(uh-'roy-oh) *n.*
A gully.
B grassland.
C coral island.

5. aquifer
('a-kwuh-fur) *n.*
A geyser.
B waterfall.
C underground water bed.

6. seismic
('siyz-mihk) *adj.*
A prone to floods.
B related to earthquakes.
C covered in lava.

7. scree
(skree) *n.*
A loose rocks.
B peninsula.
C magma flow.

8. ecology
(ih-'kah-luh-jee) *n.*
A relationship of organisms to their environment.
B cycle of ocean currents.
C composting.

9. terra firma
('ter-uh 'fur-muh) *n.*
A natural dam.
B sandbar.
C dry land.

10. cartography
(kar-'tah-gruh-fee) *n.*
A study of glaciers.
B art of mapmaking.
C science of erosion.

11. flora ('flohr-uh) *n.*
A animal life.
B plant life.
C minerals.

12. tarn (tarn) *n.*
A mountain lake.
B sinkhole.
C fossilized wood.

13. latitude
('la-tih-tood) *n.*
A distance east or west from the prime meridian.
B imaginary line through Earth's center.
C distance north or south from the equator.

14. primordial
(pry-'mohr-dee-uhl) *adj.*
A densely forested.
B on highest ground.
C from earliest times.

15. hogback
('hahg-back) *n.*
A U-turn in a river.
B steep-sided ridge.
C tributary.

"A WONDERFUL WORLD" ANSWERS

1. biosphere

B *parts of Earth that support life.*
The biosphere is home to a stunning variety of species.

2. strata

A *rock layers.*
The strata of the Grand Canyon are hundreds of millions of years old,

3. bayou

C *marshy waterway.*
Marie often paddles across the bayou in her canoe at sunrise.

4. arroyo

A *gully.*
That's my car at the bottom of the arroyo.

5. aquifer

C *underground water bed.*
The Ogallala Aquifer stretches from South Dakota to Texas.

6. seismic

B *related to earthquakes.*
After moving out west, Nick got used to regular seismic activity.

7. scree

A *loose rocks.*
Petra had to scramble through piles of scree to reach the summit.

POLAR OPPOSITES

When you were a kid, did you ever try digging to China or Australia—or whatever was down there? Points on Earth that are opposite each other (such as the North and South Poles) are called antipodes (an-'tih-poh-deez). The word comes from the Greek *anti* (opposite) and *pod* (foot), meaning "people who have their feet against our feet." So whose feet are pressed against yours? Probably no one's. In most of the continental United States, your antipode is in the Indian Ocean.

8. ecology

A *relationship of organisms to their environment.*
Scientists are studying the effect of oil spills on deep-sea ecology.

9. terra firma

C *dry land.*
After a week on the boat, Alex couldn't wait to return to terra firma.

10. cartography

B *art of mapmaking.*
"Why would anyone study cartography in the age of Google Maps?" Dora asked.

11. flora

B *plant life.*
Walt's art is inspired by the flora of Cape Cod.

12. tarn

A *mountain lake.*
A dip in a tarn is just as bracing as an espresso.

13. latitude

C *distance north or south from the equator.*
Lines of latitude are also called parallels.

14. primordial

C *from earliest times.*
This primordial forest looks like something straight out of *Game of Thrones*.

15. hogback

B *steep-sided ridge.*
I'm not sure you should take a selfie so close to the hogback's rim!

YOUR SCORE: ___ / 15

CURIOUSER & CURIOUSER

Alice's Adventures in Wonderland and other works by Lewis Carroll (aka Charles Lutwidge Dodgson) abound with terms worth knowing.

1. hookah
('hu-kuh) *n.*
A staff of a shepherdess.
B chess queen's crown.
C smoking pipe.

2. platitudes
('pla-tih-tewds) *n.*
A trite sayings.
B temperate climates.
C heaping servings.

3. welter
('wel-tur) *v.*
A toss among waves.
B droop in the sun.
C shrink in size.

4. lory
('lor-ee) *n.*
A tall tale.
B type of parrot.
C atmospheric phenomenon.

5. impertinent
(im-'pur-tuh-nunt) *adj.*
A late for a meeting.
B talking rapidly.
C rude.

6. languid
('lan-gwed) *adj.*
A speaking fluently.
B sluggish or weak.
C slightly tilted.

7. ungainly
(un-'gayn-lee) *adj.*
A not attractive.
B clumsy or awkward.
C sickly thin.

8. livery
('lih-vuh-ree) *n.*
A model boat.
B uniform.
C long, boring speech.

9. antipathies
(an-'tih-puh-thees) *n.*
A miracle cures.
B sudden storms, usually in the tropics.
C feelings of dislike.

10. will-o'-the-wisp
(will-uh-thuh-'wisp) *n.*
A fast speaker.
B rare plant.
C misleading goal or hope.

11. sally
('sa-lee) *n.*
A female rabbit.
B white smock or robe.
C witty remark.

12. griffin
('grih-fun) *n.*
A monster with wings.
B horn.
C cranky man.

13. cravat
(kruh-'vat) *n.*
A game similar to croquet.
B scarf-like necktie.
C two-person rowboat.

14. hansom
('hant-sum) *n.*
A horse-drawn carriage.
B knight or nobility.
C chimney flue.

15. sagaciously
(suh-'gay-shus-lee) *adv.*
A wisely.
B dimly or foolishly.
C ambitiously.

"CURIOUSER & CURIOUSER" ANSWERS

1. hookah
c *smoking pipe.*
Gerry found a shop downtown that offers supplies for his antique hookah.

2. platitudes
A *trite sayings.*
Our coach offered a dozen peppy platitudes like "No pain, no gain."

3. welter
A *toss among waves.*
Heading for shore, Karyn stayed focused on the buoy weltering in the distance.

4. lory
B *type of parrot.*
Mitch set off for Australia to study the lory in the wild.

5. impertinent
c *rude.*
"Would it be too impertinent to point out that I can hear you snoring six rows back?"

6. languid
B *sluggish or weak.*
By three in the afternoon, I am too languid to think about anything but coffee and a couch.

7. ungainly
B *clumsy or awkward.*
He is the most ungainly mime I've ever seen.

8. livery
B *uniform.*
The butler's rumpled livery made him a prime suspect in the disappearance of our dinner host.

9. antipathies
c *feelings of dislike.*
I'd say there were some mild antipathies between the two speakers at the city hall meeting.

10. will-o'-the-wisp
c *misleading goal or hope.*
You might follow the will-o'-the-wisp of bipartisanship regarding the new law, but you'd be foolish.

11. sally
c *witty remark.*
Aside from the occasional sally, the sportscasters had little to offer.

12. griffin
A *monster with wings.*
Felix was fascinated by the illustrations of the griffin in his mythology book.

13. cravat
B *scarf-like necktie.*
I'm going to the party as James Bond. Would he wear a cravat?

14. hansom
A *horse-drawn carriage.*
The producer of *Cinderella* was troubled by the plan to transform the hansom into a pumpkin onstage.

15. sagaciously
A *wisely.*
The critic sagaciously pointed out the faulty logic in Tara's dense first novel.

YOUR SCORE:
___ / 15

GOOD GENES

You can't pick your family, but you can at least talk about them. Here are a few familial, if sometimes unfamiliar, words to bring to the next reunion.

1. kindred
('kin-dred) *adj.*
A related by marriage.
B of the same ancestry.
C living together.

2. bairn
(bayrn) *n.*
A gap in genealogical record.
B poor relation.
C child.

3. agnate
('ag-nate) *adj.*
A related on the father's side.
B descended from royalty.
C of a child with unmarried parents.

4. sororal
(suh-'roar-ul) *adj.*
A grandmotherly.
B motherly.
C sisterly.

5. cognomen
(cog-'no-mun) *n.*
A clan emblem.
B name.
C last of the male line.

6. progeny
('proj-uh-nee) *n.*
A ancestors.
B descendants.
C extended family.

7. cousin once removed
('kuh-zen wons ri-'mooved) *n.*
A your cousin's cousin.
B your cousin's child.
C your cousin's ex-spouse.

8. nepotism
('nep-uh-tiz-um) *n.*
A marriage of first cousins.
B ninth generation.
C favoritism toward a relative.

9. congenital
(kun-'jen-uh-tul) *adj.*
A acquired in utero.
B generation-skipping.
C of a multiple birth.

10. ménage
(may-'nazh) *n.*
A marriage vow.
B household.
C golden years.

11. misopedia
(miss-oh-'pee-dee-uh or my-so-) *n.*
A hatred of children.
B middle age.
C family history.

12. pedigree
('ped-uh-gree) *n.*
A lineage.
B inheritance.
C birth announcement.

13. avuncular
(uh-'vunk-yuh-lur) *adj.*
A without cousins.
B adopted.
C like an uncle.

14. polyandry
('pah-lee-an-dree) *n.*
A having two or more husbands.
B having two or more children.
C having male and female traits.

15. kith
(kith) *n.*
A friends.
B in-laws.
C homestead.

"GOOD GENES" ANSWERS

1. kindred
B *of the same ancestry.*
Being kindred did not stop the two tribes from warring constantly.

2. bairn
C *child.*
Duncan has enjoyed playing the bagpipes ever since he was a wee bairn.

3. agnate
A *related on the father's side.*
My last name has no vowels because immigration officials misheard my agnate grandfather.

4. sororal
C *sisterly.*
After a day of refereeing sororal squabbles, the girls' mother collapsed onto the couch.

5. cognomen
B *name.*
Eugene added the cognomen "the Great" to his letterhead.

6. progeny
B *descendants.*
With seven siblings and all their spouses and progeny, we have a lot of birthdays to remember.

7. cousin once removed
B *your cousin's child.*
The university allows only two commencement guests for each graduate—what am I going to tell all my great-aunts and cousins once removed?

8. nepotism
C *favoritism toward a relative.*
When the umpire—who happened to be the base runner's dad—yelled "Safe!" the other team cried nepotism.

9. congenital
A *acquired in utero.*
Nathaniel told the gym teacher that he had a congenital heart defect just so he wouldn't have to play dodgeball.

10. ménage
B *household.*
It's not a mansion, but it's just right for our little ménage.

11. misopedia
A *hatred of children.*
W. C. Fields, who turned misopedia into comedic masterpieces, once said in a movie that yes, he loved children, "if they're properly cooked."

12. pedigree
A *lineage.*
The senator has a distinguished political pedigree, since both her father and grandfather held public office.

13. avuncular
C *like an uncle.*
The pilot's avuncular voice was reassuring to the nervous flier.

14. polyandry
A *having two or more husbands.*
Polyandry is rare in human societies, mostly because women object to picking up that many socks off the floor.

15. kith
A *friends.*
With all her kith and kin assembled, the bride got cold feet and fled the church.

YOUR SCORE:
___ / 15

KEEP IT SIMPLE

This quiz is as easy as a, b, c. All these words include those letters—in order (ignoring some repeats).

1. ambience
('am-bee-ents) *n.*
A act of listening.
B stroll.
C atmosphere.

2. diabolical
(dy-uh-'bah-lih-kuhl) *adj.*
A devilish.
B two-faced.
C acidic.

3. sabbatical
(suh-'ba-tih-kuhl) *n.*
A prayer shawl.
B strict command.
C extended leave.

4. abject
('ab-jekt) *adj.*
A lofty.
B lowly.
C central.

5. swashbuckler
('swahsh-buh-kler) *n.*
A studded belt.
B daring adventurer.
C threshing blade.

6. abacus
('a-buh-kuss) *n.*
A sundial.
B magic spell.
C ancient counting tool.

7. rambunctious
(ram-'bunk-shuss) *adj.*
A goatlike.
B unruly.
C wide-awake.

8. ambivalence
(am-'bih-vuh-lents) *n.*
A medical aid.
B contradictory feelings.
C left-handedness.

9. lambency
('lam-ben-see) *n.*
A meekness.
B desperation.
C radiance.

10. abdicate
('ab-dih-kayt) *v.*
A give up.
B start.
C decline to vote.

11. Malbec
(mal-'bek) *n.*
A coffee blend.
B French pirate.
C red wine.

12. abeyance
(uh-'bay-ents) *n.*
A following orders.
B barking.
C temporary inactivity.

13. shambolic
(sham-'bah-lik) *adj.*
A misleading.
B disorganized.
C widely shunned.

14. abscond
(ab-'skond) *v.*
A steal away.
B trip and fall.
C fail to rhyme.

15. sawbuck
('saw-buk) *n.*
A horse trainer.
B ten-dollar bill.
C tree trimmer.

"KEEP IT SIMPLE" ANSWERS

1. ambience
c *atmosphere.*
Randy's Slop House isn't much of a name, but the place actually has a nice ambience.

2. diabolical
A *devilish.*
Wile E. Coyote's diabolical schemes usually end as spectacular failures.

3. sabbatical
c *extended leave.*
Dr. Klein is taking a sabbatical this semester to finish her book.

4. abject
B *lowly.*
The sight of a spider in the bathtub made Big Joe act like an abject coward.

5. swashbuckler
B *daring adventurer.*
Robin Hood and Zorro are two famous fictional swashbucklers.

6. abacus
c *ancient counting tool.*
I couldn't do my homework because my dog ate the beads off my abacus.

7. rambunctious
B *unruly.*
Is there anything more exhausting than babysitting for a group of rambunctious 5-year-olds?

8. ambivalence
B *contradictory feelings.*
I do have some ambivalence about trapping the chipmunks in my attic.

9. lambency
c *radiance.*
By the moon's lambency, the lovers staged their secret rendezvous.

10. abdicate
A *give up.*
Having failed her accounting course, Paulina was forced to abdicate her role as class treasurer.

11. Malbec
c *red wine.*
Kendra savored a sip of Malbec then took a bite of her filet mignon.

12. abeyance
c *temporary inactivity.*
The torrential rain seems to be in abeyance, but more storms are forecast.

13. shambolic
B *disorganized.*
Kyle's bachelor pad is always in a shambolic state, with dirty socks on the floor and dishes in the sink.

14. abscond
A *steal away.*
Where's that knave who absconded with the queen's tarts?

15. sawbuck
B *ten-dollar bill.*
"In the old days, you could buy dinner and a movie for just a sawbuck," Jean grumbled as she pulled out her wallet.

YOUR SCORE:
___ / 15

WORDS TO TRAVEL BY

Before you start cramming your suitcase for that dream getaway, make sure you've got the travel lingo down. Take a tour of these terms, then jet to the next page for answers.

1. docent
('doh-sent) *n.*
A tour guide.
B side trip.
C frequent flier.

2. sojourn
('soh-jern) *v.*
A travel nonstop.
B take a guided tour.
C stay temporarily.

3. cosmopolitan
(kahz-meh-'pah-leh-tin) *adj.*
A between stops.
B worldly wise.
C of space travel.

4. prix fixe
('pree feeks or fiks) *n.*
A confirmed reservation.
B meal with a set price.
C race car.

5. couchette
(koo-'shet) *n.*
A round-trip ticket.
B French pastry.
C train's sleeping compartment.

6. funicular
(fyu-'nih-kye-ler) *n.*
A pleasure cruise.
B cable railway.
C stretch limousine.

7. jitney
('jit-nee) *n.*
A day trip.
B duty-free shop.
C small bus.

8. valise
(vuh-'lees) *n.*
A car parker.
B small suitcase.
C country cottage.

9. accommodations
(a-'ka-meh-day-shunz) *n.*
A lodging.
B travel visa.
C seating upgrade.

10. ramada
(ruh-'mah-duh) *n.*
A shelter with open sides.
B dude ranch.
C in-house maid service.

11. incidental
(in-seh-'den-tul) *adj.*
A waiting in a long line.
B minor.
C causing a scandal.

12. gallivant
('ga-le-vant) *v.*
A go by rail.
B travel for pleasure.
C go on a pilgrimage.

13. manifest
('ma-neh-fest) *n.*
A red-eye flight.
B reservation.
C passenger list.

14. rack rate
('rak rayt) *n.*
A overhead-luggage charge.
B takeoff speed.
C full price for lodging.

15. peripatetic
(per-uh-puh-'teh-tik) *adj.*
A speaking many languages.
B traveling from place to place.
C crossing a border illegally.

"WORDS TO TRAVEL BY" ANSWERS

1. docent
A *tour guide.*
I followed a docent through the museum, pretending to be with a school group.

2. sojourn
C *stay temporarily.*
Will you sojourn with us long?

3. cosmopolitan
B *worldly wise.*
Apparently, Sara wasn't cosmopolitan enough for the maître d' to seat her at the best table.

4. prix fixe
B *meal with a set price.*
Alison knew it was a prix fixe, but naturally she tried to haggle with the waiter anyway.

5. couchette
C *train's sleeping compartment.*
My couchette mates snored peacefully in their bunks.

6. funicular
B *cable railway.*
The funicular disappeared into the mist halfway up the mountain.

DOWNTIME, REDEFINED

These days, vacations come in myriad forms. A staycation is when you don't go anywhere and just enjoy free time at or near home. A paycation is when you moonlight as you travel. A daycation is a 24-hour getaway.

7. jitney
C *small bus.*
We chartered a jitney for our trip to the cape.

8. valise
B *small suitcase.*
Eric grew suspicious after finding someone else's credentials in his valise.

9. accomodations
A *lodging.*
The accomodations at the inn were not fancy but at least they were clean.

10. ramada
A *shelter with open sides.*
My ideal vacation: sipping colorful cocktails seaside under a ramada.

11. incidental
B *minor.*
Incidental items can add weight quickly, so pack wisely.

12. gallivant
B *travel for pleasure.*
Rosa has been gallivanting around Europe since her graduation.

13. manifest
C *passenger list.*
I came from such a big family, we had to keep an official manifest for every trip.

14. rack rate
C *full price for lodging.*
Savvy travelers never settle for a hotel's rack rate.

15. peripatetic
B *traveling from place to place.*
After two peripatetic years in Asia, Jason settled down.

YOUR SCORE:
___ / 15

SPACING OUT

In this cosmic vocabulary quiz , we feature words about the universe. So put on your space suit and don your thinking cap.

1. ecliptic
(ih-'klip-tik) *n.*
A a zigzag path.
B a circular path.
C the apparent path of the sun.

2. orrery
('or-er-ee) *n.*
A device that illustrates the movements of the planets.
B cluster of new stars.
C icy meteor.

3 wax (wacks) *v.*
A grow full, like the moon.
B draw together.
C give off radiation.

4. gibbous ('ji-bus, 'gi-) *adj.*
A curving.
B describing that phase of the moon when more than half is illuminated.
C traveling in a linear trajectory.

5. Polaris
(puh-'ler-us, -'la-rus) *n.*
A the evening star.
B the dog star.
C the North Star.

6. terrestrial
(tuh-'re-stree-ul, -'res-chul) *adj.*
A of the planet Earth.
B of or on the moon's surface.
C just above the visible horizon.

7. Big Dipper
(big 'di-per) *n.*
A stars in Canis Major.
B stars in Ursa Major.
C stars on Orion's belt.

8. yaw
(yaw) *v.*
A veer to the side.
B rotate on an axis.
C go into a nosedive.

9. stellar
('ste-ler) *adj.*
A vast, immense.
B of the stars.
C constantly expanding.

10. LEM
(ell ee em) *n.*
A light emitting mass.
B lunar excursion module.
C liquid engine misfire.

11. umbra ('um-brah) *n.*
A shadow caused by an eclipse.
B shield against X-rays.
C one complete orbit.

12. parsec ('par-sek) *n.*
A distance of 3.26 light-years.
B subatomic matter.
C average launching time.

13. mare (mayr) *n.*
A period of one billion years.
B dark plain on the moon.
C constellation called the Horse.

14. Kuiper belt
('kiy-per belt) *n.*
A band of stars.
B part of the Big Dipper.
C region of the solar system beyond Neptune.

15. red dwarf
(red dworf) *n.*
A nickname for Mars.
B smaller, cooler star.
C part of the Gemini constellation.

"SPACING OUT" ANSWERS

1. ecliptic
c *the apparent path of the sun.*
To spot your Zodiac constellation, look along the ecliptic.

2. orrery
A *device that illustrates the movements of the planets.*
I got my tie tangled around Neptune while spinning the orrery.

3. wax
A *grow full, like the moon.*
Finally, Nick got an answer right, and his ego waxed.

4. gibbous
B *describing that phase of the moon when more than half is illuminated.*
After one drink, Jen, like the moon, was gibbous.

5. Polaris
c *the North Star.*
Captain Jack Sparrow kept one eye on Keira Knightley and one eye on Polaris.

6. terrestrial
A *of the planet Earth.*
Whales and hippos evolved from the same terrestrial ancestor.

7. Big Dipper
B *stars in Ursa Major.*
After he walked into a pole, the stars circling Al's head resembled the Big Dipper.

8. yaw
A *veer to the side.*
After being mocked about his pointy ears, Mr. Spock put a Vulcan death grip on Mr. Sulu, causing the Enterprise to yaw.

9. stellar
B *of the stars.*
Do you know how to calculate the rate of stellar expansion?

10. LEM
B *lunar excursion module.*
Instead of flying the command module, the astronauts played poker in the LEM.

11. umbra
A *shadow caused by an eclipse.*
For some reason, the moon's umbra makes Stella bark like a dog.

12. parsec
A *distance of 3.26 light-years.*
Chewbacca joked that he wanted to eat Luke Skywalker after learning that the nearest deli was 50 parsecs away.

13. mare
B *dark plain on the moon.*
Kiki dreamed about returning to the moon with a flashlight after losing his house keys on a mare.

14. Kuiper belt
c *region of the solar system beyond Neptune.*
Many comets are formed in the Kuiper belt.

15. red dwarf
B *smaller, cooler star.*
Red dwarfs are the most plentiful type of stars in the universe.

YOUR SCORE: ___ / 15

10

Words That Are Difficult to Pronounce

SOME WORDS DON'T look the way they sound, and they don't slide smoothly off the tongue, either. Letters that sound like other letters, silent vowels and consonants, and mispronunciations we've simply accepted over the years have relegated some words to "almost impossible to say correctly" status. We've rounded up ten tricky tongue-twisters, and we've given you a guide to pronouncing them perfectly.

Colonel

SOME ENGLISH SPEAKERS know that this 16th-century word, which is derived from Middle French, is pronounced "KER-nul." However, it's easy to get confused by the first "o" sounding like an "e," the "l" that sounds like an "r," and the second "o," which is completely silent.

Isthmus

THIS TWO-SYLLABLE WORD, which is pronounced "IS-muss," refers to a narrow passage of land between two seas. It's also pretty darn confusing. Why? First off, the "th" combination doesn't even exist in some languages, which raises the difficulty level. Then, to further complicate matters, the "th" in this word is silent, so you can ignore it anyway. Still struggling? Keeping your tongue behind your teeth while speaking this word can help with pronunciation.

Scissors

YES, THIS IS A common word. However, the double consonants can make you think that it's pronounced "SKISS-ers" (when we know it's actually "SIZ-ers"). Plus it ends in an "s," which typically refers to a plural, and is called a "pair," even though it's a single instrument.

Quinoa

WHILE THE POPULARITY of this ancient grain has grown in recent years because of its superfood powers, many people still struggle with how to pronounce quinoa because of its numerous vowel blends. If you apply Standard English rules, you'd think it would be pronounced "qwin-o-ah," but it's actually a Spanish word that has numerous acceptable pronunciations, including "KEEN-wah," "ken-WAH," and even "KEN-o-ah."

Ignominious

IF SOMEONE IS despicable or dishonorable, you may call them "ig-no-MIN-ee-us." That is, if you can pronounce it properly. Despite the word's relatively short length, its five syllables—starring the letters i and o—are enough to get anyone tongue-tied.

Anemone

IF YOU'RE A FAN of *Finding Nemo*, you might remember the scene where Mr. Ray asks Nemo what type of home he lives in. Nemo's answer: "An anemonemone. Amnemonemomne." It's not surprising that even little Nemo trips over his own wildflower habitat. The vowel-heavy word looks as if it should rhyme with "tone" or "bone" and be pronounced "an-e-MOAN" or "AYN-moan," but it's actually a four-syllable word pronounced "ah-NEM-oh-nee."

Worcestershire

IT LOOKS AS IF it should be pronounced "wor-cest-er-shi-er," but it is really pronounced "WOOs-ter-sher." Worcestershire sauce originated in the town of Worcester, England, pronounced "Wooster." The term "shire" is the British word for "county," and sounds like the ending of "Hampshire."

Mischievous

LIKE "WORCESTERSHIRE," "mischievous" is one of those challenging words that many people have trouble pronouncing. In fact, you've probably heard people pronouncing the word as "mis-CHEEVE-ee-us," when it's actually a three-syllable word pronounced "MIS-chiv-us." The problem possibly lies in the fact that the old form of the word was spelled with an extra "i" at the end, which was standard until the 1700s.

Draught

THIS BRITISH WORD has a double irregularity: first with the "a-u" vowel combination and then again with the "g-h-t" consonant blend. While it looks as if it might be pronounced "drot," it's actually pronounced "draft," (like the word "laugh"), and it usually refers to an alcoholic beverage drawn from a keg.

Otorhinolaryngologist

THIS IS THE TERM given to an ear, nose, and throat doctor, and is probably one of the most difficult-to-pronounce medical specialties in the entire history of humankind. What makes it so tricky? Well, aside from the silent "h" and the irregular use of the consonant "y," the word has 21 letters and eight—yes, count 'em, eight—syllables. So if you have problems using the formal pronunciation, which is "oh-toh-rye-no-lar-ing-GOL-uh-jist," you can just refer to the doc by her more informal title: an ENT.

YIDDISH FUN

Words should be weighed, not counted, goes the Yiddish proverb. Of the thousands of words English has borrowed from other languages, Yiddish loanwords are perhaps the weightiest.

1. kvetch
(kvech) *v.*
A cook.
B complain.
C boast.

2. chutzpah
('hoot-spuh) *n.*
A sudden attack.
B filled crepe.
C gall.

3. yenta
('yen-ta) *n.*
A busybody.
B matchmaker.
C rabbi's wife.

4. plotz
(plots) *v.*
A measure.
B figure out.
C collapse.

5. meshuga
(muh-'shoog-uh) *adj.*
A worthless.
B too sweet.
C daffy.

6. nebbish
('neb-ish) *n.*
A elegantly dressed man.
B milquetoast.
C smart aleck.

7. tchotchke
('chach-kuh) *n.*
A folk dance.
B bad memory.
C knickknack.

8. schnorrer
('shnor-ur) *n.*
A loud sleeper.
B moocher.
C ladies' man.

9. oy vey
('oy 'vay) *interj.*
A Happy birthday!
B Hip hip hooray!
C Oh, woe!

10. mensch
(mench) *n.*
A coward.
B honorable person.
C ne'er-do-well.

11. schlep
(shlep) *v.*
A haul.
B insult.
C weep.

12. nudnik
('nood-nik) *n.*
A first-year student.
B bumpkin.
C bore.

13. bubkes
('bup-cuss) *n.*
A stroke of luck.
B nothing.
C term of endearment.

14. shamus
('shah-mus or 'shay-) *n.*
A detective.
B hoax.
C free-for-all.

15. mazel tov
('mah-zul 'tov) *interj.*
A Sorry, my bad!
B Welcome home!
C Best wishes!

"YIDDISH FUN" ANSWERS

1. kvetch
B *complain.*
If Bernice kvetched about her friends less, she might have more of them.

2. chutzpah
C *gall.*
After jumping the light, the other driver had the chutzpah to blame me for the accident.

3. yenta
A *busybody.*
The office romance provided irresistible fodder for the watercooler yentas.

4. plotz
C *collapse.*
When my mom sees my report card, she'll plotz.

5. meshuga
C *daffy.*
My meshuga neighbor has dressed his garden gnomes in flak jackets.

6. nebbish
B *milquetoast.*
A nebbish in an ill-fitting suit, the accountant nervously said "excuse me" to the coworker blocking the fax machine.

7. tchotchke
C *knickknack.*
Among the yard sale tchotchkes, there it was: Punchers the Lobster, one of the original Beanie Babies.

8. schnorrer
B *moocher.*
That schnorrer Artie always forgets his wallet when we dine out.

9. oy vey
C *Oh, woe!*
Dad got out of the car, looked at the flat tire, and said, "Oy vey!"

10. mensch
B *honorable person.*
The mayor is a mensch—respected even by those who disagree with him.

11. schlep
A *haul.*
Lois schlepped the newspapers to the recycling center, realizing much later that she'd tossed her husband's prize baseball card collection.

12. nudnik
C *bore.*
Don't look now, but here comes that nudnik from the IT department.

13. bubkes
B *nothing.*
They went to Vegas with a bundle and came back with bubkes.

14. shamus
A *detective.*
You don't have to be a shamus to figure out that the e-mail is a scam.

15. mazel tov
C *Best wishes!*
You got the job? Mazel tov!

YOUR SCORE:
___ / 15

PERCHANCE TO DREAM

If your bed is calling you, snuggle up with this relaxing quiz
on sleep-related terms. Answers on next page.

1. somniloquist
(sahm-'ni-luh-kwist) *n.*
A sleep talker.
B loud snorer.
C story reader.

2. eiderdown
('i-der-down) *n.*
A hotel turndown
   service.
B organic sleeping pill.
C duck-feather-filled
   comforter.

3. hypnopompic
(hip-nih-'pahm-pik) *adj.*
A brought about by
   hypnosis.
B prewaking.
C coma-like.

4. pandiculation
(pan-di-kyu-'lay-shun) *n.*
A undressing.
B closing one's eyes.
C stretching.

5. tenebrous
('te-ni-bris) *adj.*
A dark.
B prone to
   sleeplessness.
C exhausted.

6. torpor
('tor-per) *n.* a state of ...
A sluggishness.
B wakefulness.
C reverie.

7. quiescent
(kwiy-'e-sent, kwee-) *adj.*
A at rest.
B lacking sleep.
C silent.

8. bruxism
('bruk-si-zem) *n.*
A sudden waking.
B teeth grinding.
C bed-wetting.

9. coverlet
('kuh-ver-let) *n.*
A bathrobe for royalty.
B sleeping mask.
C bedspread.

10. negligee
(ne-gli-'zhay,'ne-gli-zhay) *n.*
A sleep attire
   sometimes worn
   by women.
B someone who ignores
   the need for sleep.
C extra-plush slippers.

11. soporific
(sah-pa-'ri-fik) *adj.*
A sleep-inducing.
B nightmarish.
C restless.

12. REM sleep
(rem sleep) *n.* stage of sleep
during which...
A you're most likely to
   dream.
B sleep is the deepest.
C you're least likely to
   dream.

13. siesta
(see-'e-stuh) *n.*
A mug for warm milk.
B afternoon nap.
C Spanish lullaby.

14. boudoir
('boo-dwar, boo-'dwar) *n.*
A woman's bedroom.
B four-poster bed.
C decorative pillow.

15. davenport
('da-ven-port) *n.*
A fuzzy nightcap.
B pullout sofa.
C pleasant daydream.

"PERCHANCE TO DREAM" ANSWERS

1. somniloquist
A *sleep talker.*
A somniloquist's spouse never lacks for nighttime conversation.

2. eiderdown
C *duck-feather-filled comforter.*
Noting the bed's fluffy eiderdown, Josie anticipated a cozy night.

3. hypnopompic
B *prewaking.*
After watching *Monday Night Football*, the students floated into class the next morning in a hypnopompic state.

4. pandiculation
C *stretching.*
Frank's lengthy yawn and pandiculation gave

NUMBING SLEEP

The Greek *nárkē*, meaning "numbness," is the basis (along with *lêpsis*, "seizure") for "narcolepsy," a disorder characterized by uncontrollable spells of sleep. It's also at the root of "narcotic," a drug that can induce sleep or produce a dull, pain-free (sleeplike) condition.

---

his dinner guests the hint to call it a night.

5. tenebrous
A *dark.*
Donna groped for the light switch in the tenebrous room.

6. torpor
A *state of sluggishness.*
After playing in the sun all morning, John lazed about in a torpor.

7. quiescent
A *at rest.*
The rowdy kids were finally quiescent after the TV was switched on.

8. bruxism
B *teeth grinding.*
Kyla's bruxism sounded like a chain saw.

9. coverlet
C *bedspread.*
Stephanie chose a bright purple coverlet to match the room's decor.

10. negligee
A *sleep attire sometimes worn by women.*
Lisa donned her negligee and waited for her groom in the honeymoon suite.

11. soporific
A *sleep-inducing.*
The soporific play caused many audience members to get coffee during intermission.

12. REM sleep
A *stage of sleep during which you're most likely to dream. (REM is short for "rapid eye movement," characteristic of this stage).*
Waking suddenly from her REM sleep, Jesse could recall her dream in perfect detail.

13. siesta
B *afternoon nap.*
Rob lay down for a post-lunch siesta.

14. boudoir
A *woman's bedroom.*
Sonja relaxed in her lavender-scented boudoir.

15. davenport
B *pullout sofa.*
Cormac's guest slept on the davenport.

YOUR SCORE:
___ / 15

MEASURING UP

We're counting on you to figure out these useful words about numbers, amounts, and measurements. Having trouble putting 2 and 2 together? Turn the page for answers.

1. fourscore
('fohr-skohr) *adj.*
A sixteen.
B forty.
C eighty.

2. tabulate
('ta-byuh-layt) *v.*
A rank by weight and height.
B count or arrange systematically.
C indent a column.

3. copious
('coh-pee-uhss) *adj.*
A plentiful.
B scanty.
C carefully reproduced.

4. gross
(grohss) *n.*
A 12 dozen.
B 51 percent.
C two bushels.

5. aggregate
('a-grih-get) *adj.*
A increasing exponentially.
B amounting to a whole.
C left over as a fraction.

6. googol
('goo-gaul) *n.*
A negative number.
B value of pi.
C 1 followed by 100 zeros.

7. paucity
('paw-sih-tee) *n.*
A overabundance.
B shortage.
C average.

8. myriad
('meer-ee-uhd) *adj.*
A very heavy.
B immeasurably small.
C countless.

9. troika
('troy-kuh) *n.*
A numbered wheel.
B group of three.
C ancient calculator.

10. calibrate
('ka-luh-brayt) *v.*
A adjust according to a standard.
B divide into equal parts.
C gain heat.

11. manifold
('man-uh-fold) *adj.*
A diverse.
B dwindling.
C doubled.

12. quota
('kwoh-tuh) *n.*
A estimated profit.
B bottom line.
C preset amount.

13. brace
(brayss) *n.*
A pair.
B trio.
C quartet.

14. binary
('by-ne-ree, ner-ee) *adj.*
A consisting of two parts.
B opposite.
C in equal proportion.

15. cubed
(kyoobd) *adj.*
A tripled.
B cut into thirds.
C multiplied by itself twice.

"MEASURING UP" ANSWERS

1. fourscore
c *eighty.*
That's the strangest thing I've heard in all my fourscore years.

2. tabulate
B *count or arrange systematically.*
The committee has tabulated the votes.

3. copious
A *plentiful.*
Harriet's notes from history class are copious but illegible.

4. gross
A *12 dozen.*
How many gross of cupcakes did you order for the party?

5. aggregate
B *amounting to a whole.*
Analysts are expecting the aggregate demand for electric cars to skyrocket.

6. googol
c *1 followed by 100 zeros.*
Emile's chances of dating Jacqueline are about one in a googol.

7. paucity
B *shortage.*
Given the paucity of

THE NAME IS DEEP

When the young writer Samuel Clemens worked as a Mississippi riverboat pilot, he surely saw crewmen sounding the river—measuring its depth—with the call "mark twain!" This meant they had measured two fathoms; a single fathom is six feet, and twain means "two." Clemens first used the byline Mark Twain in 1863, as a Nevada newspaper reporter.

evidence against the murder suspect, the detective let her go.

8. myriad
c *countless.*
Brooke ate myriad pumpkin-spice-flavored products this fall.

9. troika
B *group of three.*
In my opinion, Larry, Curly, and Moe are a troika of numbskulls.

10. calibrate
A *adjust according to a standard.*
The post office calibrates its scale each morning before opening for business.

11. manifold
A *diverse.*
There are manifold reasons why Cory's time machine experiment failed.

12. quota
c *preset amount.*
Are you saying one cookie is my quota?

13. brace
A *pair.*
We just adopted a brace of puppies, so it's kind of crazy around our house.

14. binary
A *consisting of two parts.*
A binary star is really two stars that revolve around each other.

15. cubed
c *multiplied by itself twice.*
Three cubed is 27, the last time I checked.

YOUR SCORE:
___ / 15

GETTING UP TO SPEED

No hurry—take your time ambling through
this quiz on words about matters both slow and fast.

1. precipitate
(pri-'si-pe-tayt) *adj.*
A gradual.
B inert.
C rash, hasty.

2. lethargic
(le-'thar-jik) *adj.*
A sluggish.
B streamlined.
C explosive.

3. drogue
(drohg) *n.*
A open speedboat.
B booster rocket.
C canvas parachute to
   slow a ship or plane.

4. tardigrade
('tar-de-grayd) *adj.*
A restrained.
B rushed.
C slow in pace.

5. velodrome
('vee- or 'veh- or 'vay-leh-
drohm) *n.*
A nuclear accelerator.
B track for cycling.
C air-speed recorder.

6. paso doble
('pah-soh 'doh-blay) *n.*
A quick march played
   at bullfights.
B shooting star.
C time-lapse motion.

7. dispatch
(di-'spatch or 'di-spatch) *n.*
A promptness or
   efficiency.
B postponement.
C impass.

8. baud
(bahd) *n. unit of ...*
A film speed.
B data transmission
   speed.
C nautical speed.

9. hang fire
(hang fyr) *v.*
A delay.
B blast off.
C streak across the sky.

10. alacrity
(uh-'lak-kre-tee) *n.*
A ignition.
B cheerful readiness.
C pause before firing.

11. tout de suite
(toot swyeet) *adv.*
A immediately.
B at a given signal.
C not in time.

12. adagio
(ah-'dah-jee-oh or -zhee-oh) *adv.*
A fast.
B without stopping.
C at a slow tempo.

13. race runner
(rays 'ruh-ner) *n.*
A red fox.
B pronghorn antelope.
C North American
   lizard.

14. celerity
(seh-'ler-eh-tee) *n.*
A gear shift.
B rapidity of motion.
C snowballing effect.

15. catalytic
(ka-teh-'li-tik) *adj.*
A causing a slowdown.
B relating to an
   increase in a
   chemical reaction.
C precisely timed.

"GETTING UP TO SPEED" ANSWERS

1. precipitate
c *rash, hasty.*
The hare made the precipitate decision to catch some z's during the race.

2. lethargic
A *sluggish.*
After a full 24 hours of travel, I am feeling extremely lethargic.

3. drogue
c *canvas parachute to slow a ship or plane.*
"You're like a drogue on a rocket. Move it!" shouted the driver.

4. tardigrade
c *slow in pace.*
The tortoise took great pride in his tardigrade gait.

5. velodrome
B *track for cycling.*
Ever the biking enthusiast, Pete enjoyed training at the local velodrome.

6. paso doble
A *quick march played at bullfights.*
The bullfighter grew anxious as the paso doble played before his debut.

7. dispatch
A *promptness or efficiency.*
After clearing out the safe, the thief left the bank with dispatch.

8. baud
B *unit of data transmission speed.*
"Mom, I could hand-deliver this message faster than your 300-baud dinosaur of a modem!"

9. hang fire
A *delay.*
The driver beckoned, but we were hanging fire at the stage door, hoping for an autograph.

10. alacrity
B *cheerful readiness.*
When Jo's brownies came out of the oven, the lazy twins suddenly moved with alacrity.

11. tout de suite
A *immediately.*
The twins' older brother was on his feet tout de suite as the aroma wafted into his room.

12. adagio
c *at a slow tempo.*
Either that violinist doesn't know adagio from allegro, or he can't keep time.

13. race runner
c *North American lizard.*
I never saw Grandma Simmons as animated as the day our race runner escaped in her house.

14. celerity
B *rapidity of motion.*
If a skunk stamps its feet and hisses, it's time to depart with celerity. Obviously, Grace's dog didn't know this.

15. catalytic
B *relating to an increase in a chemical reaction.*
To see a catalytic reaction, apply a lit match to Gary's shoe from behind.

YOUR SCORE:
___ / 15

TOOL TIME

Do you know your adze from your auger? And what exactly is a grommet? Sharpen your verbal edge by mastering these words related to construction and tools, then check the shed—or the next page—for answers.

1. calipers
('ka-le-perz) *n.*
A scissors.
B tool to measure thickness.
C waterproofing tool.

2. vise
(viys) *n.*
A clamp that holds an object in place.
B mechanism to lift a car.
C flaw in building materials.

3. adze (adz) *n.*
A ax-like tool with a curved blade.
B small rubber mallet.
C piece of scrap wood.

4. flanged
(flanjd) *adj.*
A sealed with wax.
B with a protruding rim.
C wound tightly.

5. gauge (gayj) *n.*
A deep groove.
B plumber's wrench.
C measuring instrument.

6. auger
('ah-ger) *n.*
A master woodworker.
B spiral drill bit.
C sailor's knife.

7. dowel
(dowl) *n.*
A toilet plunger.
B peg.
C paint roller.

8. ferrule
('ferr-uhl) *n.*
A beveled edge.
B tape measure.
C protective cap.

9. cambered
('kam-berd) *adj.*
A encircled.
B arched.
C stained.

10. torque
(tork) *n.*
A twisting force.
B mechanical failure.
C electrical current.

11. loupe
(loop) *n.*
A cutter.
B gripper.
C magnifier.

12. awl
(all) *n.*
A pointed tool for piercing holes.
B large wheelbarrow.
C system of pulleys.

13. casters
('kass-terz) *n.*
A swiveling wheels.
B ball bearings.
C fishing reels.

14. grommet
('grah-meht) *n.*
A ring that reinforces.
B copper pipe.
C gutter.

15. kludge
(klooj) *n.*
A blueprint.
B makeshift solution.
C tangled wire.

"TOOL TIME" ANSWERS

1. serrated
B *toothed like a saw.*
The fiery dragon's back was serrated, its claws razor-sharp.

2. vise
A *clamp that holds an object in place.*
Before sanding the board, Louisa secured it in a vise.

3. adze
A *ax-like tool with a curved blade.*
Adzes have been used to shape wood since the Stone Age.

4. flanged
B *with a protruding rim.*
Bobby's model train has flanged wheels to keep it on the tracks.

5. gauge
C *measuring instrument.*
Christine built a rain gauge in her yard.

6. auger
B *spiral drill bit.*
In the winter months, anglers use augers to bore holes in the ice.

7. dowel
B *peg.*
Ethan decided to construct the birdhouse using wooden dowels instead of nails.

8. ferrule
C *protective cap.*
Your hatchet's handle wouldn't have split if you'd braced it with a ferrule.

9. cambered
B *arched.*
The highway is cambered in the middle to promote runoff of rain.

10. torque
A *twisting force.*
If you use the wrong torque setting on your drill, you could strip the screws.

11. loupe
C *magnifier.*
After examining the antique ring with his loupe, the appraiser determined the stone was glass.

12. awl
A *pointed tool for piercing holes.*
Jerry used an awl to poke through the tough leather.

13. casters
A *swiveling wheels.*
The heavy-duty casters on the dolly helped make the move easier.

14. grommet
A *ring that reinforces.*
Ashley installed custom grommets on the shower curtain.

15. kludge
B *makeshift solution.*
I've patched together some of these cables; it's a bit of a kludge, but it just might work!

QUICK FIXES

"Jury-rigged" and "jerry-built" both mean "hastily constructed." But jury-rigged suggests a clever makeshift, perhaps deriving from the Latin *adjutare* ("to aid") or the French *jour* ("day"), suggesting a short-term fix. Jerry-built, however, implies a shoddy job, though no one's quite sure who Jerry was.

YOUR SCORE:
___ / 15

COMPLIMENTS AND INSULTS

In search of a kind word—or perhaps the perfect put-down?
Before you start doling out compliments or throwing stones,
take this quiz to brush up on words of esteem and contempt.
We won't be offended if you check the next page for answers..

1. Adonis
(uh-'dah-niss) *n.*
A handsome man.
B star player.
c evil witch.

2. windbag
('wind-bag) *n.*
A sneaky thief.
B unwelcome visitor.
c motormouth.

3. impeccable
(im-'peck-uh-bull) *adj.*
A flawless.
B unruly.
c charming.

4. adroit
(uh-'droyt) *adj.*
A idiotic.
B vulgar.
c masterful.

5. churl
(cherl) *n.*
A ill-bred person.
B friend to many.
c lazybones.

6. magnanimous
(mag-'nan-ih-muss) *adj.*
A coarse.
B self-centered.
c big-hearted.

7. poltroon
(pahl-'troon) *n.*
A criminal.
B fool.
c coward.

8. nonpareil
(non-puh-'rel) *adj.*
A unequaled.
B useless.
c sweet.

9. braggadocio
(brag-uh-'doh-see-oh) *n.*
A arrogant boaster.
B womanizer.
c conquering hero.

10. debonair
(de-be-'nayr) *adj.*
A playful.
B suave.
c childish.

11. cheapskate
('cheep-skayt) *n.*
A skilled bargainer.
B stingy person.
c sloppy dresser.

12. kibitzer
('kih-bit-ser) *n.*
A misfit.
B meddler.
c nitpicker.

13. smarmy
('smar-mee) *adj.*
A insincerely earnest.
B well dressed.
c inadequate.

14. contumely
(kon-'too-muh-lee) *n.*
A arrogant rudeness.
B ravishing beauty.
c scrumptious meal.

15. brick
(brik) *n.*
A careless person.
B reliable person.
c pigheaded person.

"COMPLIMENTS AND INSULTS" ANSWERS

1. Adonis
A *handsome man.*
Arya has fallen hard for a blue-eyed Adonis at the gym.

2. windbag
c *motormouth.*
Please don't seat me next to that windbag; he'll talk my ear off.

3. impeccable
A *flawless.*
After an impeccable performance on the balance beam, Jada got a perfect score.

4. adroit
c *masterful.*
Harry Houdini was an adroit escape artist.

5. churl
A *ill-bred person.*
Remove your elbows from the table, you churl!

6. magnanimous
c *big-hearted.*
The magnanimous dentist treated needy patients for free.

7. poltroon
c *coward.*
You're all poltroons, scared of your own shadows.

A BURN FROM THE BARD

Shakespeare was a master of colorful insults. One of his most scathing comes when Prince Henry slams Falstaff in *Henry IV:* "That trunk of humours, that bolting-hutch of beastliness, that swollen parcel of dropsies, that huge bombard of sack, that stuffed cloak-bag of guts, that roasted Manningtree ox with the pudding in his belly, that reverend vice, that gray iniquity, that father ruffian, that vanity in years?"

8. nonpareil
A *unequaled.*
Luca's baking skills are nonpareil—his cakes are too beautiful to eat.

9. braggadocio
A *arrogant boaster.*
Kate's boyfriend is a braggadocio who loves talking about his car.

10. debonair
B *suave.*
Witty and debonair, Pablo speaks three languages.

11. cheapskate
B *stingy person.*
Does reusing coffee filters make me a cheapskate?

12. kibitzer
B *meddler.*
"Maybe I'm just being a kibitzer, but I do think you should wear your blue dress instead of the red," Mom said.

13. smarmy
A *insincerely earnest.*
The heiress was wooed by smarmy suitors interested only in her money.

14. contumely
A *arrogant rudeness.*
I don't know how much more of your contumely I can take.

15. brick
B *reliable person.*
My best friend has been an absolute brick during my illness.

YOUR SCORE:
___ / 15

SIGN LANGUAGE

Signs and symbols, our human shorthand, are all around us. And if you take the word of philosopher Charles Sanders Peirce, "We think only in signs." See how many you can think of. For answers, turn the page.

1. ampersand
(ˈam-pur-sand) *n.*
A the @ sign.
B the & sign.
C the # sign.

2. totem
(ˈto-tem) *n.*
A signpost.
B emblem.
C figure of speech.

3. cachet
(ka-ˈshay) *n.*
A white flag of surrender.
B smoke signal.
C stamp of approval.

4. shibboleth
(ˈshih-ba-leth) *n.*
A figure burned in effigy.
B watchword.
C forbidden language.

5. stigma
(ˈstig-muh) *n.*
A religious rune.
B mark of disgrace.
C hieroglyph.

6. vaticinate
(ve-ˈti-suh-nayt) *v.*
A foretell.
B serve as a badge or insignia.
C break a code.

7. Ameslan
(ˈam-us-lan or ˈam-slan) *n.*
A American Sign Language.
B inventor of Braille.
C symbolic lion.

8. fusee
(fyoo-ˈzee) *n.*
A the % sign.
B warning flare.
C military tattoo.

9. logotype
(ˈlog-uh-type) *n.*
A company emblem.
B ship captain's mark.
C condensed message.

10. beck
(bek) *n.*
A design on a bottle cap.
B graffiti artist's signature.
C gesture.

11. tocsin
(ˈtock-sun) *n.*
A alarm bell.
B trumpet fanfare.
C symbol for poison.

12. auspicious
(aw-ˈspih-shus) *adj.*
A favorable.
B cryptic.
C bearing a signature.

13. diaphone
(ˈdye-uh-fone) *n.*
A directional blinker.
B signal amplifier.
C two-note foghorn.

14. metaphorical
(me-ti-ˈfor-i-kul) *adj.*
A nonverbal.
B figurative.
C enciphered.

15. colophon
(ˈka-luh-fen) *n.*
A symbol for aluminum.
B identifying mark for a printer or publisher.
C cloverleaf symbol.

"SIGN LANGUAGE" ANSWERS

1. ampersand
B *the & sign.*
The pop diva uses an ampersand in her name—R&i—but her mother still calls her Randi.

2. totem
B *emblem.*
That's Stanley, the pencil pusher in cubicle 2S-013; his personal totem is a hamster.

3. cachet
C *stamp of approval.*
The fact that he was voted Most Popular by the senior class carried no cachet in the computer club.

4. shibboleth
B *watchword.*
Shelley showed up in a wool-blend sweater, not knowing that "pashmina" was the fashion shibboleth.

5. stigma
B *mark of disgrace.*
Botching the final question in Trivial Pursuit was a stigma she continued to bear at every family gathering.

6. vaticinate
A *foretell.*
Seeing his shadow, Punxsutawney Phil vaticinates six more weeks of shoveling snow and scraping windshields.

7. Ameslan
A *American Sign Language.*
This bar band is so loud, you have to use Ameslan to converse.

8. fusee
B *warning flare.*
Rodney is a safety nut; he once set out fusees when his bike got a flat.

9. logotype
A *company emblem.*
The hippie turned business executive likes to say that the Mercedes logotype is actually the peace symbol.

10. beck
C *gesture.*
With a sidelong glance and a shy little beck, Yvette lured me toward the candy store.

11. tocsin
A *alarm bell.*
Though he's been retired from the fire department for more than 20 years, Uncle Al throws on a coat and slides down the banister whenever he hears a tocsin.

12. auspicious
A *favorable.*
I thought a Valentine's Day wedding would be auspicious.

13. diaphone
C *two-note foghorn.*
My brother-in-law thinks he's Enrico Caruso, but he sings like a diaphone.

14. metaphorical
B *figurative.*
"When I said, 'Break a leg,' I was being metaphorical," the coach told the skier after the slalom.

15. colophon
B *identifying mark used by a printer or publisher.*
Simon & Schuster's colophon is a man sowing seeds.

YOUR SCORE:
___ / 15

WALTZING THROUGH LIFE

Here we premiere an eclectic medley of musical terms—some classical, some modern, and some slangy. If you're missing a few beats, waltz over to the next page for answers.

1. clam
(klam) *n.*
A silent measure.
B wrong note.
C set of maracas.

2. legato
(lih-'gah-toh) *adv.*
A smoothly.
B quickly.
C loudly.

3. woodshed
('wood-shehd) *v.*
A serenade.
B drum loudly.
C practice an instrument.

4. busk
(busk) *v.*
A sing baritone.
B work as an accompanist.
C play for donations.

5. ska
(skah) *n.*
A hip-hop club.
B microphone stand.
C Jamaican music.

6. nonet
(noh-'net) *n.*
A ditty for kids.
B composition for nine voices.
C unrehearsed performance.

7. pipes (piyps) *n.*
A singing voice.
B tuba mouthpieces.
C emcees.

8. da capo
(dah 'kah-poh) *adv.*
A from the top.
B up-tempo.
C raised a half step.

9. beatboxer
('beet-bok-ser) *n.*
A band competition.
B vocal percussionist.
C instrument case.

10. hook
(hook) *n.*
A stolen lyric.
B saxophone line.
C catchy musical phrase.

11. tonic ('tah-nik) *n.*
A first tone of a scale.
B counterpoint.
C harmony.

12. noodle
('noo-duhl) *v.*
A change key.
B croon.
C improvise casually.

13. barrelhouse
('bear-el-hous) *n.*
A bass trombone.
B rhythmic style of jazz.
C drumroll.

14. skiffle
('skih-ful) *n.*
A swing step.
B music played on rudimentary instruments.
C fast tempo.

15. earworm
('eer-wurm) *n.*
A bassoon.
B tune that repeats in one's head.
C power chord.

"WALTZING THROUGH LIFE" ANSWERS

1. clam
B *wrong note.*
Emmett's violin solo was going wonderfully—until he hit a clam.

2. legato
A *smoothly.*
Lullabies should always be sung legato.

3. woodshed
c *practice an instrument.*
To make it to Carnegie Hall, Lydia needs to woodshed a lot more.

4. busk
c *play for donations.*
I'm between gigs right now, unless you count busking in the park.

5. ska
c *Jamaican music.*
Blake's ska band is holding open auditions this weekend.

6. nonet
B *composition for nine voices.*
Our baseball team is also a singing group; we perform only nonets!

7. pipes
A *singing voice.*
Who knew Brandon had such great pipes?

8. da capo
A *from the top.*
Even though the score already said da capo, the bandleader enjoyed bellowing, "Take it from the top!"

9. beatboxer
B *vocal percussionist.*
Marina is such an amazing beatboxer that you'd swear there was a drummer in the room.

10. hook
c *catchy musical phrase.*
The Beatles had a knack for melodic hooks.

11. tonic
A *first tone of a scale.*
"This concerto is in C major, so the tonic is C," the professor explained.

12. noodle
c *improvise casually.*
I was just noodling around on my guitar when I wrote this riff.

13. barrelhouse
B *rhythmic style of jazz.*
Cynthia played an old barrelhouse tune on the piano.

14. skiffle
B *music played on rudimentary instruments.*
Our family skiffle band features Mom on kazoo, Dad on washboard, and Uncle John on slide whistle.

15. earworm
B *tune that repeats in one's head.*
That TV jingle has become my latest earworm, and it's driving me crazy!

YOUR SCORE:
___ / 15

SING, SING, SING

Many vocal terms have their roots in the Latin verb *cantare* ("to sing"). Cantatas are pieces for singers, and *bel canto* (literally "beautiful singing" in Italian) is operatic singing. A chanson is a cabaret song, and its female singer is a chanteuse. Chants and incantations are often sung. And a long poem, whether recited or sung, may be divided into cantos.

WHOPPERS

Long words may be tricky to pronounce, but they're a great way to impress friends—or a date! These entries have at least five syllables. If they prove incomprehensible, turn the page for answers.

1. contemporary
(kon-'tem-puh-rayr-ee) *adj.*
A fleeting.
B thoughtful.
C modern.

2. insurrectionist
(in-suh-'reck-shuh-nist) *n.*
A mechanic.
B nomad.
C rebel.

3. extracurricular
(ek-struh-kuh-'rik-yuh-ler) *adj.*
A athletically inclined.
B left over.
C outside the usual course.

4. conviviality
(cun-vih-vee-'al-uh-tee) *n.*
A sleight of hand.
B merriment.
C complexity.

5. transmogrification
(tranz-mah-grih-fih-'kay-shun) *n.*
A hypnotism.
B change in form.
C sea crossing.

6. triskaidekaphobia
(tris-ky-deh-kuh-'foh-bee-uh) *n.*
A dread of magicians.
B hatred of cats.
C fear of the number 13.

7. disingenuous
(dis-in-'jen-yoo-us) *adj.*
A out of order.
B insincere.
C silent.

8. verisimilitude
(ver-uh-suh-'mih-luh-tood) *n.*
A large crowd.
B quality of seeming real.
C dizzy spell.

9. impenetrable
(im-'peh-nuh-truh-bull) *adj.*
A anxious.
B impossible to enter.
C affected by the moon.

10. superannuated
(soo-per-'an-yoo-way-ted) *adj.*
A prorated.
B outdated.
C distorted.

11. pharmacology
(far-muh-'kah-luh-jee) *n.*
A science of drugs.
B farming technique.
C study of insects.

12. heterogeneous
(heh-tuh-ruh-'jee-nee-us) *adj.*
A masculine.
B about clergy.
C diverse.

13. paraphernalia
(payr-uh-fur-'nayl-yuh) *n.*
A assorted gear.
B cranium.
C cross-stitch.

14. phantasmagoria
(fan-taz-muh-'gor-ee-uh) *n.*
A dreamlike scene.
B belief in ghosts.
C mime show.

15. idiosyncrasy
(ih-dee-uh-'sin-kruh-see) *n.*
A quirk.
B perfect timing.
C greed.

"WHOPPERS" ANSWERS

1. contemporary
c *modern.*
Joe likes contemporary art best.

2. insurrectionist
c *rebel.*
The insurrectionists overthrew the corrupt government.

3. extracurricular
c *outside the usual course.*
Troy has a variety of extracurricular interests.

4. conviviality
B *merriment.*
The village tavern is a place of conviviality.

5. transmogrification
B *change in form.*
How do you explain the transmogrification of the prince into a beast?

6. triskaidekaphobia
c *fear of the number 13.*
Many hotels go from floor 12 to 14, a nod to guests with triskaidekaphobia.

7. disingenuous
B *insincere.*
Angela's disingenuous

WORDS BY THE FOOT

The Roman poet Horace advised younger writers to avoid *sesquipedalia verba*, or "words a foot and a half long." That turn of phrase gave us a modern supersize term to describe words with a ton of syllables: sesquipedalian . Its Latin prefix *sesqui-* means "one and a half times," and *ped-* means "foot."

---

apology didn't make me feel any better.

8. verisimilitude
B *quality of seeming real.*
Archaeologists say *The Flintstones* has little historical verisimilitude.

9. impenetrable
B *impossible to enter.*
The tech department is working to make our server impenetrable to hackers.

10. superannuated
B *outdated.*
"I simply can't teach science with these superannuated textbooks!" Mr. Sanchez complained.

11. pharmacology
A *science of drugs.*
Pharmacology experts haven't tested the new drug's effectiveness in children.

12. heterogeneous
c *diverse.*
Home to millions of species, the Amazon rain forest is one of Earth's most heterogeneous places.

13. paraphernalia
A *assorted gear.*
We'll need balloons, candles, and other party paraphernalia for the birthday bash.

14. phantasmagoria
A *dreamlike scene.*
"I Am the Walrus" is a phantasmagoria of sound and imagery.

15. idiosyncrasy
A *quirk.*
Don't be boring— embrace your idiosyncrasies!

YOUR SCORE:
___ / 15

MASH-UPS

From brunch (breakfast + lunch) to Wi-Fi (wireless + fidelity), today's English language is full of hybrid words. Other examples include sitcom and Muppet, as well as those below.

1. motorcade
('moh-ter-kayd) *n.*
A breakdown.
B automatic response.
C procession of vehicles.
_____

2. radome
('ray-dohm) *n.*
A salad vegetable.
B antenna housing.
C all-night party.
_____

3. smog
(smahg) *n.*
A archaeologist.
B polluted fog.
C screen pixels.
_____

4. slurve
(slurv) *n.*
A ice-cream drink.
B automobile stunt.
C baseball pitch.
_____

5. telegenic
('te-li-je-nik) *adj.*
A suitable manner and appearance for TV.
B having ESP.
C born on foreign soil.

6. meld
(meld) *v.*
A liquefy.
B combine.
C harden with age.
_____

7. bodacious
(boh-'dey-shus) *adj.*
A remarkable.
B interfering.
C part human, part machine.
_____

8. chillax
(chi-'laks) *v.*
A ice fish.
B calm down.
C rudely insult.
_____

9. agitprop
('ah-jit-prop) *n.*
A political hype.
B building support.
C crowd control.
_____

10. bromance
('bro-mans) *n.*
A fraternity dwelling.
B gaseous element.
C close male friendship.

11. liger
('liy-ger) *n.*
A liquid measure.
B midnight snack.
C big cat.
_____

12. frenemy
('fre-nuh-mee) *n.*
A false friend.
B opposition army.
C frantic movement.
_____

13. Frankenfood
('fran-ken-food) *n.*
A dangerous eats.
B genetically engineered food.
C fusion cuisine.
_____

14. mockumentary
(mok-yoo-'men-tah-ree) *n.*
A simulated-trial manual.
B placebo.
C satirical film style.
_____

15. sysop
('siys-op) *n.*
A online administrator.
B photo shoot.
C music overdubbing.

"MASH-UPS" ANSWERS

1. motorcade
c *procession of vehicles (motor + cavalcade).*
How many insipid celebutantes are riding in the motorcade?

2. radome
B *antenna housing (radar + dome).*
The plucky parasailer passed over the radome undetected.

3. smog
B *polluted fog (smoke + fog).*
The smog exacerbated Erik's allergies so badly that he couldn't enjoy his brunch.

4. slurve
c *baseball pitch (slider + curve).*
A batter can only guesstimate where A.J.'s slurve will go.

5. telegenic
A *suitable manner and appearance for TV (television + photogenic).*
Only the most telegenic dancers appear on the show *So You Think You Can Jazzercise.*

6. meld
B *combine (melt + weld).*
Inventors melded two devices to create the camcorder.

7. bodacious
A *remarkable (bold + audacious).*
Wasn't it bodacious of Bonnie to become a paratrooper?

8. chillax
B *calm down (chill + relax).*
A puzzle addict, Daniel refused to chillax until he solved the cryptex.

9. agitprop
A *political hype (agitation + propaganda).*
No one was persuaded by the agitprop promulgated in the newscast.

10. bromance
c *close male friendship (brother + romance).*
Ben and Andy's bromance grew out of their mutual love of automobilia.

11. liger
c *big cat (lion + tiger).*
I can't go to the Cineplex; I have to feed my liger.

12. frenemy
A *false friend (friend + enemy).*
A true frenemy, Lisa poked fun at my bob before asking her hairstylist for one, too.

13. Frankenfood
B *genetically engineered food (Frankenstein + food).*
The food purists plotted ecotage against the Frankenfood conglomerate.

14. mockumentary
c *satirical film style (mock + documentary).*
Kathy urged her Labradoodle-loving sister to watch *Best in Show*, a mockumentary about five dog owners.

15. sysop
A *online administrator (system + operator).*
A savvy sysop knows how to detect malware.

YOUR SCORE:
___ / 15

TIME OF DAY

While the basics—morning, noon, evening—suffice just fine, this quiz highlights the many ways we can indicate time. Test your knowledge, then see the light of day with the answers on the next page.

1. per diem
(per 'dee-em) *adv.*
A daily.
B twice a day.
C every other day.

2. noctambulist
(nok-'tam-byoo-list) *n.*
A early riser.
B sleepwalker.
C one who fears the moon.

3. fortnight
('fort-niyt) *n.*
A wee hours.
B two weeks.
C holiday's eve.

4. soiree
(swah-'ray) *n.*
A high tea.
B birthday.
C evening party.

5. circadian
(sir-'kay-dee-en) *adj.*
A in sunlight.
B in insect season.
C in 24-hour cycles.

6. ides
(iydz) *n.*
A odd hours.
B mid-month days.
C omens at night.

7. adjourn
(uh-'jurn) *v.*
A wake up.
B exercise.
C call it a day.

8. curfew
('ker-fyoo) *n.*
A dog day.
B short nap.
C restriction at night.

9. reveille
('reh-vuh-lee) *n.*
A hourlong drill.
B wake-up call.
C noon break.

10. crepuscular
(kre-'pus-kyuh-ler) *adj.*
A at twilight.
B of holy hours.
C of morning dew.

11. repast
(ree-'past) *n.*
A prior day.
B anniversary.
C time of a meal.

12. asynchronous
(ay-'sing-kruh-nus) *adj.*
A part-time.
B not on the beat.
C not simultaneous.

13. du jour
(doo 'zhur) *adj.*
A just for today.
B within the hour.
C of legal holidays.

14. swing shift
('swing shift) *n.*
A 4 p.m. to midnight.
B midnight to dawn.
C 9 a.m. to 5 p.m.

15. advent
('ad-vent) *n.*
A commercial holiday.
B day off.
C coming or arrival.

"TIME OF DAY" ANSWERS

1. per diem
A *daily.*
Your allowance is 75 cents per diem.

2. noctambulist
B *sleepwalker.*
As a fridge-raiding noctambulist, I've wrecked my diet plan.

3. fortnight
B *two weeks.*
The roofers will be back in a fortnight to add the gutters.

4. soiree
C *evening party.*
By coincidence, six guests brought baked beans to my soiree.

NAP TIME
We think of a siesta as an afternoon nap, but originally the break was taken at noon. Siesta is Spanish and comes from the Latin *sexta*, meaning "the sixth hour." For Romans, noon was the sixth hour after sunrise, a hot time of day in the Mediterranean—and a good time to stop working and get in the shade.

5. circadian
C *in 24-hour cycles.*
We can't sleep—jet lag has skewed our circadian rhythms.

6. ides
B *mid-month days.*
The ides of March were cold and wet, and the last day was no lamb.

7. adjourn
C *call it a day.*
The committee was pooped and had to adjourn early.

8. curfew
C *restriction at night.*
I can't go out. With the SAT approaching, my parents have imposed a 9 p.m. curfew.

9. reveille
B *wake-up call.*
Buck's ring tone is a boot camp bugler's reveille.

10. crepuscular
A *at twilight.*
On the front porch, I swing to the cicadas' crepuscular serenade.

11. repast
C *time of a meal.*
Though I prefer to eat outside, on busy days I take my midday repast at my desk.

12. asynchronous
C *not simultaneous.*
The dancers' asynchronous movements looked like a mistake.

13. du jour
A *just for today.*
The restaurant's soup du jour is French onion.

14. swing shift
A *4 p.m. to midnight.*
I feel out of whack after working the swing shift.

15. advent
C *coming or arrival.*
With the advent of the holidays, we'll try to start our shopping early but will probably give in to our tradition of late gift giving!

YOUR SCORE: ___ / 15

THERE'S NO PLACE LIKE HOME

Oh my! The 80th anniversary of *The Wizard of Oz* movie occurred in 2019. To celebrate, we're featuring words that include the enchanted "o" and "z" duo.

1. woozy
('woo-zee) *adj.*
A fond of naps.
B mentally unclear.
C sneezy.

2. lollapalooza
(lah-luh-puh-'loo-zuh) *n.*
A mob scene.
B outstanding example.
C hammock.

3. schmooze
(shmooz) *v.*
A chat.
B mock.
C smear.

4. protozoan
(proh-tuh-'zoh-uhn) *n.*
A ancient times.
B one-celled creature.
C Greek sea god.

5. schemozzle
(shuh-'mah-zuhl) *n.*
A clumsy person.
B tiny pest.
C confused situation.

6. cozy
('coh-zee) *n.*
A teapot cover.
B hidden nook.
C close friend.

7. rebozo
(rih-'boh-zoh) *n.*
A caboose.
B clown suit.
C long scarf.

8. foozle
('fooh-zuhl) *v.*
A mess up.
B trick.
C lather.

9. cocozelle
(kah-kuh-'zeh-lee) *n.*
A type of zucchini.
B daring thief.
C small deer.

10. lozenge
('lah-zinj) *n.*
A local pharmacy.
B medicated candy.
C afternoon cocktail.

11. cryptozoology
(crip-tuh-zoh-'ah-luh-jee) *n.*
A science of temperature.
B history of tombs.
C study of fabled animals.

12. ooze
(ooz) *v.*
A flow slowly.
B express discomfort.
C cover with mud.

13. sozzled
('sah-zuhld) *adj.*
A infuriated.
B intoxicated.
C infatuated.

14. arroz con pollo
(uh-'roth kohn 'poh-yoh) *n.*
A chicken dish.
B citizen's arrest.
C traditional dance.

15. schnoz
(shnoz) *n.*
A punch.
B nose.
C simpleton.

"THERE'S NO PLACE LIKE HOME" ANSWERS

1. woozy
B *mentally unclear*.
Ray felt slightly woozy after his dental surgery.

2. lollapalooza
B *outstanding example*.
The Hamiltons always throw a lollapalooza of a Halloween party.

3. schmooze
A *chat*.
Who wouldn't want to schmooze with Hollywood stars at a movie premiere?

4. protozoan
B *one-celled creature*.
Under the microscope, the tiny protozoan looks like a sci-fi monster.

5. schemozzle
C *confused situation*.
This project has been a schemozzle from start to finish!

6. cozy
A *teapot cover*.
"The pot stays nice and hot," said Auntie Em, "with a woolen cozy on it."

7. rebozo
C *long scarf*.
Judy bought rebozos in a few different colors on her trip to Mexico.

THE MERRY OLD LAND OF OZ

When author L. Frank Baum was wondering what to name the magical world where he set his stories, his eye fell upon his filing cabinet, whose drawers were alphabetically labeled A–G, H–N, and O–Z. Faster than you can say Toto, he had his book's title: *The Wonderful Wizard of Oz*. It was published in 1900.

8. foozle
A *mess up*.
It was Henry's best round of golf ever—until he foozled a 2-foot putt.

9. cocozelle
A *type of zucchini*.
Mama's sauce recipe calls for three ripe cocozelles, crushed tomatoes, and a whole lot of garlic.

10. lozenge
B *medicated candy*.
I can't seem to shake this cough; I've been popping throat lozenges for weeks.

11. cryptozoology
C *study of fabled animals*.
The cryptozoology website has a page dedicated to the Loch Ness Monster.

12. ooze
A *flow slowly*.
I love to watch the chocolate ooze out of a freshly baked molten lava cake.

13. sozzled
B *intoxicated*.
The keynote speaker was too sozzled to take the podium.

14. arroz con pollo
A *chicken dish*.
As a vegan, I'll take the arroz (rice) but skip the pollo (chicken).

15. schnoz
B *nose*.
"Watch out—you almost hit me right in the schnoz!" Bert said.

YOUR SCORE:
___ / 15

SCREEN TIME

Can you speak the language of Hollywood? Go behind the scenes of the movie business in our quiz.

1. auteur
(oh-'tur) *n.*
A director with a strong personal style.
B movie buff.
C actor working for no pay.

2. boffo
('bah-foh) *adj.*
A bungled.
B out of focus.
C highly successful.

3. thespian
('thes-pee-un) *adj.*
A with subtitles added.
B pertaining to drama.
C requiring a stunt double.

4. block
(blahk) *v.*
A set positions in a scene.
B label a scene.
C edit raw footage.

5. off book
(ohf buk) *adj.*
A out of sequence.
B excluded from a shot.
C having one's lines memorized.

6. ensemble
(on-'sahm-bull) *adj.*
A perfectly synced.
B occurring during the last take.
C emphasizing the unified effort of the full cast.

7. ingenue
('ahn-juh-noo) *n.*
A role of a sweet young woman.
B musical number.
C opening shot.

8. looping ('loop-ing) *n.*
A repeating a joke.
B rolling the final credits.
C adding sound after filming.

9. foil (foyl) *n.*
A sword fight scene.
B first version of a script.
C role contrasting with another role.

10. cameo ('kam-ee-oh) *n.*
A small part played by a well-known actor.
B makeup kit.
C fish-eye lens.

11. gaffer
('gaf-ur) *n.*
A editor who corrects continuity mistakes.
B chief electrician.
C on-the-set medic.

12. montage
(mahn-'taj) *n.*
A costume collection.
B camera set on a crane.
C rapid succession of images.

13. voice-over
(vois-'oh-ver) *n.*
A dubbing of a foreign film.
B final rehearsal of lines.
C narration.

14. squib
(skwib) *n.*
A short documentary.
B artificial snow.
C fake gunshot wound.

15. denouement
(day-noo-'mahn) *n.*
A plot resolution.
B grand debut.
C framing of a shot.

"SCREEN TIME" ANSWERS

1. auteur
A *director with a strong personal style.*
Armed with his new digicam, Dad ordered us all around like an auteur on the set.

2. boffo
C *highly successful.*
He assured us that the story of the twins' birthday party would be boffo at the box office.

3. thespian
B *pertaining to drama.*
Dad's thespian dreams had been thwarted when he failed to get the lead in *Ernie Earthworm* in third grade.

4. block
A *set positions in a scene.*
He spent an hour and a half blocking the scene with the clown.

5. off book
C *having one's lines memorized.*
We were supposed to be off book on the first day of rehearsal.

6. ensemble
C *emphasizing the unified effort of the full cast.*

He had envisioned an ensemble piece, but Jingles the cocker spaniel stole the show when she licked the frosting off the cake.

7. ingenue
A *role of a sweet young woman.*
My 5-year-old cousin, originally cast as the ingenue, hit the clown with a piñata stick.

8. looping
C *adding sound after filming.*
Dad later changed the clown's response with looping.

9. foil
C *role contrasting with another role.*
The twins were natural foils for each other.

10. cameo
A *small part played by a well-known actor.*
The dog officer made a cameo when he stopped by to investigate a neighbor's complaint about Jingles.

11. gaffer
B *chief electrician.*
Uncle Larry, who had

been named gaffer, blew a fuse, and the rented bounce house collapsed.

12. montage
C *rapid succession of images.*
The movie opened with a montage of the twins' various shenanigans, including the time they painted Jingles blue.

13. voice-over
C *narration.*
Dad did the voice-over in his best James Earl Jones impression.

14. squib
C *fake gunshot wound.*
The twins rigged up squibs, complete with ketchup, under their shirts for the climactic scene.

15. denouement
A *plot resolution.*
In the Bergmanesque denouement, the boys discover that they're brothers only after they've shot each other.

YOUR SCORE:
___ / 15

SOLID FOUNDATION

They say a good vocabulary is the foundation of learning. Master these terms related to architecture and construction, and you will build yourself a fine edifice.

1. raze
(rayz) *v.*
A build up.
B dig a foundation.
C tear down.

2. dexterous
('dek-ster-us) *adj.*
A skillful.
B left-handed.
C turned clockwise.

3. jury-rig
('jur-ee-rig) *v.*
A set up permanently.
B construct in a makeshift fashion.
C glaze.

4. stud
(stuhd) *n.*
A slang for a good carpenter.
B leveling bar.
C upright post.

5. on spec
(on 'spek) *adv.*
A using blueprints.
B without a contract.
C ahead of schedule.

6. garret
('gar-it) *n.*
A attic room.
B pantry or extra kitchen room.
C basement room.

7. annex
('a-neks) *n.*
A supplementary structure.
B underground dwelling.
C foundation.

8. wainscot
('wayn-skoht) *n.*
A intricate plasterwork.
B scaffolding.
C paneled part of a wall.

9. rotunda
(roh-'tun-duh) *n.*
A central column.
B circular room.
C revolving door.

10. plumb
(plum) *adj.*
A not linked, as pipes.
B past its prime.
C vertical.

11. aviary
('ay-vee-ehr-ee) *n.*
A house for birds.
B airport terminal.
C open lobby.

12. corrugated
('kor-eh-gayt-ed) *adj.*
A with closed doors.
B rusted.
C having a wavy surface.

13. mezzanine
('meh-zeh-neen) *n.*
A lowest balcony floor.
B domed ceiling.
C marble counter.

14. cornice
('kor-nes) *n.*
A meeting of two walls.
B decorative top edge.
C steeple or spire.

15. vestibule
('ves-teh-buyl) *n.*
A dressing room.
B lobby.
C staircase.

"SOLID FOUNDATION" ANSWERS

1. raze
c *tear down.*
I hear they're going to raze the mall.

2. dexterous
A *skillful.*
Charlotte spun her web with dexterous eight-handedness.

3. jury-rig
B *construct in a makeshift fashion.*
The contractors were let go after they jury-rigged our home's first floor.

GARDEN VARIETY

A trellis is a structure of crisscrossed slats on which vines or flowers may climb. An espalier is a trellis often set against a flat wall. An arbor makes an arch of that trellis, and a pergola puts the trellis above a frame made of posts. If the structure's roof is solid instead, you have a gazebo. And if the gazebo is high on a hill, it may be called a belvedere (Italian for "beautiful view").

4. stud
c *upright post.*
Don't start hammering the wall until you locate a stud behind it.

5. on spec
B *without a contract.*
Dad is building the girls' dollhouse on spec.

6. garret
A *attic room.*
I'm not fancy—a cozy garret is all I need to finish the novel.

7. annex
A *supplementary structure.*
The children's annex was a welcome addition to the library.

8. wainscot
c *paneled part of a wall.*
Marge's kids have treated the wainscot as a crayon mural.

9. rotunda
B *circular room.*
The conflicting blueprints for the rotunda have me going in circles!

10. plumb
c *vertical.*
Our fixer-upper may need new floors, doors, and windows, but at least the walls are plumb.

11. aviary
A *house for birds.*
"Your cat hasn't taken his eyes off that aviary," Sheryl noted.

12. corrugated
c *having a wavy surface.*
Our roof is a sheet of corrugated tin.

13. mezzanine
A *lowest balcony floor.*
Sadly, our $165 seats in the mezzanine had an obstructed view.

14. cornice
B *decorative top edge.*
You're going to need an extension ladder to reach that cornice.

15. vestibule
B *lobby.*
Anxiety peaking, Claire waited more than an hour in the vestibule for her interview.

YOUR SCORE: ___ / 15

FUNNIEST ENGLISH WORDS

Inspired by *The 100 Funniest Words in English*, by Robert Beard, these picks are all a mouthful, and some even sport serious definitions (others … well, not so much).

1. flummox
('fluh-muks) *v.*
A laugh out loud.
B confuse.
C ridicule.

2. crudivore
('crew-dih-vor) *n.*
A foulmouthed person.
B garbage can.
C eater of raw food.

3. hoosegow
('hoos-gow) *n.*
A jail.
B scaredy-cat.
C strong liquor, usually moonshine.

4. skullduggery
(skul-'duh-geh-ree) *n.*
A Shakespearean prank.
B underhanded behavior.
C graveyard.

5. donnybrook
('dah-nee-bruk) *n.*
A rapid stream.
B wild brawl.
C stroke of luck.

6. cantankerous
(kan-'tan-keh-res) *adj.*
A very sore.
B hard to deal with.
C obnoxiously loud.

7. codswallop
('kahdz-wah-lep) *n.*
A sound produced by a hiccup.
B rare rainbow fish.
C nonsense.

8. doozy ('doo-zee) *n.*
A extraordinary one of its kind.
B incomprehensible song.
C double feature.

9. discombobulate
(dis-kehm-'bah-byoo-layt) *v.*
A take apart.
B fail.
C upset or frustrate.

10. hootenanny
('hoo-teh-na-nee)*n.*
A group of owls.
B folksinging event.
C child's caregiver.

11. yahoo
('yah-hoo) *n.*
A overzealous fan.
B pratfall.
C dumb person.

12. kerfuffle
(ker-'fuh-fuhl) *n.*
A failure to ignite.
B down pillow.
C disturbance.

13. absquatulate
(abz-'kwah-chew-layt) *v.*
A abscond or flee.
B stay low to the ground.
C utterly flatten.

14. mollycoddle
('mah-lee-kah-dl) *v.*
A treat with an absurd degree of attention.
B mix unwisely.
C moo or imitate a cow.

15. flibbertigibbet
(flih-ber-tee-'jih-bet) *n.*
A silly and flighty person.
B snap of the fingers.
C hex or curse.

"FUNNIEST ENGLISH WORDS" ANSWERS

1. flummox
B *confuse.*
Sarah is easily flummoxed by any changes to the schedule.

2. crudivore
C *eater of raw food.*
To help boost my health, I'm declaring myself a crudivore.

3. hoosegow
A *jail.*
After protesting a touch too loudly in court, Tara found herself in the hoosegow.

4. skullduggery
B *underhanded behavior.*
The chairman was infamous for resorting to skullduggery during contract negotiations.

5. donnybrook
B *wild brawl.*
It took four umps to quell the donnybrook at home plate.

6. cantankerous
B *hard to deal with.*
The comedian was greeted by a cantankerous crowd at his debut.

PIRATES IN THE HOUSE

Robert Beard's list of funny words also includes "filibuster," which you probably know as a long political speech. But did you know it's also related to pirates? The Spanish *filibustero* means "freebooter," a plunderer. So you might say a filibuster in Congress is a way of stealing time—legislative piracy!

7. codswallop
C *nonsense.*
"Oh, codswallop! I never went near that bowl of candy," Dad barked.

8. doozy
A *extraordinary one of its kind.*
That was a doozy of a storm—luckily, we dodged the two downed trees.

9. discombobulate
C *upset or frustrate.*
The goal of the simulator: discombobulate even the sharpest of pilots.

10. hootenanny
B *folksinging event.*
After the concert, let's head up the hill for the informal hootenanny.

11. yahoo
C *dumb person.*
Please try not to embarrass me at Sally's party, you big yahoo.

12. kerfuffle
C *disturbance.*
I was referring to that minor kerfuffle called World War II.

13. absquatulate
A *abscond or flee.*
Upon opening the door, Clare watched the new puppy absquatulate with her sneaker.

14. mollycoddle
A *treat with an absurd degree of attention.*
"Lillie's my only grandchild—I'll mollycoddle her all I want!"

15. flibbertigibbet
A *silly and flighty person.*
Do I have to spend the entire ride with that flibbertigibbet next to me?!

YOUR SCORE:
___ / 15

10

Lesser-Known Words to Use in Conversations

LET'S FACE IT: Some words in our vocabularies get used so often, they're the linguistic equivalent of a tattered T-shirt. With this list, you can give those tired-out verbs, adjectives, and nouns a well-deserved rest—and impress your friends, coworkers, and family at the same time.

Fastidious

THIS WORD MEANS excessively particular or demanding, and specifically very concerned about accuracy and detail. Bonus: "I'm a fastidious eater" sounds a lot less needy than "I'm a picky eater."

Apoplectic

YOU KNOW THE cartoon image of a red-faced man who is so angry that steam is coming out of his ears? That's what apoplectic looks like. Merriam-Webster's thesaurus defines the word as "feeling or showing anger," while the dictionary takes it up a notch with "extremely enraged" and "of a kind to cause or apparently cause stroke." Synonyms include fuming, furious, and irate. Prefer to see it used in a sentence? How about this: Sally's mother was so apoplectic when she saw the messy kitchen that she stomped her feet in a fit of rage.

Gibe

UNLESS YOU'RE A skilled comedian, gibing someone is no joke. It means "to make (someone or something) the object of unkind laughter." While a little ribbing can be acceptable during a sports competition, gibing is the type of behavior that will get you kicked out of class.

Bibelot

THOSE WHO LOVE shiny objects probably have a lot of bibelots scattered around the house. These same people likely enjoy thrifting or browsing flea markets and boutiques in search of the next addition to their bibelot collections. "Small objects displayed for their attractiveness," bibelots can be a lot of things— knickknacks, trinkets, and baubles, to name a few.

Dregs

ANYONE WHO HAS FOUND sediment at the bottom of a cup of coffee or tea has dealt with the annoying presence of dregs. It's a simple term for "matter that settles to the bottom of a body of liquid." Synonyms include grounds, sediment, or settlings. The term can also be used negatively, to describe the cast-off, trash-destined remains of a meal or experience.

Collywobbles

OH, HOW OUR grandmothers warned us about the collywobbles. Don't swim right after eating—you might get the collywobbles. Don't stuff yourself with too many sweets—collywobbles! Don't sneak too much chocolate chip cookie dough—raw eggs cause collywobbles! The collywobbles are simply "abdominal pain, especially when focused in the digestive organs." It can describe the sort of stomachache you experience after a big meal or during a bout of influenza.

Erudite

YOU'RE PROBABLY AN erudite person if you've known all the words on this list so far. Erudite people love learning. It's a quality often manifested in our English professors and leaders since those who are erudite "have or display advanced knowledge or education."

Hornswoggle

HERE'S A WORD we don't hear enough in the 21st century. It's the kind of term you might expect to read in Shakespeare's plays or a J.K. Rowling novel. First used in the 1800s (unless our sources are hornswoggling us), this funny verb means "to cause to believe what is untrue." In other words, to lie. So, the next time you realize a friend is hornswoggling you, call his bluff. Or tell a tall tale of your own and see just how long you can hornswoggle (fake out, bamboozle, or deceive) the crowd.

Sycophant

USE THIS WORD to describe a self-seeking flatterer. It's much easier to call someone out as a suck-up when you're not actually using the word suck-up.

Impiety

IF YOU'VE EVER giggled at a funeral or burped during the Christmas homily, you're guilty of impiety. Most of us have had an impious slipup or two, but making a habit of irreverence can be seen as blasphemous. Simply put, being impious is "not showing proper reverence for the holy or sacred." Impiety is in the eye of the beholder. What seems sacrilege to one could be mildly irreverent humor to another.

BATTER UP

From rookies to old-timers, benchwarmers to all-stars, our national pastime is a rich field of vocabulary. Take a hefty swing at this quiz in honor of baseball.

1. bandbox
('band-bahks) *n.*
A warm-up area for pitchers.
B bleacher section.
C small stadium.

2. cleanup
('kleen-up) *adj.*
A caught on the fly.
B fourth among batters.
C scoring zero runs.

3. pickle
('pi-kul) *n.*
A hard-to-hold bat.
B bad umpire.
C play in which a runner is caught between bases.

4. rhubarb
('roo-barb) *n.*
A heated argument.
B razzing from fans.
C thick infield grass.

5. shag
(shag) *v.*
A steal home.
B bobble a fly ball.
C practice catching in the outfield.

6. Texas leaguer
('tek-sus 'lee-ger) *n.*
A rookie player.
B double play.
C bloop hit.

7. Baltimore chop
('bohl-ti-mohr chahp) *n.*
A high-bouncing ground ball.
B weak swing.
C ballpark hot dog.

8. fireman
('fi-er-mun) *n.*
A relief pitcher.
B groundskeeper.
C third-base coach.

9. rubber game
('ruh-ber gaym) *n.*
A blowout.
B deciding game of a series.
C poorly played game.

10. gun down
(gun down) *v.*
A throw three straight strikes.
B throw out a runner.
C throw at a batter.

11. chin music
(chin 'myoo-zik) *n.*
A dispute with an umpire.
B high inside pitch.
C hometown cheers.

12. gopher ball
('go-fer bahl) *n.*
A foul fly into the stands.
B hard-hit ground ball.
C easy pitch to slug.

13. bang-bang
(bang bang) *adj.*
A close, as a play at a base.
B ricocheting.
C requiring both hands.

14. fungo
('fung-go) *n.*
A exhibition game.
B catcher's mask.
C fly ball for practice.

15. blow smoke
(blo smok) *v.*
A taunt.
B throw fast.
C relax on an off day.

"BATTER UP" ANSWERS

1. bandbox
c *small stadium.*
No wonder Joe Bailey hit 50 homers last year—look at the dinky bandbox he calls a home park.

2. cleanup
B *fourth among batters.*
Hinson, Rodriguez, and Pearson led off with walks, setting the stage for the Whammer, the league's top cleanup hitter.

3. pickle
c *play in which a runner is caught between bases.*
Smalls escaped the pickle by taking a ball to the head.

4. rhubarb
A *heated argument.*
Terry and Jimmy went jaw-to-jaw in an ugly rhubarb at home plate.

5. shag
c *practice catching in the outfield.*
How can Dugan text friends and shag flies at the same time?

6. Texas leaguer
c *bloop hit.*
Our only base runner came courtesy of a Texas leaguer that plunked between two lazy fielders.

7. Baltimore chop
A *high-bouncing ground ball.*
Porter is so quick, he can go from home to third before a Baltimore chop bounces twice.

8. fireman
A *relief pitcher.*
We still think Walker is an odd name for our ace fireman.

9. rubber game
B *deciding game of a series.*
The southpaw put out another fire to help us win the rubber game against the Knights.

10. gun down
B *throw out a runner.*
Sent down to the minors, Kinsella managed to gun down only three out of 56 base stealers all season.

11. chin music
B *high inside pitch.*
Savoy charged the mound after a little chin music from Wiggen.

12. gopher ball
c *easy pitch to slug.*
Dutch looked more like Robert Redford in *The Natural* as he whacked my gopher ball into the mezzanine.

13. bang-bang
A *close, as a play at a base.*
Another look in slo-mo clearly shows that the ump botched that bang-bang call at the plate.

14. fungo
c *fly ball for practice.*
Doc started second-guessing his rookie outfielder after watching him shag fungoes at spring training.

15. blow smoke
B *throw fast.*
Icing down his hand, the catcher told reporters that Agilar was really blowing smoke tonight.

YOUR SCORE:
___ / 15

CHANGES

"Come autumn's scathe—come winter's cold—Come change—and human fate!" Elizabeth Barrett Browning writes in "Autumn," a reminder to embrace the changes that the seasons bring. In accord, a collection of words about change. Answers on next page.

1. ameliorate
(uh-'meel-yuh-rayt) *v.*
A make better or more tolerable.
B make worse.
C turn upside down.

2. tack (tak) *v.*
A switch horses.
B follow a zigzag course.
C tailor a suit.

3. ferment
(fur-'mehnt) *n.*
A state of unrest or disorderly development.
B improvement.
C evaporation.

4. synchronize
('sin-kreh-niyz) *v.*
A cause to coincide.
B increase speed.
C move one's lips.

5. static
('sta-tik) *adj.*
A in a frenzy.
B unchanging.
C fuzzy.

6. flux
(fluhks) *n.*
A series of failures.
B continued flow.
C rapid rise.

7. vicissitudes
(vuh-'si-suh-toods) *n.*
A exact opposites.
B minor adjustments.
C ups and downs.

8. fickle
('fih-kuhl) *adj.*
A beginning to decay.
B marked by a lack of constancy.
C stuck in a rut.

9. immutable
(ih-'myu-tuh-buhl) *adj.*
A in motion.
B not susceptible to change.
C becoming a monster.

10. adapt
(uh-'dapt) *v.*
A spread gradually.
B become airborne.
C make fit, usually by alteration.

11. crescendo
(kreh-'shen-doh) *n.*
A sudden narrowing.
B gradual increase.
C change in color.

12. hiatus
(hiy-'ay-tuhs) *n.*
A growth spurt.
B interruption in time or continuity.
C change of season.

13. agitate
('a-juh-tayt) *v.*
A replace.
B break into bits.
C disturb emotionally.

14. senescent
(sih-'neh-snt) *adj.*
A getting old.
B catching fire.
C developing a fragrance.

15. incorrigible
(in-'kor-uh-juh-buhl) *adj.*
A rustproof.
B spontaneous.
C not reformable.

"CHANGES" ANSWERS

1. ameliorate
A *make better or more tolerable.*
Just 15 minutes of yoga daily ameliorates my worries.

2. tack
B *follow a zigzag course.*
Deftly, the captain tacked through the rocky shoals of the bay.

3. ferment
A *state of unrest or disorderly development.*
Henry's writer's block was followed by a creative ferment.

4. synchronize
A *cause to coincide.*
Before we begin the 5K race, let's synchronize our watches.

5. static
B *unchanging.*
Alyson found the novel's characters to be static and one-dimensional.

6. flux
B *continued flow.*
It's too soon to predict—everything's in flux.

7. vicissitudes
c *ups and downs.*
Life is anything but constant, so enjoy its vicissitudes.

8. fickle
B *marked by a lack of constancy.*
Tara described her niece as "fickle at best."

9. immutable
B *not susceptible to change.*
My upstairs tenant thinks loud music is his immutable right.

10. adapt
c *make fit, usually by alteration.*
If you want to eat vegan, I can adapt the recipe.

11. crescendo
B *gradual increase.*
The concerto ended with an unexpected yet effective crescendo.

12. hiatus
B *interruption in time or continuity.*

JUST A PHASE?
The moon is a natural symbol of change, and its shape-shifting comes in phases. As it grows from invisibility (a new moon), it is waxing; when between half and full, it is called gibbous (literally, "humpbacked"). As it shrinks again, it is waning; and when it approaches a sliver in appearance, it is a crescent.

The mayoral debate was marked by an uncomfortable hiatus before the incumbent responded.

13. agitate
c *disturb emotionally.*
Therapy sessions just agitate Karyn.

14. senescent
A *getting old.*
The rocking chair is gorgeous, but do you see me as senescent?

15. incorrigible
c *not reformable.*
I'm afraid our new puppy is simply incorrigible when it comes to sleeping on the couch.

YOUR SCORE:
___ / 15

ARABIAN SOURCES

Dozens of English words, from "admiral" to "zero," have Arabic origins. How many do you know?

1. cipher
('sye-fur) *n.*
A gentle breeze.
B musky perfume.
C encoded message.

2. nadir
('nay-deer or 'nay-der) *n.*
A hub of a wheel.
B lowest point.
C polite refusal.

3. loofah
('loo-fuh) *n.*
A sponge from a gourd.
B water pipe for smoking.
C slipper with curled toe.

4. kismet
('kiz-met) *n.*
A lovers' tryst.
B journey on foot.
C fate.

5. fakir
(fuh-'keer or 'fay-kur) *n.*
A sham or fraud.
B holy beggar.
C tassel on a fez.

6. macramé
('mack-ruh-may) *n.*
A two-masted ship.
B honeyed cereal.
C knot-tying art.

7. popinjay
('pah-pun-jay) *n.*
A conceited person.
B skewer for kebabs.
C uninvited guest.

8. mufti
('muff-tee) *n.*
A confusing situation.
B civilian dress.
C rodent.

9. sirocco
(shuh-'rah-co) *n.*
A hot, dry wind.
B head-to-foot gown.
C siege.

10. carafe
(kuh-'raf) *n.*
A slide rule.
B steep decline.
C bottle with a flared lip.

11. roc
(rock) *n.*
A flying carpet.
B narcotic plant.
C legendary bird.

12. henna
('hen-nuh) *n.*
A armed horseman.
B reddish-brown dye.
C nag.

13. fatwa
('faht-wah) *n.*
A decree.
B sneak attack.
C period of feasting.

14. alchemy
('al-kuh-mee) *n.*
A chaos.
B forerunner of chess.
C process of transmuting substances.

15. elixir
(ill-'ick-sur) *n.*
A collarbone.
B cure-all.
C happiness.

"ARABIAN SOURCES" ANSWERS

1. cipher
C *encoded message.*
I'm not sure what Peter's text message means—it's one of his usual ciphers.

2. nadir
B *lowest point.*
When the bowling alley did away with gutter guards, Claudine's score plunged to an all-time nadir.

3. loofah
A *sponge from a gourd.*
Her shower caddy is crowded with botanical shampoos and loofahs in all sizes.

4. kismet
C *fate.*
It was kismet when Pete spilled wine on another party guest; they're now married.

5. fakir
B *holy beggar.*
Louie mooches change for the vending machine like a fakir.

6. macramé
C *knot-tying art.*
My six-year-old's hair is so tangled, it looks like macramé.

7. popinjay
A *conceited person.*
The party was full of bores, morons, and popinjays.

8. mufti
B *civilian dress.*
The meter maid was grateful that no one recognized her when she was in mufti.

9. sirocco
A *hot, dry wind.*
The lone fan in the Laundromat created a sirocco that blew dryer lint around the windowless room.

10. carafe
C *bottle with a flared lip.*
The picnic was so fancy, the Kool-Aid was served in a crystal carafe.

11. roc
C *legendary bird.*
The bird feeder was empty and knocked to the ground, as if a roc had visited.

12. henna
B *reddish-brown dye.*
The chocolate Lab would have won a ribbon, but the judges found out its coat had been treated with henna.

13. fatwa
A *decree.*
The boss has issued a fatwa against lunch breaks until we've finished the Morgan report.

14. alchemy
C *process of transmuting substances.*
With a few chickpeas and a can of tomato sauce, my grandmother could work alchemy.

15. elixir
B *cure-all.*
Grandma's soup was an elixir that could cure the sniffles and the blues.

YOUR SCORE: ___ / 15

ABRACADABRA

A wave of our wand and presto! We conjure a page of magical words and phrases. Step right up and test your vocabulary—then transport yourself to the next page, where we reveal the answers.

1. levitate
('le-vih-tayt) *v.*
A defy gravity.
B weave spells.
C disappear.

2. clairvoyant
(klayr-'voy-ent) *adj.*
A in a trance.
B ghostly.
C seeing beyond ordinary perception.

3. planchette
(plan-'shet) *n.*
A sorcerer's cloak.
B Ouija board pointer.
C mischievous fairy.

4. mojo
('moh-joh) *n.*
A book of secrets.
B magical spell.
C mantra.

5. telekinetic
(te-leh-kih-'neh-tik) *adj.*
A predicting the future.
B calling on ghosts.
C using mind over matter.

6. voilà
(vwah-'lah) *interj.*
A "Begone!"
B "There it is!"
C "Open!"

7. whammy
('wa-mee) *n.*
A trapdoor.
B illusion.
C hex or curse.

8. soothsaying
('sooth-say-ing) *n.*
A prophecy.
B recitation of chants.
C revelation of a trick.

9. enthralled
(in-'thrahld, en-) *adj.*
A sawed in half.
B held spellbound.
C turned to pixie dust.

10. augur
('ah-ger) *v.*
A serve as an omen.
B bend a spoon without touching it.
C chant in a monotone.

11. shaman
('shah-men) *n.*
A fake psychic.
B healer using magic.
C genie in a bottle.

12. occult
(uh-'khult) *adj.*
A sinister.
B miraculous.
C secret.

13. invoke
(in-'vohk) *v.*
A transform.
B use ventriloquism.
C summon up, as spirits.

14. sibyl
('si-buhl) *n.*
A séance.
B fortune-teller.
C black cat.

15. pentagram
('pen-teh-gram) *n.*
A elixir.
B five-pointed star.
C enchanted staff.

"ABRACADABRA" ANSWERS

1. levitate
A *defy gravity.*
Before dunking the basketball, Michael levitates long enough to polish the rim.

2. clairvoyant
C *seeing beyond ordinary perception.*
As a bookie, I find that being clairvoyant really helps me call the races.

3. planchette
B *Ouija board pointer.*
My planchette just spelled out "You're too gullible."

4. mojo
B *magical spell.*
My mojo is working, but I still can't charm Angelina.

---

5. telekinetic
C *using mind over matter.*
Chloe employs her telekinetic powers to make the trash empty itself.

---

6. voilà
B *"There it is!"*
As he threw back the curtain, Houdini cried, "Voilà!"

---

7. whammy
C *hex or curse.*
After the magician placed a whammy on Tex, he fell into the duck pond three times.

---

8. soothsaying
A *prophecy.*
If Joe is so good at soothsaying, why does he always lose in Vegas?

---

9. enthralled
B *held spellbound.*
Paul has been totally enthralled by Jenny ever since he met her at the convention.

---

10. augur
A *serve as an omen.*
A flat tire on the first day surely augurs ill for our vacation.

---

11. shaman
B *healer using magic.*
The local shaman recited a few incantations to heal my broken nose.

---

12. occult
C *secret.*
At midnight, I was poring over an occult black-magic text.

---

13. invoke
C *summon up, as spirits.*
While studying ancient Rome, I tried to invoke the ghost of Caesar to appear before me.

---

14. sibyl
B *fortune-teller.*
My apprehension grew as the sibyl looked into her crystal ball and winced.

---

15. pentagram
B *five-pointed star.*
David said his spells don't work unless he traces a pentagram with his wand.

DIVINING DICTIONARY

When predicting the future, the suffix we use is *-mancy*, which means "divination." Pyromancy involves reading the future in flames, hydromancy in water, chiromancy in the lines on the palm of a hand, and favomancy, by reading beans scattered on the ground. Related to "mantra" and "mania," the root *-mancy* is derived from "mind."

 YOUR SCORE:
____ / 15

THE ANIMAL WITHIN

At first glance, the words in this quiz might not seem like birds of a feather. But each has an animal name (or two!) nested inside, the way "menagerie" contains "nag." So make a beeline for the quiz, try to spot the critters, then vamoose to the next page for all the answers.

1. dogma
('dog-muh) *n.*
A false belief.
B perseverance.
C established opinion.

2. cataract
('cat-uh-rakt) *n.*
A waterfall.
B tomb.
C eyeshade.

3. toponym
('tah-puh-nim) *n.*
A misprint.
B place-name.
C opposite.

4. escrow
('eh-skroh) *n.*
A money held in trust.
B gross exaggeration.
C eviction notice.

5. forbear
(for-'bair) *v.*
A hold back.
B go before.
C carry off.

6. simoleon
(suh-'moh-lee-un) *n.*
A look-alike.
B dollar.
C coincidence.

7. execrable
('ek-sih-kruh-bull) *adj.*
A discarded.
B immortal.
C horrible.

8. camellia
(kuh-'meel-yuh) *n.*
A flowering shrub.
B horned lizard.
C love song.

9. unorthodox
(un-'or-thuh-doks) *adj.*
A not conventional.
B Eastern.
C beneath the surface.

10. welkin
('wel-kin) *n.*
A fleece vest.
B sky.
C accordion.

11. epigram
('eh-puh-gram) *n.*
A long farewell.
B witty saying.
C ghostly presence.

12. malevolent
(muh-'leh-vuh-lent) *adj.*
A masculine.
B spiteful.
C good-hearted.

13. papeterie
('pap-uh-tree) *n.*
A poetic meter.
B letter jumble.
C fancy stationery.

14. demur
(dih-'mer) *v.*
A shy away from.
B take exception.
C strongly imply.

15. clamor
('klam-er) *v.*
A shine brightly.
B demand loudly.
C leave speechless.

"THE ANIMAL WITHIN" ANSWERS

1. dogma
c *established opinion.*
Galileo's ideas challenged the religious and scientific dogmas of the time.

2. cataract
A *waterfall.*
Canoeing over that cataract would be unwise.

3. toponym
B *place-name.*
Half the toponyms on this map are unpronounceable.

4. escrow
A *money held in trust.*
There's not enough in escrow to cover the taxes.

5. forbear
A *hold back.*
If you're offering my favorite cookies, how can I forbear?

6. simoleon
B *dollar.*
Reuben was down to his last simoleon when Lady Luck arrived.

THE CANINE ISLANDS

You might think the Canary Islands were named for canaries—after all, the yellow finches are indigenous to the Spanish archipelago. But "Canary" here actually refers to another animal: the dog. In Spanish, the islands are called *Islas Canarias*, derived from the Latin word for dog, a moniker bestowed by explorers who reported seeing canines there.

7. execrable
c *horrible.*
We had execrable weather last week: five rainy days in a row!

8. camellia
A *flowering shrub.*
Many people don't realize that tea is made from camellia leaves.

9. unorthodox
A *not conventional.*
Kari's unorthodox approach to investing paid off when she retired early.

10. welkin
B *sky.*
A faint rainbow stretched across the welkin.

11. epigram
B *witty saying.*
The writer Dorothy Parker was known for her biting epigrams.

12. malevolent
B *spiteful.*
Cinderella wondered why her stepsisters looked so malevolent.

13. papeterie
c *fancy stationery.*
Sonya sent her wedding guests handwritten thank-you notes on beautiful papeterie.

14. demur
B *take exception.*
You say there's no chance of winning this game—well, I demur!

15. clamor
B *demand loudly.*
The protesters clamored for the jailed activist to be released immediately.

YOUR SCORE:
___ / 15

WHAT THE DICKENS?!

When it came to ingeniously descriptive language, Charles Dickens was lummy (aka first-rate). Bryan Kozlowski compiled the most colorful terms in his book *What the Dickens?!* You might need some logic to guess the definitions.

1. sawbones
('saw-bohnz) *n.*
A doctor.
B magician.
C old nag.

2. catawampus
(kat-uh-'wom-puhs) *adj.*
A fierce.
B syrupy.
C deep and dark.

3. jog-trotty
('jahg-trah-tee) *adj.*
A monotonous.
B nervous.
C backward.

4. spoony
('spoo-nee) *adj.*
A spacious.
B pun-filled.
C lovey-dovey.

5. rantipole
('ran-tih-pohl) *n.*
A battering ram.
B fishing rod.
C ill-behaved person.

6. gum-tickler
('guhm-tihk-ler) *n.*
A funny remark.
B strong drink.
C wishbone.

7. stomachic
(stuh-'ma-kihk) *n.*
A winter coat.
B tummy medicine.
C windup toy.

8. sassigassity
(sass-ih-'gass-ih-tee) *n.*
A fancy clothes.
B cheeky attitude.
C gust of hot wind.

9. comfoozled
(kuhm-'foo-zuhld) *adj.*
A on fire.
B pampered.
C exhausted.

10. mud lark
('muhd lark) *n.*
A scavenging child.
B court judge.
C ancient scribe.

11. plenipotentiary
(pleh-nuh-puh-'tehn-shuh-ree) *n.*
A housewife.
B diplomatic agent.
C bank vault.

12. toadeater
('tohd-ee-ter) *n.*
A fawning person.
B habitual liar.
C gourmet.

13. slangular
('slang-yuh-luhr) *adj.*
A oblique.
B using street talk.
C tight around the neck.

14. marplot
('mahr-plot) *n.*
A flower garden.
B meddler.
C fruit jam.

15. heeltap
('heel-tap) *n.*
A Irish dance step.
B scoundrel.
C sip of liquor left in a glass.

"WHAT THE DICKENS! " ANSWERS

1. sawbones
A *doctor.*
Captain Kirk hired his friend McCoy as the ship's sawbones. (*The Pickwick Papers*)

2. catawampus
A *fierce.*
The catawampus storm engulfed the tiny village. (*Martin Chuzzlewit*)

3. jog-trotty
A *monotonous.*
Will Lauren ever quit that jog-trotty data-entry job? (*Bleak House*)

4. spoony
C *lovey-dovey.*
Those spoony newlyweds just won't stop canoodling! (*David Copperfield*)

5. rantipole
C *ill-behaved person.*
A gang of rantipoles vandalized the building. (*Great Expectations*)

6. gum-tickler
B *strong drink.*
Ty downed a few gum-ticklers. (*Our Mutual Friend*)

7. stomachic
B *tummy medicine.*
This new stomachic may be just the thing for your indigestion. (*David Copperfield*)

8. sassigassity
B *cheeky attitude.*
No more of your sassigassity, young lady! ("A Christmas Tree")

9. comfoozled
C *exhausted.*
We were all completely comfoozled after the 10K race. (*The Pickwick Papers*)

10. mud lark
A *scavenging child.*
Some mud lark just snatched my piece of cake! (*Our Mutual Friend*)

11. plenipotentiary
B *diplomatic agent.*
Which of those muckety-mucks is the head plenipotentiary around here? (*Great Expectations*)

12. toadeater
A *fawning person.*
You toadeaters will never disagree with your coach! (*Dombey and Son*)

13. slangular
B *using street talk.*
Lady Clara was shocked by the slangular chatter at high tea. (*Bleak House*)

14. marplot
B *meddler.*
The con men were exposed when a marplot snitched on them. (*Our Mutual Friend*)

15. heeltap
C *sip of liquor left in a glass.*
"I must go," said James Bond, downing the heeltap of his martini. (*The Pickwick Papers*)

WHAT'S IN A NAME?

Some Dickens characters have made their way into the lexicon: A scrooge is a miser (from stingy Ebenezer Scrooge), and Pecksniffian means "hypocritical" (from insincere Seth Pecksniff). Dickensian, which refers to living in decrepit conditions, owes its place to his Victorian tales.

YOUR SCORE: ___ / 15

TALK BIG

Not only do we have thousands of words to use in conversation, but we also have many to describe the very act of conversing. So the next time you're confabulating, try these words on your interlocutor.

1. gainsay
(gayn-'say) v.
A repeat.
B add, as an afterthought.
C deny.

2. badinage
(bad-uh-'nazh) n.
A swear words.
B playful back-and-forth.
C stern warning.

3. taciturn
('tass-uh-turn) adj.
A chatty.
B quiet.
C afflicted with a lisp.

4. wheedle
('wee-dull) v.
A tease.
B speak breathily.
C persuade with flattery.

5. loquacious
(low-'kway-shus) adj.
A quick to agree.
B talkative.
C to the point.

6. polemic
(puh-'lem-ick) n.
A opinionated attack.
B off-the-cuff remark.
C awkward pause.

7. maunder
('mawn-dur or 'mahn-) v.
A ramble.
B squabble.
C gurgle.

8. rodomontade
(rod-uh-mun-'tayd or -'tahd) n.
A circular argument.
B talking while walking.
C bragging.

9. repartee
(rep-ur-'tee or -ar-'tay) n.
A verbal habit, as "like" and "you know."
B witty reply.
C rhetorical question.

10. bombastic
(bahm-'bass-tick) adj.
A shocking.
B pompous.
C given to interrupting.

11. prevaricate
(prih-'var-uh-kate) v.
A scream.
B emphasize.
C tell a half-truth.

12. colloquy
('coll-uh-kwee) n.
A dialogue.
B slang usage.
C translation.

13. fustian
('fuss-chun) adj.
A obscure.
B high-flown.
C mumbled.

14. tête-à-tête
(tet-uh-'tet) n.
A comeback.
B roundtable.
C private conversation.

15. insinuate
(in-'sin-yoo-ate or -ya-wayt) v.
A make hand gestures.
B embellish.
C artfully suggest.

"TALK BIG" ANSWERS

1. gainsay
c *deny.*
It cannot be gainsaid that the sign maker who spelled "Exit" wrong is an idiot.

2. badinage
B *playful back-and-forth.*
The team's locker-room badinage is not for the squeamish.

3. taciturn
B *quiet.*
The only taciturn member of a large and boisterous family, Mavis grew up to become a psychotherapist.

4. wheedle
c *persuade with flattery.*
The saleswoman wheedled me into buying this dress.

5. loquacious
B *talkative.*
My loquacious seatmate bent my ear all the way from La Guardia to LAX.

6. polemic
A *opinionated attack.*
The meeting was interrupted by Jay's polemic against the copying machine.

7. maunder
A *ramble.*
We listened to Uncle Horace's maundering stories, one right after another.

8. rodomontade
c *bragging.*
The actress's Oscar acceptance speech was 45 seconds of unabashed rodomontade.

9. repartee
B *witty reply.*
When Curly asked, "What's that monkey got that I ain't got?" Moe's repartee was "A longer tail."

10. bombastic
B *pompous.*
The club president's speech would have seemed less bombastic without Tchaikovsky's "1812 Overture" playing in the background.

11. prevaricate
c *tell a half-truth.*
When asked if he'd broken the window, the Little Leaguer prevaricated, claiming that his aim couldn't have been that good.

12. colloquy
A *dialogue.*
The professors' highbrow colloquy quickly turned into a slugfest.

13. fustian
B *high-flown.*
The candidate's fustian oratory barely disguised his poor grasp of the issue.

14. tête-à-tête
c *private conversation.*
After a quick tête-à-tête with his attorney, the defendant decided to change his plea.

15. insinuate
c *artfully suggest.*
When my friends chipped in for my birthday present— a gift certificate for a housecleaning service—I had to wonder what they were insinuating.

YOUR SCORE:
___ / 15

STANDING TALL

The confidence you project hugely affects how others perceive you. Test yourself on these words about proof, opinion, and even doubt. Unsure of your answers? Turn the page to be certain you are right.

1. waffle
('wah-ful) *v.*
A flip-flop in opinion.
B press a point firmly.
C invent a wild story.

2. conjecture
(con-'jek-cher) *n.*
A group agreement.
B guess.
C optimistic outlook.

3. equivocal
(ih-'kwi-veh-kel) *adj.*
A open to interpretations.
B firmly settled.
C in the form of a question.

4. corroborate
(kuh-'rah-beh-rayt) *v.*
A support with evidence.
B steal another's ideas.
C pretend to be sure.

5. allegation
(a-lih-'gay-shun) *n.*
A proof.
B suspicion.
C claim.

6. precarious
(pri-'kar-ee-us) *adj.*
A false.
B depending on uncertain circumstances.
C predictable.

7. expound
(ik-'spownd) *v.*
A take back.
B carefully state.
C contradict.

8. intuition
(in-too-'ih-shun) *n.*
A instinctive knowledge.
B formal teaching.
C logical paradox.

9. indubitably
(in-'doo-beh-teh-blee) *adv.*
A certainly.
B doubtfully.
C deceitfully.

10. echt
(ekt) *adj.*
A with high hopes.
B genuine.
C in contention.

11. nebulous
('neh-byeh-les) *adj.*
A vague.
B all-knowing.
C uncertain.

12. surmise
(sir-'miyz) *v.*
A sum up.
B suppose on limited evidence.
C apply logic.

13. spurious
('spyur-ee-us) *adj.*
A sharply worded.
B false or deceitful.
C impossible to refute.

14. tentative
('ten-teh-tiv) *adj.*
A forceful.
B all-inclusive.
C hesitant.

15. apocryphal
(uh-'pah-kreh-ful) *adj.*
A mathematical.
B not fully developed, as an idea.
C of doubtful authenticity.

"STANDING TALL" ANSWERS

1. waffle
A *flip-flop in opinion.*
Quit waffling: Goobers
or Raisinets?!

2. conjecture
B *guess.*
Who will win this game
is anyone's conjecture.

3. equivocal
A *open to interpretations.*
The umpire gestured,
but his meaning was
equivocal.

4. corroborate
A *support with evidence.*
"I can corroborate
Amy's excuse," her
mom said.

5. allegation
C *claim.*
Please don't believe the
wild allegations that
Adrienne is making
about me.

6. precarious
B *depending on
uncertain circumstances.*
Everyone's job is
precarious in this poor
economy.

7. expound
B *carefully state.*
On the first day of
school, Alex's teacher

DO YOU IMPLY OR INFER?

When you're the speaker and you suggest something indirectly,
you imply it. When you are the listener and you draw a
conclusion from what someone else says, you infer it. Example:
If you say, "Everyone needs a good diet," a friend might infer
that you mean her and say, "What are you implying?"

expounded on the
basics of physics to a
befuddled classroom.

8. intuition
A *instinctive knowledge.*
A good private eye
trusts her intuition on
a case.

9. indubitably
A *certainly.*
"These footprints,
Watson," said Sherlock
Holmes, "indubitably
belong to the butler!"

10. echt
B *genuine.*
Yet again, our school
baseball team is
starting the season
without an echt
shortstop.

11. nebulous
A *vague.*
The point of practicing
seemed nebulous to
Jill until the recital
started.

12. surmise
B *suppose on limited
evidence.*
From your white
mustache, I surmise
that you've been
drinking my milk.

13. spurious
B *false or deceitful.*
Tom Sawyer played
hooky using a spurious
note from the doctor.

14. tentative
C *hesitant.*
An infant's first steps
are always tentative
and awkward.

15. apocryphal
C *of doubtful
authenticity.*
Jake's story about
having to tough it out at
camp was apocryphal.

 YOUR SCORE:
___ / 15

FAMILY GAME NIGHT

Whether your métier is crosswords, Scrabble, or Words with Friends, these terms—all short and sweet and vowel-powered—will help you (and your vocabulary) step it up when the game is on the line. Answers on the next page.

1. aerie
('eyr-ee) *n.*
A sphere of knowledge.
B bird's nest.
C feeling of weirdness.

2. ennui
(on-'wee) *n.*
A boredom.
B group of nine experts.
C dispute or feud.

3. épée
('eh-pay) *n.*
A traditional wedding dance.
B Southern word game.
C fencing sword.

4. erose
(ih-'rohs) *adj.*
A having an irregular margin, as a leaf.
B jaded.
C resembling Cupid.

5. alee
(ah-'lee) *adv.*
A as soon as possible.
B away from the wind.
C with great reluctance.

6. oryx
('or-iks) *n.*
A African antelope.
B jet-black gemstone.
C highest point.

7. etui
(ay-'twee) *n.*
A small ornamental case.
B flightless bird.
C long-standing love affair.

8. aural
('or-uhl) *adj.*
A reflecting light.
B related to the sense of hearing.
C occurring in the fall.

9. riata
(ree-'a-tuh) *n.*
A lasso.
B festival.
C break in the action.

10. wadi
('wah-dee) *n.*
A shapeless lump.
B poisonous snake.
C stream bed.

11. olio
('oh-lee-oh) *n.*
A butter substitute.
B terrible smell.
C hodgepodge.

12. arête
(uh-'rayt) *n.*
A South American cuckoo bird.
B sharp ridge.
C metrical foot in poetry.

13. outré
(oo-'tray) *adj.*
A hush-hush or illegal.
B bizarre.
C imported.

14. ogee
('oh-jee) *n.*
A bishop's robe.
B S-shaped molding.
C wild party.

15. elide
(ih-'liyd) *v.*
A omit.
B speed along smoothly.
C embellish falsely.

"FAMILY GAME NIGHT" ANSWERS

1. aerie
B *bird's nest.*
Peering over the cliff, Ernie espied an erne's aerie.

_____

2. ennui
A *boredom.*
"Are we there yet?" Lucy moaned in inane ennui.

_____

3. épée
C *fencing sword.*
Swinging his épée overhead in grossly poor sportsmanship, Josh yelled, "You can never take our title!"

_____

4. erose
A *having an irregular margin, as a leaf.*
Intending an autumnal effect, the artist chose erose edges for the new sculpture.

_____

5. alee
B *away from the wind.*
The harbormaster kept his pipe lit alee and resumed his usual pose at the dock.

6. oryx
A *African antelope.*
The horns of the oryx can be lethal and help to protect the animal from predators.

_____

7. etui
A *small ornamental case.*
Quite impressed with herself, Alice wandered around the crafts fair with her sewing kit in a handcrafted etui.

_____

8. aural
B *related to the sense of hearing.*
The speaker's voice, to put it politely, was an aural annoyance.

_____

9. riata
A *lasso.*
"Maybe I could use that riata to corral my kids!" said a weary Amy.

_____

10. wadi
C *stream bed.*
The dried-up wadi was a sad sight for the labored herd.

_____

11. olio
C *hodgepodge.*
A favorite among the neighbors, Grace's chili was known as the Outrageous Olio.

12. arête
B *sharp ridge.*
Hoping to photograph the arêtes surrounding Alaska's Taku Glacier, Alison set out from Juneau.

_____

13. outré
B *bizarre.*
What's more outré: Hillary's hair color or her hot-pink cocktail dress?

_____

14. ogee
B *S-shaped molding.*
The designer demanded an ogee edge for the countertops throughout the expansive kitchen.

_____

15. elide
A *omit.*
In an apparent error, Liam elided a few key remarks from the now-infamous speech.

YOUR SCORE:
___ / 15

MUSEUM MOTS

Planning a visit to the Louvre, the Met, London's National Gallery, or another grand museum? First take our quiz to make sure you have an artful vocabulary. Turn the page for answers.

1. graphic
('gra-fik) *adj.*
A clearly pictured.
B sculpted of marble.
C roughly composed.

2. canon
('ka-nen) *n.*
A string of images.
B standard for evaluation.
C negative review.

3. symmetry
('si-meh-tree) *n.*
A framing and matting.
B balanced proportions.
C imitation.

4. cartography
(kahr-'tah-gre-fee) *n.*
A mapmaking.
B painted wagons.
C traveling exhibits.

5. panoramic
(pan-oh-'ram-ik) *adj.*
A of film artistry.
B shown in miniature.
C sweeping.

6. opaque
(oh-'payk) *adj.*
A deceptive.
B not transparent.
C molded in plaster.

7. juxtapose
('juks-tuh-pohz) *v.*
A sit for a portrait.
B render precisely.
C place side by side.

8. kinetic
(kih-'neh-tik) *adj.*
A copied identically.
B showing movement.
C picturing countryside.

9. kitschy
('ki-chee) *adj.*
A in a collage.
B tacky.
C macraméd.

10. baroque
(buh-'rohk) *adj.*
A highly ornamented.
B plain in style.
C traditional.

11. manifesto
(ma-neh-'fes-toh) *n.*
A statement of principles.
B gallery opening.
C watercolor technique.

12. avant-garde
(ah-vahnt-'gard) *adj.*
A retro.
B scandalous.
C cutting edge.

13. aesthetics
(es-'theh-tiks) *n.*
A acid engravings.
B pleasing appearance.
C works in the outdoor air.

14. anthropomorphic
(an-throh-puh-'mohr-fik) *adj.*
A of cave art.
B made from clay.
C humanlike.

15. analogous
(uh-'na-leh-ges) *adj.*
A shapeless.
B made of wood.
C having a likeness.

"MUSEUM MOTS" ANSWERS

1. graphic
A *clearly pictured.*
The depiction of the embrace was a little too graphic for me.

2. canon
B *standard for evaluation.*
Monet's works are certainly the canon by which to measure other Impressionist paintings.

3. symmetry
B *balanced proportions.*
Dean asked, "When Picasso looked in the mirror, was his face all out of symmetry too?"

4. cartography
A *mapmaking.*
No need to test my cartography skills when I have a GPS in the car.

5. panoramic
C *sweeping.*
Eric was overwhelmed by the photograph's panoramic proportions.

6. opaque
B *not transparent.*
Notice the opaque colors in the backdrop.

SHORT AND SWEET

When people save tickets, clippings, or menus, they are collecting ephemera (from the Greek *ephemeros*, "lasting a day"). Such items may not have been made by artists, but over time they acquire value for their place in history. And a cultural trend that passes away quickly is considered ephemeral.

7. juxtapose
C *place side by side.*
Now that you've juxtaposed the photos, I agree—they're not at all alike.

8. kinetic
B *showing movement.*
I thought someone was behind me, but it was a particularly kinetic statue.

9. kitschy
B *tacky.*
Leo thinks anything that isn't Rembrandt is just kitschy.

10. baroque
A *highly ornamented.*
Alex's baroque-inspired sketches were too busy.

11. manifesto
A *statement of principles.*
Art manifestos often come across as pretentious.

12. avant-garde
C *cutting-edge.*
Holly dropped out of school to join an avant-garde painting troupe.

13. aesthetics
B *pleasing appearance.*
Ironically, Joziah's darker portraits most accurately captured the aesthetics of the city.

14. anthropomorphic
C *humanlike.*
The artist combined everyday items into an anthropomorphic figure.

15. analogous
C *having a likeness.*
Right now, my brain is analogous to that flat, empty canvas.

YOUR SCORE:
___ / 15

WORD POWER CHALLENGE SCORE SHEET

Use this score sheet to keep track of your scores as you take each quiz. Once you've completed them all, turn to page 204 to see your overall Word Power rating.

PAGE	QUIZ	YOUR SCORE
1	All in the Mind	
3	In Words We Trust	
5	The I's Have It	
7	Weather Facts	
9	The Queen's English	
11	Beauty of Words	
13	Short on Time	
15	Mixing and Mingling	
17	Going in Circles	
19	Q & A	
21	Summer Family Fun	
23	Feeling It	
25	Animal Instincts	
27	Pro and Con	
29	Myths and Meaning	
	SECTION 1 TOTAL:	

SECTION 1 TOTAL:	
SECTION 2 TOTAL:	
SECTION 3 TOTAL:	
SECTION4 TOTAL:	
SECTION 5 TOTAL:	
SECTION 6 TOTAL:	
TOTAL:	

Add up all your scores to determine
your Word Power mojo. Whether
you're a student of words or a word
champion, remember that there are
always new words to learn!

399 and below = WORD LEARNER
400-600 = STUDENT OF WORDS
600-800 = WORD MAVEN
800-1,000 = WORD NERD
1,000-1,274 = WORD CHAMPION
1,275 = WORD GRANDMASTER

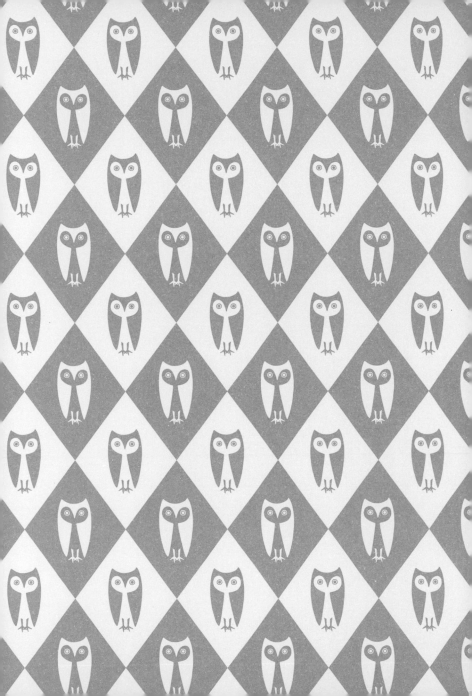